A MEDICAL AFFAIR
A STORY THAT MUST BE TOLD

ANNE MCCARTHY STRAUSS

booktrope

Booktrope Editions
Seattle WA 2013

Cover Design by Greg Simanson

Edited by Julie Klein

*This is a work of fiction. Names, characters, places, brands, media, and
incidents are either the product of the author's imagination or are used
fictitiously. Any resemblance to similarly named places or to persons living
or deceased is unintentional.*

PRINT ISBN 978-1-62015-174-7
EPUB ISBN 978-1-62015-270-6

For further information regarding permissions, please contact
info@booktrope.com.

Library of Congress Control Number: 2013917189

To every doctor's favorite patient

ACKNOWLEDGMENTS

Like most authors, I have many wonderful people to thank for helping to make my book a reality. The first is my husband, Mel Strauss, the first reader of everything I write, my staunchest supporter, and biggest fan. Thank you for believing in me.

Thank you to my agent, April Eberhardt, who so believed in *A Medical Affair* that she shopped it far longer than other agents might have. Thank you to my early editor, Kristen Weber, who helped me to shape a story into a book that would sell.

A special thanks to my very early readers and dear friends Ann Lamendola, Lorraine Austin, RN, and John Budris who gave freely of their time reading early versions and supported me with their feedback and enthusiasm.

Thank you to the highly regarded medical, legal and literary professionals David Orentlicher, Anne D. LeClaire, Lorraine Austin, and Nicole Bokat who provided endorsements for *A Medical Affair*. It is an honor to have people of your level of accomplishment support both my writing and my effort to reveal that there is no such thing as a consensual affair between a doctor and a patient.

Thank you to the countless professionals whose reams of medical and legal research enabled me to decipher the truth behind what most people have no idea can be considered a crime and the complex processes that can bring the predator to justice.

Finally, thank you to Booktrope, my publisher, and to my Booktrope team for their professionalism and friendship – Julie Klein, my editor, whose knowledge of grammar and punctuation excels; Greg Simanson, my gifted cover artist who supported a woman's right to change her mind more than once; Director of Community Management Jesse James Freeman whose responses to my emails came quickly throughout weekends and across time zones; and my proofreader and book manager Jennifer Gilbert whose enthusiasm for A Medical Affair and for life in general helped to put the book into the hands of readers everywhere.

Thank you to the brave women who shared their stories with me and trusted me to respect their anonymity. You know who you are and that, by allowing me to learn from your experiences, you are helping thousands of potential future victims.

In the interest of accuracy, the reader should note that the laws regarding doctor-patient intimate relationships vary from state to state and can be dependent on the medical professional's area of specialization. While I held as close to the law as time and place permitted, laws are constantly evolving and, in fact, some were changed during the process of my writing A Medical Affair. It should be noted that a doctor being called before the Office of Professional Medical Conduct (OPMC) and being the defendant in a civil law suit are different processes with different consequences.

To everyone who played a part in making A Medical Affair a reality, my deepest gratitude.

Nobody talks about it,
but it happens all the time.

CHAPTER 1

HEATHER

BATTLING FOR BREATH, Heather struggled toward consciousness. Her heart was racing as if she'd just run the New York City Marathon. Panicked, she willed the air to fill her lungs. *It's only a panic attack. Breathe. Just breathe.*

The clock on her night table glowed 2:14, its glaring digits pulsing the seconds at a fraction of her racing heart rate. She tried again to suck some air into her lungs. Nothing. Impulsively, she grabbed the rosary beads and cell phone from under her pillow. She crawled from the bed, navigating the unfamiliar layout on her hands and knees. Struggling in what she thought was the direction of the bathroom, she bumped into a couch. "Ouch!" The single syllable spiraled into a hoarse cough that wouldn't quit.

She changed course, hacking as she crawled along the narrow hallway back past the bedroom. Reaching the bathroom, she grasped a towel rod and pulled herself up. She fumbled for the light switch.

Her face in the mirror was barely recognizable. Sweat clung to her ashen features and drenched her hair into wet yellow strings. *Calm down. It's just a panic attack. I've had them before.* She reached into the shower stall, turning the water on full blast. Hot. Closing the bathroom door, she sank onto the lid of the toilet seat, the rosary dangling from her slender wrist. As the steam filled the bathroom, a trickle of air entered her lungs. She gasped for more.

She opened her phone. *If I call 911, I'll be dead before they get here.* "Taxi," she croaked into the mouthpiece.

* * *

The cab was waiting when Heather stumbled outside. She pulled a scrap of paper and a pencil from her purse and scribbled *Lenox Hill Hospital*. She handed it to the driver.

"Where that is?" he asked.

She tugged the scrap from his sweaty palm and wrote *Park and 77th* on its damp surface. "Go...through...the...park."

"I new in country," he said.

An illegal immigrant driving a cab in New York City? No surprise there.

"You OK?" the driver asked as she lay down on the pungent vinyl of the cab's back seat. She thought she would vomit. "Hospital," she said.

The driver floored it, reaching Lenox Hill in minutes. Heather tossed him a twenty, her heart racing even faster than before. Every breath she took required more of a struggle than the one that had preceded it.

* * *

"Dr. Davis, the patient is coming to," a female voice said as if from a distance. Heather clamped her eyes shut against the brilliant light that burned beyond her lids. *Am I dying? Am I going toward the light?* She squinted at her surroundings. There were tubes everywhere— one attached to a needle in her arm, another to a plastic thimble on her middle finger. A plastic mask was secured over her nose and lips.

"Try to breathe normally," the female voice commanded. "The nebulizer will disperse the medication along with the oxygen."

Nebulizer? Oxygen? There was an audible beep as the gurney was raised to a full upright position.

"Draw some blood," a male voice ordered. "We need a full report on arterial blood gases."

Heather reopened her eyes just a little and saw him in shadow before he came into focus. Even in her distress, she couldn't miss that this was one gorgeous man. Tall. Built. His presence alone made her feel safer. A doctor. An authority figure. *What do they think is wrong with me?*

Dr. Davis's eyes scanned the pulsating digits on one of the machines monitoring Heather's body functions. He glanced at the chart for her name. "Try to relax while I listen to your heartbeat, Heather." He noted the date: May 27, 2010.

She turned her head. The black silk chemise with pink ribbon trim she'd worn to bed hung damp and wrinkled from a hook on the wall. With hesitation, she tugged at the pink hospital gown she was wearing now. Circles of beige plastic with wires extending from them were stuck on her chest. The doctor placed his stethoscope on her left breast.

"Breathe as normally as you can," he said. His own breath grazed her cheek as he lowered his eyelids, intent on listening. His hands on her skin felt strong and sure. Safe. "Again," he said.

The doctor poked around for what seemed an eternity before saying, "Your heartbeat is a little fast."

"How fast?"

"Just slightly elevated. I've given you a shot of epinephrine. It might be making you a little shaky and raising your heart rate."

Epinephrine? Shaky? Elevated heart rate? Why?

"Try to relax," he said. "Your heart rate should return to normal range in just a few minutes." He raised himself to his full height. At least six foot two with a trim but muscular build, his olive skin was topped by a crop of thick black hair, his eyes the color of two turquoise stones. The rimless glasses perched on the tip of his nose added to his sexy command.

"I'm going to remove the nebulizer," he said as he unfastened the rubber strip holding the plastic mask in place. He lifted a device from a rolling tray beside the gurney. "This is a peak flow meter." He handed her the lightweight plastic tube. "Take the deepest breath you can. Then exhale into the meter. Seal your lips around it like you're sucking on something."

"Sucking on something?"

"A straw," he said. "Like you're sucking on a straw. Exhale as strong and long as you can. Give it all you've got."

"What's wrong with me?" she demanded before inhaling. She sealed her lips around the meter and exhaled. After a few seconds, she shook her head no, indicating she couldn't go on.

"Keep blowing," he said as she ran out of steam.

Based on his command, she struggled to exhale more air. It was impossible. She shook her head again and placed the meter in the doctor's long narrow hand. He reviewed her reading and asked, "Have you ever had an asthma attack?"

"No."

"Well, you've had one now." He stepped behind the curtain where she could hear him fumbling for supplies. When he reappeared, he was ripping open an albuterol test kit.

Her brow furrowed as she looked at him. *Asthma?*

He removed a device from the box, shook it, and sprayed it into the air. "Take this," he said. "You'll need to learn how to do on your own what the nebulizer was doing for you. Like this. Press down on the device, then seal your lips around it and breathe in."

She nodded. Taking the device, she pressed the button he'd indicated and sucked in the dispersed medication through the mouthpiece.

"Do that fifteen times," he said.

After the fifth breath, she paused for a reprieve.

"Keep at that, Heather. You need to learn to use the medication correctly," he said. "I'll be back in just a minute."

* * *

"Let's hear that heartbeat now," the doctor said as he reemerged from behind the curtain that surrounded the gurney. "Can you shift to the side and sit up fully for me?"

She struggled to turn. Her slender legs dangled from the gurney, her week-old bubble gum pink-manicured toes grazing the linoleum floor. *Chipped polish and greasy hair, and I get Dr. McDreamy.*

As he returned the stethoscope to her chest, she noticed the doctor's knee was firmly planted between her inner thighs. "Again," he said. "Breathe as deeply as you can." As he adjusted his instrument, she felt the soft cotton of his scrubs graze her left thigh.

From behind the curtained divider, a woman giggled softly.

Dr. Davis rolled his eyes. "Nurse!" he commanded. "I need you here, stat!"

Immediately, the laughter stopped, and a nurse appeared from behind the curtain.

"Has Ms. Morrison's blood sample been taken to the lab?" he asked. The irritation in his voice was unmistakable.

"Yes, Doctor."

"Tell them to put a rush on her tests."

"Right away, Doctor."

"Why would I have an asthma attack?" Heather asked. "I've never had one before."

"How old are you Heather?"

"Thirty-eight."

"Any changes in your routine during the past few days?"

"Well, I moved."

"New condo?"

"Yes, it's on West 79th." *Am I bragging?*

"Nice neighborhood," Dr. Davis acknowledged. "So nice, in fact, I bet the superintendent made sure the condo was freshly painted for you."

"Of course," she said, her shoulders relaxing. "They even let me pick the colors. Chocolate and celery. Food colors."

He looked at her quizzically, his eyebrows raised, revealing a trace of where the lines would etch his forehead in years to come.

What are you waiting for me to realize?

"It's not about the colors, Heather," he finally said. "It's about the paint."

"The paint?"

"Environmental asthma," he said. "You've got a classic case."

"Oh, no! What does that mean?"

"It's hard to say," he acknowledged. "The problem could become chronic. Or you may never have another attack again. Most likely, it'll be something between the two. If you're exposed to an irritating agent, something like paint, you may experience another attack."

An image of herself with plastic tubes up her nose and a tank on her back flashed through her mind.

"Your asthma can be controlled with medication," he said. He pulled a prescription pad and a pen from the pocket of his blue scrubs and scribbled as he spoke. "I'm writing you a prescription for the albuterol you've just learned to use."

"I'll be breathing into it constantly!" she protested.

"That one is a test kit. There's very little medication inside. We'll start you on a daily dose, but we may find you'll need it less often."

"I may not need it?" Her voice lifted.

"Hopefully, you won't."

"I've got to go to work," she said, glancing as the circular clock on the green emergency room wall ticked off the seconds. Ten minutes to five.

"Not today, you don't," he said. "Today, you rest." He handed her two prescriptions. "The hospital pharmacy will fill these. Use the albuterol four times a day for three days. After that, use it only if necessary. I'm also giving you Pulmicort to help prevent attacks. "

She laid the prescriptions on the crinkled paper that lined the exam table and took another hit from the test kit. "It's OK to go back to your condo, but keep the windows open," Dr. Davis continued. "Is there someone at home to be with you?"

She shook her head. "No. I'll be fine."

"Is there someone you can call?"

"Sure." She nodded.

He looked at her quizzically. "I'd like you to schedule a follow-up appointment at my office," he said. He pulled a business card from the pocket of his scrubs. She glanced at the raised lettering. *Jeffrey H. Davis, M.D., Upper East Side Pulmonologists, 204 East 79th Street, New York, NY 10021, 212-555-1300*, it read. *Impressive.*

"I'll be away for the next week," he said. "If you have any symptoms, call my office. I'll make sure one of the other doctors sees you right away." He cleared his throat. "Otherwise, come in after June 7."

"Do you think it's OK if I wait until you're back?"

"It should be OK," he said. "Just keep your windows open until the paint smell goes away. But this being New York, there are plenty of other allergens that could trigger an attack."

He reached toward her shoulder and gave her upper arm a reassuring squeeze. His strong hand snagged her hospital-issue gown and grazed her skin. Immediately, he returned his hand to the part of her arm that was draped by the gown.

"What's that?" he asked, glancing at her wrist.

"My rosary. It makes me feel safe."

"Whatever gets you through the night," he said with a smile.

Slipping her arms behind her back, she clasped her hands together. "Thanks, Doctor…for saving me…from the attack."

"That's my job—it's what I do." He hesitated a moment before adding, "I'll always keep you safe."

When he turned to walk away, his blue scrubs, dampened with sweat, clung to his broad shoulders. The slacks hugged the curve of his perfect ass. *When does a guy with his schedule find a chance to work out?* she wondered, taking in the view.

*   *   *

Back in her condo, Heather mentally replayed her emergency room visit dozens of times, recalling every detail. Except one. She couldn't remember if the doctor had worn a wedding band. Why hadn't she noticed? It was usually the second thing she noticed about a man, right after his eyes. Or the third—right after his ass.

CHAPTER 2

HEATHER

HEATHER LEANED AGAINST THE FLUFFY PILLOWS that lined the couch, feeling guilty for being home on a weekday. The hint of a breeze swayed the drapes ever so slightly. As she drifted in and out of sleep, she recalled the events that had preceded her asthma attack.

Yesterday had been moving day. After the moving men had unloaded Heather's belongings, she and Trista, Heather's closest friend—and until that day, her roommate—had spent the morning unpacking. They'd quit at two o'clock when, except for a dozen unpacked boxes, the place looked like home.

"When is Chas moving in?" Heather had asked as they'd sprawled on the couch, downing coffee and bagels with cream cheese from a shop down the street.

"Most of his stuff is already there," Trista had replied. "He'll make it official over the weekend."

"You know," Heather had confided, "for me, the scariest thing about living alone is the idea of sleeping with no one else in the condo."

Trista had touched her arm. "You'll be OK. Besides, it won't be long before your baby girl is here for you to focus on."

Heather had nodded enthusiastically, but she'd felt a flutter in her heart. It had been eight months since she had mailed the masses of adoption paperwork and the hefty three thousand dollar fee to Hope for Children Adoption Agency. Although she was almost assured that a healthy Chinese baby would be placed with her, it had been a long and anxious wait. Moving to the two-bedroom condo on West 79th Street was all part of the plan for adopting a daughter. Still, buying the condo was admitting that she'd never meet the right man, marry, give birth, or move to the suburbs.

"That reminds me," Trista had said. "There's something I want to give you—a housewarming gift." She had lurched from the couch, searching for her purse among the cartons. Finding her purse, she had removed a small box wrapped in floral paper and topped by a leaf-green bow. She'd resettled her buxom body on the couch, tucking a dark blond ringlet behind her ear.

Heather had opened the box and retrieved a heart-shaped locket. "You can put the baby's picture inside when you get it," Trista had said. "I hope you don't have to wait too long to wear it." Her soft brown eyes, framed by wire-rimmed glasses, glistened.

"I'll start wearing it right now," Heather had said, opening the clasp. "It can't be much longer until they place a little girl with me."

* * *

After Trista had left, Heather had continued to unpack, making lists of things she had to do. *Find gym*, she'd written, promising herself she'd be diligent about working out more than she had when she'd lived downtown. Whipping some definition into the muscles of her delicate frame might attract a man in a suit instead of the cops and firemen who always tried to date her. Those guys thought a petite woman wanted a man who would walk through fire for her, literally, if not figuratively. But despite her fragile appearance, Heather had walked through her own fires and preferred it that way.

Next she had gone through her clothes to be sure she had something to wear to work the next day. She'd chosen a crisp, tailored dress and a lightweight sweater with tiny pearl buttons—Ann Taylor in vintage.

Both Heather and her fashion sense had come a long way from years of wearing parochial school uniforms at St. Aidan's in Bridgeport, Connecticut, a small city whose major claim to fame was having been the home of P. T. Barnum and Tom Thumb. It was the kind of place where kids grew up with only one goal—getting out.

Feeling hungry, she'd headed outside in search of a nearby Chinese restaurant. She remembered seeing one called China Gold that had looked promising with a sign in the doorway that read *Food to Stay or Go*. The only remaining decision of the day had been whether she wanted sweet and sour shrimp or beef with broccoli.

She had waited forever in the tiny takeout area, soaked by a surprise late-day shower, her wet clothes clinging to her body. Finally, she had placed her order, given her name, and befriended a young man named Min who ran the takeout section. When at last Min had handed her the food, a pint of beef with broccoli and an eggroll, he'd said, "Oh, Miss Heather, you no eat very much!"

"Don't worry about me, Min," she'd said, flashing him a smile. "Have a nice evening," she'd added, stunning the young man by saying the words in Chinese.

She'd taken her selection and stepped outside. As she'd stepped into the street at 79th and Broadway, a curb-high pool of water had engulfed her foot. The rain had gotten harder, drenching her hair and the brown paper bag that held her dinner. By the time she had fumbled for her key at her mailbox in the vestibule, she was near tears. She'd clutched the mail against her chest, grateful that the post office had processed her change in address so quickly. Stepping inside the elevator, she'd pressed *seven*.

*   *   *

Inside her condo, Heather had stacked the mail on the coffee table. She'd dug through a carton and removed a plate from a two-place service of Royal Doulton china she'd bought herself for her thirty-fifth birthday—about the time she'd given up on finding a husband and before her biological clock stopped ticking. She'd sat on the sofa, removing the wooden chopsticks from their paper sleeve and placing her food on the dinner plate.

Lifting the pile of mail, she'd sighed. So *many bills, so much responsibility. And still no baby.* And then she'd seen it. The legal-sized envelope with the return address: Hope for Children Adoption Agency, Beijing, China. She'd wiped a chopstick clean, slipped it into the flap, ripped the envelope open, and read:

Dear Miss Morrison:
We are writing to tell you that Hung Wang Lin has been matched with you for adoption. Lin is ten months old, a healthy and happy girl. She weighs eighteen pounds and has been at our facility since she was a few days old.
A small picture of Lin is enclosed. Please contact our affiliate agency in New York City to confirm your interest in proceeding with the adoption process...

Tears had spilled from Heather's eyes as she looked at the tiny photo of the child. She was beautiful, with straight-cut jet black bangs and speckles of amber in her dark brown eyes. Heather had removed the locket that hung empty around her neck, grabbed a scissor, and trimmed the picture slightly before slipping it inside the heart-shaped charm. She'd closed it and kissed the heart before reclasping the locket around her neck with shaking hands.

Fumbling for the phone, she'd dropped it twice in her excitement. The second time the phone had landed on her plate, squarely in the beef with broccoli. "Shit!" She'd lifted the phone and grabbed a fistful of paper napkins to wipe away the thick brown sauce that coated it. A moment later, she'd heard Trista's voice mail message.

"Trista, call me!" Heather had enthused. "It's my baby—I got my baby!"

* * *

Now, as the living room darkened, Heather sank back on the couch pillows and recalled the beginning of her quest for Lin. She had been in Beijing on business, scouting out a facility that could host over a thousand of her company's Asian customers for their annual meeting. An American couple staying at the hotel had come to Beijing to meet their adopted child for the first time and bring her home. Heather had seen the joy in the couple's eyes as their little girl raced across the hotel lobby into their arms.

That was the day Heather's journey toward motherhood—with its seemingly endless paperwork, home visits from social workers, and finally, the letter from Hope for Children containing Lin's picture—

had begun. She had approached the representative from the agency, Susan Chin, who had delivered the child to the hotel. Susan had invited Heather to go with her the following day to visit the orphanage where the child had lived. The experience was seared on Heather's soul.

At the orphanage, Susan had introduced Heather to some of the two hundred children who were awaiting adoption. Heather saw a room full of toddlers playing and a nursery where infants were lined in cribs, some sleeping, others crying. A bevy of female caretakers in pink pantsuits tended to the children's needs, but there were hardly enough of these women to go around.

"Are they all orphans?" Heather had asked.

"Oh, no," Susan had said. "Some are orphans, but most were abandoned by their parents. Some because of disabilities, but others simply because of their gender. That is why we have so many girls. Chinese couples want sons."

Although Heather had heard this before, the reality of hearing it from a Chinese social worker in the midst of a Beijing orphanage struck hard. "I want one," she'd said immediately. "I want to adopt one of these little girls."

CHAPTER 3

JEFF

THOUGHTS OF HEATHER CLOGGED HIS MIND as Jeff stared out to sea. Behind him, the ocean parted in the wake of the ship as it headed for St. Martin. Over dinner last night, his wife Priscilla's face had morphed into Heather's, and when they made love in their stateroom, Priscilla's body had become Heather's body. And in his dreams, she was there again—or still.

Maybe I just need to get her out of my system. Fuck her and be done with it. He remembered the way her nipples had grown hard as he'd examined her, her breasts firm behind the hospital gown. He exhaled hard and imagined what it would be like to have her. *Shit! I can't fuck a patient. Not this one. She's too smart, too independent. Her chart said she was single. I might as well tear up my medical degree.*

He recalled the thrill of having sex on the couch in his office with drug reps and nurses and medical consultants. Most had been easy marks. He preferred his women to be married; it was less complicated. There had been late night sex on the tables of exam rooms and daytime sex on the couch of his private office when the surrounding exam rooms were filled with doctors and patients. Any way he could get it, sex reaffirmed life for him when his patients were deathly ill and even more so when one had died. He had to have sex as quickly as possible after a patient died. And preferably, not with his wife. It had to be with someone new, tantalizing, and life-affirming.

No one had died, but Heather Morrison stuck in his thoughts like gum on a shoe. Physically, she was exactly his type—petite and blond with big boobs. Her trust in him—her gratitude—was clear. It seemed to be coupled with an almost neurotic need for security—that sense of physical safety that only he, as her doctor, could provide. He loved the fact that taking her next breath literally depended on his professional decisions. This was why he had become a doctor and what made him feel most like a man.

Jeff knew Priscilla had put him on this ship because it was the only way she could keep him from eighteen-hour days at the office and hospital. And so, for the tenth time in as many years of marriage, Priscilla Wellington Davis had taken her husband out to sea—away from patients, colleagues, emergencies, and temptations. It was clear to Jeff that Pris couldn't have known how targeted her timing had been this time. He chuckled, wondering if he'd have been able to resist trying to see Heather immediately if he wasn't trapped at sea.

This cruise was his wife's gift for his fortieth birthday. Forty! He reached into the pocket of his Dockers, pulling out a pack of Parliaments. He glanced around to ensure that no patients or colleagues were in sight as he lit up his smoke. *Oh, right, I'm on a cruise. I don't have to play doctor here.* Fighting the ocean breeze, he struggled to light his cigarette. He inhaled the acrid smoke, longing instead for one taste of Heather.

"Don't go there," he said out loud, the wind blowing his words back at him mockingly. "She's a *patient*. A *single* patient."

"Who you talking to, Daddy?" a small voice responded.

Engrossed in his thoughts, he hadn't heard the pair of children approaching until they were running circles around him. "Dad-DEE, Dad-DEE." He reached first to catch the girl and then her brother. Beautiful children with their mother's light brown hair and his turquoise eyes, the seven-year-old twins were the perfect complement to an apparently perfect life.

"Hey, baby girl," he greeted his daughter, lifting the child in his arms.

"I thought we'd never find you!" Priscilla said, putting her arm around Jeff's waist and resting her head on his shoulder. "We've scoured every deck on the ship."

"What's so important?" he asked. "You know I couldn't escape this ship without a helicopter or a life raft."

"Exactly why we're on board," she said.

I won't give in to one of these trips next year. I get so stir-crazy.

"Dinner's early tonight, remember?" Priscilla said. "At four. With special entertainment for the children."

"Oh, right," he fumbled. It had skipped his mind entirely. "Some sort of costume party, isn't it?"

"Why else would Sam and Hannah be dressed like ragamuffins?" For the first time, he noticed the twins were wearing torn patchworked shirts and jeans rubbed with black crayon to look like grease. A far cry from the kiddie designer boy-girl clothing Priscilla normally outfitted them in.

"Jeff, where is your head today?" she asked.

"Out there somewhere," he said, indicating the vast ocean that surrounded them.

"Reel it in, honey," Priscilla said. "For the kids."

* * *

They made love quickly and quietly in their stateroom when they were certain the children were asleep in their adjoining room. Afterwards, Jeff listened to Priscilla's content postorgasmic breathing as it alternated with the roar of the higher-than-normal seas. Against the backdrop of his wife's breath, he heard Heather's relieved voice repeating, *Thanks, doctor...for saving me...* He grew hard again at the thought of eliciting such a powerful statement from another human being! *Thanks, doctor...for saving me.*

Even in the throes of an asthma attack, she had been beautiful. Despite wearing a hospital gown and not a speck of makeup, Heather Morrison was hot. Slim but curvy, delicate yet strong. A jumble of contradictions that were somehow tied together in a perfect package.

He'd felt the immediate connection between them just as much as he was sure she had—maybe more. He wanted her—and he was used to getting what he wanted. He felt the familiar warm urge in his cock, a literal ache to possess something others would say he shouldn't have.

The ship would dock at St. Martin in the morning. *Just two more of these fucking islands before I can go home,* he thought, slipping into a fantastic dream in which he finally possessed her.

CHAPTER 4

HEATHER

ON TUESDAY MORNING, Heather returned to a desk stacked with expense reports and an e-mail account that was filled to capacity. She sighed audibly as she clicked open an e-mail from her boss with the subject line: *Firm Frowns on Sick Fridays.* She read on. *Heather, as you know, yesterday was Memorial Day. Although you followed corporate policy by calling in sick on Friday morning, the company frowns on extending weekends with sick or personal time, especially on holiday weekends. Those employees wishing to take four-day weekends should schedule vacation time at least a month in advance. Jane Anderson, Vice President, Human Resources.*

Heather slammed her mouse against a mouse pad portraying the firm's logo—the only mouse pad design permitted at the firm. She fought the urge to tremble in fear as she had years before on those few occasions when she'd been summoned to Mother Superior's office. *OK, Jane, I'll schedule my next emergency room visit to suit the corporation!* She longed to work at a company that didn't have corporate travel employees report to the human resources department.

Desperate to vent, she e-mailed Miguel Estavez, her one real friend at Peters & Andrews, the stuffy international law firm where she was the director of corporate travel. *You here?* Seconds later, Miguel's auto-generated response appeared: *I will be in Mexico City on business until Tuesday, June 1. In my absence, please contact my associate Suzanne Pullman. Miguel Estavez, Associate Corporate Counsel.*

Let me know when you get into the office, Heather typed before moving on to the next e-mail. She tapped her fingernails on her desk, mentally cursing the firm's corporate culture.

A familiar voice lifted her from her frustration. "Hi, sweetie pie."

"Miguel!" She jumped up as he entered her office. It had been almost three weeks since she'd seen her friend.

"You're looking gorgeous as always," he said.

"You liar," she said. "I look like hell—barely slept last night."

"Oh, do tell! Details! Details!"

"Not *that* kind of barely slept," she said. "Insomnia."

Miguel dropped his jaw as if Heather had announced she had a case of the plague. "Oh, poor baby!" He patted her forearm with genuine concern.

"I was just excited," she said, fingering the chain around her neck. "And nervous."

"About what?" he asked, settling into the chair across from her.

She leaned over her desk, unfastening her locket. "I'm getting my baby!"

"Oh, my God! That's fabulous! When?" he asked.

"It could be close to a year," Heather said. "But at least I know who she is now." Miguel took the locket in his fingers to get a better look. "Her name is Lin."

"She is absolutely beautiful," he said. "Like her mama."

"You're too sweet," Heather replied. She sighed. "I'll have to go to China to get her."

"Cool," Miguel said. "China is a great trip."

"I know. Remember I went there last year to locate an off-site meeting site for P&A's office in Beijing? I took a few extra days for vacation and visited the orphanage Lin is coming from. That's really when this whole baby thing started."

"Duh," Miguel said, slapping the palm of his hand against his forehead. "That's right! I can hardly keep track of my travels, let alone yours. When do you pick her up, Mama?"

"I called the adoption agency's New York office on Friday. They said it could be as long as April of next year."

"Wow!" Miguel let out a soft whistle. "That will give you plenty of time to get ready."

Heather moved to the edge of her chair. "Do you think I can do it?" she asked. "Raise a child alone?"

Miguel sighed. "You've asked me that a hundred times. And a hundred times I've said there could be no better mother than you—married or single."

"I have to do it right," she said, wringing her hands. "Much better than my own parents did for me. Especially my father."

"Of course you will! No offense, sweetie, but what kind of teacher leaves his family and runs off with one of his students like your father did?"

A sad smile touched Heather's lips. "I've been wondering about that for more than twenty years."

"You'll be a great mama," Miguel said. "It's the bureaucracy of the adoption process that will be the biggest ordeal for you."

"Speaking of ordeals, I had a major one on Thursday night," Heather said. "I had an asthma attack."

"Oh, my God! I didn't know you had asthma!"

"Neither did I."

"What happened?" he asked, his eyes wide with alarm.

"I woke up on Thursday night and I couldn't breathe. I felt like I had a cinder block sitting on my chest," she said. As she recounted the cab ride to the hospital and the emergency room treatment, Miguel nodded at appropriate intervals.

"I actually passed out on the table in the emergency room. I can't remember getting from the cab to the ER," Heather said.

"Oh, sweetie! I wish I could have been there for you!" Miguel exhaled heavily and regarded his friend with his rich brown eyes framed by lashes any woman would envy.

"It wasn't *all* bad," she said. "The doctor was *hot!*"

"Leave it to you to find a man to focus on while you're clinging to life!" He winked.

"You're such a drama queen, Miguel! I wasn't clinging to life. But it *was* terrifying."

"And the hot doc?" Miguel asked.

"Don't know." She lifted the doctor's business card from where she had stood it in the keyboard of her computer. "I have to make a follow-up appointment. After that—we'll see!"

Miguel shook his head. "I can't see you with a doctor...not unless he plays in a rock band on the side."

"I know. But he *was* gorgeous." She returned the business card to her keyboard. "What about you? How was Mexico City?"

"Same as always—filthy and depressing." He tossed his head to the side, flipping a shock of patent leather black hair from his eyes. "I am so lucky my parents came to this country before I was born. Spanish Harlem is heaven compared to Mexico City."

Heather nodded. "New suit?" she asked, acknowledging Miguel's fitted grey pinstripe set off by a lime green shirt and a lime green-and-grey patterned tie.

"Do you love it?" he asked. "You know I have no self-discipline when it comes to buying clothes."

"It's great," she said. "But your crucifix is tangled in your collar."

Miguel reached for the chain and tucked it inside his collar. "Thanks, sweetie."

He's probably the most religious guy to troll the gay bars of New York, she thought as she watched him adjust his collar.

Miguel pushed a long, narrow bag he had placed on Heather's desk toward her. "I brought you this."

Removing a fifth of tequila from the bag, Heather asked, "Is there really a worm at the bottom of the bottle?"

"You'll just have to drink to the bottom to find out," Miguel said.

"Only if you join me. Are you free Fri—" She stopped midsentence as her office phone rang. The name Jane Anderson appeared on caller ID. "I've got take this, sweetie."

"Lunch later?"

"I'll e-mail you." She lifted the receiver as Miguel waved and walked away. Another great ass, but not one she would ever get a piece of.

"Heather Morrison speaking."

"Welcome back," Jane said snidely.

"Jane, I was out on Friday because..."

"It doesn't matter," Jane interrupted. "What *does* matter is that, in your absence, you failed to confirm my reservation at the Chicago Marriott."

Oh, crap! Heather clicked wildly through the task list for last Friday on her Outlook calendar. "Oh, Jane, I apologize. You see, I was..."

"Just where do you expect me to stay during the major human resources event of the year? The entire city of Chicago is booked."

Heather tugged on the heart-shaped locket that held Lin's picture. She opened one browser for Expedia.com and another for LastMinuteHotels.com. "I'll have something for you within half an hour, Jane."

Jane hung up without saying good-bye.

* * *

Heather's fingers trembled on the keyboard as she booked a room for Jane at the Chicago Marriott at twice the regular price. Then before reviewing the stack of expense reports towering on her desk, she typed the ER doctor's name into Google: Jeffrey H. Davis, M.D. She included the middle initial. Just like on the card he had given her.

Pages of results spewed onto the screen of her monitor. Quotes from Jeffrey H. Davis, M.D., in *The Journal of Respiratory Therapy* and a host of consumer magazines in articles about asthma. The last item she clicked on was the website of his practice, Upper East Side Pulmonologists, where his bio revealed that he'd earned his medical degree at the University of Southern California. He had interned at Maricopa Medical Center in Phoenix before moving to New York for a residency at Bellevue. In the picture accompanying his bio, he was wearing a suit and tie and looked to have actually had a good night's sleep. It didn't seem possible, but the photo made his appearance in the emergency room—tired and rumpled in surgical garb—pale by comparison.

She picked up her office phone and dialed Dr. Davis's office to make her follow-up appointment. She'd looked at his business card so many times, she knew the number by heart: 212-555-1300. An automated attendant answered the phone, reeling off a seemingly endless list before getting to *for Dr. Jeffrey Davis, press six*. She pressed the number, and almost immediately, a real human picked up and answered, "Dr. Davis's office."

"Hi, my name is Heather Morrison," she began. "I need to make an appointment."

"Are you a new patient?" a clipped female voice asked.

"Yes." Heather looked again at the doctor's picture on the practice's website. "He saw me in the ER at Lenox Hill last week."

"What time of day is good for you?" the receptionist continued.

"An evening would be best," Heather said.

"He's going to be booked pretty tight when he gets back into town. How does a week from Tuesday sound? At seven thirty?"

"Tuesday, the eighth?"

"That's right."

"Seven-thirty is a little late," Heather said.

"It's his last appointment of the day."

"OK, then," Heather said. "Seven-thirty it is." She entered the appointment into her Outlook calendar: *Tuesday, June 8, 2010. 7:30 p.m. Dr. Davis.*

God, please let this guy be single. And, if he's not, give me the strength to stay away from him.

CHAPTER 5

HEATHER

AFTER MASS ON THE SUNDAY BEFORE her appointment with Dr. Davis, Heather had stopped at Payless and bought a pair of black high heels and sheer pantyhose in nude. She'd taken her favorite slim black skirt and sexiest lightweight sweater to the dry cleaner. She had planned her outfit for her appointment more carefully than she did for dates.

Finally, on Tuesday, she stepped off the elevator onto the seventeenth floor of a plush building at Park Avenue and 79th Street. She trembled as she gave her name to the receptionist and signed the arrival registry with a gold pen embossed with the letters UESP, the acronym for Upper East Side Pulmonologists.

"May I use the ladies' room?" she whispered.

"Certainly," the receptionist bellowed, handing her a key ring that was literally a twelve-inch brass ruler with a tiny key dangling from the ten-inch mark. Its size all but screamed *Heather Morrison needs to pee*.

In the ladies' room, she freshened her makeup, then returned to the reception area, where she thumbed through the latest copy of *Vogue* for close to half an hour. Finally, her name was called by an obese forty-something nurse. Heather struggled to keep her balance on her cheaply crafted three-and-a-half-inch heels as she followed the nurse down the hall to the doctor's office.

Dr. Davis sat behind a huge mahogany desk, clutching the phone to his ear, engaged in a clearly serious conversation. He smiled at

Heather and indicated she should take one of the two seats opposite him. She chose the chair nearest to the door.

As he spoke into the phone, she felt his eyes rest on the tight black sweater that hugged her breasts like the skin on a grape. "Have his family notified," the doctor was saying. "I can't see him lasting more than another twenty-four hours." He raised his eyes from Heather's chest to the smile she found it impossible to contain upon seeing him again. She watched him as he conveyed what was clearly a death sentence for one of his patients.

How does he do it? Deal with death and disease day after day? She glanced at his amazing turquoise eyes, then down the arm of his starched white lab coat to his left hand. How had she missed it? No ordinary wedding band, his was embedded with at least two karats in diamonds set in yellow gold. Her throat tightened.

"Heather!" he said as he hung up the phone and reached across his desk to shake her hand. "How have you been feeling?"

She pulled her eyes from his ring with difficulty. "So much better," she said. "I haven't had another attack, thank God! That was terrifying."

"There's nothing to be afraid of anymore. I'll take care of you." It seemed more like a vow than a statement. "Any difficulty breathing?" he asked in a more casual tone.

"A bit," she said, mesmerized again by his vow to take care of her. "It usually happens at night—if I feel anxious about being alone."

"Aren't you used to being on your own?" he asked, glancing at her chart.

"No, I'm not. Until a few weeks ago, I lived with a roommate in the Village. I live alone in my new place."

She noticed his eyelids twitch in a visible reaction before his eyes once again flirted with her breasts. "Well, I imagine that is quite an adjustment for you."

"Don't get me wrong—I'm very excited about having my own place. But my asthma attack happened the first night I was alone there."

"Interesting." He tapped his fingers on the desk. The cuticles were perfectly trimmed, the nails clearly clipped professionally. "Have you been using your albuterol inhaler?"

"Only at night," she said. "During the day, I just have occasional shortness of breath. But I do use the Pulmicort every day to ward off attacks."

"Any other symptoms?" he asked. "How is your sleep, your energy level?"

"My energy level is good." She thought a moment. "Except, of course, when I haven't slept well the night before."

He ran a hand through his thick black hair. "Your sleep's not good?"

"Some nights. Since the asthma attack, I've been a bit afraid to go to sleep. Afraid I'll wake up having another attack."

"Concerns like that aren't uncommon. I can give you something to help you sleep."

"I don't think I need sleeping pills," she said.

"There are a number of new drugs with short half-lives that don't leave you feeling tired the morning after you take them. Why don't you let me help you decide what's best for you?"

"Well, you're the doctor," Heather said, glancing at the framed degrees and awards that covered the wall behind him. She looked next at a photo displayed on his desk. "Nice family picture." She felt her throat tighten more.

"Thank you." He tugged on his tie. "Taken just last week."

Heather noted the railing behind the glowing family. "Looks like it was taken on a cruise ship," she said, her heart hammering in her chest. She took in every detail of his glamorous brunette wife and two adorable children who looked to be very close in age. The doctor's hand was placed protectively on his wife's shoulder. She appeared to be almost as tall as her husband.

"Yes. The Caribbean. My wife likes to go on cruises." A distracted flicker crossed his face. She could almost hear him thinking, *I shouldn't be talking to her about this.* "It's really the only way she can nail me down." He stood and stepped around his desk. "We'll talk more inside. My nurse, Miriam, will show you to the examination room."

She watched him leave the room. *Not much point in scoping out his ass, having seen the ring on his hand. But it's so hard not to look!*

*   *   *

The massive nurse turned sideways as she came through the door of the doctor's consulting room. "Right this way, Ms. Morrison." They crossed the hall and entered a brightly lit exam room with sleek black furnishings and cutting-edge medical equipment.

"Just remove your shoes and hop on the scale," the nurse said, shifting the larger weight down to the hundred-pound mark. Heather slipped out of her pumps and stepped on the scale. Her toenails were freshly lacquered in a bright and sexy red.

"Perfect," the nurse said as she balanced the scale at 105 pounds, an envious sneer betraying her professionalism. "Maybe a few pounds underweight." After taking Heather's blood pressure, the nurse said. "I'll give you a gown. Remove your clothing from the waist up. Everything below the waist can stay on. The opening goes in the back."

Heather thanked her and took the white paper gown. The nurse waddled from the room, and the door clicked closed. Heather slipped into the paper jacket and grabbed her purse. She brushed her hair quickly and applied fresh lipstick. *Why am I doing this? He's married!* Then she waited, her heart hammering. Every few minutes, she shifted her position on the exam table, trying to find the right balance between sexy and sick.

*   *   *

It was another twenty minutes before the doctor came through the door. "I'm really sorry; this place usually runs like clockwork," he said as he checked the notes his nurse had made.

"The shortness of breath," he said. "Is there anything besides the anxiety of being alone at home that seems to bring it on?" He tugged at the stethoscope around his neck.

"Sometimes stress at work will do it. But not nearly as badly as being alone does. It's a lot like an anxiety attack. I've had anxiety attacks for years but never this bad or this often. And never at home. Now I get them almost every night. I feel like I can't get a full breath."

"The anxiety may subside once you get used to living alone," he said.

"I suppose," she said. Her face brightened. "But I won't be alone for long. I'm going to adopt a baby girl from China."

"A baby! Wow. Congratulations, I guess."

"You *guess*?" She looked at him quizzically.

"It's not easy being a single parent," he said, shining a light into first her left eye, then her right. "It's not easy being a parent, period."

"I've wanted a child forever," she said. "This may be my last chance."

"Oh, I doubt that," he said.

She smiled weakly but didn't respond. He didn't have to know about the trail of failed relationships that had convinced Heather she'd never find a decent man to marry.

He poked his stethoscope around her chest, pressing it close in four different places while he listened. She wondered if she imagined that his hand lingered on her left breast longer than any doctor's had before.

"You can relax now," he said.

She leaned forward on the table, breathing easily now. Her slender legs brushed against the smooth sheet of white paper that draped the table.

"Your heartbeat is strong. Now I'd like to check your lungs." He moved behind her, stethoscope in hand. She let the paper gown fall open to expose her back. As the cold metal touched her skin, the gown slipped off her right shoulder. *How did that happen? Did I move?* "Breathe deeply," Dr. Davis was saying, and she complied.

He positioned the stethoscope higher on her back. "Again, the deepest breath you can take. Breath in"—he was quiet for a moment—"and out."

When he was finished, she slid her shoulder back under the paper of the gown.

"Have you always been such a shallow breather?" he asked.

"I didn't know I was."

"Oh, you are. I think that may be a big part of your problem. Practice breathing from your diaphragm. Aerobic exercise would help. Or yoga."

"Maybe I *have* been a shallow breather all my life. I remember I had to stop playing basketball in junior high because I got so winded."

"Did your parents have a doctor check it out?" he asked.

"No. They didn't really go to doctors."

He was quiet for a moment as if waiting for her to offer an explanation.

"They were barely functional themselves when I was a kid," she added. She offered no more information.

The doctor cleared his throat and continued. "I think it would be best to treat your anxiety in addition to your asthma. I suspect that your asthma has an anxiety-based component. I believe you may have been mildly asthmatic for years."

"How would I not have known I had asthma?"

"Well, like you said, you chalked it up to anxiety. It sounds like it was aggravated by physical activity, which is common. But it took an environmental trigger to stimulate your first major attack. I can help you manage both the anxiety and the stimuli."

"How can you treat my anxiety? Are you a shrink, too?"

He chuckled and shook his head. His black hair shone in the fluorescent light of the room. Heather longed to reach over and touch it. "I'm no shrink," he said, "but I'm very aware of the ways the mind affects the body. Let's get your anxiety under control and see how that affects your asthma."

Heather laughed softly. "How could you possibly get my anxiety under control? I've been trying for thirty-eight years and haven't put a dent in it."

"Let's try you on Paxil. It's a selective serotonin reuptake inhibitor, an SSRI. It helps control anxiety by blocking the reabsorption of serotonin. It normalizes the brain's chemical supply faster than the other SSRIs."

"I've heard about SSRIs. But I don't know what they have to do with asthma."

"In many cases, nothing. In your case, I expect, a lot. It's certainly worth a try. I've seen it work miracles on anxiety."

"OK, if you really think so."

He bent toward her as she sat on the exam table and looked at her directly with those amazing eyes. "I really think so," he said.

She gazed back, mesmerized. "Well, OK, then." If he'd asked her to drink arsenic at that moment, she might have. As he straightened up, she felt a pull toward him, almost like a magnet. She didn't want him to back away.

"I'd like you to come back in two weeks," he said. "I want to see how the Paxil is working for your anxiety. It takes about a week or two to kick in."

"Two weeks?" She looked at him as if he'd given her a life sentence. She wanted to put him in her pocket, take him home, and take him out for a dose of professional reassurance every time she was anxious. Already she felt the beginnings of an addictive need to be in his presence. Being near him made her feel so safe.

"Tell me more about your sleep problem," he said.

"It's two things," she said. "Sometimes I can't fall asleep. Other times I fall asleep, but wake up during the night and can't go back to sleep."

"Ambien CR will take care of both of those problems."

"I really don't want to take a bunch of drugs," she insisted. "Especially sleeping pills."

"Neither of these medications is addictive in any way. I can give you some samples until you have a chance to get the prescriptions filled."

"OK," she said, still obviously hesitant.

He looked at her directly and said, "You can trust me. I really think you should try these medications."

"OK," she said again, sounding more convinced this time.

He searched through a medical supply cabinet until he located some sample boxes of Paxil. Handing her one, he grabbed a white laminate bag with a navy blue cord. *Upper East Side Pulmonologists,* the bag read in matching navy blue print.

"Shit!" he blurted as a box fell to the floor.

"Dr. Davis!" Heather exclaimed, feigning insult.

"I apologize. I just get so pressured when I'm running behind." He shoved the Ambien samples into the designer bag and said, "The Paxil will help any emotional aspect that might be influencing your asthma attacks. And the Ambien will help you to sleep."

"Thank you." She hesitated before adding, "And of course I trust you."

"If you can't trust your doctor, who can you trust?" he asked rhetorically.

It all sounded too good to be true. Anxiety—gone. Sleeping all night with no fear and no asthma. Breathing easily for the first time in her life. Dr. Davis seemed to have the answer for her every problem.

The doctor scrunched up his face as if struggling to make an important decision. Then he reached into the pocket of his lab coat and pulled out a notepad with a border of purple pills and the logo of a pharmaceutical company on the bottom of the page. He scribbled on the pad.

He tore the page off the pad and handed it to her. "My cell number," he said. "Call me anytime. Call me if you need anything more."

Heather hopped off the exam table, grabbed her purse, and shoved the paper inside. "OK," she said. "Thank you, Dr. Davis."

In an apparent effort to return their meeting to the formality of an office visit, he extended his hand to shake hers firmly. "The samples will get you started. My receptionist will have your prescriptions ready at the front desk."

* * *

Heather juggled her cell phone as she burst from the revolving doors of the doctor's office building.

"He's married!" she blurted when Trista answered the phone.

"Heather?"

"That gorgeous doctor who saw me in the emergency room is married," she stammered as she waited at Park and 79th for the *Don't Walk* sign to turn to *Walk*. She stumbled off the curb among a throng of people.

"Of course he's married," Trista was saying. "All the good ones are married."

She joined the sea of humanity that was barreling en masse across Park Avenue. "But he did do something odd."

"Odd? What?"

"He gave me his cell number."

"Your *doctor* gave you his cell number?" Trista's voice was louder than before. "What the hell is that about?"

"I don't know. Maybe so I can call him if I need medical help?"

"I never heard of a doctor making himself so...accessible," Trista replied.

"Do you think there's some other reason he gave it to me?" Heather asked, sounding hopeful.

"I have no idea, honey. What I do know is you have more important things to worry about—like taking care of your asthma and getting ready for Lin."

The cell connection floundered. The line went dead. It was just as well. *Trista is right*, Heather chided herself. *I really need to get my priorities in order now that I'm going to be a mother.*

CHAPTER 6

HEATHER

THE FEATURED BAND AT THE BLUE NOTE was taking a break, allowing Chas, the band's trumpeter, to spend time at the table with Heather and her friends. The band manager, Ian, had joined the group as he seemed to do whenever Heather went to one of Chas's shows.

Trista kissed Chas lightly on the cheek. "He blows a mean horn," she swooned, her dark blond hair spilling over her shoulders in an abundance of ringlets. Her floral skirt was full and forgiving, giving her a sexy look despite the extra twenty pounds that made their home in her stomach and thighs.

Heather tried to sneak a glance at her watch in the dim light. It had to be after midnight. "I've really got to get going," she said. She had to get up for work by seven while her friends, all musicians or artists, would no doubt sleep until noon.

"Can't you just have one drink?" Trista urged. "Jesus, you've been drinking cranberry juice all night!"

Heather shook her head no.

"How's having the baby going to affect your plans with Dr. Love?" Trista added in a whisper, using the moniker she'd adopted for Jeff Davis.

"Would you stop calling him that, please?" Heather leaned close to her friend. "Besides, we both know he's married."

"Oh, honey, you know I'm just teasing."

"How about a ride home?" Ian offered, shoveling a forkful of fried calamari into his mouth. "My car is parked on MacDougal."

"Really, that's OK," Heather said. Ian wiped his mouth with a paper napkin and tossed it onto his plate. Hard. Clearly a ride home was only the first of two rides he'd hoped to give Heather that night. "Thanks, though."

Heather walked toward Washington Square, heading for the subway station at West 4th Street. *I'm a big girl,* she reminded herself. *I don't need to sleep with some random guy to get a ride uptown.*

* * *

Almost two hours later, Heather kicked off her bed sheets and headed for the bathroom. The late night out had given her no time to wind down from the day. She'd been tossing and turning for forty-five minutes.

It was too late to take one of the sleeping pills Dr. Davis had prescribed. She opened the medicine cabinet where she had put some Valium that Trista had given her when she was recovering from her last breakup. *Why do I let the wrong men get so deep under my skin?* Trista had warned her that some diet pills she'd tried looked a lot like the Valium and could have accidentally been mixed into the vial. *Double-check every time you take a pill,* she'd warned Heather. But tonight, exhausted and desperate for sleep, Heather absentmindedly gulped down a pill with a swig of water from the bathroom sink.

It wasn't until she returned to bed that she remembered Trista's warning. She brushed the thought aside and fell asleep within minutes.

An hour later, Heather's eyes shot open in terror, her body drenched in sweat. *Oh, shit,* she thought, *here I go again.* Had she taken the wrong pill, setting off an asthma attack?

Turning on the bedside light, she reached for her inhaler. Her hands shook as she brought the device to her mouth, breathing in the medication with what little force she could muster.

She paced around the condo, inhaling the albuterol as she walked. She tried lying down, which only made it worse. *Would it be crazy to call him at this hour? Well, no, not if it's a medical emergency.* She got up and dug through her purse for the scrap of paper with Dr. Davis's cell number on it. *Call me anytime,* he had said.

His voice mail picked up immediately. "Hi, this is Jeff. I'm sorry I'm not available. Just leave your name and number, and I'll call you back as soon as I can." The message gave no emergency number to call. This was clearly his personal cell phone number.

The albuterol was helping a little. "Dr. Davis," she began. "This is Heather Morrison." She inhaled as deeply as she could. "I'm so sorry to call in the middle of the night, but I'm having an attack. I'm using the albuterol, but please call me when you get this message. My cell number is 646-555-7279."

She took an additional blast of albuterol for good measure, deciding to follow it up with a Valium and an Ambien, hoping to sleep despite the amphetamine. Next came a hot, steamy shower. *Why not? I'll take my morning shower now, kill two birds with one stone.*

She placed the cell phone on the edge of the sink where she could reach it if the doctor returned her call. It didn't ring during her shower. She returned to bed, disappointed and exhausted, and quickly fell asleep, clutching the phone in one hand and her rosary in the other.

*   *   *

Heather struggled to work the next morning, feeling more hungover from the pills than she would have if she'd been drinking all night at the club. Her morning was a grey fog until Miguel tapped on her office door.

"Hey, sweetie," he said. "How did your appointment with the pulmonologist go?"

"I'm doing OK," she replied. "But check this out—he gave me his personal cell phone number."

"Oh, boy!" Miguel rolled his eyes. As if on cue, her phone began to play "Bad Case of Loving You," the song she'd programmed to play when he called. The word *Doc* appeared in the digital display. *"Doctor, doctor, give me the news, I've got a bad case of lovin' you…"*

"Don't tell me—they're playing his song," Miguel said, recognizing the tune.

"I've got to take this, sweetie."

"Lunch in the cafeteria?"

"Absolutely. One o'clock." She opened the phone to answer as Miguel waved and walked away. "Hello, this is Heather."

"Heather," he said, "It's Jeff Davis. Are you OK?"

"I'm OK now, yes. And I'm so sorry for calling you at such a ridiculous time of night."

"There are no ridiculous times for doctors," he said. "Any hour of the day or night is fair game."

"I suppose. But I do apologize." She dropped her voice as Jane Anderson walked past her office door. "I would never have called, but I had a horrendous attack last night. I'm not sure if it was asthma or a reaction to a…well, an amphetamine."

"I'm so sorry I didn't call you back until now. I got called into the hospital last night. I lost a patient. That just never gets easier."

"Oh, I'm so sorry!"

"I didn't even listen to my messages until now. Let me make it up to you and see you, just to be sure you're all right."

"OK," she said. "I'll call your office and make an appointment."

"Who said anything about an appointment?" he asked. "Can you grab a cup of coffee with me?"

"Oops." The cell phone had nearly slipped from her quivering hand. "Where?"

"A coffee shop. Or a bookstore maybe."

"You mean like a Barnes & Noble?" she asked.

"Exactly." She heard him cough.

"There's a Barnes & Noble on East 54th," she said, glancing at the time on her computer screen: 9:45

"Would you mind coming uptown? There's a Barnes & Noble on 86th between Second and Third. I've got another patient on a respirator, and I expect his family will ask me to pull the plug within hours."

I really can't compete with that. "Of course I don't mind. I appreciate you taking the time to meet me, Dr. Davis."

"It's my pleasure, Heather. And please, do me a favor and call me Jeff."

"What time shall I meet you…Jeff?"

"About 12:15 should work. See you then."

* * *

The streets of midtown Manhattan were paralyzed by lunchtime gridlock. Taking a taxi uptown would take an eternity. The number 6 subway would get her there in minutes. Heather called Trista as she waited on the platform for the train.

"Hey, girlfriend," Trista said in greeting. "I am totally hungover."

"At least you know what brought it on. Last night I took one of those pills you gave me," Heather said. "I think I got one of your diet pills instead."

"The pills I gave you last year? You still have them?"

"A couple."

"I'm not surprised you still have them." Trista said. "I'd have polished them off months ago!"

"I know."

"Didn't I warn you that there could have been some diet pills mixed in with the Valium?" Trista asked.

"You did, and there were. I woke up at three in the morning with my heart in my throat."

"Sorry," Trista said. "Where are you?"

"I'm waiting for a train."

"How come you're going to lunch so early? Don't you usually go at one? With Miguel?"

"Yeah. But, well, the stuff in the pill made me sort of anxious—it brought on an asthma attack," Heather said.

"Oh, honey, I'm so sorry!" Trista replied.

"So I called Dr. Davis," Heather continued. "On his cell phone."

"In the middle of the night?"

"I know it was a little crazy. But he called back this morning. I'm meeting him uptown for coffee." Heather watched a roach as it scurried across the platform. Her heart jumped in fear, but snuffing out its life just wasn't her style.

"Coffee? With your doctor?"

"It does seem unusual," Heather acknowledged. "I'll let you know what happens."

"You'd better! By the way, Ian felt real bad that you didn't let him drive you home."

"Trista, I'm thirty-eight; I know what *drive you home* means."

"If you're so smart about men, why don't you get involved with somebody like Ian, who's actually available, instead of this married doctor?" Trista asked with her usual candor.

"We're not involved. We're friends," Heather shouted as the train screeched into the station.

* * *

It was 12:25 when Heather arrived at the bookstore. She scanned the café, hoping Jeff hadn't arrived first and been kept waiting for her. Seeing he wasn't there, she eyed a corner table where two young mothers were giving up the fight to converse as their wailing toddlers squirmed in their seats. Heather slid into one of their chairs while the moms were still shoving the kids' arms into pink hoodies with Kate Mack logos.

She glanced at her watch, growing uncertain that the busy doctor would even show up for her. Although he had her cell number, he could be pulling the plug on that terminally ill patient right now. Was he supposed to end a life with one hand while simultaneously calling her with the other?

Her shoulders relaxed when he appeared between the book racks, scanning the titles as if to deflect his interest from her as he approached the café.

"Dr. Davis! Jeff," she said when he arrived. She clutched the underside of the table.

"Well, somebody seems to be feeling better," he said, towering over her when she stood to greet him.

"I'm fine now...except for being embarrassed for calling you over nothing," she said.

"It wasn't nothing to you at the time. Besides, it gave me an excuse to see you before your next appointment."

She felt her pulse pound in her temples. Smiling, she sat down again.

"What can I get for you?" he asked.

"A café mocha would be great."

"My favorite as well. How about a sandwich?"

"Do you have time?"

"Everybody's got to eat," he said. "What kind would you like?"

"Anything's fine. Tuna, turkey. Whole wheat bread, if they have it."

"At your service," he said, turning toward the food counter. She hated to waste what little time they had together watching him standing in line. But they couldn't give up the table. As if reading her mind, he turned to look at her, sending a wink and a smile across the café.

* * *

It was almost ten minutes before he returned to the table with a tray holding two large café mochas, a tuna sandwich on white, a turkey sandwich on whole wheat, and a bottle of Poland Spring water. He glanced around the café before settling his gaze on their meal. "I'll be happy to share," he said, placing the items on the table. He'd even brought packets of Sweet'N Low and sugar and small tubs of half and half. "Help yourself to whatever you like."

Heather tore the top off a packet of Sweet'N Low and deposited it into the steaming coffee.

"I had you pegged as a Sweet'N Low girl," he said.

"Really?" She reached for the turkey sandwich, unwrapping it carefully. Bringing the coffee to her lips with a shaky hand, she missed her mouth. A stream of the hot liquid flowed down her white blouse. "Ouch!"

Jeff pulled a crisp handkerchief from the breast pocket of his suit jacket and moistened the edge from the bottle of Poland Spring. He reached across the table and rubbed the stain intensely. Heather shrank in horror as her nipple responded.

"All better now," he said, returning the handkerchief to his pocket. "And I see you enjoyed the stain removal as much as I did."

She bit her lower lip and blushed, mortified. "I love this stuff," she said, indicating her café mocha. "It's one of the few unhealthy things I allow myself to eat—or drink."

"So, I know you're a healthy eater," he said. "Tell me more about yourself." He bit into his tuna sandwich.

"Well, the asthma attack started…"

"Don't tell me about your asthma—I know about your asthma. Tell me about *you*. You're a fascinating woman."

"Really, I'm not," she insisted. "I'm just an ordinary girl from an ordinary family in Connecticut."

"There's nothing ordinary about you, Heather," he said. He brushed some crumbs from his fingers, glanced around, then reached for her hand. He held it gently, looking directly into her eyes. Time seemed to stand still—the noise in the restaurant dimmed to a distant lull. A moment later, he placed her hand back on the table and picked up his sandwich again. "What was it like growing up in Connecticut?" he asked.

"I grew up in Bridgeport—spent the first eighteen years of my life dying to get out. I guess we looked pretty much the classic American family of the eighties. But things aren't always what they seem."

Jeff's eyebrows shot up. "Meaning?" he asked.

"My father was a teacher at Bridgeport High. Mom worked as a matron at night at the same school. Except for my dad's drinking, everything was fine, as far as I knew, until he ran off with one of his students when I was fourteen. I have an older brother who's been married three—no, four times." She stirred her coffee with a plastic red-and-white-striped swizzle stick.

"That couldn't have been easy on you," Jeff said after a long pause. "Your dad running off…"

"It wasn't." She paused. "But at least we didn't have to deal with his alcoholism after he left." She licked a drop of coffee from the swizzle stick.

"Ever been married?" he asked.

"Nope."

"Engaged?"

"Almost. I fell hard for a guy during my last year of college. Tim Cook." She hadn't said his name in years. "I thought it was just him and me, but somehow another girl ended up pregnant with his baby. Next thing I knew, they were married."

"How'd you take that?" he asked.

"I was devastated," she admitted. "But it gave me the push I needed to move to New York and make something of my life. What about you?"

"I'm from Arizona. I grew up on a reservation," he said.

"A reservation?"

"I'm half American Indian," he said.

"Really! Now, *that's* not ordinary. *That's* fascinating."

He chuckled, coughing into his napkin. "My father-in-law doesn't think so."

"What do you mean?"

"My father-in-law is Dr. Preston Wellington. He's chief of staff at Lenox Hill. His family came over on the Mayflower. Around him, I'm known as Redskin."

"That's terrible!"

"Not really. I mean, the Indians were in America long before the Puritans." He laughed softly. "My mother was a purebred Havasupai Indian. Her husband was, too. They had five kids before he got drunk and took off one night."

"So you have four brothers and sisters?"

"No. *Five.* Five *half* brothers and sisters. I have a different father than the other kids."

Heather looked at him curiously, clearly wanting him to continue his story.

"Shortly after my father left, my mother was briefly involved with a British doctor who did some missionary work on the Havasupai Indian Reservation in Supai, Arizona. That's where I grew up. Three hundred miles from Phoenix—right at the foot of the Grand Canyon. It's absolutely beautiful, but the poverty is devastating. Eight of us lived in a tiny three-room house."

He revealed that he had been the result of the union between his mother and the British doctor, a secret she had kept hidden from everyone but him. His older brothers and sisters had chided him constantly that his skin was less golden, his hair curlier than theirs, and his turquoise eyes inexplicable. But his mother had never revealed her secret to the others.

"I was a lot smarter than the other kids in the family," he said matter-of-factly. "My mother told me, 'You must be a doctor like your father.' And one of the good things about being Indian is the government helped pay for my education."

"Your mother must be so proud of you."

"She was. My mother and I had a unique bond. She died in 1989. I was a resident at Bellevue. I haven't gone back to Arizona since her burial."

"That's sad. But at least she lived to see you become a doctor."

"Exactly. I felt I owed her that."

"What about your father?" Heather asked.

"What about him?" Jeff placed a crust on the plate, indicating he was finished.

"Have you ever looked for him?"

"No. He never knew about me. To me, he was nothing more than a sperm donor. Luckily for me, that sperm gave me the smarts to make it through med school."

"What about your brothers and sisters?"

"I don't really think of them as family. Growing up, they made me feel like an outcast in my own home. Today, they're mostly truck drivers and migrant workers in Arizona and Nevada," he said.

"You don't see them anymore?" she asked.

"No." He cleared his throat. "That part of my life is over. I've made a new life here. It sounds like I'm a lot like you. Life handed me lemons, and I made lemonade."

Heather nodded. "Do you live in the city?"

"In the thick of it. Central Park South. At Fifth Avenue," he said. Transitioning back to doctor mode, he added, "I was thinking you may need something to help with your anxiety before the Paxil starts to work. Have you ever taken Valium?"

"Of course," she said. "Hasn't everyone in New York?"

He pulled a pen and a prescription pad from his inside jacket pocket and began to write. "Five milligrams or ten?"

"Five. But I don't want to become a pill junkie."

"You won't, Heather. Trust me. I'd never let that happen to you. But a little something to help tide you over for a while can do no harm."

He handed her the prescription and stood. She stuffed the paper into her purse absentmindedly and followed him to the door. They stepped outside. Before they turned to walk in opposite directions, he said, "You know, I was lucky you had your asthma attack on that particular Thursday night. I was filling in for a colleague. My regular on-call night is Tuesday."

"Then I was lucky, too," she said.

Good-bye, Heather." He put one hand on each of her shoulders and looked at her directly with those turquoise eyes. He ran his fingers down her arms and said, "I'll see you at the office in two weeks."

She tingled under his touch. She stammered to say something, but no words came out.

Jeff turned and walked toward Third Avenue. There it was again, that perfect physique. She watched his broad shoulders and his inky black hair glistening in the sun before his image was swallowed up by the lunchtime crowd pounding the pavement.

CHAPTER 7

HEATHER

HEATHER RACED UP THE STEPS from the subway, her cell phone beeping incessantly from inside her purse. Message waiting. Buzz, buzz. Message waiting. Buzz, buzz. Car horns played a constant chorus in the midday traffic. Honk, honk. Buzz, buzz. Honk, buzz, honk, buzz, honk…

It'll have to wait, she told herself as she glanced at her watch. 1:45. *Shit!* She had a management position at Peters & Andrews, but the firm was strict about any of its employees taking extended lunch breaks unless they were with clients. She reached into her purse and clicked off the phone. Once inside her office building, she rode the elevator to the twenty-seventh floor. When the doors slid open, she burst through the glass-paneled doors of the firm, eschewing the ladies' room, although her bladder was screaming for relief.

She slipped behind her desk and slid her mouse across the corporate mouse pad. Immediately, the screen saver image of her brother Pete's four kids by three different mothers vanished, replaced by a sea of e-mails. Among them, *Girlfriend, where are you?* screamed from the subject line on a dozen e-mails from Miguel.

Oh, no, lunch with Miguel! Heather shot him an e-mail saying she'd had a minor crisis and apologizing for being such a lousy friend. *My best friend in the company, and I stand him up for lunch and cap it off with a lie! What's happening to me?*

As she worked, she pulled her cell phone from her purse, turned it back on, and pressed the message key. "You have one new message," the automated voice told her. She pressed the key a second time to listen.

"Heather, it's Jeff." She'd barely gotten back from seeing him and he was calling! Most men didn't call her back until four or five days after a date. "I just wanted to make sure you got back to your office OK. Oh, and to say how nice it was to see you. I hope we can do it again soon. Ciao."

Her hand quivered as she saved the message, knowing she'd want to listen to it again just to hear his voice. *What am I getting myself into?* She'd never been involved with a married man before. *It's wrong.* The picture of his wife and kids was embedded in her mind. *I'm not going to call him back. I don't want to be the other woman.*

* * *

Miguel's return e-mail appeared. *You OK?*

She replied immediately. *I'm fine. Got my period…no tampons in the ladies' room…ran to Duane Reade.*

* * *

On Friday morning, when Heather turned her cell phone on, there were two messages. The first one, from Trista, asked about her plans for the weekend. The next one was from Jeff.

"Hey, stranger, I'd hoped I'd hear from you by now." He paused. "I know it's short notice, but I wondered if you'd like to do a quick dinner tonight." *Quick? Quick, so you can hurry home to your wife and kids? Or maybe the hospital! Your patients need you.* "There's a great little place in Little Italy—Giuseppe's. It's on the southwest corner of Mulberry and Hester. Next to the firehouse. Please say you'll meet me there at nine."

She listened to the message a second time. "Heather, it's Jeff…" *Little Italy. Downtown where you don't know anybody. Away from your stuffy Park Avenue colleagues and Central Park South neighbors.*

She hadn't told Trista that her coffee date with Jeff had turned into lunch. And Miguel knew even less—including that Jeff was married.

Trista had already told her that getting involved with Jeff was wrong and could lead to nothing but heartache.

She listened again to Jeff's invitation on her voice mail. *What's more appealing? A microwaved Healthy Choice dinner alone while watching* Law & Order *reruns, or dinner at a great Italian bistro with Jeff?* Despite her good intentions, she returned his call. "I know the place," she told his answering machine. "I'll be there at nine." Mimicking what seemed to be his signature signoff, she repeated, "Ciao."

CHAPTER 8

HEATHER

AS THE AFTERNOON CRAWLED BY, Heather marked the seconds playing solitaire and checking the time on her computer. E-mails announcing their arrival with a ping went ignored. When Jane went into a meeting at four, Heather, anticipating her dinner with Jeff, could no longer sit still. She shoved her briefcase into a file drawer and left her computer on, grateful that it was June and she could slip out of the office without wearing a coat. Her computer would stay on all weekend.

At home, she showered and doused herself with sesame-scented oil. After slipping on a black lace underwire and matching panties, she searched through her overstuffed closet. She'd been to Giuseppe's before. The food and service were great, but the atmosphere was relaxed and casual. Jeans would be perfect. Jeff had never seen her wearing jeans, and the pair she had in mind flattered her figure more than anything she owned.

She'd seen the way his eyes had rested on her breasts when she wore her black cashmere sweater to her appointment. She had the same sweater in fuchsia. She pulled the featherweight sweater from the closet and over her head. The neckline formed a perfect frame for her gold locket. She added a black leather belt and leather boots with pointy toes and tall narrow heels. *Oh, yeah, this works.*

* * *

She took the B train to Grand Street. Her heart beat quickly with anticipation, keeping pace with the clicking of her heels as she crossed the ancient streets of the East Village. Sounds of talk and laughter spilled into the street as she opened the heavy wooden door to Giuseppe's.

She spotted him right away at a corner table near the window. "I'm meeting the gentleman over there," she told the hostess breathlessly.

He looked at her with a wink and a smile as she slid into the seat opposite him. "Hey, kid. You look like a million bucks."

"Thanks," she said, feeling suddenly shy.

"Would you like to start with some wine?"

"Sounds great."

He lifted the leather-encased wine list from the table and placed his reading glasses on the tip of his nose. "Red or white?"

"I'd like red. I'm pretty sure I'll have pasta."

"An Italian wine, no doubt. I mean, when in Rome…"

"Whatever you suggest," she said. "You're the doctor." As soon as the words escaped her lips, she wanted to take them back. It was one thing to give him all the power in medical matters. But his being a medical doctor didn't ensure that he was a wine connoisseur.

He smiled at the acknowledgment and said, "I could speak with the sommelier, but I think I can handle it. I suggest a Barolo. The Chiantis have come a long way, but you are a lady who is worthy of a Barolo."

"Why, thank you," she said, not letting on that she had no idea what a Barolo was.

"Barolos are the king of wines. Look, it says so right here." He pointed to a description on the menu next to a wine called Vietti Barolo Rocche. The price was $175 a bottle! *That would pay for groceries for weeks!*

Jeff nodded toward a waiter stationed against a nearby wall. The aging server walked briskly toward them, despite his stooped posture. "Si, signore, have you decided?"

"We'd like a bottle of the Vietti Barolo Rocche."

"Very good, signore. Pronto."

"*Grazie.*" Jeff handed the wine list to the waiter.

Heather sat back against the carved fruitwood chair and contented herself with simply being in Jeff's presence.

* * *

Moments later, the wine was carried to the table by a grey-haired man in his fifties. "I am the sommelier, signore. I don't usually serve, but I wish to compliment you on your selection," he said as he uncorked the bottle with a simple swirl of a corkscrew. He poured a small amount of the deep red wine into Jeff's glass.

Jeff swirled and sniffed the rich red liquid before lifting the glass to his lips for a sip. "Perfecto," he said in the vernacular of the sommelier.

"Oh, grazie, signore—only the best for our customers."

"It's a classic Barolo," Jeff added. "Sweet, lush, and rich—like the lady."

"Not so rich," Heather said as the smiling sommelier filled her wide-brimmed glass to the one-third mark. She sipped, skipping the swirling and sniffing that Jeff had done. The taste on her tongue was unprecedented. This was no Stone Cellars cabernet. "It's delicious. Absolutely amazing."

The sommelier ceremoniously placed the wine bottle on a tiny table that had been carried over by the hunchbacked waiter.

"I'm glad you like it," Jeff said, raising his glass to click against hers. "To your health."

"Well, that's up to you," she said.

"Let's make it a team effort," he said, his eyes darting around the room. Heather squirmed slightly in her seat and forced herself to talk about the wine. "This is wonderful. I've never had anything quite like it."

Jeff lowered his eyes from her face to her neck, then grazed her neck with his fingers. "You wear that locket all the time." He reached for it, rubbing the gold charm between his thumb and forefinger. "It must have some special meaning."

"It does."

"A Valentine's gift from an old lover?"

"No. Actually, Trista, my old roommate, gave it to me."

He raised his eyebrows. "A locket from a girlfriend?"

"Oh, don't be silly!" she answered, getting the implication. "She gave to me when I registered to adopt. And just last month, I finally got something to put inside."

"Your old roommate was a woman?" Jeff raised his eyebrows. "When you told me you had moved out on your own after living with someone for years, I assumed it was a breakup."

"Oh, no!" *Live for seven years with a man? I seldom make it to the third date!* "Just Trista." She gulped her wine, embarrassed when she realized she'd swallowed almost half the contents of the glass in a single sip.

"That heart you wear around your neck then...it isn't a treasured memoir of a past relationship?" Jeff continued.

"No. It's a treasure in anticipation of a *future* relationship." She reached for her locket, clicking it open with a manicured nail. "This is Lin, the little girl I'm adopting."

He leaned closer and took the locket in his fingers. "Sweet," he said, then closed the case. He released the locket from his fingers, letting it fall on Heather's skin. It landed backwards. The subject seemed closed.

*   *   *

After a second glass of wine, Jeff returned his reading glasses to his nose and viewed the menu with confidence. "What would you like?" he asked.

Heather tilted her menu toward him, pointing to a whole wheat pasta dish. He shook his head with a smile and said, "If all my patients were as vigilant as you are about their health, the practice would fail."

She smiled at the acknowledgment as the waiter appeared at the table. "Are you ready to order?" he asked.

"Yes, we've just decided. The lady—the healthy lady—will have the whole wheat bow tie pasta with vegetables and marinara sauce." He faked a bodily quiver as if in reaction to her healthy choice. "I, on the other hand, would like the penne a la vodka."

*   *   *

The tables were close together in typical Italian restaurant fashion. When the diners at the two tables nearest them left simultaneously, Jeff reached across the table for Heather's hand. Now it was her eyes that were darting around the restaurant. "Should you be doing that here?" she asked. Her fork slipped gently onto the white linen tablecloth.

"I just had to touch you—if only for a second." He looked at her with an expression of longing, then freed her hand.

Heather lifted her fork and raised a single piece of bow tie pasta to her mouth. She chewed it thoroughly and swallowed hard. "You're married, Jeff. Why are we, you know, starting to sort of hang out together?"

He leaned toward her. "Put down your fork," he said. When she complied, he took her hand in his once more. "We're hanging out together because we like each other."

She didn't respond.

"Don't we?" he asked.

"Yes." Her voice was barely audible.

"My marriage has been dead for years, but I can't leave. I like you, you like me. Logically, it makes perfect sense."

Heather nodded, a lump forming in her throat. He made it sound so rational, so calculated. Perhaps detecting the sad look that crossed her face, he added, "Of course, this is only the beginning. Anything can happen."

*   *   *

As they resumed their meal, Jeff asked, "What do you do? I mean when you're not seducing vulnerable doctors over dinner?"

"I'm not seducing you!" she said, giving his arm a playful shove.

"Your presence itself is seductive," he said.

She felt her neck stiffen, uneasy with Jeff's highbrow flirtation. Her typical dates expressed their interest by buying her a beer. "I organize corporate events. And make travel arrangements for the people in my company. You know, making reservations, processing expense reports."

"For what kind of firm?" he asked.

"A law firm—Peters & Andrews."

"I know them," he said. "International corporate law. Those guys must do a lot of traveling."

"Those guys—and women—travel constantly," she said. "I travel quite a bit myself."

"That sounds fascinating. Where have you been?"

"Everywhere. Every continent except Antarctica."

"Tell me about it," he said. And she did as they shared their food, talking and laughing softly like lovers.

*   *   *

After their dinner plates had been removed, Jeff reached for Heather's hand again. "This went too fast. Shall we linger over dessert?"

"I'll stay, but I try not to eat dessert."

"How about an espresso, then?"

"Sounds perfect."

He placed their order for two espressos and a crème brûlée with two spoons. Turning his attention back to Heather, he asked, "Have you ever been with anyone like me?"

"Someone married? No way!"

"I'm not talking about marital status. Have you ever been with someone you could lean on, who you trusted, who knew what was best for you?" He squeezed her hand tighter. "Someone who had your best interests at heart, not his own?"

"No."

"Well, you are now. I can help you. I can help you with your asthma attacks—with the emotional and physical things that bring them on. You trust me, don't you?"

"Of course I trust you!" she said. And then, a bit lower. "You're my *doctor*."

"Exactly. So I probably know what's best for you, too. We're good for each other, Heather. You'll see."

*   *   *

Jeff sat close to Heather on the cab ride uptown, their outer thighs pressed together. As the cab turned sharply north on Seventh Avenue, they tipped to the left. He put his arm around her shoulders protectively and left it there until they arrived at her building.

"Remember, you have an appointment on Tuesday evening," he said.

"It's a week from Tuesday," Heather said.

"Call the office and reschedule," he said. "That's too long a time between appointments." He winked. "In the meantime, if you have any issues—medical or otherwise—call me." He kissed her lightly on the lips. "Now, go upstairs before I insist on going with you."

She struggled from the cab to the curb and closed the door. Jeff smiled at her from the back seat. Then the driver whisked the cab away until there was nothing left of it but the glow of its brake lights when it stopped for a red light at Broadway.

*   *   *

Heather told Trista about her dinner with Jeff as they trolled for bargains on Canal Street the following day.

"This can't end well," Trista warned.

"I know that," Heather said, absentmindedly picking through a stack of cashmere shawls.

"I'm sorry, honey, but this doctor seems about as legitimate as that so-called cashmere."

"I know this isn't really cashmere." Heather pulled a black shawl from the bottom of the pile. "But he's really a doctor."

Trista touched the shawl's material as Heather offered it. "I know he's a doctor. I also know doctors aren't supposed to fool around with their patients."

"We're not fooling around." Heather turned away sharply, digging through her purse for small bills.

"Twenty dollar for shawl," said a toothless vendor draped in Indian garb.

"I'll give you fifteen," Heather said.

"Fifteen, OK," the woman said with a sigh.

Heather handed her the money.

"A four-hundred-dollar dinner and you're not fooling around?" Trista added.

"That's right," Heather said, draping her new purchase across her shoulders.

"Believe me. You will be," Trista said, reaching into her purse for a pack of cigarettes. "Within a week. Probably less."

* * *

It was an unfamiliar number but with the same exchange as Jeff's office phone number. Heather lifted her cell from its temporary perch as a paperweight for the corporate American Express bills and answered.

"Heather, it's Jeff. I'm calling about your appointment," he said in a muffled tone as if he was trying not to be heard. "I had an emergency at the hospital—actually three emergencies. Fairly typical."

Oh, poor baby, she longed to say. *You work so hard.* Instead, she listened, simply saying, "OK."

"I'm running hopelessly behind. I can have the appointment rescheduled or see you late tonight."

"How late?"

"Can you come in at nine?"

"Nine? You have office hours until after nine o'clock?"

"Well, no, that's the thing. If you want to come in that late, it's fine with me. But I really need to let my staff go home by eight o'clock. Technically, office hours end at seven thirty on Tuesdays."

She heard what he wasn't saying loud and clear. "I'll be there at nine," she said.

She returned her attention to balancing the American Express bills against employee expense reports. Focusing was hard—the idea that she would be alone with Jeff in his office was totally distracting. They'd shared two meals, a lot of conversation, and one sweet kiss. But they'd never been alone together. Not this way. Not yet.

* * *

When she arrived at Upper East Side Pulmonologists at nine o'clock, the door to the reception area was locked. She knocked on the glass. Nothing. She waited, then knocked again, harder this time. Jeff appeared, unlocking the door from inside.

"So, you're the doctor *and* the receptionist tonight?" she teased.

"That's what happens when it gets so late. I hope this isn't too inconvenient."

"It's fine," she said, following him down the familiar hallway. They passed the consultation room and went straight to the exam room.

"Have a seat," Jeff said, indicating the exam table.

Heather hopped on the table. "Oh," she said. "I need an exam gown!"

"That's just a formality," Jeff answered. "We can do this through your blouse. Just unbutton the first few buttons."

He watched her intently as she undid the top three buttons of her black silk blouse. When she was finished, he took his stethoscope and placed it on her chest. The steel instrument was cold. His hand was brushing her breast. He moved the stethoscope to listen to another heart chamber. His face was so close she could feel his breath. As he moved the stethoscope a third time, his hand lingered over her left breast before cupping it. This time, the intent of his gesture was clear.

They kissed for real this time, their lips pressed moist and hard to each other's, their tongues swirling and sucking a part of each other that seemed like an extension of themselves.

There was something familiar about the taste of his mouth, some distant memory that she couldn't quite place. Perched on the exam table, she wrapped her legs around his waist and started to unknot his tie. *Such a sexy thing,* she thought as she struggled with the unfamiliar Windsor knot. *None of the guys I date wear ties.*

Jeff opened the remaining buttons on her blouse and slipped it off her shoulders. As he unfastened her bra, his lips came to her nipple. "Mmmmm," he sighed, as if tasting chocolate for the first time.

Slowly, gingerly, she tugged at his zipper. After a brief snag, it opened smoothly. She slipped his slacks over his perfect ass, pulling them down. She heard his shoes drop to the floor, first one then the other. He stepped from his slacks, and they fell to the floor. She heard his belt buckle clink against the sterile linoleum.

Sliding off the table, she fell to her knees, face-to-face with his underwear. *Polo,* it said front and center. *Designer underwear.* The briefs were bright and white, smelling slightly of bleach. For a moment, she hated herself, imagining his wife washing her husband's briefs to a brilliant white so they'd be all nice and clean for his lover. And then she realized, O*h, no, this woman doesn't do laundry...she has a maid.* Somehow, the thought made her feel less guilty. She slipped the briefs to the floor and took him in her mouth.

Abruptly, he pushed her head away. "Stop!" he said. "Stop now or I won't be able to do anything for you." With that, he lifted her up, returning her to her perch on his exam table. He lifted her legs, one at a time, draping one over each of his shoulders before thrusting himself inside her.

The impact of the position was amazing, allowing her to feel him deep inside her in a way she had never experienced a man and letting him touch and pleasure her freely with his fingers at the same time. The crisp white paper lining the table crinkled and crackled beneath her as the impact of his thrusts moved her ecstatic body up and down on the table.

And then she heard his grunts. One. Two. Three. Each the same length, each the same tempo. Deep, guttural sounds breaking from his soul.

*   *   *

Within minutes, they were pulling their clothes back on. The clock on the wall ticked toward ten o'clock. She wanted to pull him toward her again, tell him how she needed him. But it was clear that Jeff had someplace else to be. "I'm sorry I have to race off like this, baby," he said as he buttoned his shirt.

"I understand," she said as lightly as she could. Recalling the familiar taste in his mouth, she asked, "When are you going to tell me that you smoke?"

"How do you know that?" he asked.

"I can taste it."

He scrambled for his suit jacket from among the pile of their clothes. Pulling a pack of Parliaments from the inside pocket, he removed one from the box. "Sorry. But now that you know, I won't have to hide it from you." He ran the cigarette under his nostrils, inhaling its scent. "But there is nothing like a cigarette after sex."

"I know," she said.

"You *know*?" He raised his eyebrows in surprise. "Your medical history doesn't say that you smoke."

"I *smoked*. Past tense. Parliaments. Just like you."

He tapped his cigarette against the back of his hand, his frustration visible. She could see he wanted it bad.

"How much do you smoke?" she continued.

"Pack a day, maybe two." It seemed unfathomable. A renowned pulmonologist with a two-pack-a-day habit? "It was impossible not to smoke on the reservation," he explained. "They practically gave cigarettes away for free there."

"That was a long time ago," she said. "You really need to quit. You're a doctor...a *lung* doctor."

"Quitting cigarettes would be like quitting you. Impossible." He flicked off the light above the exam table.

She got the message. It was time to go. She grabbed her purse and headed for the doorway. He hugged her one more time. "I've wanted you since the first moment I saw you," he whispered.

"During an asthma attack?"

"That was actually part of your appeal," he said. "I wanted to help you—to take care of you. I still do."

CHAPTER 9

HEATHER

"IT HAPPENED," HEATHER TOLD TRISTA as they stood side by side trying to decipher the meaning of an abstract painting.

"In the painting?" Trista frowned at the image.

"No. In his office. That's why I'm late."

"Oh!" Trista grabbed Heather's arm. "You mean *it*?" She leaned closer to whisper in her friend's ear. "You had sex with him?"

"Right."

"I need a cigarette for this," Trista said. "Let's go outside."

Heather linked arms with Trista as they headed from the gallery and whispered, "Why do *you* always have to smoke after *I* have sex?"

Laughing hysterically, the two women made their way through the gathering of artists, dealers, and collectors at the opening night exhibit until they reached the exit. When they stepped outside the gallery, they were met by a strong breeze and about half a dozen smokers lining the pavement.

Trista struggled against a gust of summer breeze to light her cigarette. "You had sex with this guy? I thought you had an appointment."

"Well...yeah. Exactly." Heather pushed the hair from her face, but the humid breeze blew it back immediately.

"You did it in his *office*?"

"Yes, I just told you."

"That's right. How was it?" Trista inhaled deeply.

"Amazing. Completely amazing." Heather leaned her head back against the glass pane of the gallery's storefront and gazed at the halo of a nearby streetlamp. A smile turned up the corners of her mouth as she remembered.

"It's always amazing when they're married or otherwise unavailable," Trista said.

"I wasn't even thinking about that. He is an amazing *lover*." Heather hugged herself to keep warm. "And the position! I was lying on his exam table and he was standing. I've never felt a man so deep inside me."

"Well, duh!" Trista said.

"Duh?"

"They have tables like that in sex clubs for that very reason," Trista whispered.

"You've gone to sex clubs?" Heather replied loudly. A few heads turned and looked toward the two women.

Trista linked arms with Heather and took a few steps away. "Nooooo! I've read about it."

Heather inhaled the smoke-filled air. "I think you've read about everything imaginable." She adjusted a purse strap that was digging into her shoulder. "Or heard about it on NPR."

"I know about a lot of stuff." Trista exhaled, waving the smoke away from her friend's face. "And, honey, I don't want to burst your bubble, but I don't think doctors are supposed to do that."

"Doctors aren't supposed to have sex? Or affairs?"

"Of course they have affairs. But not with their patients. It's unethical."

"How is it unethical?"

"I saw it on some news show. Actually, it's not only unethical; it's illegal in some states. Because you put yourself into their care."

"Oh, come on! You're telling me I had illegal sex? Like with a male prostitute?"

"No, of course not," Trista replied.

"How do you know all this stuff?" Heather asked. "Sex club furnishings? Doctors having sex with their patients?"

"I saw a show—20/20? One of those. The doctor-patient relationship is considered a fiduciary relationship."

"You mean, like, because he's the superior being, he's supposed to know better?" Heather asked, her voice dripping with sarcasm.

"Yeah, pretty much. Look online. Google 'professional boundary violations.' That was one of the terms they used a lot in the story."

"You're such a news junkie!" Heather said, giving her friend a playful shove.

"Have you talked to him since?" Trista asked.

"God, it only happened an hour ago! But actually, he did call when I was in the taxi on my way over here," Heather beamed.

"Good postcoital etiquette. Nice touch." The smoke rings she was blowing dissipated almost immediately after they escaped her lips into the humid air. "So now what happens?"

Heather lowered her head. "I have no idea."

"Honey, you're gonna get hurt."

"I don't have any expectations." Heather insisted. "I've got my baby coming. There don't appear to be any sane and available straight men in the entire city. This is a chance for sex and passion. Sure, I wish he wasn't married. But he is. I'll just have to live with it."

"That'll change. Once you're more hooked into him emotionally, you'll be begging him to leave his wife," Trista said.

"Can we not jump that far ahead? Let me *please* just enjoy this phase of the affair before the agony kicks in." Heather dug her hands deep into her pockets.

"Sure, honey." Trista dropped her cigarette to the sidewalk, extinguishing it with a firm press from the sole of her stiletto-heeled shoe. "Let's head back inside. It's muggy out here."

*   *   *

As Heather waited for the train in the nearly deserted Houston Street station, she felt a hand touch her arm. Panicked, she turned quickly. "Miguel!" she gasped. "You scared the hell out of me! What are you doing here?"

"Dignity meeting," he said, referring to the organization of gay Catholics whose meetings he attended regularly. "And you?"

"I was at the opening of an art show. Trista is one of the featured artists."

The subway pulled in. Dozens of people got off the train, but there were few to get on. Only two people shared the car with Heather and Miguel as the train pulled out of the station. At the far end of the car, an elderly white woman's age-spotted hands fingered rosary beads as her lips moved in tandem with her silent prayers. Much closer to them, a weathered older man wore the scent of homelessness and the uniform of a Vietnam veteran—tattered jeans with American flag patches at the knees and an ancient leather jacket.

Heather put a hand on Miguel's shoulder for balance as the train sped along the tracks. "I have to tell you something," she said directly into his ear.

He looked at her, his raised eyebrows inviting her to continue.

"I had sex with Jeff tonight," she said.

"The doctor?"

She nodded.

Miguel let out a low whistle. The homeless man looked up, then just as quickly zoned out again. "Oh, baby!" Miguel said. "Your place or his?"

"His. His office actually."

"He can't take you to his bachelor pad?" Miguel quizzed.

Heather bit her lower lip.

"Heather! Making love is a beautiful thing," Miguel said. "Why do you seem so sad?"

"Because there is no bachelor pad." Her lip quivered. "He's married."

"*Mierda!*" He slapped his hand against his forehead. "He is *married*?"

"Please don't hate me," Heather begged.

"I don't hate you."

"I just can't seem to help myself," Heather said.

"I understand how that can be," Miguel admitted. "What I don't understand is why you didn't tell me he was married in the first place."

"I was afraid you'd judge me. You're the only person I know who's a better Catholic than I am."

Miguel placed a protective arm around her. "*Judge not lest ye be judged,* the Bible says. I would never judge you…but I am concerned that this man, this Jeff, will break your heart."

She rested her head on her friend's broad shoulder as the train rounded a curve. "So am I," she said.

*   *   *

On Friday night after work, Heather crashed on the couch as soon as she got home, exhausted from a particularly grueling week at the office. Flipping on the evening news, she dumped the contents of her purse on the coffee table and grabbed her cell phone to check voice mail. "You have one message," the familiar digitized voice told her. She sank into the couch grinning broadly as she listened to Jeff's voice.

"Hey, gorgeous," he began. "I'm in my office, finishing up some paperwork—looking out the window at New York's amazing skyline. Buildings are growing dark—everyone must want to leave work to enjoy an early summer weekend. I wish you were here with me." She saved the message, knowing she'd listen to it again and again. She pressed redial to call him back. He answered on the first ring.

"It's Heather," she said.

"Hey, baby. I must've just missed you. How are you feeling?"

"I feel great. Fine. Just tired."

"Really? I was hoping you were a little under the weather," he said.

"Why would you hope that?" she asked.

"If you weren't feeling well, I'd say maybe you could use a house call."

She bolted upright on the couch, the hairs on her arms standing at attention. "You're kidding!" she said. "A *house call*? You? Here?"

"I'd like to be."

"In that case, Doctor, I'm *dying!* How quickly can you be here? I may have only moments left."

"Then I'll be there in moments," he said. "I know where you live from dropping you off last week. All I need is your condo number."

"It's 704."

"Ah, 704. My new lucky number," he said, clicking off.

Suddenly energized, Heather raced from room to room, straightening things. She tossed a quilt over a stack of self-help books that had toppled beside her bed. She touched up her makeup, brushed her hair, and changed into sexy underwear before slipping back into her white linen suit. *Let him think I wear underwear like this all the time.*

She had barely rebuttoned her blouse when the intercom buzzed. She flew across the living room and pressed the speaker button. "Who's there?" she asked.

"It's Dr. D.," he replied. "I'm here to make a house call."

She giggled as she pressed the button that unlocked the door seven floors below. This playing doctor was more fun than it had ever been as a child.

A minute later, she was opening the door to Jeff. They fell into each other's arms in the doorway, moving quickly to the couch. On the way there, he looked around, assessed his surroundings, and said, "Nice digs, kid."

"Thanks. I like it."

He lowered her onto the couch, covering her body with his own like a cozy quilt. As he kissed her, she struggled to her elbows. "Let's take a walk down the hall. It's more comfortable in the bedroom."

"I've got a better idea than walking," he said, untangling himself from the jumble of tangled appendages they had formed. He stood and lifted her in his arms, carrying her down the hall, covering her face with kisses. He laid her on the bed.

The next forty minutes were heaven.

*   *   *

When it was over, he reached impulsively for a cigarette. "Do you have a fire escape—somewhere I can smoke?"

"You can smoke here." She reached for a ceramic tray on the night table where she stored the jewelry she wore during the day before going to sleep. "You can use this as an ashtray." She dumped the accumulation of treasures on the night table. She slid the tray in front of her rosary, embarrassed at the thought of his seeing the beads there. "It's OK."

"You're sure?" he asked, bringing a cigarette to his lips.

"I'm sure."

He reached for his jacket and pulled a cheap yellow lighter from its pocket. Lighting up, he inhaled with deep satisfaction.

"You make it sound so good."

"I love smoking. Couldn't give it up if my life depended on it. And of course, I realize it might some day."

She reached for his cigarette. "Let me try."

"Old addicts can't have one of anything." He held the cigarette out of her reach. "Not one drink, one pill, or one drag."

She wrestled him for the cigarette. He let her win without much of a fight.

"I haven't had one of these in nearly ten years," she said, hesitating, the cigarette pressed against her lips. Then with the determination of a swimmer charging into frigid water, she inhaled. She held the smoke inside and felt a long-ago glow of satisfaction. Slowly, deliberately, she exhaled the smoke from her nostrils.

"Was it good for you?" Jeff asked.

"Fabulous." She leaned back on the pillows. "The cigarette was good, too. I am a little dizzy, though."

"That's to be expected. Another pack or so and it'll seem like you never quit."

"Oh, I don't plan to…"

"In case you change your mind." He placed his pack of Parliaments on her night table. "Just use your inhaler more often if you're going to be smoking."

She took another cigarette from the pack and lit it with the tip of Jeff's.

* * *

As they held each other after a second round of lovemaking, Jeff's stomach let out a loud growl. "You're starving!" Heather said.

"And embarrassed," he said, patting his stomach.

"Don't be," she said, jumping from bed. "Let's order some Chinese food."

"I love Chinese food," he called after her as she raced toward the kitchen to find a menu from China Gold. "How did you know?"

"Come out here and tell me what you'd like," she called back, pulling the menu from a cabinet and heading into the living room.

Jeff smoothed his hair as he joined Heather on the couch. She handed him the menu. "What would you like?" she asked.

"Now that's refreshing," he said, taking the menu from her hand. "My wife, Priscilla, is a total control freak. She'd never ask me what I want. She'd just order something she likes and expect me and the kids to eat it or go to bed without our supper."

"That's terrible!" Heather said.

He stopped studying the menu and placed it on the coffee table.

"That's nothing. Just a very minor example of how controlling she is," he said bitterly. "She treats me like I'm her third child. I make life-and-death decisions every day, but my opinion doesn't seem to count at home."

"That must be hard for you," Heather said, stroking his hair.

"A woman who was raised with four houses, each with a full staff of servants, apparently develops a sense of entitlement," Jeff said. "When I was growing up, we weren't always sure there'd be enough food to go around."

"Well, you do come from two different worlds."

He sighed. "We're still living in different worlds, despite living under the same roof."

"You looked happy in that photo on your desk—the one taken on the cruise," Heather ventured.

"Trapping me on those damn cruises is a classic example of the way Priscilla Wellington Davis controls my life," he said. "She claimed that last cruise was a gift for my fortieth birthday. But the truth is, she knows cruises are the only way she can keep me away from the office and the hospital. They put me in a place I can't escape without a helicopter or a life raft."

"Happy belated birthday," Heather said in response.

Jeff smiled. "I swear I won't give in to another one of those trips. I get so stir-crazy."

"Your kids looked like they were enjoying themselves in the picture."

"Sam and Hannah," he sighed. "My twins. They're seven years old. Already they're addicted to cruises and kiddy designer clothes."

"I guess that's the way Priscilla likes to dress them." The moment the words escaped her lips, she tried to pull them back with a deep inhalation of smoke. It was none of her business. And Jeff's wife's name felt odd on her lips.

"It is," Jeff replied. "Priscilla's family is a bunch of snobs. Although I do admit that the lifestyle has its pluses. I could never live this way on my own."

"What way?"

"Well, let's see. Besides the penthouse on Central Park South, we have homes in Southampton, Aspen, and Boca Raton. But then there are the countless social functions we're forced to attend. Everybody trying to outdo each other with the trophy wife in the designer gown. So many commitments..."

"I think it sounds glamorous." She took another drag.

"Believe me, Heather, it gets old really fast."

Heather stretched her legs out and laid them over Jeff's.

"But the biggest hook is the children," he continued. "I never really understood unconditional love until I had my kids." A slight smile touched his lips.

"I feel that way about my daughter," Heather said. "I haven't even met her, but in my mind, she's already my little girl. I can't wait until she's finally here."

"When?"

"Probably April of next year."

"How are you going to manage? I mean, you can't stop working, can you?" he asked.

"Oh, no way! *I'm* not a socialite. There's a group of women on the Upper West Side that I met through a chapter of Single Mothers by Choice who are adopting girls from China. We've found a nanny who will watch all the girls. She's Chinese, so the girls will learn both Chinese and English. It's all falling into place."

Jeff returned his attention to the trifold Chinese menu. He opened it and held it at arm's length, reading with the enthusiasm of a kid in a candy store. "So, what's *your* favorite?" he asked.

"I like everything. As long as I start out with an eggroll and end with a fortune cookie, it doesn't matter what comes in between."

"How about General Tso's chicken?" he asked.

"Not exactly the healthiest choice on the menu." She brushed her hair from her eyes.

"That's true of most things. The most tempting choices are seldom what's best for us."

She nodded in agreement. "I'll have a little of the chicken. But let's get some shrimp with broccoli for those of us who are health conscious." She reached for the pack of cigarettes and the ceramic tray containing ashes and cigarette butts that Jeff had carried from the bedroom. "Or were until today." She lit another cigarette with his lighter. A BiC. Not exactly what she'd expect a Park Avenue doctor to use. "How do you stay in shape eating things like steak and fried chicken?"

He tapped the ash from his cigarette. "These will increase the metabolism of the average adult by seven percent," he said. "And as for my workout—I think you just saw me go through it. Deep orgasmic breathing is extremely healthy."

She laughed in amazement. She'd heard that doctors made the worst patients but had never considered that while they were looking out for the health of their patients, they might fail to take care of their own.

"I'll call the restaurant," she said, pulling her cell phone from the pocket of a short black silk robe. She placed the order. "Thirty minutes will be fine," she said, hanging up.

"Come back into the bedroom with me," he said.

"Don't tempt me," she answered, tousling his hair as he nibbled her neck. "Maybe after dinner. You know people always get hungry shortly after eating Chinese food."

"I'm hungry for you again and it hasn't even been twenty minutes," he said.

"I can't get enough of you either. How late can you stay?"

A troubled expression furrowed his brow. "I'm sorry, baby, but I'll have to get going right after we eat."

*   *   *

While they waited for the food to arrive, Jeff reviewed the series of travel photos that lined Heather's hallway. There was a shot of her seated at a table at the Jules Verne restaurant on the second level of the Eiffel Tower with the chef and maitre d' standing behind her. Another photo showed Heather waving from the deck of a ferry with the Sydney Opera House in the background. One photo showed her among a small group of tourists along the Great Wall of China.

"That was the trip where I visited the orphanage where Lin is now."

"Lin?"

"My daughter."

"Of course," he said, moving quickly to the photo taken in Paris. "Hobnobbing with the chef, I see." "That's the best part of my job," she said. "I check out all the accommodations and suppliers well in advance of corporate events. It's a job that allows me to go to some amazing places."

"I'll say," Jeff said, moving on to a shot taken in London.

"It's one of the perks of the job—maybe the only perk," Heather said.

"Don't knock it," he said. "A business trip for a doctor is a consult at a hospital across town. *You're* the one with the glamorous job."

* * *

Heather spread the just-delivered food on the coffee table. "I've been getting takeout from this restaurant since I moved here, but this is the first time I've ever ordered in. They probably thought I was homeless before tonight." She laughed lightly.

They fed each other with chopsticks and fingers, finishing every morsel from the Royal Doulton plates on which Heather had placed the food. Finally, they nibbled on fortune cookies and prepared to read each other's fortunes. After Heather told Jeff, "You have a proud but stubborn personality," he nodded as if in agreement, then looked at her fortune and frowned.

"Oh, now you *have* to read it," she insisted, trying to snatch the tiny paper from his hand.

"I'll read it. But you have to remember, there's no truth to these things."

"OK," she said skeptically.

"You are lucky in business, unlucky in love," he read.

She frowned.

"You OK, baby?" he asked.

"I've got a bit of a migraine."

"From that silly fortune?"

"No. Probably because I forgot to order no MSG in the food."

"Let me help," he said, pulling a prescription pad from his pocket.

He scribbled quickly and placed the paper on the coffee table, his thumbprint embedded on it with the greasy sauce of his General Tso's chicken. Glancing at it, Heather saw he'd prescribed ten milligrams of Vicodin four times a day.

"Really, Jeff, it's just a headache," she said. "I always get them after I've had MSG."

"There's no reason you have to *keep* getting them," he said.

Although they continued to playfully feed each other a dessert of litchi nuts, Heather's heart was no longer in it. Sex. Dinner. Gone. Trista had been right. She *was* setting herself up for heartache.

Chapter 10

Heather

DURING THE SUMMER, Jeff's calls had been occasional—maybe twice a week. But as the months wore on, their relationship had escalated to *seeing* each other at least twice a week, and his phone calls came every day—except weekends. They'd developed standing appointments on Tuesday nights when Heather would meet him for sex at his office. Their escapades included watching porn together on Jeff's office computer, playing doctor and other activities that, in Heather's mind, bordered on kinky. Yet she never questioned his desires—if he'd asked her to jump out the seventeenth floor window of his office, she'd have been on the ledge in seconds. On Thursdays, they'd visit an out-of-the-way restaurant, avoiding trendy places in an unspoken effort to avoid being seen by anyone either of them knew.

* * *

A few nights before Halloween, they drove around the Upper West Side before settling on a tiny French restaurant on Ninth Avenue for their Thursday night dinner.

"I have to go to Austin next week," Heather said over steak au poivre.

"Why?"

"Just a conference."

Their legs were intertwined beneath the tiny bistro table. Jeff added pressure to their grip and said, "I need to make love to you before you leave."

Heather returned the grip on his leg. "Come back to my condo after we eat."

"I'd rather go to my office. We'll miss our Tuesday night appointment next week if you're away," he said. They rushed through their meal and, fueled by anticipation, got into Jeff's black Mercedes with the M.D. license plates. Jeff was talking dirty to her when he was interrupted by the all-too-familiar buzz of his phone. He looked at caller ID and shook his head. "Dr. Davis," he said, after flipping the phone open.

He weaved through traffic as he sped down Broadway. "Call her family." He slammed on the brakes as a light turned red ahead. "And increase her morphine. My instructions are in her chart." The car stopped, and he listened for a moment before saying, "I'll be there in fifteen minutes."

They both remained silent until he turned onto 79th Street.

"I guess you know what that was about," Jeff said.

"Emergency at the hospital." Heather was starting to know the drill.

"That's life with a doctor, baby. At least I got to take my girl out for a nice dinner."

"Yeah, it was great. Thank you. But how am I going to get through a week without making love with you?"

"I don't know, baby. How am I?"

Double-parking in front of Heather's building, he turned on the car's hazard lights. Horns began to blare behind them. Heather closed her eyes when Jeff reached across the car for one last kiss good-night. Apparently spotting their silhouettes, the driver of the Humvee behind them leaned steadily against his horn. He didn't stop until Heather had stepped from the car on the passenger side.

"Good-night, baby," she heard Jeff call from the Mercedes. "Have a safe trip."

In her other ear, the driver of the Humvee was shouting, "Come on, lady; get a room!"

Heather turned up her collar against a cool evening breeze. She stepped inside her building, entering 4-5-4-1 to unlock the door to the vestibule.

*   *   *

I miss him already, she thought, replaying his most recent voice mail. Her cell phone voice mail was full, but as always, she couldn't bring herself to erase Jeff's messages. Instead, she opened her desk drawer and removed a tiny digital recorder. Putting her phone on speaker, she turned on the recorder and played back Jeff's most recent messages from her voice mail as the recorder captured them.

When she was finished, she turned the recorder back to the messages she'd saved at the beginning of their relationship. She brushed her teeth, then brought the recorder into her bedroom. After crawling into bed, she pressed play.

"Heather, it's Jeff," the first message began. "I just wanted to make sure you got back to your office OK. Oh, and to say how nice it was to see you. I hope we can do something like that again soon. Ciao." It was the first message he'd left her after meeting her at Barnes & Noble the first time. A smile touched her lips at the memory.

She began to listen to dozens more messages she'd recorded on the machine.

"I'm looking out the window of my office. The lights of the city are twinkling all around me. Usually when I look out this window, it just looks like New York. Tonight, knowing you're out there, that one of those lights is yours, it feels lonely. I wish you were here with me. Or I was there with you."

"What are your fantasies? I asked you first, you have to tell."

In one message he sang the words to "My Girl" in an off-key voice. *"I've got sunshine on a cloudy day…"*

Some of the messages were short and sweet.

"Just wanted to say hi. Sorry I missed you. I'll call you later. Ciao."

Other messages were the kinds of complaints that couples share.

"I had the day from hell today. Six hospital admissions— unbelievable…"

"Hey, babe, I swear my entire office staff is nuts…"

As she dozed off, the recorder was replaying the messages for a second time. *"I've got sunshine on a cloudy day…"*

CHAPTER 11

HEATHER

"DOCTOR, DOCTOR, GIVE ME THE NEWS..."

"Hey," Heather said, flipping open her cell phone. She checked the time on her office computer: 9:22 a.m. "This is a nice surprise."

"Remember what I said when I dropped you off last night?" Jeff asked.

"About what?"

"About not being able to wait until you get back from Austin to make love to you."

"Sure. I remember. I feel the same way."

"Great minds think alike," he said. "Meet me in the lobby of my building at eight o'clock tonight."

"But it's Friday! And it's Halloween weekend. Don't you have to go home early tonight?"

"All the more reason the office will be empty," he said. "You're not going to Austin until I get a chance to be alone with you. Understood?"

"Absolutely, Doctor," she said. "You know what's best!"

*   *   *

They rode the elevator to Jeff's seventeenth floor office standing side by side like two strangers. They both knew elevators everywhere in the city were monitored by video cameras. But the second Jeff closed the door to his waiting room behind them, he was tearing at Heather's clothes like a child unwrapping a birthday present.

He backed her down the hallway and into an exam room. Within seconds she was on his exam table, her slacks and panties in a heap beside Jeff's clothes on the floor. "Wrap your legs around my neck, baby," he said. "And tell me how much you like it that way."

"I love it that way," she murmured. "It lets me feel you so deep inside me."

"How do you feel it?" he asked as he entered her.

"Deep," she repeated. "Deep, deep, deep."

Unable to hold back, Jeff came with a shudder within minutes. As she held his quivering body, now pressed on top of hers on the exam table, she glanced over his shoulder. "What the hell is that?" she asked.

"What's what?" he asked, jerking to attention.

"What's that?" She pointed a quivering finger toward a storage cabinet a few feet across the room. From behind what must have been a small hole in the door of the cabinet, a tiny red light directed toward the exam table held steady.

Jeff walked toward the cabinet. "Oh, that!" He reached for a brass handle and opened the cabinet door. Was his hand shaking?

He removed a DVD from a recorder stashed inside the cabinet. "Sometimes we record procedures on DVD for our residents to review." He picked his slacks up off the floor and pulled his keys from the pocket.

"Why do you keep the recorder in the cabinet?" Heather asked.

"It's less obtrusive back here," Jeff said. "Of course, we obtain signed consents from patients who are being recorded, but I've found they're more comfortable if the recording apparatus isn't so obvious to them."

"Why is it on now?"

"Dr. Cooperman was recording a demonstration of how to use a peak flow meter in here this afternoon. She must've forgotten to turn the recorder off. Don't worry, though. It isn't recording anymore. The DVD ran out of time hours ago."

He crossed the floor and unlocked a file cabinet. He put the DVD inside and slammed the door shut. He locked the file cabinet.

Tossing his keys on the counter, he moved back toward Heather and asked, "Now where were we?"

Heather slid off the table and started pulling on her clothes. "I should get going," she said.

*   *   *

After Jeff dropped her off, Heather gulped two Valium to calm her nerves. She pulled a cigarette from one of the packs Jeff had developed a habit of leaving behind.

She wanted to believe Jeff's story about the DVD recorder, but she just wasn't buying it. It seemed more like a precalculated effort to record their sexual activity without her knowledge. How many times had he done it? And why couldn't she be straight with him about her suspicions? If it had been any other man she'd dated, she would have confronted him, destroyed the tape, and refused to see him again. But she froze at the idea of confronting Jeff. Why?

Maybe it's because he's married, she thought as she searched for a match. *He could dump me anytime and still have his family life, his great homes, his children, even his wife. But I'd have nothing. I'd be alone.*

Heather dumped the accumulation of jewelry from the tray on her night table and headed for the kitchen. She found her collection of matchbooks stored in a tin can over the stove. She'd collected matchbooks for years, although she'd had no need for them. They were just souvenirs. *Maybe now that I'm smoking the cigarettes Jeff leaves behind, I'll get a chance to use some of these matches.* She spilled the contents of the tin onto the bistro table. Gordon's Steakhouse. Kitty O'Shea's Pub. Sarah & Thomas, June 26, 2004. Before lighting up, she took a strong toke from her inhaler for good measure.

The first drag made her dizzy. After that, it was easy.

Why did I pretend I bought that story about Jeff filming procedures for medical students? Please! He wouldn't have to hide his recorder for that! Why didn't I tell him I was on to him? She tapped a long ash into the tray and took another drag. *Could this be an example of what Trista had mentioned? That doctors aren't supposed to fool around with their patients? What was that phrase she had used? Professional boundary violations!*

*   *   *

Moving to her computer, she googled the term. Pages of results spewed out on the computer screen. The most interesting link was to a website called OnYourSide.net. She clicked her mouse and lit another cigarette.

"There have been appalling news stories about doctors forcing themselves on their patients. Whether they touch them inappropriately when the patient is under sedation or violently rape them, society reacts with shock. But you rarely read about patients who willingly become sexually or romantically involved with their professional medical practitioners. In truth, this is a common practice, but it is just as inappropriate as violent rape.

"While a patient may feel flattered to receive special attention from his or her doctor, in truth, the patient is being exploited. The fiduciary nature of the doctor-patient relationship creates a fundamental imbalance of power. Very often, patients develop feelings of trust, intimacy, and emotional dependence with their doctors. This process is called transference. It places patients in a vulnerable position in relation to the professional. Such a vulnerability and imbalance of power make consensual sex between a doctor and a patient impossible."

She trolled the site, intrigued by every page.

"Doctors take an oath to act in their patient's best interest. They promise not to exploit or abuse patients in any way. This includes the strict requirement that professionals maintain boundaries…"

* * *

All the stories of the men and women who had become sexually involved with their doctors had one thing in common: Each one of them had believed the affair to be consensual. Many were initially flattered by the attention. All of them had ended up devastated.

Heather flicked the ashes from her cigarette as she read about one woman's experience with her psychologist: *"I admired my doctor so much that I was flattered when he told me he found me attractive. I felt like a teenager in the beginning. Now I cry all the time; I can't stop."*

"I cry all the time." Oh my God. *That woman is a mess!* Heather moved on to a comment from a woman who'd had an affair with her general practitioner. *"At first, my doctor really helped me through a very*

difficult part of my life—the loss of my sister. One day, he leaned toward me and kissed me during my appointment. The next thing I knew, we were making love right there in his office. I knew it was wrong, but for some reason, I just couldn't tell him no. That was the beginning of what later became the worst nightmare of my life." For Heather, that vignette hit even closer to home.

She clicked on the site's discussion of transference: *Transference generally manifests as an erotic attraction toward the caregiver. However, transference can be seen in many other forms, such as rage, hatred, mistrust, parentification, or extreme dependence."*

Heather wondered if she was, in fact, experiencing this transference phenomenon. If so, who was it she was projecting Jeff to be? Her father? Her father wasn't the nicest man who'd ever walked the planet. She remembered him as quiet and brooding and stingy with his emotions. But until he left the family, Heather had taken the feeling of safety she had when he was around for granted. After he left, she had been stricken with terror—panic attacks, insomnia, and a physically hollow feeling within herself that nothing seemed to fill.

She scoured the site further and discovered another condition—countertransference. It was described as the redirection of the feelings of the authority figure toward a client, often resulting in their emotional entanglement with a client. Could that be happening to Jeff?

Hours later, feeling winded and exhausted, Heather clicked off the Internet and turned off the desk light. She continued to sit, staring at her reflection in the vague glare of the screen, listening to the computer as it shut itself down. Her face in the screen portrayed her mood—disbelieving. If what she'd read was true, her affair with Jeff violated every code of medical ethics. How could she have had no idea? How could *no one* seem to have any idea? Did he, in fact, know he was risking everything—his reputation, his livelihood, his license to make a living—by becoming involved with her? Or did he know and believe that the rules didn't apply to him?

CHAPTER 12

HEATHER

AN INSTANT MESSAGE FROM MIGUEL popped up on Heather's computer screen on the Friday after Thanksgiving. *Want one of my turkey sandwiches for lunch?*

Sure. Noon? I'm starving, Heather responded immediately.

It's a date, he replied.

* * *

The cafeteria was quiet as Miguel ceremoniously produced their lunch. He had brought turkey-embellished paper plates with matching napkins, two sandwiches on white bread bursting with turkey, a Tupperware container packed with cranberry sauce, and another filled with stuffing. "You haven't tasted stuffing until you've had my mother's Mexican stuffing," he said as he returned from the cafeteria microwave and piled the stuffing high on top of a paper plate portraying a turkey in full-feathered regalia.

"This is wonderful," Heather said, as Miguel prepared the feast. "It's the closest thing I've had to a Thanksgiving celebration."

He looked at her with soulful eyes and asked, "What do you mean? I thought you were spending Thanksgiving at your mother's in Connecticut."

"I told my mother I was having dinner at Trista's. The truth is, Jeff had said he'd come over for a while."

"What happened?" Miguel asked.

"He never showed up."

Miguel's brow tightened, and a look of fury came over his face. She added, "He never called either."

"Even though he promised to come by on Thanksgiving?" Miguel lifted a forkful of stuffing to his lips.

"Yeah, he did. But he can't always keep his promises because of the…circumstances." She ripped small shreds off her paper napkin, depositing the remnants on her plate.

"I would like to beat the crap out of him!" Miguel declared, pretending to roll up the sleeves of his Hugo Boss suit jacket.

"It's my own fault." Heather reached for the sparkling jeweled cufflink that embellished the cuff of her friend's shirt. "I set myself up for this. I knew he was married."

"But he said he would come over yesterday," Miguel insisted.

"He said he'd *try*. He probably had an emergency at the hospital."

"So now you are defending him? *Mierda!*" He put down his sandwich. "Sweetie, you are way too emotionally invested in this guy."

Heather tapped her fingernails on the Formica table top. "I'm starting to realize that," she said.

Miguel nodded in commiseration. "Do not let him hurt you, Heather. You have to be stronger than this passion. And it is so very hard when you are in love."

"I didn't say I was in love!"

"No, you did not say it in words. But you are. Otherwise, you would not be in so much pain."

"I'm in pain, all right," she admitted. "I really thought I could do this and keep my wits about me. But when he pushes me away, it makes me crazy." She took the last bite of her sandwich and crumpled the aluminum foil that had wrapped it. Forming the foil into a ball, she tossed it toward a nearby wastebasket. It hit the rim and fell to the floor.

"Foul play, girlfriend," Miguel called her shot.

"Foul play, indeed," she agreed.

*   *   *

"This might make you feel better," Miguel said as he produced another Tupperware container from his insulated lunch tote.

"There's more?" Heather placed a hand on her full belly.

"Is it Thanksgiving without homemade pumpkin pie?"

"Not really," she said as Miguel placed a heaping serving of pie on her paper plate. As she devoured the pie, she considered taking Miguel into her confidence about her suspicions that Jeff was surreptitiously recording their sex life. Since she'd discovered Jeff's concealed DVD recorder, she'd checked regularly for the glowing red light emanating from the storage cabinet during their Tuesday night appointments. For the first couple of weeks after she'd mentioned it, the light had been off. She'd actually started to consider that Jeff's story about recording medical procedures was true. But last week, as Jeff had pressed her body against the cold tile floor of the exam room, she'd gazed up and around. And there it had been, high on the wall across the room, that flickering red light that said nothing but spoke volumes.

"Miguel," she began. "I...."

An unexpected ping emitted from her friend's Blackberry.

"Oh, my God!" Miguel leapt from his chair. "I have a meeting with Mr. Andrews in exactly two minutes! Would you mind cleaning this up, sweetie?"

"Of course not," she said, her thoughts switching gears. "You brought the food. It seems only fair that I should clean up."

*   *   *

When she got back to her desk, Heather checked her cell phone messages. Nothing. Storming into the ladies' room, cell phone in hand, she was relieved to find the room empty. She slipped into a stall and pressed Jeff's stored number. To her amazement, he answered.

"I need to see you," she said without introduction.

"Sure, baby, name your time."

"That's just it, Jeff," she hissed. "I *did* name my time."

"Heather, I'm at the hospital," he said, lowering his voice. "I can't have conversations like this here."

"O.K. Where *can* you have this conversation?"

"There's a lot going on here," he said. "Holidays seem to be one of the worst times for people with pulmonary disease. I'll call you when there's a reprieve. I'm guessing around five o'clock. Can we do a really fast coffee at Barnes & Noble?"

"Sure. Just give me about twenty minutes' notice to get there."

*　*　*

At 5:45, Heather squeezed her way into an uptown subway. Jeff hadn't called, and his cell phone had gone straight to voice mail when she called him. Maybe he would simply show up.

She bought a café mocha and a copy of *The New York Times*. Half an hour after she arrived, she saw Jeff entering the bookstore, cell phone at his ear. Seeing her, he closed his phone and approached her table. "I was just calling you," he said.

Heather pushed aside the newspaper she was only pretending to read. Jeff sat down. "What is it you wanted to talk to me about?" He took her hand. Immediately, her anger quelled, replaced by the feeling of safety in his presence. For a moment, she hated him for the effect he had on her.

Her voice quivered as she said, "Jeff, when you say you're going to do something, I need you to do it."

"What didn't I do?" he asked, freeing her hand.

"You promised to call me on Thanksgiving. You said you'd say you had an emergency and come by for an hour or so. Do you remember saying that?"

"I remember. And I tried, Heather. But Thanksgiving turned out to be crazy." He looked away. "I do always respond immediately to my patients. I'm not as good with personal things."

"Are you forgetting I'm your patient?"

"No," he said. "But this wasn't a medical matter. " Ironically, Jeff's phone vibrated in his pocket. He removed it, checked the number, and let the call go to voice mail.

"Look Jeff, I don't need you to call me every day." She reached for his hand. He held hers halfheartedly. "What I need is for you to call when you *say* you'll call. I may not be saving lives, but I have a life too."

"I know, baby, I know. I'm really sorry."

"I stayed home alone on Thanksgiving, hoping to have that time with you," Heather said. "I had invitations from Trista and from Miguel. But no; I said no. Hell, I even turned down my mother!"

"Oh, God. You must hate me."

"I don't hate you." She bit her lip. "That's the problem."

"I just couldn't get a moment of privacy on Thanksgiving," he said, shaking his head. "We went to Priscilla's father's place. The cook burned the turkey—nearly set the penthouse up in flames. He fired her on the spot. Old bastard was probably trying to impress his girlfriend of the week."

Heather frowned at the feeble explanation. Jeff continued. "Anyway, the place was a mess, all gooey pots and pans. We ended up going to Tavern on the Green for dinner. No one but Preston Wellington could have gotten a table there for Thanksgiving dinner without a reservation."

He reached for her coffee, asking with his eyes before taking a sip. "What did you end up doing for Thanksgiving dinner?"

"Swanson's turkey potpie."

Jeff put down the coffee cup with an audible thud. "Oh, shit, Heather, that's terrible. I'm so sorry. I swear I'll make it up to you."

"How can you possibly make it up to me? Thanksgiving's over."

He squeezed her hand. "How does a night at the Mercer Hotel sound?"

"Oh, my God!" The words raced from her lips. "Can you get away? Will you stay with me all night?"

"Yes, baby," he whispered. "This Saturday night. All night long."

CHAPTER 13

HEATHER

AS THEY STEPPED FROM THE CAB at the entrance to the Mercer Hotel, Jeff carried Heather's small overnight bag that contained her sexy nightclothes, her makeup, and her toiletries. Her heart fell as she realized that he hadn't brought along a bag of his own.

There were only a handful of people in the lobby as Jeff and Heather approached the reception desk. "We'd like to register, please," Jeff said smoothly to the clerk, an ebony-skinned woman with startling green eyes.

"Certainly, sir. May I have your name?"

"Robinson," Jeff said without batting an eye. "Mr. and Mrs. Charles Robinson."

Of course! Heather thought, feeling suddenly numb. *No way he could register under his real name.* She wondered briefly how one registered at a hotel using one name while paying with a credit card with another name before concluding that was really Jeff's problem, not hers. She took up the bulk of the slack in this relationship; let him deal with some of the technicalities for a change.

* * *

Once in their room, all memory of her lonely Thanksgiving disappeared. Jeff had gifted her with a vibrator on the cab ride over—

colossal in size. After placing it on a nightstand, Heather slipped into the bathroom and returned wearing a black bustier, red thong, fishnet stockings, and five-inch heels. It hadn't taken her long to learn just how to raise the doctor's temperature—and more. Together, they did things she'd always fantasized doing with a man. But until Jeff, Heather had never found that level of trust that let her push her sexuality to its limits.

Feeling nervous and exposed, Heather reached for the hotel terrycloth bathrobe hanging on the back of the door. *No! I know by now that he wants a sexually confident woman.* Assuming an assured demeanor to hide the scared little girl inside her, she opened the door. Her heels clicked on the floor with the steps of a confident woman.

"Oh, God, what you do to me..." he breathed, tugging at his tie.

"Allow me," she offered, untying the knot easily by now. She unbuttoned his jacket and unzipped his slacks.

A steady buzzing filled the air as Jeff reached for the vibrator and turned it on high. As she slipped his slacks off him, he teased her with the tip of the dildo, moving it up and down her thighs but stopping short of the places that would make her scream with delight. He continued to tease her with the vibrator as he fell to his knees, nibbling the garters that hung from her corset. He bit her stockings free, dragging each down the length of her leg with his teeth. She came like thunder before he had even touched her most sensitive parts.

Suddenly, there was a knock at the door.

"Holy shit!" Heather exclaimed.

"It's OK," Jeff said. "I ordered some champagne. That must be room service."

Kicking off her stilettos, Heather dove into the bed where the room service clerk wouldn't see what she was wearing. Jeff opened the door.

"Good evening, Mr. Robinson. Your champagne is here. Cristal, as you requested, sir." The bellman carried a huge silver tray on his shoulder. He placed it on the coffee table. "May I open it for you?" he asked.

"I'd prefer to do it myself," Jeff said. "Thank you." He handed the man a folded bill and ushered him to the door.

Jeff popped the champagne cork and set aside the pair of frosted flutes. With the bottle in hand, he came to the bed. With a swift tug, he removed Heather's thong. Placing his strong hand between her thighs, he spread them apart using just his thumb and his pinky. "I don't know about you, baby," he said, as the champagne trickled between her legs, "but I won't be needing a glass."

*   *   *

When it was over, Heather drifted toward sleep, wrapped protectively in Jeff's arms. Every muscle in her body was relaxed; her breathing was deep and even. What was this strange feeling? *I feel safe,* she realized. *Safe for the first time since Daddy left home.*

*   *   *

Heather stirred in her sleep as the bed beneath her began to vibrate. Reaching for Jeff, she wrapped her legs around him, pressing her groin against him. He pulled away. Flipping on the light, he fumbled through the bedclothes for the source of the sound. With a sigh of frustration, he pulled his cell phone from the tangled mass of sheets and checked caller ID.

"What is it, Pris?" he asked, sounding irritated.

A moment passed. "Yeah, you did wake me up. I was catching a catnap in the on-call bunks." He moved from the bed to the bathroom, closing the door. *Did he really need to go or was he looking for privacy?* Heather wondered. The toilet flushed. *Was it part of his act?*

He returned to the room, rubbing his scalp through his thick hair and shaking his head. "My little girl is sick," he said. "She's got a temperature of 104. I really need to go home and check on her."

"I understand," Heather signed. "But it still sucks."

"I shouldn't, but I'll stay a few more minutes," he said, as if looking for redemption. When she nodded, he raised her to her knees, straddling her from behind. Their bodies rocked together, slowly at first, then with increasing passion. The heart-shaped locket holding Lin's picture slapped back and forth from Heather's chin to her collarbone as they moved together.

When Jeff was gone, Heather struggled for sleep. She hugged his pillow and inhaled the citrusy scent of his aftershave. But the pillow and the scent weren't enough for her. Reluctantly, she reached for the vibrator, slipping it inside without turning it on. *Only hours since he gave it to me, and already I'm using it as a substitute for him.*

CHAPTER 14

HEATHER

ALL DAY AT WORK, Heather anticipated dinner with Miguel's extended family at his mother's Spanish Harlem apartment. Visions of meals she'd enjoyed at Sophia's home filled her mind. The hostess would probably start with one of her delightful salads—white cheese and tomato was Heather's favorite. There was always a selection of entrees: chicken and rice, fish stew, beef with bananas. Plantains with everything. Stuffed peppers. She'd bought an apple pie at a posh bakery at lunchtime—always her gift at Sophia's as the only guest born in America. Except, of course, for the kids. Miguel had sixteen nieces and nephews and more on the way.

Miguel called at ten after four. "It's a good thing I'm gay," he began in a hushed tone. "I'd make a terrible husband."

Heather eyed the pie box with disappointment. "You can't make it, can you?"

"It's the client from hell. The gringo from Dallas who always wants to practice his high school Spanish with me. *Mierda!* How can it be that in 2010 I am the only Spanish-speaking attorney in a gigantic law firm in New York City?"

"Probably because you're the only one who *admits* to speaking Spanish."

"This gringo, this client, he doesn't speak enough Spanish to find his way out of my neighborhood. But he always insists we go to a Mexican restaurant where he can order in Spanish. Any of the other attorneys could go with him. But, no, he has latched onto me like I'm his new best friend."

"Damn, I was looking forward to your mom's cooking. And to hanging out with your sisters!" She clicked on her Outlook calendar, deleting "Dinner at Sophia's" with a single click.

"That's why I'm calling…besides to say what a creep I am. You go uptown without me. My mama loves you—she still wants you to come. And she is making her arroz con pollo."

"You're killing me. But I don't want to go without you. I had really wanted to tell you about my night with Jeff at the Mercer."

"Was it wonderful?" he asked.

"Yeah. It was great. Until two in the morning when he went home, claiming his daughter was sick."

Miguel emitted an audible sigh. "Maybe I can get out of this client dinner," he said.

"No, Miguel, really, it's OK."

"But my sisters will be there and their babies—my niece Emma is walking now; you must see her. I will come as soon as this damn dinner is over."

"Really, it's OK. I'm tired anyway. And they'll all feel like they have to speak English if I'm there."

"Speaking English in America is not a bad thing," he said.

"No, honey. I'll just go home."

"I feel terrible."

"It's not your fault. It's your *job*."

"I'll bring some leftovers for your lunch tomorrow."

"Sure. A lunch of leftovers sounds great. Your mom's leftovers are the next best thing to her fresh meals."

"You're killing me with guilt! We may as well be married!"

"I don't mean to. Really. I'm just disappointed. And I'm so upset about what happened with Jeff."

"I know, sweetie," Miguel said. "If you won't go to my mama's place without me, try to drown yourself in some reality TV."

"My own reality is about all I can take at the moment."

She heard him clicking through his computer, counting aloud: "Four, three, two…"

"What are you doing—preparing for takeoff?" she asked.

"Even better," he said. "I'm counting back from Christmas. Do you know what this Sunday is?"

"No idea."

"It's the second Sunday of Advent! Our favorite season at church!"

"It *is* Advent," she realized.

"Pink and purple candles, Christmas hymns," he said. "Let's go to Mass together on Sunday!"

"You're not going to stand me up, are you?" Heather teased.

"Of course not."

"Being stood up for Mass by a gay man would be the ultimate humiliation," she said, her sense of humor giving her the first lift of the phone call.

"Five o'clock Mass at Blessed Sacrament?" he asked.

"I can come uptown to Holy Redeemer," she offered.

"The church is being renovated. As it is, there's standing room only at Holy Redeemer every Sunday. Let's go to your church and hope for a seat."

"OK. Thanks, Miguel. I'll see you at lunch tomorrow."

Heather clicked her folders closed. Outlook. Expense reports. Check requests. Suddenly she realized her boss was standing beside her. She hadn't even heard Jane come into her office.

"You might want to work on those files this evening," Jane said, looking over Heather's shoulder at her computer screen.

"I'll get to them tomorrow morning. First thing," Heather said, her hand quivering on her mouse.

"You've fallen behind on a number of deadlines recently," Jane said. "I'm not the only one who's noticed. People don't like to wait to have their expenses reimbursed. You really might want to think about staying and working on the expense reports tonight."

Heather bit her lip. "I have plans," she said.

Jane crossed her arms. "With the economy the way it is, you need to be more vigilant about your job than ever. We all do."

"I know that, Jane." Heather pulled her purse from her file drawer.

"Don't forget we had this conversation," Jane replied. "Good-night."

"Good-night," Heather said, pushing her way past Jane, who had stepped back to the doorway of her office.

*   *   *

Instead of heading for the subway, Heather walked along East 54th Street to Barnes & Noble. Obsessed with relationship self-help books since reading *Men Are From Mars, Women Are From Venus* in her early twenties, she was an addict in need of a fix. Her mission was to find a book that would help her to deal with—maybe even leave—her affair with a married man.

The selection of books on the topic was vast. Even if a book couldn't take away her pain, one thing was for certain—there was a huge market for the subject. She had plenty of company.

Her eyes scanned a long shelf lined with books with such titles as *The Other Woman's Guide to Infidelity, Single Woman–Married Man*, and *Being the Other Woman*. Finally, she settled on a paperback that, like most of the books, had a pink cover. The title, *When You're In Love with a Married Man*, gave her hope the author was someone who would understand.

The cashier at the counter looked from the jacket of the book to Heather's face and back again. Heather lowered her eyes and handed the woman a ten and a twenty, leaving her credit card in her wallet. No point in leaving a digital trail of her purchase.

*   *   *

At home, Heather changed into sweats. Still feeling chilly, she added a bathrobe. She moved to the kitchen and found a can of black bean soup. She heated it and stood at the counter, eating her soup directly from the pot. *Having a child will be so good for me. I won't raise Lin to eat directly from the stove or in front of the television. We'll sit down every night and have a proper dinner at the table.* She glanced at the tiny bistro table where she'd already strapped a bright pink booster seat. Lin wouldn't be there until the spring, but Heather wanted everything to be ready and waiting for her.

She really wasn't hungry for anything other than Mexican food. The can of black bean soup had sufficed. She shoved the white pie box with its knotted string into her tiny freezer and called Trista.

"Hey," Trista said. "What's up?"

"Miguel stood me up for dinner."

"That's too bad. Want to go clubbing with me instead?"

"On a Tuesday? No thanks."

"Chas is playing at a club in Brooklyn. I'm on my way there now."

"You're such a groupie," Heather teased.

"Just trying to be supportive," Trista said. "And hold the *real* groupies at bay."

"Miguel's not the only one who stood me up," Heather said. "Jeff left me at the Mercer. At two in the morning. He claimed his wife called and said their little girl was sick."

Trista paused before asking, "Do you believe him?"

"I'm not sure."

"I'm sorry, honey," Trista said. "But I'm not really surprised. You need to move on with your life."

"I'm trying," Heather said. "I bought a self-help book."

"I thought you'd already cornered the market on those."

"This one's different—it's specifically about relationships between single women and married men."

"Good luck with that," Trista said. "It's gonna be a quiet night without Miguel's family."

"Yeah, I know. I was…" Through the phone, Heather heard the warning signals that the subway doors at Trista's end were about to close. Then nothing. The A train traveled deep underground through the West Village. Only a cell phone with mammoth signal strength could hold a connection there.

* * *

She wondered what Jeff was doing. *It can't hurt to call him. If he's at the hospital, his phone will probably be off. I'll just leave a message. Tell him I'm thinking of him—try to act like I'm not hurt or mad about his leaving me at the hotel.* She reached for the phone and pressed his name.

He answered on the first ring. "Dr. Davis speaking."

"Hi, it's me," she said, using what had quickly become her standard line.

"Er, yes, what seems to be the problem?"

"The problem? Jeff? There's no problem."

"I see."

"It's *me*, Heather!"

"Yes, I'm aware of that. I can't check the record right now. I'm having dinner with my family."

As if on cue, a small voice chanted in the background, "Who is it, Daddy? Who's on the tel'phone?"

"Oh, God, ohmygod, Jeff, I'm so sorry! Didn't you notice it was me calling?"

"Call me again if the situation changes," he said curtly.

"Daddy who…?" the small voice insisted.

"Good-night," Jeff said.

Dammit, now I've done it! Called him in the middle of dinner with his wife and kids! She held her head in her hands, then reconsidered. *Hey, wait, it's not my fault. He has to realize I couldn't have known. He should have noticed my number and not answered the call.*

*   *   *

She headed toward the bedroom. Flopping on the bed, she propped the pillows behind her head and settled in with *In Love with a Married Man*. She moved the ashtray to the edge of the nightstand and lit a cigarette.

The pink book cover portrayed the image of a hand wearing a wide gold wedding band—distinctly male. A ringless female hand reached toward it. The message was clear. Heather flipped the book over and re-read the back cover: *The author wishes to help those women who are already involved with a married man. Her hope is to help those women to resolve their affairs and put their lives back together. Daring, funny, with just the right touch of guilt,* In Love with a Married Man *goes where few books have dared.*

Finally. Heather breathed a deep sigh and adjusted the pillow to cradle her head. *Someone who understands.*

*   *   *

An hour later, Heather was wiping tears from her eyes as she completed the third vignette about a woman who had loved a married man...and lost. *That won't happen to me. All the women in the book pressured their lovers to leave their wives. I'd never do that with Jeff. Besides, I won't be lonely like this when Lin's here.* The agency had said it would probably be April before Heather went to China to formalize the adoption and bring Lin home. She counted the months off on her fingers. Tomorrow was December first, then January, February...five months until she would bring her little girl home. Lin would be twenty-one months old.

She tried to sleep, but the sound of Jeff's child's voice kept her awake as surely as if he'd been in the room. Routinely, she reached for the Ambien Jeff had prescribed. She swallowed two of the sleeping pills, images of Jeff dining with his family invading her thoughts. *Who is it, Daddy...who is it, Daddy...Daddy...Daddy...Daddy.*

CHAPTER 15

HEATHER

HEADING FOR BLESSED SACRAMENT, Heather stopped at a stationer on the corner of Broadway and 73rd. She started to walk in, then paused. Buying a pack of cigarettes was different than bumming them from Jeff. It would be admitting she'd started to smoke again. She struggled into the shop, half frozen by hesitation. Her eyes traveled to the variously-colored packs of cigarettes displayed behind the counter. The clerk moved in front of the display, oblivious to the turmoil brewing in his prospective customer's mind. There was no sign to indicate the cost of a pack.

After the last customer in line had paid, Heather impulsively stepped up to the checkout. "A pack of Parliaments, please." She tugged a five dollar bill from her purse.

"Hard or soft?" the clerk asked gruffly.

"Hard. A box."

The clerk turned and grabbed the blue-and-white box from its location. Turning back to face Heather, he mumbled, "Six seventy-five."

Six seventy-five? Holy shit! Six dollars and seventy five cents for one pack of cigarettes? She pulled two ragged singles from her wallet, then stepped outside, clutching her box of Parliaments and her single quarter in change.

*   *   *

Miguel was waiting on the steps of the church as Heather hurried up West 70th Street. A brisk wind blew his jet black hair backward, exposing the exquisite chiseling of his features.

Heather raced up the church steps, struggling in her high heels. "Will we have to stand?" she asked, glancing at her watch. Ten minutes to five.

"There are still plenty of seats. I checked just a minute ago," Miguel said. He extended his arm toward her and asked, "Shall we?"

Smiling in acknowledgement, Heather slipped her arm into his and walked securely into the church and down the main aisle. As they walked reverently, arm in arm, she imagined she was what she longed to be—part of a happily married couple. Despite his fur-trimmed leather jacket and the slight but unmistakable swagger of his hips, they could have been a couple. In New York City, married couples came in all varieties: gay husband, straight wife; rich old husband, gorgeous young wife; androgynous couples of undetermined sexuality.

They both genuflected before slipping into a pew toward the center of the church. As Heather sat beside her friend, the sinking sunlight of early December filtered through the stained glass windows, playing on her fingers, turning them alternately to the dazzling colors of the windows—blue, red, green, yellow.

The organ started softly overhead, its pitch growing steadily deeper and louder. The entire church vibrated in response. The congregants stood while the procession came down the aisle and sang the hymn, "O Come, O Come, Emmanuel," an Advent classic that referred to the Christians awaiting the birth of Christ on Christmas. A grey-haired woman in a starched cotton shirtdress led the procession. She carried a missal, held open as if it were a platter of hors d'oeuvres she was serving to a guest. Next came the altar boys, sneakers peeking from beneath their floor-length red gowns, topped by white tunics. The priest, a convert from Mumbai, whose heavily-accented sermons Heather could never decipher, followed, clad in brilliant purple vestments etched with gold.

"Great outfit," Miguel whispered as the priest passed their pew. Heather smiled as the procession made its way toward the alter, where an Advent wreath was the centerpiece—a massive circle of pine planted with candles three feet high, three purple, one pink.

* * *

Heather was deeply engrossed in the words of the Apostles' Creed when she felt the familiar vibration in her purse. Her phone! She didn't get many calls on Sundays. Curious, she slipped her hand into her purse and checked the display. *Jeff*, it said. Jeff? On a Sunday evening? The unexpressed rule was that Sunday was the day he spent with his wife and kids. Was something wrong? Or was he miraculously free on a weekend?

She returned the phone to her purse unanswered and continued to pray… "I believe in the Holy Spirit, the holy Catholic Church…"

* * *

When it came time to receive communion, Heather bent forward and lifted the kneeler, feeling conspicuous for remaining in the pew.

"You're not receiving?" Miguel asked, the word *communion* implied in his Catholic-speak.

"I can't receive." She brought her lips directly to his ear. *"I'm having an affair!"*

Miguel placed a protective arm around her and whispered. "It's just a ritual, sweetie." He gave a gentle tug to the sleeve of her black cashmere coat. "Come on. I'll stand between you and the devil."

* * *

When Mass was over, the church emptied quickly, the congregants following the priest and his assistants down the aisle on a thick wave of incense. Heather and Miguel joined the procession of people pressed tightly against each other until the funnel of humanity spilled open on the steps of the church.

"Starbucks?" asked Miguel.

"Just let me check this message. I got a call during Mass."

Miguel kicked a stone around the concrete while Heather listened to Jeff's message: "Major surprise. I've got a free night. I hope I'm not being presumptuous, but I'm heading over to your place now. Be ready for me, baby."

She pressed redial. He answered immediately, saying, "I'm almost there."

"But I'm not, Jeff," she said. "I'm at church—just got out of Mass. Can you meet me here? It's Blessed Sacrament—on 70th, just west of Broadway. You can't miss it—it's a big old Gothic church."

"I'll be there before you can say *Hail Mary*," he said, and clicked off.

Shoving her phone back into her purse, Heather looked at Miguel, asking with her eyes what he wanted to do.

"Sorry, sweetie, I'm not gonna hang around for this," he said.

"Oh, Miguel," she sighed. "I don't mean to dump you."

"No problem. Our plans were for Mass. Not for Mass and coffee. I'm just not ready to meet this guy yet—especially right after Mass."

"I understand." She hugged him tight. "See you tomorrow," she whispered into his fur collar before he swaggered down the church steps and up the street. Along the way, he passed Jeff, but of course, neither of them knew it.

* * *

Jeff spotted Heather on the church steps and raced toward her. "It's freezing out here," he said. "Let's go into the church until we decide what to do."

Once inside, she glanced around at the pews, empty but for a homeless couple and a white-haired lady lighting a candle.

"When's the next Mass?" Jeff asked.

"This was the last Mass of the day."

Jeff kissed her cheek and steered her by her elbow around the perimeter of the church. "When's the last time you went to confession?" he asked.

"Years."

"Don't you think maybe you're a bit overdue?" He stopped in front of a confessional and reached for the knob of an ornately-carved mahogany door that guarded the middle section where the priest sat while hearing confessions.

"Jeff, you can't go in there!"

"Then maybe I can go in here." He moved in front of one of the two side sections that framed the center and pushed aside a red velvet drape. "And you can tell me your sins."

"Are you crazy?" Heather stammered.

He kissed her. His kiss was tender on her lips. "Come inside. Just for a minute. So I can kiss you in private...*really* kiss you."

She stood defiant outside the confessional. Jeff took her hand and gave it a gentle tug.

Once inside the confessional, his kiss grew more insistent. Heather kept her eyes open, trying to distract herself from his kiss by examining the details of the confessional. Mahogany carved into figures of saints capped by halos and surrounded by swirls. The grated confessional screen. The sliver of light at the hem of the velvet drape that dimmed as the church lights were lowered for the night.

Jeff pressed her back against the grated screen. He placed a foot on the kneeler, giving himself better leverage to press himself against her. She stiffened, but he didn't seem to notice. Reaching through her heavy coat, he lifted her skirt, inching his fingers slowly higher along her inner thigh. When he reached inside her panties, his hands felt rough. Old. Like someone else's hands.

"Stop!" she gasped. "Let me out of here!"

"What's wrong?"

"I don't know." She panted in desperation.

"Where's your inhaler?" he asked, snapping back instantly to doctor mode.

She pointed to her purse on the floor of the confessional. He grabbed the purse and poked it and his head outside the velvet drape. He dug through her things until his hands found the inhaler. Pulling aside the drape, he held the inhaler to her mouth. "Breathe in," he said. "Hold it."

By the third inhalation, she was breathing normally again. They stepped into the now empty church. Even the homeless couple had left.

Arm in arm with Jeff, Heather dragged her feet up the aisle, reviewing their moments in the confessional. Those hands. His voice had changed. He was someone else. *Oh, my God.* She shuddered as the image came to her, stark and alive for the first time in thirty years. *Father Hamilton! Father Hamilton did the same thing to me when I was a child!*

CHAPTER 16

HEATHER

HEATHER HAD SET HER ALARM CLOCK half an hour early, giving herself time to call her mother before going to work. Coffee mug in hand, she settled on the sofa, wrapped in a plaid flannel bathrobe.

"Hi, Mom, it's me, Hea—"

"Heather." Her mother completed her daughter's name in a smoke-filled exhale, punctuated by a smoker's cough. "*I* remember *your* name. I just didn't realize you remembered mine." A vacuum cleaner wheezed to a halt at the other end of the line. "When you backed out of visiting on Thanksgiving, I wondered if I'd ever see you again."

"Mom, I—"

"Thanksgiving is the one time of year I know what's left of my family will be together," her mother went on. "Not Christmas. Not Mother's Day. Thanksgiving Day. Even your brother was here with that what's her name, the one he's married to now."

"Her name is Jen, Mom. And if she's good enough for Pete, we should get used to having her around for a while."

"Well, at least she showed up! Unlike some people."

"I'm sorry, Mom. Something came up. It seemed important at the time."

"More important than you mother? It had to be a man." There was a deep inhale followed by a full exhalation. Heather could almost see her mother lighting another cigarette and dropping into the aged recliner she'd gotten at Goodwill when Heather was in grade school.

Heather glanced around her living room, mentally contrasting her surroundings with those of her childhood home. She admired her sleek, modern furnishings and the series of colorful Delacroix prints that were framed, matted, and tastefully interspersed throughout the room. The living room in her mother's house was a hodgepodge of sagging chairs and a sofa covered with tattered, unmatched slipcovers. There were grease spots where her father's Brylcreem-swathed head had rested decades before and burn holes from cigarettes on each arm of every piece of furniture. She visualized her mother, probably wearing a stained house coat, and a sink full of unwashed dishes in the kitchen. "It's not important now, Mom."

"But it was important enough then. Important enough to leave your mother alone on Thanksgiving."

"You just said Pete and Jen were there!"

"What if they hadn't shown up? How would it have been for a woman to spend Thanksgiving totally alone?"

Heather recalled sitting in this very room watching a TiVo replay of the Thanksgiving Day parade while eating a turkey potpie. *I could tell you a lot about that myself.* She pulled off her socks. Her toenails were screaming for a pedicure. "I'm sorry, Mom. Really, I am. But that's not why I called."

"Then to what do I owe the honor of hearing from my daughter, the executive?"

"I'm hardly an executive," Heather reminded her mother for what seemed like the thousandth time.

"You work in an office. You walk around with a briefcase, not a pail and broom. Pardon me if I think that makes you an executive."

Heather sighed. "You have a nice pension now from being a cleaning lady for the school district for all those years. Try to look on the bright side."

For decades, Heather's mother, Margaret, had cleaned toilets in the same high school where her husband was a history teacher with a reputation for fraternizing with his female students. Heather waited for her mother's usual feedback about how humiliating it had been to have such a lowly job, a philandering husband, and now a pension that barely kept her in cigarettes. But all she heard were the steady inhales and exhales of a smoker who would probably die with a cigarette in her hand. Heather shuddered at the thought of the already half empty pack in her own purse and swore it would be the last one she bought.

"The reason I called is—well, it's awkward," Heather said.

"Oh, God, you're pregnant!"

"No, Mom. Not this time. Not any of the thousands of times you've asked me over the years."

"What, then?"

Heather stood up in a vain attempt to give herself some of the power she didn't feel. "Did anything, well, funny happen to me when I was a little girl?"

"Sure. Lots of funny things happened. You and Petey were a laugh riot as kids. Kept the whole neighborhood in stitches with your antics."

Heather sat back down on the couch and picked at her shabby pedicure. Chips of red nail polish fell to the floor. "I don't mean funny. I mean scary. Inappropriate."

Her mother sighed in exasperation. "I don't know how you got where you are in life if you don't know how to say what you mean."

It was Heather's invitation to jump right in. "Remember that priest who was so friendly with the family?"

"Father Hamilton!" Her mother's voice perked up as if she were speaking of God himself.

"Right, Father Hamilton." Heather could barely get the name past her lips. She reached for her inhaler as she began to wheeze.

"You all right, honey?" her mother asked, sounding suddenly concerned. That's what it had always taken to get attention in her family—physical symptoms. Emotional upset was simply swept under the rug with the day's dust.

"I'm OK. Just let me say something. That priest. I remember he used to come to the house for dinner."

"Every Sunday afternoon," her mother said proudly. "It was such an honor!"

"Did you ever leave me alone with him?"

"Well, I don't know. I suppose. You and your brother used to keep him entertained. Your father usually snuck into the backyard for a shot of bourbon from that flask he always hid in his trouser pocket. And I never let Father see me in the kitchen. So yeah, maybe there were times you were alone with him."

As she braced herself for the next question, Heather's throat tightened. "Did I ever seem upset?" The words out, she broke into a hacking cough.

"What is the matter with you? It sounds like pneumonia."

"I'm fine," Heather insisted, holding the phone away while she puffed again on the inhaler.

"You should rub some of that Vicks VapoRub on your chest and get in bed with a vaporizer on," her mother said.

"No, Mom, I should go to a doctor."

"A doctor! Go on! Doctors are for people who have diseases — cancer and stuff. People like us, we can take care of ourselves. Don't go wasting some important doctor's time when all you need is a little rest."

"I need more than rest, Mom. I need medication."

"I never gave either one of my kids an aspirin, and you know it. Why are you talking about taking medicine?"

"Because I have asthma. I haven't mentioned it because I didn't want to worry you."

"Oh, that asthma's all in people's heads. And if you do have it, it's because you live in that dirty city."

It was hopeless. Denial was her mother's mantra. Denial about her husband's drinking and womanizing. Denial about her kids' illnesses. It was a wonder Heather and Pete had lived until puberty. Other than the requisite vaccinations the school insisted they receive, they had rarely been to a doctor. Their mother had insisted on home remedies for everything, holding the sanctity of a doctor's time right up there with that of her other idols, priests.

"Did I ever seem upset after Father Hamilton left? Like if I'd been alone with him while you were cooking dinner?" Heather continued.

"Heather Alice Morrison! I hope you're not saying what I think you're saying." Her mother's tone was harsh.

"Mom, do you read the paper?"

"I read the *Post*. And I watch Oprah."

"Has Oprah ever done a show on pedophile priests?" Heather blurted out.

"Some of those shows are just made up. They pay people to come on and say the most awful things. People will do anything for money."

Heather seized her mother's devotion to Oprah as her ace in the hole. "Maybe on Jerry Springer, Mom. But on Oprah?"

"Well, if Oprah did a show on such an awful thing, she must believe it herself. But ..."

Heather interrupted. "I think Father Hamilton abused me. More than once. I think he went around molesting little kids. I'm sure I wasn't the only one."

"Heather, you're speaking about a Catholic priest! A man of God!" Her mother spoke sharply, her sentence ending in a coughing fit that rattled into the phone. "It's sinful to even *think* such a thing."

"Then why was he run out of town when I was in the eighth grade?" Heather asked.

"He wasn't run out of town. He was transferred to St. Benedict's," her mother replied.

"For an administrative position," Heather added. "No contact with kids. And a daily gig saying the seven-thirty morning Mass. Nobody at that Mass but old people."

"Where did you get all these sinful ideas about Father Hamilton?"

"It doesn't matter. But I did get some information on pedophile priests on the Internet."

"The Internet! Just another tool of the devil!"

The telltale interruption in her mother's words told Heather she had another call. "Hold on, Mom. Someone else is beeping in."

"How I hate that call wa..."

"Hello," Heather said.

"What happened to you in that church last night?" Jeff asked.

"Oh, it was no big deal."

"No big deal! It took half your inhaler to get you breathing right again!"

"I thought it was the *patient* who usually exaggerated their symptoms," Heather said. "Not the doctor. Hold on a second." She clicked back to her mother. "Mom, I'm sorry, I've got to take this call. It's a work thing. I'll call you this weekend."

"Don't bother to call if you're going to bring up this blasphemy about Father Hamilton."

"I'll never bring it up again." She hung up and reconnected with Jeff. "So what's up?"

"That's what I was trying to find out from you—what was up last night. When we got outside the church, you sprinted up the street like a marathoner...like you couldn't wait to get away from me."

"I was upset," Heather replied as Jeff stayed quiet, waiting. "What happened in the confessional brought something back to me."

"Repressed memory?" he asked.

"I can't talk about it now. I have to get to work. But it did take me three Ambien to get to sleep."

"Maybe we'll have to up your dosage."

"Is that your answer for everything?"

"Not always," he said. "But this repressed memory sounds like something you should talk about."

"With you?"

"Sure. Was it something I did that brought it on?"

"Let's just say a confessional isn't an appropriate venue for making love. I'll talk to you later."

Heather ended the call. She sat on the couch, staring at the phone in her hands. Closing her eyes, she tried to remember things she had to know but didn't want to believe.

CHAPTER 17

JEFF

MIKE DOMMER HAD BEEN A RESIDENT with Jeff at Bellevue. Still single and still at Bellevue at forty-one, Mike was a serial womanizer. He headed up the hospital's emergency room, probably the most active ER in the city.

"Breakfast at Tiffany's?" Mike teased when Jeff reached the table, signature bag in hand.

"Christmas present for the wife," Jeff said. "I'm just coming from there. It's a madhouse." He placed the Tiffany's bag on the table and gripped his friend's hand. "How long's it been?"

Mike signaled for the waiter. "Since last Christmas season," he said. "Right here at Bemelmans at the Carlyle."

"Time's going too fast," Jeff said. The waiter arrived. "Dewar's on the rocks, please."

"Another vodka gimlet," Mike added.

Jeff leaned back in the ample leather chair. He took in the upscale surroundings—the rich mahogany of the lengthy bar, the mural-covered walls, and the affluent clientele. A satisfied smile touched his lips.

"I met a woman at a club downtown last night," Mike was saying. "As soon as I told her what I do for a living, she was calling a cab from her cell to take me to her place."

"You're a doctor!" Jeff said in a mock-female voice. "In the emergency room? Oh, my God, the things you must see!"

The two men laughed. Then reassuming his regular voice, Jeff leaned toward his friend and asked, "Ever been attracted to a patient?"

"Come on, man, you can't do that," Mike answered. "It's way too risky. Besides, I don't have that problem where I work. The ER at Bellevue is hardly a mecca for hot babes."

"I remember," Jeff said.

"But once I'm out of there, telling any woman what I do seems to be the ultimate aphrodisiac. Just those three words, *I'm a doctor*, can cut right past twenty minutes of foreplay."

"One of the job's many perks," Jeff said.

The waiter returned. Jeff ordered the Angus beef burger, Mike, the triple decker club.

"Excellent," the waiter said as each order was placed—as if they'd ordered haute cuisine.

"Now, why are you asking about being attracted to a patient?" Mike asked. "I hope you haven't done anything stupid."

"I would if I let myself. But I learned a long time ago to compartmentalize my feelings."

"Liar," said Mike. "You've already had sex with her, haven't you?"

"Yeah." Jeff took a long drink of his scotch.

"Be careful, man. I just heard about a doc in Texas who lost his license. A patient who became his lover reported him to the medical board."

"The laws are tougher in Texas," Jeff said. "And Heather's too crazy about me to ever report me. Besides, I'm sure she doesn't know anything about professional boundary violations."

"Remember the words of the Hippocratic oath, my friend." Mike raised his glass for a toast. "First do no harm," he said, his glass clicking with Jeff's.

"First do no harm," Jeff repeated, less enthusiastically. "And if you do, be damn sure you don't get caught."

Jeff tapped his fingers on the tabletop, craving nicotine. *How could a city as progressive as New York ban smoking in bars, of all places?* "I went through the psych rotation in med school. I learned enough to recognize that she's a classic codependent. Divorced parents. Alcoholic father. A series of bad relationships."

Mike glanced around at the well-dressed couples and the ladies who lunch in the room. "If I didn't know you better, I'd say you've actually got feelings for her."

"Maybe. I've always been one for a good lay, but the chemistry between Heather and me is amazing."

"Just be careful, man," Mike said. "Between that marriage of yours and your practice, you've got way too much to lose."

The waiter returned and placed their orders on the table. "By the way," Jeff said, "one of my pharmaceutical reps gave me a tip. Her company's doing trials with a new breast cancer drug; should be out in the fall."

"What house does she work for?" Mike asked.

"Lilly. She says their investor relations guy expects the stock to triple within six months of its coming on the market."

Mike let out a low whistle. "I'll call my broker on Monday morning. And as usual, we never had this conversation."

"What conversation? I'm not gonna become the Martha Stewart of medicine!" Jeff said.

"Hey, weren't you screwing a drug rep?" Mike asked, stabbing a French fry.

"There've been a few. But Anna's an old standby." Jeff sipped his scotch.

"That's the sort of woman you should be having sex with," Mike said. "Not some patient who's got you all googly-eyed."

"Hey, man," Jeff said. "I know what I'm doing."

They clapped their right hands together over the table and said in unison, "I'm a doctor!"

Two older women in Chanel suits looked over from the next table and frowned at the display.

"Sorry, ladies," Jeff said, assuming his professional decorum. He flashed his smile, and they visibly fell under his spell.

"No problem," one of them said. "No problem, Doctor."

Turning back to his friend, Jeff said softly, "Works every time."

Mike nodded, then flashed his friend a worried look. "Watch yourself, my friend. Fucking a patient is professional suicide."

CHAPTER 18

HEATHER

THE PROMISE OF CHRISTMAS had transformed Barnes & Noble into a fantasyland. As Heather waited for Jeff to arrive, throngs of Saturday afternoon shoppers crammed the aisles, looking for the classic last-minute gift—a book. A simple inscription on the first page made books look like personalized gifts that had been thoughtfully selected far in advance of the holidays.

Heather focused on her magazine, averting her eyes from the angry looks on the faces of exhausted shoppers who coveted her table. She sat alone without even a cup of coffee, pretending to read *Cosmopolitan*'s advice on "Eight Ways to Bring Him from the Christmas Tree to the Bedroom." *God, I've read a different version of this same article in this magazine every December for the past twenty years!* She flipped to the next page: "Twelve Perfect Last-Minute Gifts." At the top of the list—*a thoughtful book.*

She checked her watch: 5:40. Jeff had agreed to meet her at the bookstore by 5:15. She tried to focus on the peaceful New Age arrangement of "The Little Drummer Boy." Her eyes scanned half a dozen customers juggling their shopping bags in an effort to down a cup of coffee while standing up.

She checked her watch again: 5:47.

"You know I'm always late. Sorry again," Jeff was saying.

"Good Lord! Where did you come from?" Heather asked, looking up at him.

"It's so damn mobbed in here; I snuck down the least-crowded aisle—travel." He pulled off his black leather gloves and laid them on his side of the table.

"Café mocha?" Jeff asked.

"No. Eggnog."

He nodded, pushing out his lower lip. "Appropriate. Whipped cream?"

"Of course!"

"OK, sweet tooth," he said.

"It's my only weakness," she reminded him.

He leaned across the table. "I thought I was your only weakness."

"OK," she said. "Maybe I have two."

* * *

Jeff returned with a tray topped by a steaming café mocha, an eggnog, and a pair of brownies. He arranged the items on the table. "I hope this won't ruin your dinner."

"This *is* my dinner."

"Mine, too. I'm on my way to the hospital after this," he said.

"On a Saturday night?"

He pressed his back against the chair and waved his spoon as he said, "People have no consideration that way. COPD, cancer, asthma—whatever. They just don't seem to care if they drag their doctor into the hospital at a civilized time like eight o'clock on a weekday morning or on a Saturday evening."

"OK, OK, I get it. But weren't you supposed to go to some black tie thing tonight?"

"Oh, yes. The hospital's holiday ball," he said. "Truth is, I'd rather be performing emergency surgery. But Priscilla insisted that I meet her at the ball whenever I finish at the hospital."

"That shouldn't be so bad; you might even have a good time."

"Sometimes I like to sleep." He glanced around before reaching for her hand. "Especially with you." He took a swig of coffee and glanced at the magazine Heather had been reading. "*Cosmo*?" he said. "I should have known. You're my *Cosmo* girl—I should write a thank-you note to the editors."

"Yeah, except you couldn't sign your name to it."

"Come on, Heather. What's with you tonight? Why are you zinging me? I was trying to pay you a compliment."

She pushed her eggnog away. "I know. I'm sorry. Christmas always gets to me. All the happy family focus and me, as always, alone."

"I figured you'd spend Christmas in Connecticut with your family," he said.

"Exactly," she answered. "Thirty-eight years old and spending Christmas with my mother." Ironically, the overhead speakers were now emitting "I'll be Home for Christmas." An employee dressed like an elf in green tights and a red tunic walked past their table carrying a stack of trays.

Jeff sipped his coffee. "It sure looks like Christmas in here."

"It does," Heather said. She paused, her heart fluttering. "I was wondering how *we* would celebrate Christmas...*our* Christmas."

"We'll definitely have a very special celebration of our own...but you know it can't be on Christmas Day, baby."

"Of course I know." Despite her best intentions, tears spilled over her lower eyelids.

Jeff wiped her tears away with a paper napkin. "Don't do that, baby. You know I can't promise you Christmas Day itself. Even if I could, I wouldn't. I don't want to chance having a repeat of what happened on Thanksgiving."

Remembering how hurt and angry she'd been on Thanksgiving stopped the flow of her tears.

"Neither do I," she said. "And now that you've confirmed I definitely won't see you on Christmas Day, I guess I'll go to Connecticut for sure. Mom's pretty pissed off at me, though."

"Why?"

"Oh, just a phone call we had."

"Oh, God, you didn't tell her about us, did you?" he asked, dropping her hand.

"Of course not. That's all she'd need to hear. *By the way, Mom, I'm involved with a married man.*"

"What did you do to piss off your mom?" he asked.

"I said something about the memory that being in the confessional with you triggered."

"Are you ever going to talk about exactly what you remembered in there?" he asked. "It's important that you talk about it."

Heather didn't want to talk about her sudden certainty that she had been sexually abused by Father Hamilton as a little girl. No! She felt it made her look pathetic and scarred. She wanted Jeff to see her as the woman she'd grown up to be, not the terrified little girl who lived in her memory.

"I'm fine," she said. "It just made me so nervous to be making out in the confessional. It would have been so easy for us to have gotten caught."

He asked her in a whisper, "Doesn't the idea of almost getting caught turn you on a little?"

"No!" She picked up a pencil she'd been using to fill in her answers to one of *Cosmopolitan*'s infamous quizzes while she'd been waiting for Jeff. She pressed the pencil between her thumb and forefinger. "Caught by a priest? In a church? No way!"

"I'm sorry, then," Jeff said. "That kind of thing appeals to some people. Tell me about the memory that was triggered in the confessional instead."

She sighed in defeat. "OK. Here's what I know. When I was growing up, there was this priest in our parish, Father Hamilton. He was old and creepy, but my mother seemed to think he was God himself."

"Go on," Jeff said encouragingly.

"Mom would invite him over for dinner on Sundays. She'd make my brother and me sit in the living room with him while she got dinner ready. Dad was usually out back nipping on his stash of Wild Turkey."

"Did this priest violate you? Or your brother?"

Heather looked away. "I don't know," she said. "But I know that when I was in that confessional with you, I had this overwhelming feeling that I was with someone else—not you. Someone old. And disgusting."

"It sounds to me like this bastard molested you," Jeff said.

I *told* you—I don't know what happened. I'm just sure *something* did. And that it was with Father Hamilton."

"I can help you with this," Jeff said. "Being involved with me—an authority figure—might be good for you."

Heather felt her face flush. "Not to belittle your profession, Doctor, but I don't think of you as an authority figure. I think of you as a lover."

"I'm not trying to impress you, Heather. I'm just asking you to trust me on this. I told you I'd always take care of you. I believe that I can take care of you both physically and emotionally. And that your asthma definitely has an emotional component."

Given the trauma of her recovering memory, physical and emotional care by a doctor held a tremendous appeal to Heather. On the other hand, what she'd read on OnYourSide.net gave Jeff's words an almost predictable familiarity. "What do you mean?" she asked.

He cleared his throat. Coughed. "The experience you had with the priest."

She looked at him quizzically.

"You can't recover from this experience—whatever it was—until you remember what actually happened. One way that helps a lot of people is to reenact a repressed experience."

"How can I reenact an experience if I don't know what the experience was?"

"You reenact it to the best of your ability. Doing that may trigger more details." The sharp angles of his argyle sweater grazed the table between them. "Think about this. You've heard of the rebirthing process some psychologists use to help patients recall their births in order to make a new start?"

She shook her head. "This is shrink stuff. You're not a shrink."

"Rebirthing is all about breathing. Breathing is about the lungs. I'm a pulmonologist. It's all connected, baby. I'm just trying to help you."

She twisted her hands.

"I thought you were into this new agey alternative stuff," Jeff said.

She shrugged her shoulders and looked away. "Some of it."

Jeff leaned across the table. "Think about what happened in the confessional. It's the same idea as rebirthing. I—an authority figure or whoever you think of me as—touched you. I touched you in a confessional—perhaps the same place Father Hamilton touched you. Or maybe it was just the association of a confessional with a priest. The psychology comes into play when you repeat the activity with the intention of triggering the repressed memory."

"I don't think I can do that. It would freak me out completely."

"Yes, it would. But I'd be there with you to calm you down. You'd freak out once, but after that, I expect you'd never be haunted again," he said.

"Not ever?"

"A lot of my patients have asthma symptoms that are based entirely on emotions. I have to know a lot about psychology," Jeff said in his doctorly tone.

"Fair enough. But what you're proposing about a reenactment— that totally creeps me out." She shook her head.

"How about some Tuesday night at my office? We could try to take it further to trigger the repressed memory there."

"Take it further? *You're* the one who's crazy!"

"Baby, I'm not trying to play out some fantasy. I'm trying to *help* you."

"By letting you grope me like a pedophile priest?" The heads of two women at the next table snapped toward them. Heather lowered her voice. "Just forget I ever told you about it. I, in turn, will try to forget you ever suggested such a sick solution to a woman who was most likely violated as a child by one of the most trusted people she knew."

She pushed back her chair and propelled her fists into the sleeves of her jacket. "Let's go outside," she said. "I need a cigarette."

"*You* need a cigarette?"

Heather nodded.

"You're smoking pretty steadily now, aren't you?" he asked.

She stood and pulled on her coat. "Pack a day," she said. "Maybe more."

*　*　*

Heather and Jeff made their way through the throng on East 86th Street, a cloud of cigarette smoke billowing around their heads. Jeff cupped his cigarette in a gloved hand between inhales; Heather waved hers freely about, punctuating her sentences with its tip.

Reluctantly accepting the reality that there was no way she and Jeff could spend time together on Christmas, Heather had agreed that she would visit her mother.

"We'll celebrate on December 23," Jeff promised after mentally calculating the date. "On one of our regular Thursday nights together. We'll celebrate both Christmas and New Year's Eve—presents *and* champagne toasts."

Heather took a stab at proposing a celebration somewhere other than in her condo. "I've never been to Tavern on the Green at Christmas," she said. "I've heard it's an absolute wonderland."

Jeff inhaled deeply, holding the smoke in his lungs for a long moment before exhaling. "Why don't we have Tavern on the Green come to West 79th Street?"

"How?"

"Well, Tavern doesn't do take-out, but I have connections there. I can arrange to have the entire feast delivered to your condo— Christmas goose, plum pudding, the works. All you need to provide is the atmosphere."

"I can't compete with their atmosphere," she said. "I've heard they have entire rooms filled with trees, a trillion lights, fabulous ornaments, wooden soldiers…"

He stopped walking, dropped his cigarette to the ground, and took Heather's face between his hands. "Your face in the light of a single strand of Christmas lights would be just as beautiful to me."

Silently, she recalled the story Jeff had told her about his well-connected father-in-law moving Thanksgiving dinner to Tavern on the Green at the last minute. She knew why Jeff couldn't take her there.

"OK," she said. "Tavern on the Green at my place it is."

*   *   *

After Jeff's urging her to reenact her experience with Father Hamilton, Heather couldn't get the subject off her mind. Before going to bed, she returned to OnYourSide.net to search for material on men and women who had been violated by priests as children. The stories made her stomach lurch. She noticed the site had a bulletin board where registered visitors could post e-mails to each other. *It can't hurt to sign up.* She filled in the registration information, entered a user name and password, and clicked to agree with the bulletin board's posting rules.

Lighting a cigarette with a shaking hand, she began her first post.

I'm a woman in my thirties who was immediately attracted to a doctor who took care of me in a NYC ER. He diagnosed me with asthma and referred me to his private practice. Within weeks we were having an affair. I thought it was all consensual until I found your website. Now I'm not so sure. BTW, he's married, I'm single...never thought I'd have an affair with a married man. That's bad enough, but having read through this site, there's a part of me that wonders if I'm being exploited.

She pressed *Enter*. Immediately, her post appeared on the screen.

CHAPTER 19

HEATHER

JEFF ARRIVED PROMPTLY AT SEVEN on Thursday evening. They spent an hour cuddling and talking, Heather stretched out on the couch, Jeff cradling her head in his lap. There was no rush to the bedroom to make love—this night he'd promised to stay until long after dinner.

A few minutes after eight o'clock, the delivery Jeff had arranged from Tavern on the Green arrived. It was a classic Christmas feast made up of roast duck with plum sauce with sweet potato pancakes and winter vegetables. The foods were wrapped so beautifully, they could have been Christmas presents.

Heather had brought the bistro set from the kitchen into the living room, banishing Lin's booster seat to the back room that would be her bedroom. She'd purchased a red velvet table cloth and gold linen napkins. Tapered green candles flickered on the small table set with her two place settings of Royal Doulton. She and Jeff began the meal with chestnut truffle soup, still warm when she scooped it into bowls from a metal soup crock, firmly sealed and etched with the restaurant's logo, ToG.

"The soup is amazing," Heather replied. "Everything is amazing… absolutely perfect."

Jeff nodded in agreement. "It's sweet the way you appreciate things that someone else might take for granted," he said.

"Someone else? Like Priscilla?"

"Let's not spoil a perfect evening with talk of Priscilla. But yes, she has been catered to all her life. She has no idea what it's like to live in the real world." He scraped his bowl for any remaining truffles and deftly changed the subject. "If you think the soup was good, wait until you taste the duck!" He stood and said, "I can serve."

Heather jumped up from the table, racing to the counter where the rest of the meal awaited them. "I'll do that, Jeff. I'm the hostess."

"Let's do it together," he said, stepping behind her and reaching around to cup her breasts in his hands.

His breath was warm on her neck. Heather reached for the green cellophane over silver aluminum foil that wrapped the duck. The meat was still warm, too. Jeff held her from behind, pressing himself against her, clearly excited. As she savored the moment, she heard the familiar vibration of his cell phone erupt from his pocket.

"Oh, God, no," he said, burying his head in her neck as he reach for the phone. Checking caller ID, he said, "It's the fucking hospital."

"I thought someone was covering for you."

"Dr. Davis," he said into the phone. He covered the mouthpiece and whispered to Heather, "Except for one patient."

She rested her head against his shoulder as she heard him say, "Push ten milligrams of Valium to start. Tell him I'll be there in twenty minutes." Jeff clicked off. "It's Tom Driver," he said. "The actor who won the Academy Award last year."

"I know who he is."

"Well, I removed a tumor from his lung yesterday. The lab results just came back. It's cancer. Stage three. Pretty serious stuff." Jeff grabbed a piece of foil from the food wrappings, rolled it into a ball, and slammed it against Heather's kitchen wall. "Fuck!" The rigid foil ball hit hard, then slid to the floor.

Heather picked up the foil and dropped it into the garbage. "That *is* awful. But I'm not sure what it has to do with our dinner."

"What it has to do with our dinner is that I promised Tom I'd personally give him the results of the biopsy as soon as I got them. It's my duty as his doctor. I just didn't think they'd come in so soon."

"Can't you go after we eat? What's a couple of hours?"

"A couple of hours is an eternity for someone waiting for the results of a biopsy," he said.

She couldn't argue with that. She got his coat and walked him to the door, where they kissed once more, lightly this time, on the lips.

*   *   *

After Jeff left, Heather placed the meal, still warm in all its fancy packaging, in the fridge and freezer. There was a tub of rich vanilla ice cream packed in a Styrofoam container and poached pears with ginger sauce on a silver aluminum tray topped by green-tinted plastic and encircled by a red ribbon. There were half a dozen tiny white bags, each containing a gingerbread man, each bag tied closed with a red bow.

She was numb as she put the feast away. Instead, of the planned perfect evening with Jeff, she would be alone. And the remaining chestnut soup would do as dinner.

CHAPTER 20

HEATHER

IT WAS BARELY EIGHT O'CLOCK on Christmas morning when Heather heard the intercom buzz. *That's all I need. Christmas pranksters while I'm trying to catch the train.* She ignored the intercom, continuing to toss sweats and underwear on top of the tiny, carefully wrapped packages, each containing a gift card, that already lined her suitcase. Small in size, adding no bulk or weight to her baggage, there was a gift card for a craft shop in Bridgeport that her sister-in-law frequented, one for a local steak and brewery for her brother, and a gift card for Borders for her mother. She knew her brother would spend the bulk of his gift on beer and anticipated her mother's response to be something like, "A bookstore? You can get books for free at the library."

* * *

The intercom buzzed again. Irritated, Heather raced through the living room, pressed the speaker and demanded, "Who is it?"

"Santa Claus."

"Jeff?"

She heard the wind rush through the speaker, howling outside the vestibule door.

"Let me in," he said. "I'm freezing."

Heather pressed a button that released the lock on the lobby door seven floors below. Racing to the bathroom, she quickly combed her hair while simultaneously rinsing her mouth with mouthwash.

Jeff knocked only once before she opened the door. She held him close. "You're here!" she murmured into his overcoat. "You're here for Christmas!" Lifting her face to kiss him, she saw his expression. "My God, Jeff, what's wrong?"

"I lost a patient," he said, tears filling his eyes. "A twenty-five-year-old man—on Christmas morning. I just came from the hospital."

"Oh, my poor baby," she said, taking him into her arms.

"I had to tell his parents and his fiancée," Jeff muttered into her shoulder.

"God!" She took his hand and led him to the couch. "I'll never understand how you can do those things." Touching his cheek gave her a perfect view of her wrist. She glanced at her watch: 8:22.

"Let me make love to you," Jeff said.

The train to Bridgeport left Grand Central at 9:38. Was it possible to reassure him with sex and still grab a taxi by nine o'clock?

He reached for the tiny pearl buttons on her red satin blouse. "You look so Christmassy," he said. "Light the tree. Make it feel like Christmas *should* feel." She fumbled for the electric cord to turn on the Christmas lights on her tree as Jeff reached the last of her pearl buttons. He slipped the blouse off her shoulders, revealing a red lace bra. "What do you know—it's Christmas underneath, too."

They made love in the surreal glow of the multicolored lights on her tiny artificial tree. A mix of rain and hail carried by terrific winds slammed against the windows, painting a dismal backdrop. When their lovemaking was over, Jeff held her as if his own life depended on it. She thought about the postings on OnYourSide.net—they seemed like fiction. *Those women are all crazy,* she thought, *cast off by men with power. Men who fell out of love with them.*

* * *

They lay on the couch, intertwined like one of the twisted pretzels that were sold by street vendors throughout the city. "I can't tell where I end and you begin," she whispered before they both nodded off. Just moments later she heard Jeff's phone.

He pulled his slacks from the floor, the phone vibrating in the pocket. He glanced at caller ID. "I've got to take this," he said. Then flipping open the phone, he answered, "Hi, Pris."

Heather could hear the female voice at the other end of the connection. It sounded high pitched and angry, but she couldn't make out the words. She glanced at her watch: 9:40. The train to Bridgeport would be pulling out of the tunnel at Grand Central at that very moment.

"I'm still at the hospital," Jeff said. "The patient is lingering."

Heather picked up her satin blouse from the floor and draped it over her body.

"Go to Christmas services with your father and the kids," Jeff was saying. Heather tried not to listen as he added, "Pris, that's exactly why I can't leave. Nobody else wants to be here on Christmas either."

She got up and picked up the rest of her clothes.

"Sorry," Jeff said. "Saving lives takes precedence." He flipped the phone closed and tossed it on top of the pile of his clothes on the floor. "Now, where were we?" he asked.

"I thought the patient died," Heather replied.

"He did. But I just bought us a little more time. Now, come back here." He reached into the pocket of his slacks again and pulled out a wrapped gift box. "I brought your present."

"You brought it to the hospital with you?"

"I knew I was going to *try* to see you today." He handed her the rectangular-shaped box. "Open it."

"Let me put some clothes on first."

"No! This is perfect. Open it just like you are—wearing nothing but the blouse over your shoulders and your gorgeous skin."

"And my locket," she said, deliberately fingering the golden heart that held Lin's picture.

She balanced the gift box on her thighs and untied the red ribbon. She slipped a red-lacquered fingernail under the emerald green paper and lifted the folded flap of foil from the underside of the box. First one side, then the other. Beneath the green wrapping paper, she saw the trademark blue. "Oh my God, it's from Tiffany!"

"Only the best for you." He snuggled beside her, his face glowing with anxious anticipation. "You're my Christmas angel."

Her hands trembled as she tried to pull the top off the box. Jeff covered her hands with his. "Here, let me help you," he said. Together, they lifted the shiny blue cover off the box. Jeff removed the black velvet jewelry box inside and placed it in Heather's hand. She flipped the top open. Inside was a black pearl pendant set in platinum.

"Oh, my God," she said in one breath. "It's stunning—elegant." *And so not me.*

Jeff reached behind her neck and deftly undid the clasp that held her heart-shaped locket in place. As he laid it on the coffee table, the locket snapped open, revealing Lin's face, shiny black hair, and amber-flecked eyes. He took the black pearl pendant from Heather's hand and clasped it around her neck. "There!" he said. "Now that's much more in line with the sophisticated New York woman that you are."

Heather glanced at her locket on the coffee table. For just a moment, a ray of sunlight broke through the clouds outside, dancing on Lin's pretty face. The glint of gold around the child's face flickered in the sunlight. Just as quickly, it was gone.

* * *

Feeling suddenly naked, Heather slipped her arms into her blouse and reached for her underpants. "I have something for you, too," she said as she stood to pull her panties into place. "Let me go get it."

"You've already given me all I need."

She felt her cheeks flush. "Hold on," she said before turning to race down the hall.

She'd wrapped the small box in silver metallic paper surrounded by a slender red ribbon tied in a square knot—no bow. Jeff opened the box to reveal a cigarette lighter Heather had felt compelled to buy when she saw it in the window of a smoke shop on Fifth Avenue. "This flame will light in a tornado," the salesman had insisted, flicking the lighter as he blew directly on the flame. Heather recalled Jeff complaining about lighting a cigarette against the wind on the balcony where Priscilla insisted he do his smoking. "And the face of the lighter is fourteen-karat gold," the salesman had said. Both facts were conveyed in the cost. The clerk had asked her if she wanted it engraved. Sadly, she'd declined. She'd expected the clerk knew why.

Jeff took the lighter in his hand, flicking it on and off like a child with a toy. "Don't you want me to stop smoking—like everyone else does?" he asked.

"Of course I want you to stop, but I'm not going to nag you. Besides, now you've got me smoking."

"It's beautiful," he said, ignoring Heather's comment about her own smoking. "Really classy. Just like you."

The card was plain—a red parchment rectangle—but the sentiment inside was unique. *This flame will burn wherever you go—like the flame in my heart that burns for you,* she had written. *Merry Christmas. Heather.*

"Wow, that's really sweet," he said. "I'm sorry, but I'm not much of a card giver. I didn't get one for you."

"Don't be silly." Her fingers touched the smooth surface of the pearl. "This is more than enough."

*   *   *

Hours later, on the two o'clock train to Bridgeport, Heather opened her change purse to check that the heart-shaped locket was still there where she'd tucked it away so she could show her family Lin's picture. She removed it and slipped it into the pocket of her skirt before reaching for her cell phone and pressing *Mom.* "I'll be in Bridgeport in twenty minutes," she told her mother. "Pete should probably head to the station now."

CHAPTER 21

HEATHER

THE IMPROMPTU COUPLING on Christmas Day had thrown a monkey wrench into Heather's plans. She had been late for her family's celebration of Christmas in Connecticut. As a result, her mother was cranky. By the time she arrived, her brother Pete had drunk enough eggnog for Santa and all his elves, and two of his four kids were coming down with a stomach virus. Given Pete's level of intoxication, Heather opted not to ask him about any memories he might have harbored of Father Hamilton. It seemed like no time to open that can of worms.

"Sit down and eat," their mother insisted the minute Heather and Pete returned from the train station. Heather had wisely designated herself as the driver for the trip back to the house when Pete had staggered toward her and greeted her with a hug that smelled like a fraternity house on a Sunday morning.

Heather's mother removed her apron. "Me and Jen finished up the cooking while Petey went to the station," she added.

"Where's that other six-pack?" Pete asked no one in particular as he searched through his mother's refrigerator. His wife ignored him until he began to find the individual beer cans tucked behind various items in the fridge. "Why do you try to trick me like this?" he snarled in Jen's direction as he pulled two cans from behind a gallon of milk. "Don't you know by now you can't win?"

"Yeah, I've known that for a long time now," Jen shot back.

"Children, behave!" their mother said, her reaction slipping back through the decades. "It's Christmas!"

Heather brushed her mother's cheeks with her lips and pulled off her coat. "Hi, Mom," she said.

"Just call me Lady Margaret," her mother said in response. "As you can see, I live in the lap of luxury."

"Come on, Mom," Heather said, rubbing her mother's back. "It's Christmas."

"Just put all your stuff in the bedroom for now," Margaret said. "It's time to eat."

The turkey, frozen since Margaret had received it at Thanksgiving from the school where she used to work, was crammed on a wreath-trimmed platter in the center of the tiny kitchen table, surrounded by condiments, mashed potatoes, and heated canned string beans. A card table had been set up for the children near the kitchen door that led to the living room. It was surrounded by four grey metal folding chairs that Heather recognized from the church basement at St. Aiden's circa 1980. She figured her mother had probably been gifted with the chairs in recognition for her thirty years of service as an altar lady, one of a dozen or so unpaid women who dusted the statues, polished the chalice, and arranged fresh flowers on the altar every week.

"Everybody sit down or it'll be stone cold," Margaret said. Pete's youngest son appeared in the kitchen doorway, wiping his mouth with a red hand towel from the bathroom, clearly having just thrown up. "Except you, Patrick. You go lie down on Nana's bed with your brother until you feel better."

The family sat down and began to serve themselves. Jen alternated between feeding herself at the adult table and cutting her kids' meat at the children's table. The turkey was overcooked and cold, the mashed potatoes replete with lumps.

"Great dinner, Mom," Pete said, green beans spewing from his lips.

Ever been to Balthazar? Heather caught herself thinking. It had been sheer luck that Tim had knocked up Tara while Heather was working her way through her last year at the University of Bridgeport in 1992. Otherwise Tim would have married her instead of Tara, and her life would have been no different than her brother's. "Yeah, Mom. Everything's really delicious," she said.

* * *

During the gift exchange, Heather's gifts were accepted as she had anticipated. Her brother and his wife spouted gratitude for their gift certificates. As expected, her mother mentioned the library when she opened her fifty-dollar Borders gift card. And each of the kids, having received a crisp twenty-dollar bill from Aunt Heather, thought he or she was the richest person on the planet. Heather had received a basket of beauty products from her mother—none of which she used. Pete and Jen gave her a matching set of pink mittens, a scarf, and a cap.

She thought about the necklace Jeff had given her, replacing her locket without question. And the way he had appeared at her door unannounced—was it a sexy Christmas surprise or thoughtless interference with her plans for Christmas Day? But despite her mixed emotions, she physically ached to return to New York to enjoy the after-Christmas celebration they had planned.

*   *   *

Heather made her announcement over a dessert of vanilla ice cream and Christmas cookies.

"I have a very exciting surprise for all of you," she said, running her fingers along the edge of a gingerbread man.

"Don't tell me," her mother replied sarcastically, "You're moving back to Connecticut."

"No, Mom. I don't think that's likely to happen." She broke an arm off the gingerbread man, chewed it, and swallowed. "But you, Jen and Pete, are going to be an aunt and uncle. Mom, you're going to be a grandmother again. And, kids, you're going to have a new little cousin."

Her mother blessed herself and shouted, "I *asked* you if you were pregnant!"

"Mom, I am *not* pregnant. I'm adopting a baby. A little girl from China. Her name is Lin." She removed her locket from the pocket of her skirt, opened it, and placed it in the center of the table.

"Why can't you get married and have your own babies like normal people?" her mother asked. She dropped her spoon into her ice cream bowl with a clatter.

Heather bit the inside of her lip until she tasted blood. "Do you have any idea how many children in this world need a home?"

"OK. Maybe. So *get married* and then adopt a child."

"I haven't had any offers of marriage lately, Mom. In fact, I haven't had any offers for a date."

Her mother sighed and pressed a hand against her chest. "That's because all the men in that filthy city are homosexuals."

"That's not true." Heather played with the ends of the pink scarf she'd wrapped around her neck in the hope that Pete and Jen would think she liked it. *Do the people who give me gifts know me at all?*

Jen picked up the locket and looked at Lin's picture. "She's adorable," she said. Pete washed down a spoonful of ice cream with a swig of beer.

"Well, if you have to adopt a child, can't you get an American one?" her mother asked. "Everyone will know this little Chinese girl isn't really yours."

"She'll be mine as much as if I'd given birth to her. And if I adopted a child in this country, the odds are overwhelming that he or she would be African American."

"Lord, have mercy!" Margaret said, lifting the locket and looking at the child more closely. "Her name is Lin you say? For Linda?"

"No, Mom. It's Lin. Just Lin. Spelled L-I-N. And she's your granddaughter."

CHAPTER 22

HEATHER

THE IDEA OF PHYSICALLY EXPLORING with Jeff the possibility of an abusive sexual encounter with Father Hamilton felt like pointing a gun to her head. "I don't want to do this," Heather said when Jeff opened his office door to her on the Tuesday night after Christmas. "The thought of it terrifies me."

"That's exactly why you *should* do it," he said, placing his arms around her. "It was a big step for you to agree to do it."

Heather had only relented to get Jeff to stop nagging her. "I would be better off if I'd never suspected anything," she said.

He steered her toward the exam room. "On the contrary," he said. "Once you know what happened, we can *do* something about it. We can address the behavior and the symptoms it's caused. If that bastard priest did molest you, it would affect every aspect of your life."

"Why are you so interested in this?" Heather asked, remembering that moment in the confessional with Jeff when the vague image of Father Hamilton's ancient hands touching her young body had first invaded her memory.

"Because I want to help you." Now in his exam room, he brushed the hair from her shoulders protectively. "Because it's becoming more and more clear to me that your asthma is triggered by a lot more than environmental factors. And there's little doubt in my mind that it stems from deep-seated emotional issues from your childhood."

He propped her unwilling body onto his exam table. Since the moments in the confessional, Heather had been obsessed with wondering if the priest had done more than touch her. Had he actually raped her? "Really, Jeff, I don't want to know any more about what happened."

"Shhhhh," he said. He put a hand on each of her shoulders, gently pressing her body back on the exam table. "Let me help you, baby."

"No! Jeff, I'm not going to do this. Pretending to have sex with a priest is sick."

"We don't know that this will lead to having sex," he reminded her. "It's a reenactment. Hopefully, your original experience will come back to you, and we'll act it out just as it happened when you were a child. If that means having sex, it's only to unblock your memory."

"But sex with…" Her voice trailed off.

"I'm not viewing this as having sex," he insisted. "And you shouldn't be either. I want to trigger your memory so you don't have to live with this unresolved nightmare anymore." He looked at her directly in the bright light of the exam room. He took her purse, opened it and retrieved her inhaler. "Use this so you don't have an attack if the reenactment gets too upsetting."

Heather took the inhaler and breathed in the medication. Once. Twice. Five times. She handed the device back to Jeff.

Jeff's body stiffened as he assumed the personality of the pedophile priest. His voice sounded different as he said, "Tell me why you weren't at Mass on Sunday, Heather."

"I was sick," Heather said in a childish voice.

"Are you telling the truth?" Jeff asked.

"Yes," she said.

"Are you a good girl?" he asked.

"Yes, Father."

"Then open your legs for me. You remember how."

Her whole body trembled as she followed his orders.

More quickly than usual, Jeff came with a shudder. Heather merely shuddered inside at the memories the reenactment had triggered. The second he'd entered her, she knew for certain this had happened before. She had wanted to ask him to stop, but she'd been helpless to say anything at all.

* * *

"Settle down, baby. You'll feel better soon," Jeff said when it was over.

"I know." She brushed a tear away. "You told me the immediate aftermath of the reenactment is hard—that the benefit comes later."

"Exactly right. You're a good patient."

She shifted her gaze from his face. As he began to pull his clothes on, she looked around the room, almost gasping aloud when she saw it. The tiny red light behind the wall cabinet where Jeff kept his DVD recorder was glowing. He had recorded the reenactment of her having sex with Father Hamilton. Every second of it.

CHAPTER 23

HEATHER

CONVINCED THAT JEFF'S RECORDING of the reenactment had been intentional, Heather raced to her computer the minute she got home. As the machine booted up, she removed her trench coat, drenched from a cold and unrelenting rain, and dropped it in a heap on the floor.

She hadn't revisited OnYourSide.net since she'd entered her post. Since then, Jeff had been almost singularly focused on the emotional component of her asthma, culminating with the reenactment of a hideous childhood experience in the name of therapy. Recording the encounter had brought his behavior to yet another level. *I need help,* she thought. *Help that maybe this website can give me.*

She clicked to the bulletin board where she'd posted her query. She was surprised and excited to see there were eleven responses. She read through them one by one, finding overwhelming support interspersed with a few from clearly disturbed women and a couple from voyeurs.

I've been involved with my cardiologist for twelve years, wrote one. *He says he'll never leave his wife. Still, I can't make myself break it off. I'm so in love with him. I'm forty-eight now and feel I've run out of options. Get out now before you lose your youth chasing a dream that will never come true.*

Another comment read: *A doctor having sex—even so-called consensual sex—with a patient is against every code of medical ethics. Tell this guy to take a hike—and find yourself another doctor.*

The next response came from a sicko proposing a threesome. Heather shook her head in disgust and moved on to the last posted message. A woman named Suzanne had written: *Because your doctor treated you for asthma, I expect he is a pulmonologist. You said you were in a hospital in New York. I'm respectful of the privacy rules of this website, but at the same time, I can't stand the thought that the doctor I was involved with might be a serial abuser. I already know of one other woman who was involved with him. So to start, I'll just ask you this: Does his first name begin with J?*

Heather clicked back to the bulletin board rules and read *Please do not name a perpetrator in this forum. Because OnYourSide.net is not able to verify any claims anonymously posted on this forum, we ask that you do not post any defamatory messages that give the name of the perpetrator. Thank you for understanding.*

Heather returned to Suzanne's message. Her heart raced wildly as she typed *Yes. His first name begins with J. Last name starts with D.* She lit a cigarette with shaking hands. *He's part American Indian.* Then to avoid further postings on OnYourSide.net, she typed her personal e-mail address and added *Write to me as soon as you see this!*

She wrapped herself in a flannel robe and began to pack her suitcase. An impromptu business trip to London had come out of nowhere the day before. Peters & Andrews had already slashed its staff by fifteen percent due to the bleak world economy. Dismal revenues for the fourth quarter from the European offices meant more heads would roll. Heather was tasked with locating the proper venue in which CEO Jake Warner and Jane Anderson, as head of human resources, would conduct layoffs of the European staff in April if the financial results for the first quarter were as poor as expected.

After packing, she returned to her computer. An e-mail from a Suzanne Fisher with the subject line *Your Inquiry on OnYourSide.net* had just arrived. Heather clicked it open immediately.

Dear Heather, Suzanne had written. *My doctor does indeed have the initials J.D. His name is Jeff Davis, just to make it crystal clear. I'm sure he's the same man you're involved with.*

I'd like to meet with you. Please let me know if you feel you're ready for that.

Sincerely, Suze.

Heather's heart raced as she reread Suzanne's e-mail. This was real. She reached for her purse as she read, removing her inhaler and Valium vial. She had no doubt that Jeff had had an affair with this woman—this patient. Her hand shook as she pressed the print button on her computer, then she curled up on the couch with it, reading it repeatedly. She cried softly at first, eventually convulsing in sobs. She swallowed two Valium and used her inhaler before returning to the computer to respond to Suzanne.

Suze, she wrote, *thank you for writing to me. I'm a little hesitant to meet you since I'm still involved with Jeff. I really don't want to believe any of this is happening. But I am curious. Would you e-mail me again? Heather.*

She lit a cigarette and watched her reflection in the computer monitor. The tip of her cigarette brightened as she inhaled, lighting up her image in the monitor. She saw herself, still young and pretty, and remembered the warning from the older woman on OnYourSide.net who had written *get out now before you lose your youth chasing a dream that will never come true.* She exhaled, blowing the smoke against the monitor.

Unexpectedly, an instant message appeared: *How about a bench in Central Park? Tomorrow at three? I'll bring my poodle FiFi so you'll recognize me. Suze.*

Heather's flight to London was leaving JFK at nine o'clock tomorrow night. If she left work by two thirty, she could meet Suzanne and still get to the airport on time.

Her hands quivered on the keyboard as she typed: *OK.*

She turned off the computer, downed two Ambien with a sip of milk, and stumbled, barely conscious, to the bedroom, where she fell into a dreamless sleep.

*   *   *

Heather would have recognized Suzanne even without her poodle. Impeccably dressed, her posture erect as a dancer's, Suzanne wore the uniform of an Upper East Side woman who'd married well: designer jeans, a camel's hair jacket, and a cashmere scarf around her neck. Like Heather, she was slender and blond.

As Heather approached the park bench where Suzanne was ensconced, FiFi began to tug on her leather Swarovski crystal-encrusted leash, yipping loudly.

"Suzanne?" Heather ventured.

"Suze, please, it's Suze," the other woman said. She stood, adjusting her scarf around her neck and shoulders. "FiFi, sit!" she commanded as the dog's leash tangled around her legs. "You can see I'm not used to walking her."

"Cute dog," Heather said, patting FiFi's head.

Suze and Heather sat together on the bench, and FiFi settled in the grass, sniffing at Heather's suede boots.

"I'm so glad you agreed to meet me, Heather," Suze said, tugging nervously on her leather gloves. Heather pulled her black pea coat tightly around herself, wishing she'd worn the zip-in lining.

"I don't want to believe the man you were involved with was Jeff." Heather's voice shook. "What we have together seems so special... so unique."

A flicker of recognition filled Suzanne's features with empathy. "I'm not trying to convince you," she said. "My intention is to spare you and any of Jeff's future victims from heartache. And I'd like to see him pay for what he's done. I already know another woman who was involved with him."

"How many of us *are* there?"

"At least one other."

"How do you know?" Heather asked.

Suzanne wrapped FiFi's leash securely around her gloved hand. "One time when I was waiting in Dr. Davis's—Jeff's—reception area, I saw a woman I recognized. She had been a freshman at Barnard when I was a senior. I recognized her accent when she spoke to the receptionist."

"Accent?"

"She was a Southern girl from Charleston. I went over to her and asked if she'd gone to Barnard. After that, we became friendly. We did a few things together socially. Eventually, it came out that we were both involved with the doctor."

"At the same time?"

"Within a year of each other. I met Melissa in Jeff's office last summer. My involvement with him started in July."

"How long did it last?"

"Less than six months. Melissa got involved with him in February. She didn't tell me about it until last May—when it was over."

That's when he started seeing me. Oh, God! Could he really be a serial womanizer?

Suze leaned close to Heather and whispered, even though there was no one nearby. "Are you going to report him?"

Heather felt her neck muscles tightening. "Report him?"

"To the OPMC," Suze said. "The Office of Professional Medical Conduct. They conduct investigations for the New York State Medical Board. All the information and forms are on OnYourSide.net."

Heather shook her head, uncertain of a plan. "I don't know. When I thought I was the only one, I actually thought he was in love with me." Saying the words out loud made her feel like a fool.

Suze touched—almost tugged—the sleeve of Heather's jacket. "I could never go public with this," she said. "I've got my marriage at stake, financial security for my children. We have four kids. But if you take that bastard down, I'll head your cheerleading squad."

CHAPTER 24

JEFF

AFTER THE HOSPITAL'S NEW YEAR'S EVE BALL at the Waldorf, Jeff sat stiffly in the library at home, staring at the art collection lining the walls. He and Priscilla had left the party fairly late, at one in the morning, and Jeff was too keyed up from socializing to go to bed for the night. On top of that, his service had called to inform him that one of his patients had died a few minutes before midnight.

The clicking of her heels against the marble foyer floor heralded Priscilla's arrival long before she entered the room. "I didn't know you were in here," she said.

He glanced at his watch. "I'm too wound up to go to bed."

"Me, too," Priscilla said. She settled on a damask chaise, the silk drapes surrounding the floor-to-ceiling windows behind her, framing her image. "Jeffrey, you know I don't like you smoking in the apartment."

In the chair across from her, Jeff crossed and recrossed his legs, trying in vain to relax. He stabbed out his cigarette in a crystal ashtray. Immediately, he slipped another from the pack and lifted the cigarette lighter Heather had given him for Christmas to its tip.

"Nice lighter," Priscilla said.

"Grateful patient," Jeff replied, by way of explanation.

"A patient gave you a cigarette lighter!" She bolted from the chaise and grabbed the lighter. "You told a patient that you smoke?"

Jeff sipped some brandy from a Waterford glass he'd set on the coffee table beside the ashtray and tried to appear cool while his brain raced for the lie that would redeem him. "Really wealthy patient with chronic COPD," he said. "I sent him to our smoking cessation clinic. It worked, and his COPD improved dramatically. He gave me the lighter because it's valuable, and he said, because of me, he'll never need to use it again."

Priscilla examined the lighter under the glow of the bone china table lamp. "This is a very expensive cigarette lighter," she said. "My father had the same type of lighter before he quit smoking. I'm guessing this is worth well over a thousand dollars."

Heather spent a thousand dollars on my Christmas gift? Holy shit! "Like I said, Pris, this patient was even more loaded than most of my patients."

He stepped to the bar and carried the full carafe of brandy back to the table beside his chair. Tonight he knew he'd want enough of it that crossing back and forth between the chair and the wet bar would be too much effort. Mike Dommer had been at the ball at the Waldorf with a nurse from Lenox Hill who couldn't have been more than twenty-four. Her youthful sexiness combined with the loss of his patient had Jeff in desperate need of a sexual release. Since sex wasn't likely to be an option, he'd chosen alcohol.

"Great party," he said. "Unfortunately, while we were there, I got word that a patient died on me."

"Jeffrey, they don't die *on* you."

"You know what I mean. It just reminds me of mortality. The finality of things."

"Medicine is a bizarre career choice for someone with the mortality issues you have," she said, words she'd repeated hundreds of times during their marriage. Probably translating his words into a bid for sex, she folded the corner of a page in Vanity Fair. She pushed herself up from the chair, holding her magazine. "I'll see you in the bedroom. I have a bit of headache. Good-night, dear."

He lifted his glass, toasting her back as she left the room. *Priscilla. Heather. Anna. Pathetic. Screwing three women and I still can't get laid!*

CHAPTER 25

HEATHER

HEATHER WALKED ALONG THE EDGE of the vast loft space that Trista shared with a dozen other artists. They were a cooperative of painters and sculptors, each with their own unique style. Sunlight flooded the studio, beaming in from floor-to-ceiling windows with a southern exposure.

As Heather approached her friend's space, Trista turned off the small battery-operated radio from which the midday news on NPR provided a quiet hum in the background.

"Hey," Trista said. "You're late. I'm starving."

"Sorry. I waited forever for the subway connection at 14th Street."

"No problem," Trista said. She hugged her friend with her elbows, careful not to touch her with her paint-splattered hands. "I bet you didn't have problems like that on the tube in London."

"I had no problems at all in London; it was a great trip," Heather said.

Trista mixed a dab of cobalt blue watercolor paint into some cadmium yellow to create a perfect leaf green. "What did you do?"

"*London!*" Heather said. "I did *London*." She sat down on an inverted milk crate and continued. "Let's see. I found the perfect spot for the corporate meetings the very first day. So I spent the next two days of the trip hopping on and off a big red double-decker bus that toured the city. I saw two shows. It was a great trip!"

"Wow! You packed a lot into a few days."

"I did. It was wonderful," Heather said. She paced behind her friend, assessing her work. "That's really beautiful, Trista. Such great colors!"

"Thanks, sweetie. And what about you? "How's it going with Dr. Love?"

"Things with *Jeff* are great," she lied. "I don't think you've seen this great necklace he gave me for Christmas."

Trista wiped the paint off her hands and reached over to touch the pearl in its exquisite setting. "Do you like it?" she asked Heather. "I mean, it's so...sophisticated."

Heather took the pearl between her fingers. "OK, so maybe it's not a hundred percent me. But it's from him, so it's special."

"I don't think it's *one* percent you," Trista answered. "And I don't mean to sound like a jealous lover, but where's the locket I gave you?"

Heather shrugged. "Well, I can't wear them together. They're completely different from each other."

"More importantly, where's Lin's picture?" Trista asked.

"It's at home in the locket—in the ashtray on my nightstand."

"In the *ashtray*? I know you keep a little tray on your night table where you put your jewelry. You never called it an ashtray."

Guilt engulfed Heather's face as she opened her purse and removed a pack of cigarettes.

"What are you doing with those?" Trista demanded.

"Jeff smokes. Being around him kind of got me started again."

Trista splattered paint on the drop cloth on the floor. "You're seeing a married pulmonologist who smokes? And now *you're* smoking again? Perfect!"

Heather nodded. She eased another crate across the paint-splattered floor with her foot and sat down.

"I'll try not to lecture you about the married thing," Trista said. "But I remember the agony you went through when you quit smoking the first time." Trista twisted a paper towel into a point. She stood and touched it to the painting. "It's not going to be any easier the next time."

"I know," Heather acknowledged before quickly changing the subject. She ached to tell Trista about her meeting with Suzanne, the repressed memory of being violated by Father Hamilton, and Jeff's surreptitious recordings of their sex life. But if she told Trista, there would be no taking it back. Maybe just a little information. "I've been doing a little detective work," she began.

Trista splashed a dab of white into cadmium red, blending them into the perfect shade of pink. "What kind of detective work?"

"On the Internet. That website I found—OnYourSide.net—it has a forum section where you can chat with people."

Trista stopped painting. "Who have you been talking to online?"

Heather bit her lower lip. "I met another woman online. She claimed to have had an affair with her doctor who happened to be a pulmonologist in New York. He sounded exactly like Jeff."

Trista dampened a piece of paper towel and stabbed at her painting. "People can say *anything* on the Internet." She tossed the paint-stained paper towel into a communal garbage can and pulled up another inverted crate. She sat down beside Heather. "What did you do?" Trista asked.

"I just asked her to e-mail me instead of posting on OnYourSide.net. The website is really careful that no doctors get named on their site. It could get innocent people into a lot of trouble."

"So what do you know about this woman?" Trista asked.

"Well, she told me that she lives in New York and had an affair with her pulmonologist. For all I know, she could have been some rich trophy wife with nothing to do but play on the Internet all day. I sent her an e-mail before I went to London, asking if the doctor she'd been involved with had the initials J.D. and was part American Indian."

Trista was waiting for more.

Instinctively, Heather decided to come clean. "I met her," she said.

"Dear God, Heather, you've got to stop this. If not Jeff, then the cyberstalking!"

"Suzanne gave me Jeff's full name. It's definitely him. And she says there's another woman who was involved with him, too."

"This Suzanne sounds as crazy as Jeff has made you."

"I don't want to believe her," Heather said.

Trista glanced at the pack of Parliaments in her friend's hand. "Oh, sweetie, I wish you'd just throw out those cigarettes and that guy along with them! Why would you want him if, on top of everything else, he's got a bunch of other women?"

"There's more." Heather looked around the studio, deflecting her gaze from Trista. "Suzanne thinks I should report Jeff."

"To whom?"

"The Office of Professional Medical Conduct. They handle complaints made to the New York State Medical Board."

"Would you do that?" Trista asked.

"At this point, I just don't know."

"If she's so anxious to turn him in, why doesn't she do it herself?" Trista asked.

"She's married," Heather explained. "There could be some publicity." She got up from the crate. "I just don't know who he is anymore! But I am sure it's over between him and his wife."

"Has he said so?" Trista asked.

"Not really. But I can tell by the stories he tells about her and by the way he acts toward her."

Trista placed her hands on her hips. "You only know what *he* tells *you*."

"I've heard the way he speaks to her on the phone. He's always in a hurry to get off the phone, always frustrated by her responses, whatever they are."

"Does he get frustrated with you?"

"I don't think so. I try really hard not to do anything that would frustrate him."

Trista stood, her shoulders sagging, her paintbrush still in her hand. A speck of red paint dripped onto the drop cloth at her feet. She removed the floral painting from the easel and stood it against the wall to dry. In its place, she put a nude scene of a couple intertwined in a flurry of flowing white sheets. "This is one of my favorites," she said. "It's almost finished."

"It looks finished to me," Heather said. "What do you have to do—paint clothes on them?"

Trista laughed lightly and shook her head. "That's why I'm the artist and you're the travel expert." She studied her painting. "The light on his back is totally wrong." She moved the easel to adjust the way the light fell on her work. "Why else do you think it's over between Jeff and his wife?"

"He lies to her all the time," Heather said.

"That's not a good sign. It probably just means he's a liar in general."

"Why do you always burst my bubble?" Heather pouted. "Can't you be on my side for a change?"

Trista put down her paintbrush. "Honey," she said, "I *am* on your side. You're my friend, and I love you enough to tell you the truth. Telling the truth is what friends do."

"Even if it hurts?"

"*Especially* if it hurts." Trista adjusted her easel again. "Now tell me what he lies to his wife about."

"About everything," Heather said. "Where he is. On Christmas, he told her a patient who had died was still alive. He said that's why he needed to be at the hospital, but he was with me."

"Oh, honey, you just don't get it, do you? People are either liars, or they're not. If he's lying to her, he's lying to you, too."

CHAPTER 26

JEFF

JEFF CALLED HEATHER LATE MONDAY AFTERNOON. "Meet me at Bryant Park?" he asked. "Around seven?"

"Sure," she replied, pleased at the unscheduled date, and his meeting her in Midtown suggested that he might be growing considerate of her location and her schedule.

Instead of heading for dinner, they simply bought hot chocolate and big salty pretzels from the vendors who lined the park. They settled themselves at a concrete table on the concourse.

Jeff took a bite of his pretzel and started to chew. He chewed repeatedly, appearing to struggle to swallow the dough. He coughed, placed a paper napkin over his mouth, and wrapped the moistened pretzel remains, leaving the rest of the uneaten pretzel in a brown paper bag, a grease stain pooling at its base.

Heather was anxious to tell him that she'd booked the Churchill Hotel in London for the company meeting in April. She twisted her hands in nervous anticipation, knowing she planned to ask him to join her there. He could tell his wife he was going to a medical convention and fly to London for the weekend after her company meeting was over. It would be perfect, she thought, the first time they'd ever travel together!

"What's the matter?" Heather asked. "Why aren't you eating?"

Jeff gave a brief glance to passersby before lighting up a cigarette against the strong wind with the lighter Heather had given him for

Christmas. When he exhaled the acrid smoke, it mixed with his frosted breath in a thick cloud of grey vapor.

Heather anchored the brown paper bag that held her pretzel against the wind with her almost-full cup of hot chocolate.

"We have to talk," he said.

"OK," she replied, her heart starting to hammer.

"Priscilla found out," he said.

"Found out what?" Breathing was a struggle.

Jeff looked down at the concrete table. "She found out about *us*."

"How could that happen?" she asked, arching her back in a sudden panic. She reached for Jeff's hand, knocking over her hot chocolate in the process. The steaming liquid spilled on her tights-clad leg, burning like hell. "Shit!" she cried.

Jeff jumped up. "Let me take a look at that," he said.

"No!" Heather insisted. The burning in her heart was a lot more painful than the one on her leg. "It's fine." She rested her calf on her opposite thigh and rubbed it gently. "What happened?" she asked.

"She found a bill," he said.

"What bill?" Jeff had always used cash when they went out.

"My American Express bill. The one with the Tiffany's charge on it." He rubbed the filter of his cigarette between his thumb and forefinger. "The bill for your necklace."

Heather reached for the rich black pearl that was tucked behind a thick wool scarf that circled her neck. Her fingerless leather gloves let her feel the pearl's smooth surface against her fingertips, causing her elbow to jut into the walkway. Just then, a group of kids wearing NYU jackets and carrying ice skates swarmed past, knocking into her elbow.

"Excuse us."

"Sorry, ma'am."

Ma'am? The term made her feel old. She turned back to Jeff. "How did she…"

"She was paying the bills," he said. "I could have sworn I'd used my AmEx card from the practice for your gift. But obviously, I didn't." Jeff reached for her gloved hand. "I'm sorry, baby. I'm just as upset as you are about this whole thing. I can't imagine not being with you."

"What are you talking about—not being together? This is an isolated occurrence. Just think of some story and keep things between us the way they are. We can still be together."

"Baby, I can't risk it. There's just too much at stake."

Tears spiked from her eyes. "What are you talking about? I thought we were different, special..." she said, thinking of the other women who she still wouldn't let herself believe had been in his life.

"We *are* special, Heather," he said. He dropped his cigarette, stubbed it out with the heel of his shoe, and took her hand. "But nobody is special enough to compete with the Wellington family." He squeezed her hand in emphasis. "Nobody."

"The Wellingtons?" she asked, her throat tightening.

"Priscilla's family," he said. "They basically own Lenox Hill. They own me." Heather was struggling to breathe. "Use your inhaler," he said.

She ignored his instruction. If it was over between them, what was the point in breathing?

He stood, rounded the table, and bent to kiss her forehead. "I know I never said it, but I *do* love you, baby." He turned and walked away, his perfect physique towering over the skaters and sightseers that filled the park.

*   *   *

It was Friday afternoon—four days since she'd seen him. He hadn't called.

Heather had replayed the conversation over and over again in her mind. She recalled Jeff's gestures, his tone, as he told her he couldn't see her anymore—and why.

At first, she'd been certain he'd call her, telling her he'd made a dreadful mistake and begging for forgiveness. As the week wore on, she battled with herself constantly to keep from calling him. She couldn't hold out anymore.

She closed her office door, snapped her phone open, and whispered "Call Jeff" into the mouthpiece. His phone didn't ring. Instead, it was immediately answered by an automated recording. *You have reached a nonworking number at Verizon Wireless,* a digitized female voice stated. *No further information is available about this number. If you feel you have reached this number in error, please try again.* The recording clicked off. Nothing.

She stabbed the dial pad, looking for Jeff's office number. The numbers did their digital dance before a brief ring bridged the connection to the practice's voice mail message. *You have reached the offices of Upper East Side Pulmonologists. If this is a medical emergency, please hang up and dial 212-555-2309. If you are calling to make an appointment...*

Heather shut the phone. *This can't be happening.* But Jeff's message was becoming painfully clear.

CHAPTER 27

HEATHER

BY ELEVEN O'CLOCK FRIDAY NIGHT, Heather was losing her mind. Miguel had offered to spend the evening with her after she'd told him about the breakup, but she'd declined. Now, as she continued to call Jeff's cell number, praying that it had simply been out of order, she longed for the comfort of Miguel's presence.

She dialed Miguel and got voice mail. Obsessively, she redialed Jeff's number. *You have reached a nonworking number at Verizon Wireless.* She stared at the phone, willing it to make contact with Jeff. *He can't have meant it's over. I have to let him know I'm not that strong, not strong enough to stay away...that I'll see him on whatever terms he wants.*

She lifted the phone again, this time to call Trista. Heather was sobbing.

"Do you want me to come over?" Trista asked.

"No, it's OK." Heather had called her friend at least three times a day during the week of the breakup. Even in her desperate state, she was aware that she was pushing the friendship.

"Honey, you've got to get hold of yourself," Trista said.

"He changed his cell number!" Heather wailed in response.

"You're kidding!" Trista exclaimed. Heather could almost hear her friend thinking just how serious this was and reaching carefully for her words. "You need to let go," Trista continued. "And if you can't let go, you've got to fight back."

Heather lay back on the couch, the flow of tears pooling in her ears. "What do you mean, fight back?"

"I don't know," Trista said. "Maybe you *should* think about reporting him to the medical board. Maybe that other woman you met *isn't* crazy. And by now, you and I both know that he could lose his medical license for having sex with patients."

"I *have* been thinking about filling in the form on OnYourSide.net," Heather said. "I couldn't bring myself to do it before we broke up. Now I'm actually starting to consider it."

"You go, girl!" Trista cheered.

"I told you Suzanne thought I should report him," Heather continued.

"That's Mrs. Upper East Side, right?"

"Right. She also gave me the e-mail address of the other woman she said had an affair with Jeff. Her name is Melissa. I e-mailed her my phone number and she called me. I'm having coffee with her on Sunday." Heather rolled onto her stomach, propping herself up on her elbows.

"I'm not sure if that's a good thing or a bad thing," Trista said. "If nailing Jeff's ass is what's motivating you, go for it. But if it's an obsession, you need to start letting go. You don't need anyone's story but your own to report him to the medical board, especially if these women aren't willing to talk."

"Well, I know Suzanne isn't willing to risk her marriage," Heather said. "I'm not sure about Melissa yet, but it's probably the same for her. Suzanne told me she's married, too."

"Just make sure you take all this detective work beyond commiserating with them because you were all screwed by the same man," Trista said. "No pun intended." She cleared her throat. "By the way, I took a look at that website—OnYourSide.net. You're right that you can report him to the medical board for violating medical ethics. But you can also file a civil case against him. If you win that, it could mean a lifetime of financial security."

"I don't want his money," Heather said.

"You might want to rethink that," Trista said.

Heather walked over to her laptop and turned it on. "Why? Getting rich off this was never my intention. I loved him."

"I know, honey," Trista said. "I'm just saying you have options."

"I've done enough research to know that it's always unethical for a doctor to have an affair with a patient. And that it's actually illegal in many states."

"I saw that, too," Trista said.

Heather wiped a tear from her eye as the Office of Professional Medical Conduct website appeared on the computer screen. She clicked to the page that contained the complaint form that would initiate a report to the medical board. "I'm thinking about reporting him. It's just so hard. I'm so depressed."

"We need to get you out of that condo. What are you doing tomorrow?"

"No idea." She stared at the form on her computer screen.

Trista sighed long and hard into the phone. "You need to have plans. Otherwise you'll stay in and get even more depressed. You might do something stupid, like call him."

"*Hello?* The whole problem is that I *can't* call him. I told you he changed his cell number."

"I know. But that's not the *whole* problem. It's this obsession. You need to deal with it." Trista was quiet for a moment at the other end of the line. Heather could hear her digging through her purse or a drawer. "I know! Let's get those free pedicures I got for Christmas. I've got the coupons."

Heather pulled off an argyle sock and looked at her toenails. They were long, and the red polish she'd applied for Christmas was badly chipped. "Nobody will be seeing my toenails," she said.

"Do *you* see them?" Trista asked.

"Well, yeah, when I take off my socks."

"That's reason enough. Who's more important than you?"

"Fine, we'll get our pedicures." Heather tugged her sock back over her foot. It was cold in the condo.

"The salon is at 52 Mott Street in Chinatown. Between Hester and Grand. They don't take appointments. How about if I just meet you there at eleven tomorrow?"

"OK."

"Will you be OK until then?"

Heather clicked *print*. Within a second, the OPMC complaint form was spewing out of the printer. She reached for the bottle of Ambien and quietly emptied three pills into her hand. "I'll be fine until morning," she said.

CHAPTER 28

HEATHER

DESPITE THE TRIPLE DOSE OF AMBIEN, Heather woke up at ten minutes to three. She stared at the ceiling, counted sheep, and reviewed every possible misstep she might have made with Jeff that could have caused him to dump her. Despite his assurance that his only motive was to keep his marriage together, she still believed the breakup was her fault.

Hours passed. The streetlights flickered off, and the sky began to brighten. Still, Heather tossed and turned, praying for sleep. At seven o'clock, she gave up, kicking the covers to the floor, and tried to start her day. She took a cup of strong coffee to the computer. She saw the OPMC complaint form she had printed last night lying beside the computer. *This form can also be filled out online*, it said in tiny letters on the bottom of the page. She accessed the form on the OPMC website, but her hands were shaking so badly, she could barely type her own name.

Valium will help me settle down without putting me to sleep. She returned to the bedroom and dug through her oversized purse until she found the Valium among the multiple vials of various pills she had gotten from Jeff. Suddenly, she froze in panic. *Where will I get my meds with Jeff out of my life?*

Her fingers fumbled as she twisted open the plastic vial. She poured two yellow five- milligram tablets into her hand and closed the vial. Returning to the living room, she tossed the pills into her mouth and downed them with a swig of cold coffee.

Her fingers still quivered when she returned to the OPMC form, but within a few minutes she was at least able to type. After she completed the form, she moved on to another task she would have to complete if she took action against Jeff.

*   *   *

Grabbing her digital recorder, she hit *play*. She took a tissue from her purse, blowing her nose as she made her way through the series of recorded messages that she'd saved initially just to hear the sound of his voice.

It took nearly an hour to play all the messages. When she was finished, she pressed *record* and put her cell phone voice mail on speaker. She began recording after the most recent message she'd copied had left off. She focused on the messages she'd thought of as sexy, only now realizing that they might also be incriminating.

"I can't stop thinking about being with you last night. Did I ever tell you you're the most beautiful woman in the world?"

"I know you're out there somewhere, baby. I'm imagining being cuddled up there next to you. Can't wait till next time."

When she was finished, she reached for an old audiocassette recorder. Slipping a tape into the recorder, she set it to *record* while she replayed Jeff's messages aloud from the digital recorder.

By the time she had copied the very last message finalizing the plans for their meeting last Monday in Bryant Park, she was devastated and ready for sleep. She lay down on the couch for a quick nap, after which she planned to shower and head downtown to meet Trista. Instead, she fell—finally—into a deep sleep. She dreamed the breakup was all a bad dream, that she and Jeff were still together and were, in fact, planning a future as a couple. In sleep, a smile touched her lips for the first time since the breakup.

It was a hard dream to wake up from. The Ambien hangover coupled with a Valium chaser didn't make it any easier. But her cell phone was ringing, and she had the feeling it had rung a few times before. *It must be Jeff,* she thought, even though the ringtone wasn't "Bad Case of Loving You," but the European double ring she'd installed during her trip to England.

"Jeff?" she said, after knocking a full ashtray to the floor as she reached for the phone.

"Where are you?" demanded a familiar female voice.

"Mom?" Heather ventured.

"Not quite. It's me—Trista."

"Hi, honey, what's happening?" Heather asked.

"What's happening? Maybe you should tell me what's happening. I've been calling you for an hour! It's almost noon."

"Holy shit!" Heather said as reality filtered its way through her dreams. With it came the memory that it was over between her and Jeff. Her heart pounded in her chest as she remembered the pedicures that were supposed to provide a pick-me-up from her heartache. "I'm so sorry. I couldn't sleep last night, and I finally fell asleep on the couch this morning."

Trista emitted a long and frustrated sigh into the phone. "Any chance you could get down to Mott Street within an hour or two? I'm starving—got to get something to eat. Do you want to meet me for dim sum at the Mandarin Cafe?"

"No. You go ahead," Heather said.

"Are you sure? You've got to eat, too."

"No," Heather said. "The truth is, I've barely eaten all week. I'm nauseous all the time. I'll just meet you at Fancy Nail. I can be there by two."

Trista sighed again. "OK. I'll see you at two. Eat something. I'm worried about you."

CHAPTER 29

HEATHER

FANCY NAIL SALON HAD EVERY AMENITY of the posh spas at a fraction of the cost. An additional twist was that all the salon workers were male. Heather liked that aspect because the men worked quietly without the constant chatter in Korean she could barely tolerate in more traditional salons.

"I always think the women in those places are talking about me," Heather said as she settled into the cushy pedicure chair beside Trista's.

The male attendant gently placed her feet in the water. "Water feel OK?" he asked.

"Perfect," Heather said.

"You soak now," he said, and walked to the front of the store.

"Who gave you these coupons for Christmas?" Heather asked, considering the purplish-red tone she had selected. "One of your gay friends?"

"Shhhhhhhhhh!" Trista said, adjusting the vibration selection on the chair to *knead*. "No, actually, it was an attorney who bought a bunch of my prints of the city bridges to decorate his offices."

Heather felt the warm water swirl around her feet and between her toes. She watched as the vibrating motion of the chair propelled her friend's upper body forward, held it in position, then slowly lowered her back at an angle. "Ummmm," Trista moaned as the massage balls inside the chair worked the knots from her upper back.

"That looks like a great setting," Heather said.

Reaching over to her chair, Trista pressed the number five on Heather's control. Her chair began to vibrate, its apparatus massaging the small of her back and working its way upwards. "Heaven," Heather declared.

"I'm really worried about you," Trista said as the attendant returned and lifted her feet one by one from the water before wrapping them in a thick red towel. Another attendant sat at Heather's feet, shaking the bottle of polish she had chosen. "This your color?" he asked. She nodded.

"It's not like you to sleep through something we've planned," Trista said. "In fact, I don't think you've ever done anything like that."

"You're right, I haven't," Heather said. "I've been so depressed since Jeff ended things. I'm feeling a little spacey."

Trista peeked down at the bright red polish she'd chosen as it was painted on her toenails. "Are you feeling spacey because of the breakup? Or is there more to this?"

"Like what?" Heather asked, her voice a little too loud.

"Hey, now, don't get defensive," Trista said. "I'm not accusing you of anything."

Heather remained quiet.

"How long have you been having trouble sleeping?" Trista ventured.

Heather lowered her voice. "Jeff started giving me sleeping pills a few months ago. I began relying on them. Now I can't sleep unless I take them. Sometimes I can't even sleep when I take them."

"Oh, honey, you've got to stop taking that stuff!" Trista said. "You've got to get hold of yourself. If you keep going at this rate, you'll be addicted to Jeff *and* to whatever medicine he prescribed for you. Were there more medications?"

Heather nodded. "Lots more."

"What are they?" Trista sat bolt upright despite the vibrations of the chair.

"I'll show you in a minute."

"*Show* me?" Trista asked.

"When I got up this morning, I couldn't stop thinking about what you'd said last night about reporting Jeff to the medical board," Heather said. "I started to fill out the OPMC's complaint form from the OnYourSide.net site. I've got a copy in here somewhere." Heather rummaged through her purse and pulled the folded form from inside. She spread it out on her thighs and glanced at the first paragraph: *All reports of misconduct are kept confidential and are protected from disclosure according to New York State Public Health Law. Any person who reports or provides information to the Board for Professional Medical Conduct in good faith, and without malice, shall not be subject to an action for civil damages or other relief as the result of making the report.*

Below that Heather had filled in the requested data, including her name and contact information as well as Jeff's. Under the section headed *Complainant*, she'd filled in her date of birth and Social Security number. She handed the form to Trista and said. "I'm going to finish filling this out and send it in."

"Describe your complaint as completely as you can," Trista read aloud.

"Do you think I should do it?"

"Of course I think you should do it." Trista handed the form back to Heather. "Jeff totally violated medical ethics by having a relationship with you. He may have gotten you hooked on prescription meds. He made you half crazy!"

Heather smiled at her friend as Trista concluded, "I hate this guy. I hate this guy for breaking my best friend's heart."

Heather took a magazine from the stack beside the pedicure chair. She took a pen from her purse and laid the OPMC form on top of the copy of *Glamour*. The next blank section on the form said, *Describe your complaint as completely as you can.* She wrote:

I met Dr. Davis in the emergency room at Lenox Hill Hospital in May 2010 where he treated me for asthma. I had been his patient for about a month when he asked me to have coffee with him. Within two weeks of that, we had sexual relations in his office. Our affair continued for six months. He also encouraged me to reenact an experience I had as a child—I was molested by a priest. Dr. Davis said that repeating the experience with him would help me psychologically and ease my anxiety. Anxiety is one of the things that triggers my asthma.

During my relationship with Dr. Davis, in addition to the asthma medication that I needed, he also prescribed antidepressants, pain relievers, tranquilizers, and sleeping pills, all of which I felt I didn't need. I now rely on all these medications.

When she was finished, she handed the form to Trista for review. "It's all in there—the drugs, everything."

Trista read every word, then looked up and asked, "Are you really going to mail this?"

In response, Heather pulled a stamped envelope addressed to the Office of Professional Medical Conduct, New York State Department of Health in Troy, New York, from her purse. She reached for the complaint form, folded it, and placed it in the envelope.

"That looks like a yes," Trista said as they gathered their possessions and headed for the dryers.

"You want flip-flops?" the attendant asked.

They both nodded.

"One more dollar, please."

*   *   *

Half an hour later, as Heather and Trista shuffled down Mott Street in their flip-flops, a light snow began to fall. They found a stationery store with an ancient copy machine that charged five cents a page. Heather made copies of the form, bought a pack of Parliaments, and stepped back outside with Trista. Then, wearing jeans, a ski jacket, and a pair of Fancy Nail Salon flip-flops, she sealed the envelope and slipped it into a mailbox on the corner of Mott and Bayard Streets.

Now there truly was no turning back.

CHAPTER 30

HEATHER

ON SUNDAY MORNING, Heather woke at eight thirty to the ringing of her alarm clock. *Why do I have the clock set on a Sunday?* A second helping of Valium and Ambien had all but erased any memory of Saturday. What she did remember was the plans that she had made with Melissa, the second woman who claimed to have had an affair with Jeff.

When the two women had spoken by phone during the week, Melissa had insisted on meeting far from her neighborhood. "It would have to be someplace where I'd be sure no one I know would see me," she'd said.

"Where do you live?" Heather had asked.

"Upper East Side."

"Ever go to Harlem?" Heather had asked.

"No," Melissa had said.

Heather had heard the trepidation in the other woman's voice.

"Harlem has changed a lot—since Bill Clinton put his office space there, anyway." She'd headed for her computer and clicked her way through the restaurant guide on *New York* Magazine's website. "There's a great African coffee shop in Harlem," she'd said, clicking for the address and a subway map. "It's called Kitu Koffee. With a K. It's on Broadway and West 116th. The Seventh Avenue local train will drop you right down the street."

"I guess I can be pretty sure I won't run into anyone I know up there," Melissa had said.

"How's eleven thirty Sunday morning?" Heather had asked.

"Sounds perfect," Melissa had said with a touch of a Southern drawl.

* * *

As Heather dressed for her meeting with Melissa, she felt a literal aching in her heart. She coughed to try to clear the pain to no avail. This was no chest cold—it was a broken heart.

He can't mean it, he'll come back, she told herself as she slipped a black turtleneck sweater over her head. With a start, she remembered accessing the Office of Professional Medical Conduct complaint form through the OnYourSide website. She vaguely recalled beginning to fill out the complaint form in a Valium-fogged and angry impulse. She remembered filling in the rest of the information with a green ballpoint pen at Fancy Nail Salon. And dropping the form in a sealed envelope into a mailbox in Chinatown.

Heather rushed to her desk in the living room with a surge of hope. *Maybe I didn't put a stamp on the envelope!* But when she looked down at her desk, the first thing she saw was a small book of stamps. The book was folded open, and the top corner stamp had been removed. Ironically, the stamps portrayed an assortment of roses with the word *Love* on the lower left corner.

She sank onto the desk chair, elbows propped on the desk, her face in her hands. *What the hell have I done? He'll never forgive me; he'll never take me back.* She looked at her toenails for confirmation. Purplish-red and perfectly manicured. It had all really happened. It wasn't a dream.

* * *

Kitu Koffee was located less than two blocks from the 116th Street station. Telling the hostess that she was meeting a friend, Heather was escorted to a table for two in the midst of the restaurant.

"Your waitress will be with you in a moment," the hostess said as Heather removed her coat and settled into an elaborately carved wooden chair. The tables were draped in linen in bright African-influenced shades of blue and orange.

Scents of spices wafted through the air as Heather settled at the table. She recognized the smells of cinnamon, saffron, and ginger coming from plates of food as they were carried past her table on their way to other patrons.

A little girl with ebony skin and almond eyes peeked through the palm leaves that offered privacy between the tables and smiled shyly at Heather. Dressed in a frilly pink dress, her kinky hair tamed into pigtails tied with satin ribbons, she sat with her family, celebrating what appeared to be a grandfather's birthday. Heather smiled back and thought of the thrill of dressing Lin up and taking her to restaurants when she was a little older.

Heather scanned the coffee menu. All of the African coffees were described as deeply dark and rich. Café European was also listed. European coffee was about the richest she could stomach.

As if on cue, a young waitress appeared at the table. "My name is Elizabeth," she said in the perfectly clipped enunciation of a West African girlhood. "Today I shall be your waitress." Elizabeth pushed up the wide wrist of the sleeve of her traditional African garb to reveal an order pad. Holding her pencil like a child holds a crayon, she asked, "Would you want coffee until your friend is arrived?"

"Yes, please," Heather said. "Café European."

"A pot, Madame?"

"No, thank you. Just a cup for now."

*   *   *

Heather knew Melissa the minute she arrived. Aside from being one of the few fair-skinned people in the shop, like Suzanne, Melissa bore a striking resemblance to Heather. She was blond and petite with a look of uncertainty that furrowed the brow of her otherwise perfect face. Her clothes could have come from the cover of *Vogue*. She carried herself like a model as she was escorted to Heather's table.

"Heather?" Melissa asked.

Heather nodded. "Melissa?"

The women smiled in recognition, bonding immediately in their shared circumstance. But when Melissa slipped off a rich maroon coat with a Burberry plaid lining, Heather immediately noticed one way Melissa's appearance was different than her own.

Melissa was pregnant. She looked to be close to term, her belly full, cradling the child within. Melissa sat opposite Heather, pushing the chair back from the table to accommodate the curve of her belly. "It really was good of you to meet me," she said. "It can't have been easy for you to contact me."

"It's something I had to do," Heather replied. "I need to find out if Jeff is abusing his patients. I really wanted to believe this guy was for real."

"He's charismatic," Melissa agreed. "And he does make you feel like you're the only woman in the world—for a while, anyway."

As they spoke, Heather mentally calculated the timing of Melissa's affair with Jeff with the stage of her pregnancy. February through May. This could definitely be his baby. "By the way," she said. "Congratulations. When is your baby due?"

"Any day now."

The waitress returned, and Melissa ordered an individual pot of Ethiopian café arabica. Heather asked for a second cup of café European. Examining the menu, Heather selected bananas in jackets; Melissa simply ordered toast.

Once her coffee arrived, Melissa appeared to relax a bit. As she lifted the steaming brew to her mouth, her shoulders dropped at least three inches from their previous position at the base of her earlobes. She returned the mug to its saucer and leaned across the table.

Feeling the time to ask was now or never, Heather whispered, "Did he ever have sex with you on his exam table?"

"All the time," Melissa said, without hesitation. "I think it gave him the ultimate feeling of control—*I'm your doctor, and I'm nailing you right here on the same table where I examine my patients.*"

"I think so, too," Heather said, sickened that Jeff hadn't even varied his modus operandi. Except, of course, for changing partners. "There's something else I'd like to ask you."

Melissa reached for Heather's arm, grazing the rim of her coffee mug. Her emerald-cut engagement ring, easily three karats, clinked against the colorful ceramic. "Anything. We've slept with the same man. Maybe even both thought we loved him. We've already shared the ultimate intimacy. There really is nothing you can't ask me."

Heather struggled to begin, her hesitation still strong despite Melissa's words. After a few false starts, she managed to ask, "Did Jeff use protection when you were together?"

Melissa squirmed visibly in her seat, her fully belly grazing the table. "No. I tried to insist but he always assured me it was OK—"

"—that you were the only one," Heather said, continuing Melissa's sentence. "That he wasn't even sleeping with his wife. That if either of you had an STD, he would know."

"It was the same with me," Heather said. "I was so sucked in by his God complex, I probably actually believed he could magically know if he was sick. Now I realize he's such a narcissist, he simply doesn't care what consequences his thoughtlessness could have on other people."

They raised their coffee mugs and smiled across the linen-draped table at the irony of it all.

"And of course, he believes he's so high and mighty, an STD isn't even a threat to him," Melissa said. "Still, your breakup was so recent. I'm not really sure you're over him."

"I'm trying really hard to be," Heather replied. *Why am I hesitating to tell her that I mailed the letter to the OPMC? And how can I be vacillating between heartache that Jeff broke up with me and wanting to ruin his life?* She tugged anxiously on her cloth napkin. "But now that I've talked with you and with Suzanne, it's also clear that Jeff is a sex addict and chronic cheater. I know he'll never leave his wife."

The women sipped their coffee and nibbled at their food. Eventually, Melissa spoke. "The only thing that finally convinced me to end it was when I caught him with another woman."

"Suzanne?"

Melissa shook her head. "I caught them in person."

Heather's mug clattered toward the table, making an audible hit against its coordinating saucer. "In *person*? You *saw* them?"

Melissa nodded, her eyes dampened by unshed tears.

"During your affair?"

Melissa nodded again. "He had me so twisted. I would have done anything for him. In fact, I hate to admit this, but I played right into one of his fantasies." She lowered her voice and leaned toward Heather. "He had this thing about a woman in a raincoat with nothing underneath."

Heather shook her head, her foot tapping audibly against the tile floor. "That's not even original."

Melissa looked down into her brimming mug of coffee. "My husband was out of town. I decided to pay Jeff a surprise visit on his late night."

Heather's heart felt like it would burst from her chest. She swore her heartbeat was straining the seams of her sweater. "Tuesday."

"Right," Melissa said, still staring into her mug. "And the office door was unlocked. I heard it as soon as I opened the door. The sounds were unmistakable. I walked into his exam room and confronted him right then and there in the altogether with his briefs around his ankles."

"Good for you!" Heather said.

"The other woman," Melissa said. "He called her Anna."

Heather shook her head in disbelief. *How many women had there been?*

"What did you do after you caught him in the act?" Heather asked.

"After that night, I never took another one of his calls. I got another pulmonologist for my asthma and a new cell phone number."

She's a stronger woman than I am, Heather thought.

"I can't tell you how much I want to bring that bastard down," Melissa was saying. "But I won't risk my marriage doing it. But if you decide to do it, I'll support you in any way I can."

It was the same thing Suzanne had said.

"I filed a complaint with the medical board," Heather finally acknowledged. "I mailed it yesterday."

"Thank you!" Melissa exclaimed. "I just can't begin to thank you enough."

"It was one of the hardest things I've ever done," Heather said. "But I know it was the right thing to do."

Melissa smiled tightly. "I'll do anything in the world to help you, as long as I don't have to admit that I fell for him myself. I wish I could do more."

"I understand," Heather said.

Melissa picked up the check that the waitress had left a few minutes before. Opening her purse, she slipped some crisp bills beneath the check. "I need to get going. I told my husband I was going to church."

"Thanks for coming," Heather said, standing as Melissa did and touching her arm. "Thanks for everything."

"Remember," Melissa said. "I'm counting on you. You're the only one I know who can bring him down—the only one with nothing to lose."

Heather's eyes dropped to Melissa's curved belly as she struggled to button her coat over it.

"You're so fair," Heather said. "The baby is bound to be blond and beautiful, if you and your husband have the same coloring."

"My husband is Asian," Melissa said.

*   *   *

After Melissa left, Heather stayed behind in the restaurant. She went through the motions of taking care of the bill. Smile. Pay. Tip. She lifted the two crisp tens Melissa had left on the tray. Adding two of her own, she returned them to the gold-trimmed jade tray that held the bill. Her legs were weak and shaking, her knees grazing the bottom of the table.

She stood and left the restaurant. Instead of heading for the subway, she walked a few blocks until she saw a Rite Aid drugstore. She went inside and bought two gigantic bags of M&M's—one plain, one peanut.

"Sweet tooth got ya, sister?" the checkout clerk asked.

"I just need chocolate," Heather said.

"Got to be a man, then," the clerk said, two gold front teeth centering a friendly smile.

Heather felt a bond with the woman, a bond with every woman who had ever been wronged by a man. "Isn't it always?" she asked, not needing a reply.

*   *   *

One block turned into another. Barely noticing how different this part of the city was from her own, Heather trudged forward, shoveling the candy into her mouth. Shoveling, chewing, swallowing. She felt like she was walking beside herself, an unsettling feeling at best, calmed only slightly by the chocolate.

Melissa had said her affair with Jeff had lasted over six months; Suzanne's had lasted only three. Heather counted back the months since July. *Clearly I've met my expiration date, too.*

Surrounded by the brilliant sights and sounds of Harlem, she saw nothing and heard less. It was just her and her two gigantic bags of M&M's shoved inside a plastic Rite Aid shopping bag. Red, yellow, green, blue. *When had they started adding blue to the mix?*

She walked as if on autopilot, navigating the streets and sidewalks, robotically obeying the *Walk* and *Don't Walk* signs, crossing the streets with the crowds. Along the way, she stuffed one candy after another between her lips, filling the cavernous emptiness inside her with anything that tasted remotely like love.

CHAPTER 31

HEATHER

HEATHER HAD WALKED EVERY STEP of the way home from Harlem—thirty city blocks. But once outside her building, instead of going inside, she'd continued on to the 72nd Street entrance to Central Park. She'd stopped at a second pharmacy on 76th Street to refuel with a third bag of M&M's—this one plain.

Every couple of hours, she added a yellow Valium to the mix. Nothing really fazed her when she took those magic pills—not even walking through an almost empty Central Park on a cold winter day. She traversed the winding pathway through leafless trees and empty benches until exiting the park at Central Park South. Even after all he'd done—the surreptitious recordings of their sexual encounters, the other women, the outrageous violations of medical ethics—she couldn't let go. All she wanted was to see him. Just a glimpse. She had to see him.

She headed toward Fifth Avenue and stationed herself across the street from Jeff's building. Maybe, just maybe, he'd walk outside to get a pack of cigarettes. Or drive by in his black Mercedes with the M.D. license plates.

After two hours huddled at the entrance to an electronics store, Heather gave up. All of her extremities, even her face, were numb from the cold. She couldn't feel her feet or legs, and yet they carried her all the way back across Central Park South and up Broadway to 79th Street.

* * *

Heather was nauseous and restless when she finally reached her building at six o'clock. She fumbled at the dark entryway to find her key, making a mental note to tell the superintendent that a light bulb had burned out.

As she paced her condo, she replayed in her mind the conversations with Melissa and Suzanne. Swallowing yet another Valium with a sip of tea, she opened a spiral notebook and tore out a page.

I still love him, she scribbled on the top line of the page. She doodled some daisies in the margin, then wrote, *What is the matter with me?* She sketched another daisy on the center of the page. Beneath it, she started a list. *Conflicted,* she wrote. On the line beneath it, she wrote LOVE HIM. A few lines down, she printed HATE HIM.

As the Valium coursed through her bloodstream, she began to feel OK about having sent the complaint form to the OPMC. She turned to her computer and returned to OnYourSide.net.

She clicked first on *Resources.* Under that she chose *Find Attorney.* The page showed a map of the U.S. She clicked on *New York.* There were three attorney recommendations in New York State. One was upstate in Binghamton; the other two had offices in Manhattan. Thinking she recognized the name William M. DelFlorio from newspaper articles she had read, Heather clicked on the link to his website.

DelFlorio was described as a staunch defender of the rights of those whose boundaries had been violated by people who had been entrusted to their care—psychologists, social workers, drug and alcohol abuse counselors, marriage counselors, clergypersons, and doctors. He was licensed to practice in New York, Massachusetts, and half a dozen other states. His website had a prominent link to OnYourSide.net.

He's the one for me, Heather thought as she wrote his number on a yellow sticky and pressed it on the outside of her briefcase. *I'll call his office tomorrow to make an appointment.*

* * *

William DelFlorio's next available appointment was on Thursday, January 29.

Heather struggled through each day at work, her thoughts consumed with her need to see Jeff again, to believe he wasn't the serial womanizer and violator of medical ethics that he appeared to be. She marked the days until her appointment with DelFlorio on the calendar of scenes from England that she had bought in London. Ten, nine, eight...

She knew she couldn't hold on much longer.

CHAPTER 32

HEATHER

HEATHER HAD BOUGHT THE PAINT the day after Jeff told her their affair had to end. She'd stored it in the foyer closet, waiting until the time was right. Tonight was the right time.

Meticulously, she lined the floor of Lin's room with drop cloths to protect their wood surfaces. She pushed and pulled the furniture into the middle of the room and tossed some plastic tarps over it. She was breathless, and she hadn't even begun. *God, I'm out of shape. It's been weeks since I've had that deep aerobic orgasmic breathing!*

She mixed the paint in the bathroom, stirring the fluid with a wooden stick until it took on the consistency of lobster bisque. She carried the bucket back to Lin's room and stared at the walls. They were a pale sage green, a perfectly acceptable color for a little girl's room. The new paint was bright yellow, the color of smiley faces from the sixties.

She hadn't used her asthma medications in a few days. Increasingly short of breath, she dragged the ladder she'd borrowed from building maintenance down the hall and into the room that would be Lin's. And closed the door.

She stashed her cell phone and an inhaler in the bib of her denim overalls in case she chickened out. Leaning over the paint bucket, she breathed in the fumes deliberately. She took the brush and bucket, climbed the ladder, and balanced the paint on its top ledge. Her strokes were fast and angry, then slow and deliberate. After a while things began to blur, and her body ached. Each breath was a struggle. But she kept going. She was still at it at midnight, mixing, painting, rolling.

Finally, satisfied that her symptoms were at the appropriate level, she started down the ladder to continue her plan. She would shower, freshen her makeup and put on a sexy red teddy. Then, after checking to make sure each window was shut tight, she would leave Lin's bedroom door open, crawl into her bed, and call for an ambulance.

The fumes from the paint were overwhelming in the small room. Her legs shook as her feet tried to find their way down the steps of the ladder. She was so dizzy. Another step. She missed. She fell to the floor, hitting her head, the ladder crashing behind her. She felt the sticky paint splash her skin.

She reached into the bib of her overalls for her phone. It wasn't there! *It must've flown out when I fell.* Her inhaler was gone, too. And her head hurt. A lot.

She scanned the floor for her phone. Across the room its metallic surface caught the light from the naked light bulb overhead. As she crawled toward it, she noticed she wasn't doing a great job of painting. And she was no longer sure about the color.

But it wasn't about the color—it was about the paint. The paint that would bring on an asthma attack strong enough to send her to the emergency room at Lenox Hill on a Tuesday, Jeff's on-call night. The paint that would bring him back to her.

* * *

"Heather?" Miguel was saying.

"Help me," Heather said into the phone. Her voice was weak, barely audible.

"What's wrong?" Miguel asked, his tone suddenly shaky. "Did you get mugged?"

There was no answer.

* * *

Heather opened her eyes against blazing overhead fluorescent lighting. She was lying down; she guessed that she was in a hospital. *Thank God. Jeff will be here soon.*

Miguel was standing over her bedside. There was a handsome man standing anxiously behind him, but it wasn't Jeff. No sign of Miguel's phone either.

"Weren't we just talking on the phone?" she asked.

"That was hours ago, sweetie." Miguel pushed Heather's damp hair off her sweating forehead. "You're in the hospital now."

She looked at the dingy mustard yellow walls, stained with the splatters of old blood and coffee. The level of noise in the background told her she wasn't at Lenox Hill. "What hospital is this?"

"Mount Sinai."

She started to sit up, but Miguel held his hand up firmly in front of her chest to stop her. "Mount Sinai? Why isn't it Lenox Hill?"

"The ambulance takes people to the nearest hospital," the handsome stranger said. He extended a broad, youthful hand, but instead of shaking Heather's hand, he brushed his fingers against her forearm. "I know that from playing a doctor on the soaps."

"There was an ambulance? How did I get an ambulance?" she asked.

"You called my cell," Miguel explained. "I was on a date with Jackson." He nodded toward the soap opera actor. "Our first." Heather saw him turn and wink at Jackson, who smiled back, displaying a perfect set of porcelain veneers. "He's an actor," Miguel reminded Heather proudly. "On 'Young Love.'"

If teeth could talk, I'd already know that.

Miguel smoothed the hospital sheet that covered Heather from her feet to her neck. "I usually turn my phone off when I'm out. But for some reason, I forgot. I felt it vibrate and saw it was you calling. It was after midnight; I thought you might be in trouble."

She reached awkwardly for his hand, trying not to tangle the IV tubes or loosen the needle that pierced her vein. "Then what happened?" she whispered.

"You said 'Help me.' After that, there was just this horrible gasping. Jackson called 911 from his cell while I tried to keep you on the phone."

Heather shot Jackson a look of gratitude.

"I don't remember any of this," she struggled to say.

"Here, inhale this," Miguel said, bringing the familiar albuterol inhaler to her mouth. "They just took the nebulizer off you a few minutes ago." *How long has it been since I've used my medication?* "The doctor said you should start to inhale it once you came to."

"What doctor? Jeff?"

"Jackson insisted on coming with me," Miguel was saying. *Is he ignoring me? Didn't I just ask about Jeff?* "Most guys would have said 'See ya' and hung out at the club to see if they could pick somebody else up."

Heather took another inhale of the albuterol. "Jackson sounds like a special guy. Cute, too." She looked around again. "But where's Jeff?"

"Honey, we just told you," Miguel said. "You're at Mount Sinai. The pulmonologist has already been here."

She nodded and wiped away a tear. *Jesus, I nearly killed myself, and I still haven't figured out a way to see Jeff.*

Miguel continued the story, telling Heather how he and Jackson had raced for her condo. "Thank God I remembered your code."

"Yeah, 4-5-4-1," Heather repeated by rote.

"I know. Otherwise, I don't know what would have happened."

Heather inhaled the medication. "Who got there first?"

"We did," Miguel said. "On a Saturday night in Manhattan, there's no way an ambulance can outrun the subway. Your door was unlocked."

"I left it unlocked so you could get in and take me to the hospital— to Lenox Hill!"

"You were in no shape for us to take you to the hospital. You needed an ambulance," Miguel said.

She nodded weakly in acknowledgement.

"The ambulance got there a few minutes after we did. Jackson and I rode over here with you."

Miguel reached for Jackson's hand with his right hand. His left hand was still clutching Heather's. The two men stood and Heather lay like a perfect trio of construction paper circles kids make in kindergarten—a circle of friends.

"I had a plan," Heather said.

"You *planned* this?"

"I needed to see Jeff. I was going to call you and ask you to take me to Lenox Hill."

"Sweetie, you nearly killed yourself. No man is worth that."

As if on cue, Jackson began softly humming "The Things We Do for Love."

Heather glanced beyond the two men. Her overalls were lying beneath a clear plastic bag marked *Patient Belongings*. One denim leg hung to the floor, its hem coated in sticky brilliant yellow paint that was barely dry.

"Take a look at yourself," Miguel was saying.

Heather freed her hand from his and used her left arm—the one unencumbered by an IV—to peel the hospital sheet off her chest. She tugged at the neckline of a blue plaid hospital gown. Her chest was bruised and splattered with paint. "What the—"

*　*　*

"Ah, Ms. Morrison, you are awake now." Heather squinted in an attempt to read the name on the doctor's ID badge. *Chandra Sharma, M.D.* it read beneath the postage stamp-sized likeness of this dark-skinned Indian man. "I am the pulmonologist on call tonight."

"Where's Dr. Davis?" she croaked.

"I am Dr. Sharma. We do not have Dr. Davis here on staff."

Miguel stepped in, reminding her yet again that this wasn't Lenox Hill.

This was a nightmare—the antithesis of the night she'd met Jeff in an emergency room across town. The total reverse of her plan to reenact the magic of that night and make Jeff fall in love with her again.

"Where's Dr. Davis?" she repeated.

"I am Dr. Chandra Sharma. Do not worry. I can help you."

"But I want to be at Lenox Hill." She began to sob. "I want to be where Jeff is."

"Please do not speak," Dr. Sharma implored. "Or cry. You need all of your oxygen simply for breathing."

One attempt to inhale told Heather the doctor was right.

* * *

Within two hours, Heather was breathing normally. Physically, she was well enough to go home. She had a concussion, but rest would take care of that. But her mental health was another question.

Dr. Sharma returned to her bedside, where Miguel and Jackson remained. The doctor turned his back to her, his white lab coat stretched tight across his wide backside. "She is not stable mentally," she heard him tell Miguel. "My suggestion is that we admit her for psychiatric observation. Even if this behavior was not a suicide attempt, she is a very troubled woman."

I can't have Jeff find out I'm in the psych ward in this horrible hospital. He'll think I'm crazy.

Miguel glanced over Dr. Sharma's shoulder. His eyes met Heather's. He winked, realizing she was listening to the conversation. He stepped around the doctor and approached her. "Do you want to go to home, sweetie? I'll stay with you."

She pictured her bedroom. The mocha-colored sheets and chocolate-embroidered duvet in which they had become entangled. The half dozen pillows that always ended up on the floor. "I can't. I can't sleep in the bed where Jeff and I made love."

Miguel nodded in acknowledgement. "Sleep on the couch."

The lumpy hospital pillow kneaded her skull. She shook her head.

"You did it there, too," he said, more of a statement than a question.

She nodded, the lumps in the pillow pressing against her scalp.

"Did you hear what the doctor was saying?"

Her eyes filled with tears, telling him she had.

"Do you want to go to the psych unit? If you admit yourself, you can sign yourself out whenever you want to. Or I can sign you in. The minute you say you want to leave, I'll be here."

"I don't know." Tears rolled down her face. "I just don't know what to do."

CHAPTER 33

HEATHER

CHARLOTTE ROSNER, M.D., wore a white lab coat and tailored black slacks. Her mostly grey hair was tucked in a bun at the nape of her neck. "Hello, Heather. I'm Dr. Rosner," she said as Heather sat across from her in the doctor's shabby hospital office. Cinder blocks painted the color of oranges served as walls, and the doctor's battered desk was made of steel and covered with scratches and a frayed brown blotter. "From what we could glean about what brought you here last night, the psych team determined that I was the doctor best qualified to manage your case. I specialize in boundary violations by professionals of all kinds."

Heather nodded and bit her lower lip. *Yes, they sure hit the nail on the head with that one.*

"So you must know the man I did this for was my doctor," Heather said.

"Yes," Dr. Rosner said. "I talked with your friend Miguel outside the ER. He told me a little bit of the history. Not too much. Just enough so that I could understand and help you."

"This boundary abuse you specialize in. Is it exclusively in doctor-patient relationships?" Heather asked.

"I specialize in boundary abuse by anyone in a position of authority. A teacher. A clergy person. A scout leader. A relative. I do a lot of work with children. Let's face it—when you're a child, virtually everyone is an authority figure."

Heather's thoughts flashed to Father Hamilton and Jeff's insistence that she replay the scenes in which the priest had abused her. "Have you worked with other women who have become involved with their doctors?" she asked.

Dr. Rosner smiled. "Every day of my professional life." She leaned forward and looked at Heather with genuine concern. "Nobody talks about it, but it happens all the time."

Feeling exposed, Heather tugged at the sleeve of her hospital gown. "I don't think I can function until I get Jeff—my doctor—out of my system."

"I believe you can function," the doctor said. "You may require additional care. But in my opinion, you don't need hospitalization. The patients here are seriously messed up."

Startled yet comforted by the doctor's choice of words, Heather felt the tension ease from her body.

Dr. Rosner continued. "In my professional opinion, you don't need to spend time in the psychiatric unit. But I would like to see you as an outpatient through my private practice. I've helped a lot of people with relationship addictions, many of which were boundary violation cases."

Heather glanced at the doctor's left hand. No wedding band. What did a fifty-something shrink without a husband know about relationships?

As if reading the doubt in her mind, the doctor reached across her small desk and briefly touched Heather's hand. "I know I can help you," she said. "If you'll let me." She took back her hand and opened a notebook. "Tell me what happened last night."

"Jeff is a pulmonologist," Heather began. Even in the terrifying environment of this office deep in the bowels of Mount Sinai's psychiatric ward, she liked and trusted Dr. Rosner immediately. "I met him in the ER at Lenox Hill when I had my first asthma attack."

"What brought on that first attack?" the doctor asked, scribbling in a marble notebook—the kind Heather had used in Catholic grade school.

"It happened the first night I spent at my newly painted condo," Heather said. I think it was the fresh paint. Realizing that Dr. Rosner was waiting for more, she continued. "Jeff broke up with me two weeks ago. He changed his cell phone number. I thought if I had another asthma attack, Miguel would take me back to Lenox Hill. So I painted a room in my condo on Tuesday night. Tuesdays are Jeff's nights on call."

"But you ended up here," the doctor said.

"I called Miguel when the attack started to get bad," Heather said, tugging on her hair. "But I passed out before I could ask him to take me to Lenox Hill. In the meantime, he called an ambulance, and they took me here."

"How do you feel now about your plan having gone awry?" Dr. Rosner asked.

"Relieved, actually. At this point, I realize Jeff would probably have known it was all a ruse. He would have thought I was crazy."

Dr. Rosner tapped her short, polished nails on the brown blotter. "I'm glad it worked out for you."

"So am I!" Heather said.

"I'll sign your release papers," Dr. Rosner said. "But I do need you to promise me a few things." As she spoke, Dr. Rosner made notes on a fresh sheet of paper in her marble notebook. "First, promise me you will never do anything as dangerous as what you did last night, that you'll take your asthma medications and stay away from things that trigger your attacks."

Heather nodded.

The doctor wrote *two* on the page. "And I'd like you to make a follow-up appointment with me within ten days. You can take one of my business cards—they're right there on the desk. Call the number for my private practice."

"Will you have to notify Jeff about what I did?" Heather asked.

Dr. Rosner slid her notebook across her blotter. She wrote *three* as she said, "Not if you get a new pulmonologist immediately. You can see Dr. Sharma or any other doctor you choose." She wrote *new pulmonologist* next to the *three*, tore the page from the notebook, and handed the paper with its tattered edge to Heather.

"Consider it done," Heather promised. "All of it."

* * *

Heather called Miguel from her cell phone in the hospital lobby. The paint had dried on her overalls, but she still felt she looked like exactly what she was—a woman who had just come within a hair of committing herself to a psych ward. "I'm ready to leave," she said.

"When?" Miguel asked.

"I'm actually out—they released me. I'll take a taxi home."

"No, I'll come and get you," Miguel insisted. "I can be there in fifteen minutes."

"You're such a sweetheart."

"And I don't want you to be alone tonight," he continued. "I'll sleep on the couch at your place."

"What about your friend—Jackson, wasn't it?"

"Right. It's Jackson. "

"Don't you want to go out with him tonight?"

"I can't see him every night." Miguel chuckled. "I'm playing hard to get."

Heather clicked off and sat back in a chair covered in turquoise vinyl, feeling grateful for the blessing of having wonderful friends like Miguel and Trista. *Trista! Oh my God! I haven't told her what happened.* She pressed Trista's number and settled in for a talk while she waited for Miguel to arrive.

CHAPTER 34

HEATHER

BILL DELFLORIO'S TAILORED SUIT, coiffed hair, and manicured fingernails could not disguise the fact that he'd grown up on the rough streets of Red Hook, Brooklyn. When he opened his mouth, his accent gave him away. And the way he moved—defensively, as if he expected to be jumped from behind at any moment—gave him the posture of a large leopard about to turn and pounce on its prey.

Laminated awards, diplomas, and framed photos of DelFlorio standing beside such noted dignitaries as Mayor Michael Bloomberg and Secretary of State Hillary Clinton filled the wall behind his large mahogany desk. They referred to him as William M. DelFlorio, J.D. But to those who knew him best, he'd always been DelFlorio or just plain Bill.

DelFlorio stood as his assistant ushered Heather into the room. "Good morning, Ms. Morrison. Your coming here was a very brave thing to do," he said.

Heather settled into the chair opposite him. At least a dozen framed family photos were displayed on the desk. "It wasn't easy to come here," she said, her hands shaking uncontrollably.

DelFlorio reached toward an elaborately carved mahogany box. Lifting its glass top, he selected one of a collection of at least twenty pipes. "Would it bother you if I smoked my pipe?"

"Not at all. Although it would have a few months ago."

He tilted his head. "What do you mean?"

"A few months ago, I was an ex-smoker—hadn't had a cigarette in ten years. Now I'm back up to over a pack a day."

"Was it the stress of the relationship with Dr. Davis that brought that on?" DelFlorio asked, grabbing a pair of reading glasses and a yellow legal pad, then scribbling wildly.

"It added to it, I'm sure," Heather said. "But what got me started was the fact that Jeff—Dr. Davis—smokes, probably a couple of packs a day."

DelFlorio glanced at his notes. "This guy's a pulmonologist," he confirmed. "A pulmonologist with a two-pack a day habit!" He smiled. "If I were in any other line of business, I'd find that hard to believe." He filled his pipe, saying, "Sorry to hear about your smoking relapse, but please feel free to join me."

"I'd love a cigarette," Heather said, reaching into her purse. "But is it OK to smoke in offices in the city?"

"It's OK if you own the building," DelFlorio said.

* * *

"Tell me what happened, Heather. Everything. From the beginning," DelFlorio said.

"In detail?" she asked.

"Vivid detail," he said.

Oh, God, she thought, *I don't want to do this. I want to walk out of here and have this whole thing just go away.*

"Remember," DelFlorio was saying, "I don't do this for some sick, vicarious thrill. I'm a happily married man with seven kids. And more importantly, I'm an ethical attorney with a passion for protecting my clients from boundary violations by professionals. I'm not some horny priest who gets off hearing people talk about their sex lives in the confessional."

The irony of DelFlorio's analogy sent a shudder through Heather's body. She tried to speak, but the room was screaming silence.

"Maybe it will help if I guide you through this," DelFlorio said. "When was the first time you and Dr. Davis had sexual intercourse?"

"Last July. Early July."

"And where were you at the time?"

"We were in his office."

DelFlorio shook his head and asked, "Where exactly in his office?"

Heather looked away, humiliated. "On the exam table. I mean, *I* was on the exam table. He was standing."

If Heather could have read Bill DelFlorio's mind, she would have heard him thinking, *Cheap bastards, these abusing docs—don't even take their conquests to a nice hotel. The exam table! The ultimate doctor in control, patient as conquest venue.* "Why were you in his office?" he asked.

"I'd had an appointment scheduled for earlier in the evening. And he was running late. He actually called me himself to reschedule the appointment. He told me beforehand that we would be alone in the office."

DelFlorio relit his pipe. "And you didn't find that a little strange?"

"I wasn't concerned. I trusted him. After all, he was a *doctor!* My doctor." She tapped a long ash from her cigarette into a huge cut glass ashtray on the desk.

"The last thing I want to do is pressure you," DelFlorio said in as gentle a tone as his Brooklyn gruffness could convey. "It's up to you entirely whether or not to pursue this. As I told you on the phone, there is no charge for this consultation, and if you wish to make a claim against Dr. Davis, I'll handle everything on a contingency basis. But in making your decision, consider what his actions have cost you. Remember that, because of your doctor-patient relationship, what he did was not only in the toilet ethically, it was against the law. And if he opened a case for mental health care law by treating you for psychological issues as well—particularly if he claimed the sex act was therapeutic—he's committed a far more serious crime."

Wondering if the attorney had read her mind, Heather reached into her purse and fingered her inhaler.

"Unfortunately," DelFlorio continued, "Dr. Davis isn't a psychotherapist. The laws and codes of ethics on sexual misconduct are very specific—and very strict—for mental health care workers. Generally, only psychotherapists are trained in the transference phenomenon and the devastating effects that can result when a therapist crosses the line from doctor to lover—or even friend. Unfortunately, the laws are less stringent, almost nonexistent, for non-mental health care professionals."

"Does that mean we don't have a case?" Heather asked.

"Not at all," DelFlorio replied, spilling some ashes into the cut glass ashtray. "It just means it will be more difficult. Psychotherapists are specifically trained to know that having sex with a patient is out of the question. They call it *professional incest*—the phrase itself sounds nasty. But other medical professionals aren't usually taught about transference. So even though they may know that having a sexual relationship with a patient is not a good idea, they may not understand the consequences of their actions."

"Oh, please!" Heather sighed. "How could someone—anyone—be smart enough to be a doctor and not smart enough to realize it's not a good idea to have sex with their patients?"

"The law and common sense aren't always in sync," said DelFlorio. He shook his head. "But at least the American Medical Association has it right. The AMA Council on Ethical and Judicial Affairs states categorically that sexual contact that occurs concurrent with the physician-patient relationship constitutes sexual misconduct. So the good news is, you could report Dr. Davis to the Office of Professional Medical Conduct—the OPMC. It could cost him his license."

Heather bit her lower lip. "Actually, I already reported him to the OPMC. It was kind of impulsive. It was right after I found out he'd changed his cell number."

DelFlorio ran his hands through his coif of curly brown hair flecked with grey. "Ideally, it would have been better to initiate a civil case first. Getting a letter from the OPMC might buy him time, give him a chance to get his ducks in a row before we serve him with papers—should you choose to take that route. And assuming we can gather solid proof of your affair."

Heather squirmed in her chair.

"To prove that there truly was an affair, I need evidence," DelFlorio said. "Hard evidence. Without hard evidence that you had sexual relations with Dr. Davis, I can assure you he'll deny the whole thing. They all do."

"I recorded every phone message he ever left me," Heather offered. She reached into her purse and removed the two cassette tapes. She placed them on DelFlorio's desk.

The attorney lifted the two tapes in their plastic cases. "Is there a recording of you and Dr. Davis having sex on one of these?"

Her eyes widened in amazement. "Of course not! They're *phone* messages."

DelFlorio slid a DVD in a plastic case across his desk. Heather lifted it and read the handwritten label. *Maurice and me having sex*, it said.

"This is what I mean by hard evidence," DelFlorio said.

"Oh, my God!" She put the DVD back on the desk and wiped her hands on her sleeves.

"Do you think you could come up with anything like that?" he asked.

The tiny red light of Jeff's DVD recorder flickered in Heather's memory. There was no doubt in her mind that Jeff had recorded some of their sex sessions—even the one where he had reenacted her abuse by Father Hamilton. But how could she get her hands on them?

"There's a remote possibility I could get something like that," she said.

"Try to find a way," DelFlorio insisted. "Evidence like that—or the *threat* of evidence like that—is almost essential to a case like this. Otherwise, you'll have no case for sexual misconduct. He'll deny it. I've seen it happen a thousand times."

"I'm no attorney, but wouldn't that be entrapment?" she asked.

"It's not entrapment unless I *ask* you to *record* sexual activity. Otherwise, it's just a sex tape—something a lot of people make without any suggestions from anyone." DelFlorio pushed the cassette tapes to a corner of his desk. "Sometimes the evidence I need gets a little tacky. I apologize for that."

"Wow," Heather said, pulling her fingers through her hair. "I really thought that the recordings of Jeff's phone messages would be all the evidence I'd need."

"I'll certainly listen to these," DelFlorio said. "But I expect what's said on them is not even close to what we'll need." He hesitated a moment before he continued. "You should know this. The people I represent are the good guys. Sometimes I bend the truth a little to help them. It's nothing that keeps me awake at night."

Heather could hear her blood pulsing through her ears. *What am I getting myself into?*

DelFlorio cleared his throat. "You said Dr. Davis changed his cell number. I expect it was he who ended the relationship."

She nodded again.

"When did it end?"

"A few weeks ago. Jeff told me his wife had found out about us. He said it was over. Just like that—no warning."

"That must have made you crazy," DelFlorio said.

"Crazy? I'll say. I spent Tuesday night and Wednesday in the emergency room at Mount Sinai. I almost checked myself into their psychiatric unit."

"Bad for you." DelFlorio wrote something down. "Good for your case. Was it a suicide attempt?"

"No. It may have looked that way, but it really wasn't a suicide attempt at all. It was an attempt to see Jeff. I painted a room with the door closed so I could induce an asthma attack and go to the ER at Lenox Hill. That's how I met Jeff in the first place. I was having an asthma attack, and I went to Lenox Hill. But this time, the ambulance took me to Mount Sinai." As if to demonstrate that she really was asthmatic, Heather brought her inhaler to her mouth and breathed in. Another freshly lit cigarette burned in DeFlorio's ashtray.

"As far as what put you in that hospital, in my courtroom, it was a suicide attempt," DelFlorio said. "A suicide attempt puts your damages way up there. We need to convey how the affair and its termination left you a devastated victim—not simply a jilted lover."

"Believe me, I won't have to *pretend* to be the devastated victim," Heather said. "But I don't want to come off as stupid."

"I understand," DelFlorio said. "It doesn't matter if you're a rocket scientist and Davis graduated at the bottom of his med school class. Under the law, the onus is on the doctor to do what's best for his patient. It's the imbalance of power that makes the doctor-patient affair sanctionable. That's why sex with a patient is never OK." He twisted a pencil tightly between his fingers. It snapped in two. He looked at his hands, his face emitting surprise. "*Never.*"

Stunned by the strength of DelFlorio's convictions, Heather felt a jolt go through her entire body.

He resumed speaking. "As I said, pursuing this through the OPMC could result in his license being suspended or even revoked. But it won't put money in your pocket."

"Mr. DelFlorio, I'm not in this for money."

He continued as if Heather hadn't said a word. "Pursuing a sexual misconduct case in civil court won't make you rich unless the doctor himself is exceptionally wealthy. Doctor-patient affairs happen so frequently that most malpractice insurance policies cap awards for physician sexual misconduct at twenty-five thousand. If the insurance companies didn't put so low a cap on sexual misconduct—and if there were more brave women like you who were willing to prosecute—I'd wager medical insurance companies would go broke in a heartbeat."

"It's that common?"

DelFlorio nodded. "I've had doctors tell me that up to thirty percent of their colleagues have slept with one or more of their patients. It's so common that we'll need to come up with some additional claims of malpractice to make money on this. Somehow I doubt that's going to be a problem. Almost invariably, when there is a deeply personal relationship between a physician and a patient, the doctor is guilty of additional improprieties that also constitute malpractice."

Heather rolled her eyes.

"I'll run an asset check quickly, before he gets the letter of complaint from the OPMC," DelFlorio said. "We don't want to give him a chance to hide his assets."

"It would take a long time to hide all the family assets. His wife's family is loaded. He's married to Priscilla Wellington—old New York money."

"Any relation to Preston Wellington—the chief of staff at Lenox Hill?"

"He's her father."

DelFlorio raised his eyes and a smile touched his lips. "Then you're right. They definitely have money—lots of money."

Heather poured a second mug of coffee from a tray of coffee and pastries DelFlorio's assistant had left in the room. She passed on the pastries. The thought of eating made her stomach turn.

DelFlorio leaned across his desk. Pastry crumbs clung to his mustache. "Another thing you may want to consider is the damage Dr. Davis has done if yours was not an isolated occurrence." He wiped his mouth with a candy-cane embossed paper napkin, clearly left over from the holidays.

"There *have* been others," Heather said, stabbing out her cigarette. A few ashes continued to glow.

"How do you know that?"

"Same place I found you. OnYourSide.net. I found two other women who had affairs with Jeff. I've met both of them."

DelFlorio let out a low whistle. "You're way ahead of most clients on an initial consultation," he said. "You've not only found out about the OPMC, you've filed a complaint with them! And now you're telling me that you've actually *met* women who were also sexually involved with Dr. Davis?"

She nodded. "Is that a bad thing?"

"It's not that it's a bad thing," DelFlorio said. "But you have to be careful. Contact with other victims of the same professional could be perceived as conspiring with them."

Heather shook her head. "That's not likely to happen. Neither of these women will allow me to name them. They're both married. They're not willing to risk their marriages by reporting him."

"Were these women also Davis's patients?" DelFlorio asked before polishing off a cherry Danish in two bites.

"Yes. Both of them."

DelFlorio cracked his knuckles. "It concerns me that this man has had so much sexual activity with patients. It sounds to me like he's a serial abuser."

"It's starting to seem like he may be."

"It's actually not unusual for a sexually abusive doctor to be a serial abuser. These are guys who've let the M.D. title go to their heads— they truly seem to believe the rules don't apply to them." DelFlorio leaned his large body over his desk. "Cases like yours remind the rest of them that the rules do indeed apply to them. Your case could be worth millions."

Heather twisted a lock of hair around her finger. "Really, I don't care about financial restitution," she said.

DelFlorio stood, his large body casting a gigantic shadow across the dark wood flooring of his office. "You should," he said. "You could actually sue the whole practice. If you won, you'd probably never have to work another day in your life."

"I don't *want* to sue the whole practice. It's not about the money. It's about Jeff and what he did to me."

"If it's not about money, think about the message you'd be sending. Most patients have no idea of the ethical and criminal violations their doctor commits by becoming involved with them sexually. In fact, if their doctor pays special attention to them, they're likely to take it as a compliment."

Heather clenched her teeth. "You're right," she said. "That's exactly how I felt in the beginning."

"What Dr. Davis did was wrong, terribly wrong," DelFlorio continued. "But, legally, as his employer, the practice itself has certain responsibilities. You really should consider suing the firm itself."

"On what grounds?" Heather asked.

"The practice could be held responsible for negligent hiring and inappropriate supervision of its employees," DelFlorio said.

"Trust me, Mr. DelFlorio," Heather replied. "I don't want to go there."

"Fair enough," DelFlorio conceded. "For now. But if it's not money that's driving you, what is?"

"It's the impact this whole thing has had on me. And now the breakup is turning me into someone I don't even know. I mean, Jeff was someone who I confided in, who counseled me, gave me medication. I trusted him with my life. He wasn't just anybody—he was my *doctor*."

"That's the dynamic," DelFlorio said. "The doctor/patient relationship is a unique relationship, a fiduciary relationship. That is the very reason the law protects the patient."

"I don't *feel* protected. I feel totally abandoned. This whole thing has really brought me to my knees. I used to be so much stronger than this."

DelFlorio raised his eyes to look at her over his reading glasses. "Have you ever felt this way before?"

"I've felt bad when men have dumped me. But never to this extent."

"Were there any specific relationships that left you feeling especially hurt and betrayed—more like what you're feeling now?"

"I felt like this when my father left my mother," Heather said, reaching for another cigarette.

"How old were you when that happened?"

"Fourteen. He married a seventeen-year-old girl who was a student in his history class."

"Another clear case of boundary violation. It seems this sort of thing has been an ongoing theme in your life. It almost made an experience like you had with Dr. Davis inevitable. Would you say you transferred your feelings for your father onto Dr. Davis?"

"No. No, I really don't think I did." She thought again of Father Hamilton.

"I've mentioned transference," DelFlorio said. "You haven't asked me what it means."

"I know what it means. I've learned a lot about transference and its impact on the doctor-patient relationship—mostly on the Internet. And transference in other relationships as well."

DelFlorio's eyebrows were approaching his hairline.

"I'm not making this very clear, am I?" Heather asked.

"You're doing fine," he said unconvincingly. "Just take your time."

Heather hunched in the chair and looked away. Almost in a whisper she said, "I was molested as a child…by a priest."

"I'm sorry. That's a terrible thing. But consider this—we've learned that close to ninety percent of women who have sexual relations with their doctors were molested as children."

Heather felt her jaw drop.

"Talk to me, Heather," DelFlorio said. "I've heard it all. There's nothing you can say that would shock me."

"When I told Dr. Davis I'd been molested by a priest, he said it would be therapeutic to reenact the experience."

"Did you do this?"

Heather lowered her eyes. "Yes," she said softly.

"That son of a bitch!" DelFlorio said. "That's a hideous thing Davis put you through. But it makes for a brilliant case of a medical doctor stepping into a psychotherapeutic role and using sex as an element of his so-called treatment. It makes the potential of a case against him huge."

"Does it?"

"Absolutely," DelFlorio said. "Patients transfer feelings about significant others in their past onto the professional during psychotherapy far more than in any other medical field. I'm no therapist, but it seems to me that the feelings you transferred to Dr. Davis were the result of what that awful priest did to you years ago."

* * *

An hour later, Heather was on her third cup of coffee.

"Odds are there are women all over the city who have been sexually violated by Dr. Davis," DelFlorio was saying. "I suspect one article in *The New York Post* would have them coming out of the woodwork."

"An article? In the *Post*?"

DelFlorio looked as excited as a kid from the Bronx at his first Yankees game. "The *Post* loves this stuff. A doctor getting his license suspended or revoked for sexual misconduct would be a page one story in that rag."

"Mr. DelFlorio, I had hoped to do this without any publicity. Keep it out of court. And certainly out of the papers." Heather's eyes were rimmed with tears. DelFlorio handed her a box of tissues.

"The risk of publicity is there, even if you settle out of court," he said. "Once a case is filed, the filing can be accessed. There are journalists whose sole purpose in life is to lurk around courthouses waiting to report on juicy cases." DelFlorio took a long swig of coffee. "Let's talk about the other areas of malpractice that might be part of this case."

"OK" she said, shifting on her chair.

"Tell me about the medications Dr. Davis prescribed for you."

"Let's see. He prescribed a lot of medications, not just for my asthma. From the start, he asked me about my life, my emotions. I mean, I guess emotions can affect asthma, but within a couple of weeks, he had me on antidepressants, tranquilizers, and powerful painkillers. And sleeping pills."

"What specifically?"

"First, there was Paxil—in case my asthma attacks were being brought on by anxiety. And Ambien to help me sleep. Then Valium for my nerves. And finally, the Vicodin."

"Putting you on Paxil and Valium will strengthen the claim that he treated you as a psychotherapist," DelFlorio said. "The drugs he prescribed are powerful stuff. Are you still taking them?"

"Yes. At first I took them because Jeff prescribed them. Now I can't seem to manage without them."

"I'm sorry, Heather," DelFlorio said. "But again, while this is bad for you, it's good for your case." He reviewed the list he'd made of the medications Heather had named. "Dr. Davis prescribed antianxiety medication and a steady diet of tranquilizers." He sat back in his leather executive chair and asked, "Did he ever refer you to a psychiatrist?"

"No," Heather said softly. "He believed he could help me with my emotional problems. He said it was OK to do that because they were one of the triggers for my asthma."

DelFlorio looked at Heather and shook his head. "Reenacting your childhood abuse was the worst form of malpractice imaginable. It goes way beyond failure to refer."

Heather tugged on a dangling earring and asked, "What is failure to refer?"

"Failure to refer is treating you with psychiatric drugs while failing to refer you to a psychologist or psychiatrist. It's malpractice. Additionally, because he claimed to be treating you for psychological problems himself, we may be able to hold him to the same standard set for psychologists and psychiatrists." He tapped his pen lightly against his forehead. "Unfortunately, I'm not aware of any cases in New York where medical doctors who weren't psychiatrists were brought to trial for sexual misconduct."

Heather looked away.

DelFlorio continued. "What did he prescribe the Vicodin for?"

"Migraines."

"Does the Vicodin help your migraines?" he asked, scribbling again on his yellow legal pad.

"In a way. It doesn't always make the headache go away, but it kind of makes me not mind that I have it."

"How did you treat your migraines before Dr. Davis prescribed the Vicodin?"

"Excedrin Migraine. Over-the-counter."

"How did that work?"

"It worked just fine."

"So, he prescribed numerous medications, two of which you probably didn't need—drugs that are highly addictive?"

DelFlorio turned a page in his yellow legal pad with his stubby fingers. He rotated the pad so it faced Heather, writing the words upside down so she could read them:

Care.

Cause.

Injury.

"To prove malpractice, we'll have to establish three things: breach of the standard of care, causation, and injury. The first one is usually the toughest. Breach of the standard of care means we have to prove the doctor made a mistake—a mistake that a prudent doctor would not have made under the same circumstances. The trick here is that it usually requires an expert witness—generally another doctor in the same area of specialization. But doctors don't like to testify against each other. They have a code of silence—sort of a brotherhood, like cops and firemen. "

Heather nodded.

"We could probably go after him for improper prescribing practices. That's some pretty powerful stuff he gave you."

I know that now, Heather thought, counting the hours since she'd had her last Valium and Vicodin. A glass of water DelFlorio's assistant had given her was within arm's reach. She took a sip but chose not to slip her hand into her purse for her next round of pills. She wiped a light sweat from her forehead with a shaking hand and looked at DelFlorio's list. "What about cause?" she asked.

"Cause, or causation, is proving that the doctor made a mistake that injured you." He circled the word *cause* on the legal pad with his Waterman pen. "Clearly, the emotional turmoil that resulted from this affair might be considered an injury. And your dependence on the medications he prescribed—medications that you didn't even need—is injury as well. Here again, you need an expert witness to testify. And the state monitors prescription records. We can get those for backup if necessary."

"Some of the medications he gave me were samples," Heather said.

"Jesus!" DelFlorio exclaimed, his Brooklyn background rising to the surface. "Bastard tried to cover all his bases."

"There were plenty of prescriptions, too," Heather added. "I had them all filled at the same Rite Aid drugstore."

"Great! We'll see what kind of records he kept. And how they match up with your pharmacy records. We can probably get him for faulty record-keeping, too. Finally, there is injury—in your case, emotional injury. And his clear violation of the most basic medical premise, the commitment to do a patient no harm." He circled the word injury on his list. "In a case against a doctor, a civil injury is any breach of the standard of care. Whether you're interested in a big settlement or not, this doctor should pay for what he's done. Not only should his license be suspended, if not revoked entirely, he should have to dig deep into his own pocket—not just some insurance company's resources—to make restitution. That's why I think you should strongly consider a civil suit."

"I don't even know if I can make it through the medical board hearing," Heather said, her body flooding with exhaustion, "let alone a trial."

"You're doing fine, Heather," DelFlorio assured her. "We'll take it one step at a time. But if you want to pursue a civil action, we will need to act quickly before he hears from the medical board. We don't want to give him a chance to go changing your medical records."

DelFlorio walked to the window, pushing aside a drape to take in more of the dismal day. "There are a lot of crazies out there. Unfortunately, in my experience, I've found that a good percentage of doctors fall into the crazy category."

Returning to his desk, he checked his Blackberry. "My calendar is jammed. Can we iron out the rest of the details a week from Saturday?"

"What time?" Heather asked.

"Bright and early. Nine o'clock. It could take the better part of the day."

"I have an appointment that morning," she said, recalling her session with Dr. Rosner.

"What time can you be here?"

"Probably by ten thirty."

"Just get here as early as you can. Meanwhile, I'll go ahead and file the initial papers in civil court. I have no doubt that you'll come through with the evidence we need. Bring anything you have with you on Saturday."

CHAPTER 35

HEATHER

AS HEATHER WALKED DOWN FIFTH AVENUE, she called Miguel.

"How are you doing?" he asked with concern. "You weren't up when I left your place. I thought it best to let you sleep."

"Thanks, sweetie. Thanks for staying with me," Heather said. "Listen. I just got out of my appointment with that malpractice attorney—William DelFlorio."

"Right, yes. How did it go?"

"It went really well. This guy knows his stuff. I like him."

"Great! It's very important to have a good rapport with your attorney. Is he going to pursue a civil action?" Miguel asked.

"I'm struggling with that," Heather said. "We talked about it. But a civil suit could really destroy Jeff."

"Destroy him?" Miguel demanded. "Destroy him as much as you nearly destroyed yourself? Heather, you could have died!"

"I know, honey, I know. Still, I'm so torn about this whole thing. Part of me has a fantasy that Jeff will come back to me."

"Heather, you must stop this. Why would you want this man in your life? Besides, you've already filed with the medical board. It's too late to turn back."

"If he came back to me, I might deny everything I said in the report to the medical board—say we had a fight and I submitted the report in a drunken stupor. Would they throw the case away if I did that?"

"It *is* possible. But that's not the point! You have to stop thinking about him this way. The man did a terrible thing to you! He has no loyalty to his family, no respect for the patients who put themselves in his care!"

Heather turned her collar up against a fine mist that was falling. "You're right, Miguel. It's just so hard."

"I know, sweetie, I know. Do you need me to stay with you again tonight?"

"No," she said. "I'll be OK. But there is one more thing."

"What is that?" he asked patiently.

"I lost the key to my filing cabinet. Do you know how I can get it open without a key?"

"You should be able to do it with a paper clip. Open the clip so it's straight. Then jiggle the end inside the hole where you would put the key. If you come at it from just the right angle, the lock should open."

"Thanks! I'll try that."

She heard him sigh. "But you don't have to do this yourself. Someone on the maintenance staff here at the office should be able to fix it."

"The filing cabinet isn't at work. It's at home," Heather said.

"There's no filing cabinet in your condo."

Oh, shit! Miguel knew every inch of her condo. "Sure there is," she said. "It's…" Then she clicked off the phone, swamped by guilt that she was pretending the call had been cut off.

* * *

Heather had walked a full block before her phone rang. *Miguel,* it read on caller ID. *Oh, shit! I may as well take his call and get it over with!* "Hi," she said.

"One more thing," he said. "Have you called the office since this whole asthma attack and hospitalization thing happened?"

"Holy shit!" She stopped dead in the middle of crossing West 43rd Street. The crowd split and funneled around her as if she was a rock wedged in a flowing stream.

"No!" she exclaimed. "I completely forgot to call."

* * *

A conversation with Jane Anderson after two unauthorized sick days was more than Heather could manage while walking uptown clutching her cell phone. She ducked into a Starbucks and ordered a café mocha. She leaned against a standing bar and sipped the steaming drink. It didn't taste the same without Jeff. She pressed Jane's number with a quivering finger.

"Jane Anderson," the human resources manager said.

"Jane, it's Heather Morrison. I'm terribly sorry I haven't called in the past few days, but I've been in the hospital."

"Oh," Jane said, sounding caught off guard. "Are you all right?"

"I'm fine now," Heather said. "I had an acute asthma attack on Tuesday night. The hospital held me for observation."

"I see. Can you tell me what hospital you were admitted to—just in case we need to verify this?"

"Mount Sinai," Heather said, steaming as much as her coffee.

"Do they have telephones at Mount Sinai?" Jane asked.

"They do, Jane, but I assure you I was in no shape to call."

"Can you manage to be here tomorrow? It'll be Friday, and people will be looking for their expense checks."

"Yes," Heather promised. "I'll be in tomorrow."

*   *   *

"Shortly after eleven on Friday morning, after a few hours of aimlessly shuffling papers and cruising the Internet, Heather slipped away from her desk and rode the elevator to the ground floor of her office building to give in to her urge for a cigarette."

The elevator was empty. She glanced at the light of the video camera tucked in the ceiling. She knew everything that was happening in every elevator in the building could be seen live by the two security guards manning the desk in the lobby. Feeling mildly self-conscious, she fumbled in her purse for her inhaler. She'd only completed two of the prescribed five inhales when the elevator announced with an electronic chime that it had reached the first floor. She stashed the inhaler back into her purse and pulled out a pack of Parliaments and a BiC lighter. Waving hello to the guards at the security desk, she pulled a single cigarette from the pack. So what if the men had seen her using the inhaler on her way to a cigarette break? There was no doubt in her mind they'd seen things that were a lot more interesting—and a lot worse.

Stepping through an automatic door, she turned the collar of her suit jacket up against the January wind. She'd purposely left her coat behind hoping that no one—Jane in particular—would notice that she'd slipped out.

She used to silently mock the swarm of nicotine addicts who stood outside the building inhaling their cigarettes like patients on life support sucking on respirators for survival. Now she was one of them. Still, she avoided talking with the other smokers. Doing so would be making a commitment to a team she didn't want to be on.

Back upstairs, she returned to her desk. There were three e-mails from Jane. *Damn! I can't be out of here for ten minutes!*

She heard Jane's unmistakable footsteps in the hall. Flat shoes, quick steps, one foot a little slower than the other. Heather smoothed her hair and sat up as straight as she could.

"Have you finished the weekly expense reports?" Jane asked.

Heather nodded, despite knowing that the stack of files on her desk remained untouched.

"I need to see you in my office. Right away," Jane added.

Heather walked into Jane's office on legs that felt like jelly.

She faced Jane from the opposite side of her oblong-shaped desk. Jane cleared her throat awkwardly. "I think you know why we're here." Jane brushed a tendril of grey hair from her forehead. "As we've discussed before, your attendance has been a problem recently. You've missed some deadlines, and your work hasn't been up to par. But your most recent faux pas is the pièce de résistance!"

"My faux pas?"

"The arrangements you were supposed to make for the quarterly meetings in London in April."

Supposed to make? "I made them," Heather said. "In person—when I was over there earlier this month."

"I know you went to London," Jane acknowledged. "I know you told me you'd made arrangements at the Churchill Hotel. Did you sign anything?"

"No, Jane. The contract exceeded the fifty thousand dollars I'm authorized to sign for. You know those expenses need the signature of a vice president. I faxed the contracts to you."

"Unfortunately, I never received that fax," Jane said. "I called the hotel yesterday to discuss details and learned that the dates on which we planned to hold our meetings have been booked by another company."

"I faxed the contract, Jane! I remember doing it as if it was yesterday."

"Did you get a confirmation of that fax?" Jane asked. "Perhaps something you've filed somewhere?"

Heather remembered that the contract had been hopelessly long, at least fourteen pages. As she'd sent it, she was mentally mapping out a tour of the places she and Jeff would go if he joined her in London. Had she waited for the confirmation fax in her hurry to rush out to preview those places? Probably not. Now it seemed that her impatience had cost her dearly. Chances were the fax had not gone through. Suddenly terrified, she brushed an unexpected tear from her eye.

"You're not making this easy for me," Jane said. "Despite what you may think, I *do* have feelings."

Heather looked at Jane with surprise bordering on disbelief.

Jane took a breath and lowered her eyes. "Unfortunately, Mr. Andrews doesn't have that same level of compassion."

Mr. Andrews! Holy shit! Why is the CEO of the firm getting involved in issues that are between me and my boss?

"Mr. Andrews was thrilled when I told him we'd be at the Churchill. It's his favorite hotel in all of London. He made other commitments in Europe around the dates."

"What did you tell him about the contract with the hotel?" Heather asked.

"I told him the truth. That you hadn't told me to expect a fax of the contract for my signature—and that I'd never received one. That, as a result, the dates I believed were booked for us were taken by another company." Jane folded her hands on her desk. "Let's face it, Heather. It's clear your mind has been focused on things other than your job for about six months now. Your attendance has suffered. You've made mistakes. Mr. Andrews himself asked me to let you go." Jane placed a thick folder labeled *Severance Agreement* on the desk between them.

Heather reached for the ominous looking folder. "May I take this home and look at it?"

Jane hesitated. "We typically ask employees to sign all the documents before collecting their personal items and leaving the building," she said.

Heather clutched the file to her chest and looked at Jane with pleading eyes. "Please," she said. "I just can't deal with this now."

Jane nodded. "I understand," she said. "Please make copies of all the documents after you sign them and return the originals to me by the end of next week."

"I will," Heather promised.

Jane stood up and brushed some imaginary lint from the jacket of her navy blue suit. "Will you need help transporting your personal items?" she asked.

"No," Heather said. "Even after twelve years, I really don't have that much here." She turned, headed for her office, and grabbed her coat and purse.

Somehow Heather made her way to the elevator past the cubicles of curious colleagues who'd never shown much interest in her before. Now as she left Peters & Andrews for the last time, one arm in a sleeve of her coat, her purse draped over her other shoulder and the beige manila folder clutched to her chest, every eye in the place was on her.

CHAPTER 36

HEATHER

THE LIGHT WAS DIM in the vestibule of Heather's building as she collected her mail. She grabbed a bunch of flyers and put them directly into the trash bin. Removing a stack of bills from the mailbox, she noticed that one was from Upper East Side Pulmonologists. *Why are they billing me? I always make my co-pay at the office.*

Upstairs in her condo, Heather lay down on the couch and stacked the mail on her stomach. She opened the envelope from Jeff's practice first. Tearing into it through the return address, she removed a single sheet of paper. It was a letter, not a bill.

> *Dear Ms. Morrison,*
>
> *We are writing to notify you that your status as a patient at Upper East Side Pulmonologists will be terminated effective March 1, 2011. We will be glad to provide a referral to a suitable doctor for your needs and transfer your records at no cost to you.*
>
> *New York State law requires that a physician whose services are no longer available to a patient notify the patient at least four weeks prior to termination of treatment. If you require the assistance of our practice prior to March 1, 2011, please call the office to make an appointment.*

Heather crumpled the letter into a ball, dropped it on the floor, and reached for her purse. She found her pills and cigarettes quickly.

How dare he upstage me when I was about to find another doctor and dismiss him as my doctor! He must want to push me completely out of his life. It's just like when he changed his cell phone number! She swallowed two Valium without water, lit a cigarette, and curled up in a fetal position on the couch. She felt so hopeless she actually considered sucking her thumb.

She had four weeks to get inside his office and find the DVD that would ruin him forever.

*   *   *

Facing Jeff as a patient would be impossible. Besides, for reasons she'd never understood, her Tuesday night trysts with Jeff had usually happened in Dr. Cooperman's exam room. That's where Heather hoped to find the DVD. So on Monday morning, she booked an appointment with Dr. Cooperman. The doctor could see her the following afternoon—Tuesday.

After making the appointment, she spent hours on the phone with both Trista and Miguel telling them that she had lost her job. Miguel was livid, but he explained that because New York is an employment-at-will state, companies can let people go for no reason and without warning.

Trista was also furious. "How could they do that to you?" she demanded.

"They can do it—and they did," Heather said.

"Where's the security in that?" Trista asked.

"There isn't any," Heather said.

*   *   *

"Dr. Cooperman will be with you shortly," Miriam said, handing Heather a white paper gown. "Everything off above the waist, opening in the back." The nurse's white oxfords squeaked as she turned and left the exam room. The door clicked closed behind her.

Immediately Heather leapt off the exam table. She pulled one of the half dozen large paper clips from her purse. Just in case, she had brought along a couple of small ones, too. Shaping the clip into a straight line, she headed for the file cabinet where Jeff had stored the DVD the night she'd discovered the recorder was on. She clutched the paper gown that draped her upper body.

Kneeling down, Heather inserted the paper clip into the lock. Nothing. She jiggled it furiously, her wide eyes alternating between the lock and the door to the exam room. Her eyelids twitched.

She removed the paper clip from the lock and inserted it again, this time at an angle. She jiggled the clip inside the lock. After a series of clicks, the file drawer slid open. Sure enough, the drawer contained dozens of DVDs, arranged alphabetically--*Benign Lung Tumors, Collapsed Lung, Lung Cancer, Measuring Lung Function, Mesothelioma.* Heather could hear Jeff's intermittent smoker's cough coming from his office on the other side of the wall. She removed the stack of medical DVDs from the file drawer and laid them on the floor.

The file drawer had a false bottom—a sheet of metal with a U-shaped cutout just large enough for a fingertip. Heather slipped her finger into it and removed the flooring from the drawer. Beneath it were more DVDs, each marked with a woman's name. There were dozens, stored with the same meticulous alphabetizing as the medical tapes: *Anna A., Barbara C., Beth M., Caroline J., Denise S., Donna S.* She scanned further for familiar names: *Heather M., Melissa C., Suzanne M.*

With a quivering hand, she pulled the tape marked with her name. She returned the false flooring and the stack of medical DVDs to the drawer in as neat a fashion as she could manage.

There was a light knock on the door. *Holy shit!* Clutching the DVD to her chest, Heather tore across the room, grabbed her purse, and hopped on the exam table.

"Ms. Morrison? I'm Dr. Janice Cooperman."

Heather extended one hand as she pushed the DVD deep inside her purse with the other.

"I'll take that for you," Dr. Cooperman offered. Heather handed her purse to the doctor.

"Thanks," Heather nodded.

Dr. Cooperman flipped through Heather's chart. Smoothing a few stray hairs back into her perky blond ponytail, she asked, "How can I help you today?"

"I had a very bad asthma attack last week that put me in the ER," Heather explained.

"At Lenox Hill?" Dr. Cooperman asked.

"No. The ambulance took me to Mount Sinai."

"Let's listen to your heart and lungs," the doctor said, placing her stethoscope against Heather's chest, "and we can determine if you're back to normal." When she was finished, she took Heather's pulse. "Your pulse and heartbeat are rapid," she said.

Well, yeah, I just picked the lock to that file cabinet over there, and there's a tape in my purse of your colleague and me having sex.

"Have you been taking your medications?" Dr. Cooperman asked.

"Usually. Sometimes I forget or I'm too busy."

"It's vital that you take your medicine," the doctor said, "especially so soon after an attack severe enough to put you in the ER."

Dr. Cooperman pulled her collar from the beige tubing of her stethoscope and continued the exam. "Your lungs sound fairly good," she said. "I do detect a bit of hyperventilation, and your blood pressure's higher than I'd like it to be."

Believe me, it'll drop thirty points the minute I get out of here.

The doctor lowered her voice. "I see here that this is your final appointment with our practice. There are three referrals here. Dr. Davis felt you might prefer Dr. Lillian Epstein."

Why? Because she's a woman and she won't try to fuck me?

*   *   *

Heather clutched her purse tightly to her chest as she blindly followed the nurse down the hall. When they'd almost reached the reception area, Jeff stepped out of another exam room. Seeing Heather, he cleared his throat nervously, brushed his hand through his thick black hair, and walked into his office. As if in testament to the finality of things between them, he closed the door behind him. Click. It's over.

CHAPTER 37

HEATHER

HEATHER MENTALLY RECOUNTED her Saturday morning appointment with Dr. Charlotte Rosner as she rode the train downtown from the doctor's West 93rd Street office, headed to the meeting with her attorney. She had hated to leave the session with Dr. Rosner.

In place of the lab coat and tailored black slacks she'd worn at the hospital, Dr. Rosner had worn a floor-length caftan. An aging child of the sixties, the doctor had started the session by telling Heather about her own background.

"In classic psychotherapy, the therapist never reveals anything about herself," Dr. Rosner had said. "I feel that approach only exacerbates the doctor-as-authority, patient-as-needy dynamic. I believe that softening the doctor-patient border from the beginning makes boundary violation far less likely."

It was a far cry from the model in which Heather's mother had placed the doctor on a pedestal while the patient worshiped at what Margaret perceived as his all-knowing feet. The patient knew nothing about the doctor except that he'd studied medicine. And in Heather's mother's model, the doctor was always a man.

"I've been at Mount Sinai for eight years—since my divorce," Dr. Rosner had continued. "My divorce was the most painful event I've ever experienced. And it was highly publicized in California. My former husband is a pastor of a well-known church on the West Coast. Diamond Deity has quite a following. Despite my training in psychiatry, I spent years looking away while he had affair after affair with his congregants."

The doctor had explained that the experience confirmed her belief that, no matter how painful the situation, there is often some gain—or at least a lesson—to be learned from it. "My husband's relationships with his parishioners led me to my research on boundary violations," she'd said.

The doctor had repeated what DelFlorio had told her—that virtually every woman who becomes involved in an affair with her doctor was sexually abused as a child.

"That's overwhelming," Heather had said. But she hadn't felt ready to tell the doctor about Father Hamilton—or the reenactment Jeff had encouraged.

"Tell me about the first time you met Jeff," Dr. Rosner had asked.

"I met him in the emergency room at Lenox Hill," Heather had said. "I'd had an asthma attack—my first. When I opened my eyes at the hospital, Jeff was bringing me to."

"That's pretty powerful stuff," Dr. Rosner had said.

"Absolutely," Heather had said. "I would have died if he hadn't saved me."

Dr. Rosner had shaken her head. "That's not entirely accurate. You might have died if *any medically trained person* hadn't intervened."

Heather had thought about the doctor's comment for a moment.

"I gather it was he who initiated the affair?" Dr. Rosner had continued.

Heather had nodded. "It didn't start out with sex. He asked me out for coffee. It did seem a little weird to me, his being my doctor..."

"You mentioned reading about transference and boundary violations on the website OnYourSide.net. I'm so glad you found that excellent resource. Did it help you to understand why, as your doctor, he never should have even asked you to have coffee with him?"

Heather had nodded. "I didn't have any idea that what was going on between Jeff and me was a violation of his professional ethics. Absolutely no idea. I only wish I'd known. It would have spared me so much misery."

The doctor had continued. "And Jeff was married, yes?"

"Yes."

"Was that part of his appeal? The longing for what you couldn't have?"

"I really don't think so. In fact, I always looked down on women who had affairs with married men."

"So you yourself had never been involved with a married man before?"

"That's right. I always thought it was wrong."

"What was it about Jeff that made you willing to bend this lifetime rule?"

"I didn't know. I still don't."

"Could it have been his power over you—the transference?"

"Maybe. From the start, he made me feel so safe. I literally felt like my life was in his hands. So yes, maybe."

"And the dynamic of the relationship," Dr. Rosner had continued. "Have you ever had a relationship where you did more of the caretaking, where it was the man who was needy?"

"Unfortunately, that's the story of my life," Heather had said. "I always fall for men who need fixing. Weak men who lean on *me*."

"So this relationship dynamic was different for you."

"Very."

"Did you enjoy not having to be the strong one in the relationship, not being leaned on by him for your strength?"

"I loved it. It made me feel so protected."

"Transference usually manifests as an erotic attraction," Dr. Rosner had continued. "But it can take many forms. Extreme dependence or even placing the doctor or therapist in a godlike status is common."

In parting, Dr. Rosner had outlined a plan to work on with Heather to achieve closure and acceptance that her relationship with Jeff was over. "It will be painful," she'd said. "But you need to go through the pain before you close the door. If you close it too soon, what you leave on the other side will always be scratching at the door. You'll make the same mistakes again and again."

* * *

Heather followed DelFlorio into his office. She sat in the same chair opposite him as she had on her first visit. "I've got what you asked for," she said. "But before I give it to you, would you mind if I used this?" She displayed her inhaler. "The ladies room was locked."

"You're practically addicted to that inhaler, aren't you?" he asked.

"Not *practically* addicted," she said. She turned her head, inhaled, and held her breath. "*Totally* addicted," she added as she exhaled. She took a few more inhalations. When she turned back toward DelFlorio, she had the encased DVD in her hand.

DelFlorio smiled and nodded, clearly pleased. "Does he do the thing where he talks to you like he's a priest on that?" he asked.

She slid the DVD across the glass that topped the desk. The DVD landed squarely in front of DelFlorio. "I *said* that I'd gotten what you asked for."

"Well done, Heather. I know it wasn't an easy thing for you to do." DeFlorio opened his desk drawer and slipped the DVD inside without lifting it.

"I can't stand the thought of anyone seeing that!" She rocked back and forth in the seat she'd taken on the other side of his desk. "I haven't even *told* anyone but you that he did this. No one. It's beyond embarrassing. He recorded sex with me—and a lot of other women—without my knowledge."

"He made the recording *without your knowledge?*"

"That's right."

"No. That's wrong. Very, very wrong. Bastard!" DelFlorio said. "The fact that I have this is probably all the ammunition I need. When the time is right, Dr. Davis will be told that I have this DVD. He'll be told that it shows him having sex with you and pretending to be a priest. And that it was recorded without your permission." He looked at her with a slight smile, his eyes crinkled at the corners. "By the way, how did you get the tape?"

Heather reached into her purse, retrieving the straightened paper clip. She held it up for him to see. "I had my final appointment at the practice last week—with one of his colleagues. I snuck it out of the file cabinet where I'd seen him stash it."

"Your final appointment?" he asked.

She handed DelFlorio the letter from Upper East Side Pulmonologists terminating her treatment.

DelFlorio glanced at the letter. "I see he's playing defense already. Odds are he's expecting you to go after him legally." He pushed the sleeves of a hunter green cashmere sweater up from his wrists, revealing hairy forearms. "Let's get to work," he said. "It's clear you've done your homework. I did mine, too. I did a thorough search for complaints filed against this guy Davis. It didn't surprise me that nothing came up. I expect he chooses his victims very carefully."

Heather hugged herself and rocked back and forth in the chair.

"But rest assured," DelFlorio continued, "doctors will almost always settle out of court—no matter what it costs them—to minimize publicity."

"I thought you said that once a case was filed, it became a matter of public record," Heather said.

"It does. But there's generally not much publicity unless the case is taken to court," DelFlorio explained. "Civil cases differ from complaints reported to the medical board. The results of medical board hearings are kept private unless the doctor is disciplined, but there's talk in Albany about changing the law. For now, though, no one can get to those records unless disciplinary action has been taken. In either case, you would need a sharp reporter who's hell-bent on cracking a story like this to bring it into the public eye."

"I'm very nervous about that. I really can't have my name smeared all over the papers." Heather rubbed her hands together to keep warm. It felt like the heat in the office building had been lowered for the weekend.

"I expect the doctor will feel even more strongly about that than you do," DelFlorio said. "He'll likely do anything to avoid publicity."

Heather nodded, slipping her coat back over her shoulders.

"You've probably heard it said that the wheels of justice move slowly," DelFlorio continued. "Unfortunately, that expression is extremely accurate. It's only been a week since I initiated the suit. But it could be a month before papers are served against Dr. Davis. And it could take four months to a year to get this matter on a judge's docket."

Heather nodded, mentally calculating how she would juggle Lin's adoption, her search for a new job, the civil suit, and the review by the medical board. She rubbed an aching muscle at the back of her neck. "OK," she said.

"As I told you last time," he said, "the papers I filed after your initial visit initiate a suit against Dr. Davis for sexual misconduct, breach of the standard of care, faulty record-keeping, and improper prescribing practices." He twisted his diamond-encrusted wedding band around his finger a few times. "But this next part is key. Because the rules regarding what's acceptable and what's not are crystal clear in psychotherapy, I wanted to be sure you could provide evidence of Jeff acting in a therapeutic manner toward you on the DVD. And putting that 'therapy' into a sexual context, in my opinion, really knocks it out of the water. Because he treated you in a psychotherapeutic manner, I feel he should be held to the same standard as a psychiatrist would be for the sexual impropriety. I'll make that case for you in court."

"Makes sense to me," Heather said.

"Another thing. You are clearly an educated and savvy young woman. Ordinarily, that's a good thing. But in a sexual malpractice case, it could work against you. We'll need to work on that. Cases like these tend to have less value if it looks like they involve a sexual relationship between two equals. But if the patient appears to be extraordinarily dependent on and in a significant transferential relationship with the professional, the case will have much greater value."

"How equal does a woman who painted her way into a psychiatric unit look?" Heather asked.

"Exactly. We need to play up those things and play them to the hilt."

"That won't take much acting on my part," Heather sighed. "I may be sensible otherwise, but when it comes to Jeff, I have absolutely no sense whatsoever. Even now, I'm still torn about bringing a lawsuit against him."

"That's typical. But as far as I'm concerned, Jeff Davis is just another sick bastard in a white lab coat—no insult to your taste in men intended." He scratched his head. "Anyway, you go ahead and be yourself when you're with me. But when we're in the company of anyone on the defense team, I need you to play to your weaknesses. Don't speak so eloquently or act as knowledgeable as you are. We'll work on it. But I can tell you as sure as I'm sitting here, this approach will pay off for you in spades."

"But Jeff knows my personality."

DelFlorio shook his head. "Doesn't matter. In front of his defense team, you're a timid woman who was overwhelmed by the interest this big important doctor took in you. You got me?"

"I've got you."

DelFlorio shifted his weight. "Let's talk some more about damages. How secure is your job?"

"That's the other thing I have to tell you. I got fired."

"I'm sorry to hear that." He started to write again. "But on the other hand, if losing your job had anything to do with your relationship with Davis, it could be seen as a real damage."

"Losing my job had *everything* to do with my being involved with Jeff. Before I met him, I was a model employee. I probably hadn't taken more than five days off in my twelve years with the firm. After we got involved, I started missing work, being irresponsible when I was there. Frankly, I deserved to get fired."

"Actually," DelFlorio said, "from a legal perspective, this is a good thing. In fact, you might want to consider holding off on a job search until the case is over."

"I can't be without a job with Lin coming," Heather said, tugging at the chain around her neck.

DelFlorio looked at Heather blankly. "Who's Lin?" he asked.

"The little girl I'm adopting from China. I'm going to pick her up in—"

"*Adopting?* You're *adopting* a child?"

"Yes. I must have told you." She opened her locket. "Here, look at her picture."

"Holy shit," DelFlorio said. "I can't even look. Oh, my God, I had no idea."

"No idea about what?" Heather demanded. *What is the matter?*

"This child—I had no idea you were in the process of adopting."

"I must have told you. I've told everyone."

He shook his head.

"Why is this such a big deal? Tell me!" Heather implored. She reached across his desk, knocking over one of the photos of his seven children in the process.

"It's a big deal," DelFlorio said. "It's a big deal because your involvement in a lawsuit of this nature will almost certainly cause the adoption agency to rescind your eligibility as an adoptive parent."

*   *   *

Heather pounded frantically on the phone number of the adoption agency as she rode the elevator to the lobby of DelFlorio's building. A recording greeted her: "You have reached Hope for Children Adoption Agency, where every child has a chance for—" She slammed the phone closed. *Of course. It's Saturday.*

As the elevator announced its arrival on the first floor with a chime, Heather called the adoption agency a second time. This time she listened through the entire recording. Still no one answered. She wouldn't leave a message. She'd call them again first thing Monday morning.

Tears streamed freely down her cheeks as she walked. She made no effort to hide them from passersby. What she'd heard ten minutes ago had put her in a place as dark as the night she woke up in the emergency room at Mount Sinai. Maybe darker.

The thought of losing Lin before she even had her was more than Heather could bear. She called Trista and Miguel and got voice mail for both. She left messages telling them what had happened.

Riding the subway uptown, Heather reviewed the dreadful possibility DelFlorio had just drawn. She wanted to blame him, but she knew it wasn't his fault. She hadn't told him about the adoption, and there was no reason for him to have asked if she was in the process of adopting.

The question on the adoption form seeped its way back into her mind. *Are you now or have you ever been involved in a lawsuit?* It had stood out to her because it had seemed almost silly at the time she was filing the initial adoption papers. Before meeting Jeff, her closest encounter with the law had been a ticket at the Bridgeport train station for parking without a permit.

She thought about the explanation DelFlorio had given for why her being involved in a lawsuit could end her eligibility as a suitable adoptive parent. "Adoption agencies run on shoestrings," he'd said. "And Americans are notorious for their frivolous lawsuits. That's why agencies eliminate prospective parents with litigation histories— for fear of a lawsuit if the adoption sours. It's their way of avoiding the expense and negative publicity of litigation."

Naturally, she'd asked DelFlorio if there was something—anything—they could do to halt the legal process. He'd said that because the complaint and the lawsuit had both been filed, it would be extremely difficult to halt the action on either of them. Even if he were able to do that, the records would remain.

The wheels of justice—however slow—had been set in motion. There could be no turning back.

*   *   *

Heather called Hope for Children Adoption Agency at the stroke of nine Monday morning.

"Good morning, Hope for Children Agency," said an accented voice in a perky tone.

"Carol Chung, please," Heather said.

"Who is this calling?"

"Tell her Heather Morrison is calling. It's urgent."

Carol was on the line within seconds. "Miss Morrison, what is wrong? You have a problem?"

"I need to come in and see you," Heather replied. "Are you available this morning?"

"I can make myself available, if there is an emergency," Carol said.

Is there an emergency? Both her lawsuit and her complaint to the medical board were in files somewhere, just waiting to be reviewed and assessed by paralegals. She'd lost her job. She had to get to China and adopt Lin before any word of the ugly scandal of her affair with Jeff or of her job loss was accessed by the investigators at Hope for Children.

"There is an emergency," Heather said. "Because of it, I must try to get to China earlier than scheduled and adopt my daughter."

"Oh, no, I am very sorry," Carol said. "We cannot make changes to the schedule. We have never done something like this before."

Heather had spent the weekend devising a plan she would use if she had no other option. "May I come in and see you?" she asked, certain now that she'd have to resort to her plan, the only story she could come up with that might work. "It is a major emergency."

"OK. Can you come in this morning?" Carol asked. "Eleven o'clock?"

"I'll be there," Heather said. "Thank you *so much.*"

CHAPTER 38

HEATHER

AS SHE CHECKED IN WITH THE RECEPTIONIST at Hope for Children, rain dripped from Heather's trench coat. She was wet and freezing and miserable, but she was in a race against time to adopt Lin. A little rain wouldn't stop her. Nothing would.

The receptionist, whose nameplate read *June Huai*, walked around her desk and frowned at the pool of raindrops gathering on the floor around Heather. "You are Miss Morrison? Please, let me take your coat."

Heather's foot tapped impatiently against the floor.

After what seemed an eternity, Heather followed June down the narrow hall to an open door with a nameplate that said *Carol Chung, Chief Administrator*. Carol stood and shook Heather's hand with a firm grip. "It is a pleasure to finally meet you," she said. "I see so much paperwork and clients have their interviews with our social workers before I finally have the opportunity to meet our adoptive parents in person."

"It is good to meet you," Heather said. "Unfortunately, the circumstances are not good."

June left the room, and Carol and Heather seated themselves on opposite sides of Carol's desk. "How can I help you, Miss Morrison?" June asked. "What is this emergency?"

Heather planted herself solidly in the chair and prepared to tell the lie of a lifetime. "My mother is dying," she said.

"Oh! I am very sorry!" Carol exclaimed.

"My mother has battled breast cancer for many years. She is in hospice now. The doctors say she has only a few weeks left to live."

"I am very sorry," Carol said again.

"As you know, I have been approved to adopt Hung Wang Lin. I keep her picture here." Heather touched her locket with a fingertip. "Of course, I have shown Lin's picture to my mother. It is my mother's wish—her dying wish—to meet her granddaughter."

A gentle smile touched Carol's lips.

Maybe I'm getting through to her with the emotional hook, Heather thought, filling with hope.

"As you know, we go to great lengths to arrange for our adoptive parents to fly to Beijing together," Carol said. "We have made arrangements for all the parents to have a meeting at the Civil Affairs Bureau in the provinces where each child resides." She glanced at Heather's file. "You will go to the Civil Affairs Bureau in Beijing. They will certify your daughter's birth certificate. Some of the members of your party will have to fly to other provinces. All of the parents adopting in Beijing will stay together in the same hotel there. We have also arranged for your group to travel to the Children's Welfare Institute, where your child is being housed. Then you will all return to the hotel with your children. It is a wonderful experience to share with other adoptive parents."

"I know. The agency's care and attention to detail is one of the reasons I chose Hope for Children," Heather said, making every effort to flatter Carol. "And, of course, I realize how special it would be to do these things with the other adoptive parents. But now it is more important that my mother can see Lin…before she…before she dies."

Heather's voice shook. She was not used to lying. But the quiver in her voice might give credence to her words.

"Yes," Carol said. "I understand. But I don't know if I can help. Hope for Children has taken great care to prepare your preliminary itinerary. Other agencies leave parents floundering to find flights and hotels and to figure out parts of the adoption process on their own. You have paid for all of the extra care our agency provides. The funds are nonrefundable."

"I know that your service is unmatched and that I have paid for all of this," Heather said. "But I am willing to spend my own money to fly to Beijing and Guangzhou on my own, if you will allow me to pick Lin up earlier than has been scheduled." She pulled a tissue from her purse and wiped her eyes. "My mother is dying! Please! Please try to help me!"

"I *do* want to help you, Miss Morrison. But I'm not sure I can. We have never had such an exceptional situation." Carol flipped to the month of April in a large datebook on her desk. "Our agency is taking care of all of these details for over three dozen adoptions being done in your group. It looks like we are very close to finalizing the dates. Within a week or two, we should be able to give you the finalized itinerary for an April adoption."

Heather knew she couldn't wait that long. "When is my interview with the Civil Affairs Bureau scheduled?"

Carol reviewed her notes closely. "It will most likely be on Wednesday, April 7, at ten in the morning."

"Can you change it to some time this week or next?" Heather asked. "Can you change all the appointments—the Civil Affairs Bureau, the Children's Welfare Institute, the interview at the U.S. consulate in Guangzhou? Please!"

Carol shrugged her shoulders. "Because of the extreme circumstances, I will try. Call me tomorrow morning, and I will tell you if I've been able to make any progress."

CHAPTER 39

JEFF

WHILE HEATHER WAS STRUGGLING against time to salvage Lin's adoption, Jeff was enjoying a late and solitary lunch at Bemelmans at the Carlyle. Because his afternoon schedule was unusually light, he allowed himself the luxury of two double scotches with his Angus burger.

When Jeff returned to his office, his mail was stacked neatly in the middle of his desk. As always, Barbara had sliced each envelope with a letter opener and attached its contents with a paper clip. On the bottom of the pile were stacks of trade magazines and newsletters he never had time to read. He reached toward the pile. On the bottom, beneath the magazines, was an envelope Barbara had failed to open. A flicker of annoyance furrowed his brow. Lifting the letter, he checked the return address. It read: *Office of Professional Medical Conduct–OPMC, New York State Department of Health.*

Holy shit. It was a moment every doctor feared. Jeff's hand, suddenly clammy and unsteady, reached for his letter opener. It slipped from his hand, crashing on the glass desktop that covered his mahogany desk. He ripped the envelope open with his hands, pulled out the letter, and began to read.

> *Dear Dr. Davis:*
> *This letter is to inform you that a complaint has been filed against you by a patient claiming sexual misconduct. Supplemental charges include failure to refer, improper*

prescribing practices, and poor record-keeping. We are currently
conducting an investigation of this complaint.

If we find that disciplinary action is warranted, you will
have an opportunity to present your case at an initial hearing.
Please be advised that you may seek counsel in this matter.

A hearing to determine the accuracy of said allegation
will be held on Wednesday, March 23, 2011, at 10:00 a.m.

As was typical with the OPMC, the complainant was not named.
It didn't matter. Jeff knew who had made the report. *Heather.* All
the other patients he'd had sex with had been married to wealthy,
high-profile men. None would have risked her marriage to seek a bit
of revenge.

Jeff pressed his assistant's extension number. "Barbara, would
you come in here and take a letter?"

He knew the drill. Denying an indiscretion reported by a patient
was a doctor's standard response to a complaint from the OPMC.
But he also knew that these investigations rarely ended with the doctor
simply denying the charges.

He knew what would happen next.

CHAPTER 40

HEATHER

EVEN AFTER HAVING SPENT NEARLY two hours at the adoption agency with Carol Chung on Monday, Heather was still uncertain she would be able to get to Beijing before someone at the agency discovered the lawsuit DelFlorio had filed. She had to make the adoption official before she risked becoming what the agency would term an "unsuitable adoptive parent."

She spent most of Tuesday scouring the Internet for airfares to China. The airline tickets alone cost fifteen hundred dollars. She went through the preliminary itinerary Hope for Children had sent, trying to imagine how she could manage the many appointments she had to attend on her own. Guangzhou appeared to be a two-hour flight from Beijing. How could she get from place to place and handle all these appointments when she spoke very little Chinese? She chain-smoked as she struggled to recreate a new itinerary based on the one the agency had prepared.

Heather was pacing the living room when her phone began to vibrate on the coffee table. She ran to the table, ashtray in hand, and picked up the phone, holding her cigarette between her teeth. "Hello," she said.

It was Carol Chung. "I have good news for you," she said. "I have managed to arrange for you to meet with the agent in charge of your adoption at the Civil Affairs Bureau in Beijing. The meeting is on Thursday, February 18, at two o'clock in the afternoon. This, of course, is Beijing time."

Heather's heart felt like it would burst from her chest. "Thank you, Carol. I can't thank you enough!"

"There is more," Carol continued. "Miss Chu will be able to certify the birth certificate of Hung Wang Lin. But I am still working on the arrangements for your meetings at the Children's Welfare Institute, where you will be given your child, and at the U.S. Consulate in Guangzhou."

"Thank you," Heather said again. "Thank you so much!"

"Have you made your flight reservations? And your hotel?"

"I was waiting to hear from you so I would know when I should go."

"I recommend that you stay at the Hua Fu International Hotel. It is near the Children's Welfare Institute, the orphanage where Lin is living. Even more important, this is the hotel where we house our parents who are adopting in Beijing. There may be people working there who are familiar with Hope for Children agency and will be able to help you."

"Oh, Carol, thank you for helping me!" Heather sank to the couch, tears streaming down her face.

"I am doing my best for you, Heather," Carol said. "Your mother's serious illness is an extreme circumstance. But there are many appointments I must arrange. And I am having trouble reaching our contact at Lin's orphanage and at the U.S. Consulate in Guangzhou."

"But the first step—the first appointment—is supposed to be at the Civil Affairs Bureau, right?" Heather asked, studying the group itinerary.

"Yes."

"I will fly to Beijing as soon as possible," Heather said. "I'll make my flight and hotel reservations. Can you arrange the other appointments while I'm travelling? I'll check with you by e-mail as soon as I arrive at the hotel in Beijing."

"It is a risky plan," Carol said. "There is no guarantee that our representatives at these agencies will be available to meet with you and surrender your baby to you during the time you are in China. But, yes, if you wish, I will go along with this."

Heather took the information she had scribbled down during the conversation and headed for her computer to make air and hotel reservations. Her plan was working! She would have Lin in her arms and home in New York before anyone could put a stop to it!

CHAPTER 41

HEATHER

HEATHER ARRIVED IN BEIJING at seven o'clock on Tuesday evening. The flight had been grueling, as she'd expected it would be. She'd kept herself going by taking some Valium and Ambien each time she changed planes. Valium to relax, Ambien to sleep. She had looked at Lin's photo in the locket dozens of times throughout the flights. Every time she saw her child's face, she felt she could endure any journey to get to her.

Beijing Capital International Airport was like Times Square on New Year's Eve. Heather followed the herd from her plane, breathing an audible sigh of relief when she saw signs in English below the Chinese characters. Exit. In. Out. Customs. Food. Toilet.

* * *

"Business or pleasure?" the customs agent growled.

"Business," Heather stammered. "I am here for business."

"You have with you business documents?" he asked.

Heather thought of the reams of adoption papers in her carry-on bag. Not wanting to deal any further with the language barrier and the customs process, she simply said, "No."

The agent stamped her passport and waved her on her way.

Heather passed through the doors between customs and baggage claim. Behind the ropes stood a bevy of taxi drivers, each holding a sign with a name on it. *Which one is the driver the adoption agency sent for me?* She scanned the names, finally spotting a short, slender man wearing blue jeans and a black ski jacket. He held a rumpled piece of paper on which she could barely make out her name: *Hetter Marson.* She rushed toward him, her body flooding with relief.

"Hi, I'm Heather Morrison," she said.

"You go Hua Fu Hotel," he said. It was a statement, not a question.

"Yes. Please."

*   *   *

Forty minutes and probably five miles later, a bellhop took Heather's suitcase and carried it into the hotel. He greeted her in flawless English. Heather checked in and was escorted to her room. She was seven thousand miles from home but felt comfortable at once, at home.

*   *   *

In her room, Heather hung the crisp navy blue suit she would wear to the Civil Affairs Bureau tomorrow. It was just the right look, she thought, for an American woman being entrusted with the care of a small Chinese girl. When she was finished, she lay down on the bed for what she expected would be a catnap. When she awoke, it was eight o'clock in the morning. She was starving. She made tea from a pot in the room. She sipped the green tea scented with jasmine and ate a few fortune cookies as she looked out the ninth floor window at the mass of traffic and pedestrian chaos below.

*   *   *

As she left the hotel, she felt recharged. She was going to adopt her baby! She damned Jeff for breaking her heart, but she believed that, in Lin, she would find a love that would never have to end.

A bilingual doorman flagged down a taxi for her, instructing the driver to take Heather to the Civil Affairs Bureau. Once there, she entered a reception area that was bursting with couples waiting for marriage licenses and couples who were waiting to adopt. She stood in line, shifting her weight from one foot to the other, in front of a sign reading *Adoption*. Behind a counter with an iron grate, an efficient-looking Chinese woman shuffled papers and spoke to the adoptive parents in flawless English.

"How can I help you?" the woman asked when Heather reached the grate. She wore a name tag that identified her as Lillian Chow Din.

"I'm here to have my daughter's birth certificate certified," Heather said. "Her name is Hung Wang Lin."

The woman shuffled through a file drawer, finally arriving at a file folder labeled *H*. She pulled a manila folder from it and placed it on the counter between herself and Heather. The file was covered with yellow stickies filled with notes in Chinese. "For Hung Wang Lin, you will see Miss Wu. Come with me, please."

Lillian Chow Din pointed to a doorway at the far end of the counter. "I will meet you there," she said. A moment later, Heather could hear her opening a series of locks. She opened the door, and Heather stepped into a long, narrow hallway. Lillian Chow Din locked the door behind them and led Heather through a maze of corridors. Finally, they arrived at a door with a name plaque that read *Dee Sim Wu, Chief Administrator*.

When Heather entered the room, Miss Wu stood, circled her desk, and bowed. Awkwardly, Heather did the same.

"Please sit down," Miss Wu said.

Heather took the seat Miss Wu had indicated, sat down, and crossed her legs. Her right foot bounced up and down in anticipation.

"Miss Morrison, you are here to certify the birth certificate of Hung Wang Lin?" the administrator asked.

"Yes," Heather said. "I am very excited to meet her."

As Miss Wu smiled in return, there was a knock at the door. "I am sorry," she said. "My meetings are meant to be undisturbed." She called something out in Chinese that Heather assumed meant "come in," because a moment later, a young Chinese woman opened the door. She walked over to Miss Wu with a short stack of papers in her hand. Holding the papers upright so Heather couldn't see them, the two women spoke rapidly in Chinese. After a conversation that lasted five minutes, Miss Wu put the papers inside Lin's file, closed the file, and dismissed the young woman.

Miss Wu pulled her chair closer to her desk and looked squarely at Heather. "Miss Morrison," she said. "Something has come up that might make us modify our plans."

"Modify our plans?" Heather asked, reaching for her inhaler.

"There are questions that have come up very recently—just today, in fact. We will need more information," Miss Wu said.

Heather felt herself breaking out into a visible sweat. "What kind of questions? Maybe I can answer them for you now."

"Oh, no, it is nothing like that," Miss Wu said. "We need more information from the U.S. Do not worry. The information will be here soon."

On the desk in front of Miss Wu was a certificate with Chinese lettering and festive scrolls. "This is the birth certificate of Hung Wang Lin," she said. "But because of this new information, we cannot certify it today." She rolled up Lin's birth certificate and tied it with a piece of red satin ribbon.

"I don't understand. Everything had been cleared for me to take my child home to the U.S.," Heather said, looking for an opportunity to discreetly turn her head and use her inhaler.

"The questions. As I said, they are new," Miss Wu replied.

New questions. Anything could have happened in the three days since I left New York. Did they find out I made up the story about my dying mother? Did they find out I lost my job? Or that I filed charges against Jeff? The complaint to the medical board was to remain sealed unless a disciplinary board found him guilty of violating medical ethics. The civil suit had been filed only two weeks ago. What was wrong?

Miss Wu continued. "We will take you to the Children's Welfare Institute where Lin is living. It is called Tongling House. It is not far from here. You can meet her."

Heather's heart fluttered. Maybe it was just some sort of bureaucratic delay.

* * *

Tongling House was only a few miles from the Civil Affairs Bureau. On the way there, Heather sat silently with Miss Wu in the back seat of a chauffer-driven black American-made sedan. Beside her on the seat was a duffel bag stuffed with toys and clothes— things she had planned to give to Lin before they traveled from Tongling House back to Heather's hotel. But now it was clear that the trip to the hotel was not going to happen today. Heather felt the blood pulsing through her ears as she continued to wonder why.

The car pulled into a circular driveway in front of an institutional-looking brown brick building. A Chinese flag attached to a flagpole on the front lawn flapped in the strong wind. At the entrance beneath a large sign with huge Chinese characters were small letters spelling out *Tongling House*.

The two women waited in a drably-furnished room. Miss Wu sat silently and perfectly erect on a chair with a tattered green slipcover. "They have gone to get her," was all she said during the ten minutes the women sat in the room.

Heather gave no reply beyond a nod. Afraid to say anything that might further jeopardize her eligibility for the adoption, she sat silently until she heard two sets of footsteps on the linoleum flooring in the hall. One set was clipped and quick; the other was a shuffle— as if the person walking was barely lifting her feet from the floor. After a brief knock, the door to the waiting room swung open. A different woman, wearing the same pink uniform as the woman who had let them in, entered the room. Holding her hand was a tiny girl—at nineteen months, no longer the baby in the photo in Heather's locket, but a toddler.

Miss Wu exchanged words with the other woman who appeared to speak no English. Finally, Miss Wu stopped speaking and took the child's hand. She approached Heather and said, "This is Hung Wang Lin." She bent toward the child and said something in Chinese.

Immediately, Lin shook her head no and started to cry.

"This is not unusual," Miss Wu told Heather. "The children are often very shy with new people, especially with people who do not look like those they are used to."

Heather nodded and reached for the girl's hand. *"Ni hao,"* she said in greeting, one of the many Chinese words and expressions she had studied. She longed to say *Don't cry. I am your mother.* But she

•

didn't know how to say the words so that Lin would understand. Besides, she wasn't yet Lin's mother and was terrified that she never would be.

Heather unzipped the black duffle bag she was carrying. Reaching inside, she removed two dolls—a baby doll from American Girl and Princess Ariel from the Disney store.

"*Wa wa, wa wa!*" Lin exclaimed, reaching first for the baby doll. She held it to her chest and rocked back and forth in a comforting motion. "*Wa wa,*" she said again, removing a tiny bottle attached with Velcro to the baby doll's clothing. She held the bottle to the doll's mouth, jamming it repeatedly against its lips.

The woman in the pink uniform said something to Lin in Chinese. A moment later, the child walked over to Heather, placed the doll on her lap and said, "*Xiexie.*"

"She is saying *thank you,*" Miss Wu confirmed.

"*Xiexie,*" Heather said. "*Xiexie,* Lin." She looked anxiously at Miss Wu and the woman in the pink uniform.

Lin returned to sitting on the floor, bringing the two dolls with her.

"Do you want to play dolls?" Heather asked. "*Wa wa?*" she added, knowing the words Lin said before meant dollies.

The child brought her doll over to Heather in a hopping motion typical of children playing with dolls anywhere in the world. Lin tapped the Ariel doll's head with the baby doll's and handed it to Heather. Heather tapped back. Lin began to laugh, a soft giggly laugh that was the universal laughter of a child.

"Can she sit on my lap?" Heather asked Miss Wu.

The woman in pink said something to Lin. In response, Lin put down her baby doll and climbed on Heather's lap. Heather felt her baby soft skin and smelled the fresh scent of lemon in her shiny black hair. The child turned to Heather and looked at her with dark brown eyes speckled with amber. Heather hugged her and said in a whisper loud enough for the others to hear, "*Wo men ai ni. Wo shi ni de ma ma.*"

"Ma ma," Lin repeated. "Ma ma, Ma ma, Ma ma…"

"Do not confuse her," Miss Wu interjected. "You may tell Lin that you love her and you are her mother after the adoption is finalized."

*   *   *

In the car on the way back, Miss Wu explained, "Our protocol is very strict. Because we have not yet certified Lin's birth certificate and she is not with us, we cannot take you to your hotel. We will put you in a taxi and give the driver the address of your hotel. You come back tomorrow. Maybe we have everything fixed for adoption."

Heather closed her eyes, picturing her beautiful daughter. She remembered the feel of her skin, the smell of her hair. But most of all, she remembered the word that Lin had repeated that was the same in English and Chinese—"Ma Ma." Lin had said the word a dozen times, probably having no idea what it meant.

If only she didn't have to wait. If only these people would certify Lin's birth certificate, Heather and Lin could be on the next flight to Guangzhou for an immigration interview at the U.S. Consulate. She was certain something had gone terribly wrong.

When she returned to the hotel, Heather had no interest in eating. Instead, she headed for a computer kiosk and checked her e-mail. Finding nothing of interest, she prepared e-mails to send to Trista, Miguel, and Carol Chung at Hope for Children in New York.

The e-mails to Trista and Miguel were the same. In the subject line, she typed *Lin*. Her message followed: *I met my beautiful little girl today. But I wasn't allowed to have the adoption certified or to bring her back to the hotel with me. I was told that the Civil Affairs Bureau had "new information." Whatever this information is, they won't let me complete the adoption and take Lin until it is resolved. I am going out of my mind. They can't possibly know about my job loss or the lawsuit I filed against Jeff, but what else could it be? I'll write again as soon as I know more.*

Dear Miss Chung, she wrote in the e-mail to Carol Chung. *I arrived at the Civil Affairs Bureau today as instructed. I was told by the chief administrator there, Miss Dee Sim Wu, that they have some "new information" that is preventing the certification of Lin's birth certificate. Miss Wu accompanied me to Tongling House, the orphanage where Lin is living. I met Lin briefly. But I was not allowed to bring her back to the hotel with me. I have no idea why.*

Please, please let me know what is wrong and how it can be resolved. Now that I have met and held my little girl, I love and want her even more than before.

Heather tapped the mouse pad. Within seconds, her e-mail had landed in Carol Chung's mailbox halfway around the world.

CHAPTER 42

DINA CAVALI

WHILE HEATHER WAS EN ROUTE to Beijing, Dina Cavali, one of the toughest reporters in New York, was hard at work in her tiny cubicle at *The New York Post*. Her colleague Jack Horowitz passed her work space while shoving his arms into the sleeves of his jacket.

"Hey, did you see my article on today's *front page*?" Dina teased her fellow reporter. Her black trench coat hung from a hook in her cubicle, still wet from the rain outside.

"What's that, six front-pagers for you, four for me so far this year?" replied Jack, like Dina, a seasoned reporter at the *Post*, New York's oldest and sleaziest daily newspaper.

"Yep," Dina said, tossing a Hermes scarf over her shoulder. "Better get cracking or *you'll* be taking *me* to dinner at the restaurant of my choice next January." She pulled a lipstick from her massive purse and painted her lips cherry red.

"I'm on my way to a fire on 14th Street. I'll beat you to the front page tomorrow for sure, if there are any fatalities," Jack said.

"Don't count your chickens," Dina warned, pushing her red hair from her forehead. "I'm on to something good."

"Seriously, Dina, that's quite a story in today's paper," Jack acknowledged. "It's not every day that the New York Health Department agrees to allow medical misconduct charges to become public record even before a hearing takes place."

"About fucking time, I might add." Dina's laptop kicked into gear. She clicked from the original draft of her story to the online version. "Fucking Newman," she said, referring to the paper's most ominous editor. "I swear that man lives to kill my best sentences."

"It's still a great story," Jack said, folding his copy of yesterday's paper. "It's Newman's job to keep editorializing—something you're way too free with—out of the news."

"Hey, whose side are you on?" She grabbed a stress ball from her desk and bounced it off her colleague's head.

"Whoa. All I'm saying is if you wanted to editorialize, you should have worked in the op ed department." Jack tossed the stress ball onto Dina's desk.

"And you say that how often? Every day?" she asked rhetorically, before settling in to read her page-one story once again. *Under the terms of a patient safety bill agreement signed on Monday by Governor David Paterson, doctors who are charged with misconduct will no longer have their names protected when complaints are filed. In addition, they will be given only one day to produce office records requested by investigators. Under the terms of the bill, misconduct charges reported to the Office of Professional Medical Conduct (OPMC) will become public records without exception. Previously, complaints to the OPMC remained confidential until the doctor was formally disciplined. If the charges were dismissed, misconduct charges remained sealed. The OPMC is the disciplinary arm of the state health department that investigates complaints about physicians and monitors practitioners who have been charged with misconduct.*

"Reporting the change in the law was one thing. Now I've got to get my hands on a real case involving real people," she said.

"Well, good luck with it," Jack said. "Gotta run. This one's a three-alarmer."

"Later, Horowitz," Dina said, thinking, *It's a good generic story, but if I can personalize it, it will be a great story.* "Where there's smoke, there's fire."

* * *

Dina's goal, the story she lived to write, would be one about a female patient charging a male doctor with sexual misconduct. She read on, silently applauding herself for the thorough research and meticulous wording of the article that had kept her at the office until nearly midnight on Monday. She had outlined the specifics with bullets in a sidebar. Frustrated, she focused on the last bullet: *New York will remain one of the few states that do not conduct their physician disciplinary hearings in public.*

Damn, she thought. *I don't like that one. I love being in the courtroom. Being inside a medical board hearing would be even better!*

As a reporter, Dina knew that, in the past, doctors who were reported to the OPMC for sexual misconduct had settled such cases quietly, paying off their lovers and keeping their malpractice records clear. Those days were gone now! Dina felt like she was on the cusp of writing her best story ever. She just had to find a case in its early stages that had the potential to bring down the high and mighty.

She clicked onto the OPMC website and searched under pending rulings. Only one claim came up, but one was all Dina needed to personalize her story. *Physician: Jeffrey H. Davis, Complainant: Heather Morrison,* she read. *Complaint: Sexual misconduct.*

Certain that a woman who had filed with the OPMC would also file a civil suit against her doctor, Dina clicked on the website for New York City Civil Court. She accessed the page for cases filed and searched for the story of a lifetime. She entered the name *Heather Morrison* into the search engine. The case came up within seconds: Morrison v. Davis. *This one will be my baby,* Dina thought. *I just need the details.*

Dina made a quick call to the Thirty-Eighth Judicial District in lower Manhattan. A male voice answered.

"Eric?" she said. "It's Dina Cavali at the *Post*. I seem to remember that you owe me a favor."

Within seconds, Eric Crane, a friend from grad school, had e-mailed Dina a copy of the plaintiff's verified complaint for the Morrison v. Davis case. She struggled to control her excitement as she read it.

> *Plaintiff: Heather Morrison*
> *Defendant: Jeffrey Davis, M.D.*
> *Date of Filing: January 27, 2011*
> *Charges: sexual misconduct, failure to refer, improper prescribing practices, poor record-keeping*
> *The plaintiff, Heather Morrison, 38, has filed charges against the defendant, Jeffrey Davis, M.D., 40, for the following acts of medical malpractice:*

Sexual misconduct: Plaintiff claims that during the period beginning June 23, 2010, and ending January 11, 2011, she and Dr. Davis engaged in a sexual relationship. Plaintiff claims that sexual activity occurred at her home, a hotel, and at the doctor's medical office located at 204 East 79th Street, New York, New York.

During this period Dr. Davis, a pulmonologist, was treating Ms. Morrison for asthma. Dr. Davis, although having limited training in the field of psychiatry, also treated Ms. Morrison for psychological problems, insisting on reenactment with him of an incident of molestation that occurred during the plaintiff's childhood.

Failure to refer: Despite treating Ms. Morrison for psychiatric conditions, Dr. Davis failed to refer her to a psychologist or psychiatrist.

Improper prescribing practices: During the period in question, Dr. Davis prescribed large doses of Ambien, Valium, and Vicodin to the patient.

Poor record-keeping: Dr. Davis's records fail to include his treatment of Ms. Morrison for psychological issues. His records for pharmaceutical drugs prescribed to Ms. Morrison are not properly or thoroughly recorded in his medical records.

*   *   *

Oh, God, this is good, Dina thought as she printed out the page. *I can't wait to make a front-pager out of this one!*

CHAPTER 43

JEFF

JEFF ENTERED HIS OFFICE on Wednesday morning the same way he always did. He walked past the reception area, smiling a good morning at whichever of the six receptionists—one for each member of the practice—looked his way. Most mornings, each of the receptionists was busy at work, either on the phone or computer or speaking with patients in person.

But this morning was different. A trio of receptionists, including his own, Barbara Donnolly, was standing in a group looking at a newspaper. The younger receptionist, Jen Maynard, was reading aloud from the paper. As soon as they spotted Jeff, they separated and returned to their desks. Jen tucked the newspaper somewhere behind her desk, out of Jeff's sight.

They couldn't know about the complaint he'd received from the medical board, Jeff told himself. Only Barbara might have suspected, having seen the envelope with the return address of the OPMC. And he knew she would not have breathed a word of it to her coworkers.

As he walked down the hall to his office, he nearly collided with Dr. Cooperman. "Oh, excuse me, Dr. Davis!" she said. There was something in the way she was looking at him that made Jeff uncomfortable.

Jeff shook his head as he entered his office, wondering why everyone seemed a little off this morning.

* * *

By the time he'd seen twelve patients in a two-hour period, Jeff felt like he'd already put in a full day. As he headed toward his office for a brief break between patients, he felt his cell phone vibrate in the pocket of his slacks. It was Mike Dommer.

"What's up, Dommer?" he asked, closing the door. "People going crazy at Bellevue?"

"*You'll* go crazy when you see the cover of *The New York Post*," Mike said.

"You know I don't read that rag," Jeff replied, scanning his appointment schedule. Clara Dixon, the world's greatest hypochondriac, was scheduled five minutes from now at eleven o'clock.

"Well, you should read it today," Mike said. "The cover story is all about you—and Heather. Now go get the paper, man."

Jeff felt a chill of fear. "I've got a faster way," he said. Turning to his computer, he searched for *The New York Post* homepage. The page was taking forever to load.

"Just check out the story, Jeff."

When the website finally appeared, Jeff clicked on the link to *Today's Issue*. Headlines in bold print screamed, *Lung Doc Charged with Playing Doctor with Patient*.

"Holy shit, man," Jeff said. "Let me read this."

"I can't believe you haven't seen it yet," Mike replied.

Jeff scanned the article:

A thirty-eight-year-old asthma patient has filed charges of sexual misconduct against Jeffrey Davis, M.D., forty, a partner in the prestigious medical firm, Upper East Side Pulmonologists. The charges, made by Heather Morrison, until recently the director of corporate travel at the law firm of Peters & Andrews, also include failure to refer, improper prescribing practices, and poor record-keeping.

Morrison is represented by William M. DelFlorio, a hard-hitting personal injury attorney with a roster of celebrity clients and a history of winning cases. DelFlorio made only one statement to the press, saying that the Post's questions were premature. "If such a case has been filed—and I'm not saying whether or not it has—the case would be in its infancy," he said. "According to the filing time line the reporter provided, a defendant, if there is one, would not even have been served at this juncture."

Jeff read on. *A review of records filed with the Office of Professional Medical Conduct (OPMC) reveals that Heather Morrison has also filed a complaint with the New York State Department of Health, alleging…*

Jeff looked at the byline. Dina Cavali. "This reporter," he said. "Where the hell did she get this information?"

"I'm guessing great connections and a First Amendment that ensures freedom of the press," Mike said.

"I haven't even gotten a summons and complaint on this," Jeff said.

"Listen, pal, I've got to get back to the ER," Mike was saying. "Let me know if there's anything I can do to help."

"I might need a place to sleep," Jeff said, only half kidding.

"Whatever you need, man. I'm there for you." Mike ended the call.

Oh, my God, Jeff thought. *Priscilla is bound to hear about this.* He buried his head in his left hand, still holding the cell phone with his right. *It's over. Everything's over. My marriage. My practice. My life.*

* * *

Jeff's intercom buzzed. "Ms. Dixon is waiting in the exam room," Barbara said.

"Thanks, Barbara. I'll be with her in two minutes." Jeff returned his stethoscope to his neck, smoothed his white lab coat, and headed for the exam room.

"What seems to be the problem this time?" he asked as he entered the room, not even offering a *good morning*.

Clara Dixon's head jerked in reaction. "I've had some new symptoms," she said. "That chronic cough I have?"

Jeff nodded.

"Well I seem to be coughing up some mucus now. I never had that problem before."

Jeff began to perform the same examination on Clara that he'd conducted at least two dozen times before, never finding any legitimate ailment. After listening to her breathing, he said, "Look, Clara. I work with people every day who are suffering from lung cancer, COPD, and asthma so bad they can't walk from their beds to the bathroom. One or more of my hospitalized patients dies every day of the week."

He leaned against a counter, his body stiff with tension. "Meanwhile, you torment yourself imagining illnesses that don't even exist."

"But you give me medications!" Clara said.

"I give you medications to placate you, but nothing ever works because *there's nothing wrong with you!*"

"Well, this time, there *is* something wrong with me," Clara insisted. "I have this mucus."

"Is the mucus light green or dark green?" Jeff asked, probing Clara's mouth with a tongue depressor.

"It's light," she said when he removed the depressor.

"Clara," he said, "We all have mucus. I have mucus, my secretary has mucus, my wife has mucus. In fact, Clara, mucus is good. Mucus is a protective lubricant that coats the cells and glands of the mucous membranes. That's a good thing. And light mucus is especially good because, unlike dark green mucus, it carries no infection. I see no indication of anything except some minor postnasal drip—not even sufficient enough to require nose drops. I will tell you, though, that postnasal drip *can* cause bad breath. So why don't you pick up a bottle of Listerine on your way home and stop worrying about it?"

*   *   *

Jeff left the exam room. He needed a cigarette. But there was no way he could walk past a waiting room full of patients and sneak into the alley where he usually caught his daytime smokes. He thought about the staff lavatory. Although he'd never dared to smoke in there before, he needed a cigarette desperately.

He headed for the far end of the hall. No one was in the lavatory. *Thank God!* But how could he be sure no one would detect the smell of smoke? He closed the door behind him in the tiny room. Slipping a flattened pack of cigarettes and the lighter Heather had given him from a front pocket of his slacks, he knelt down on the bathroom floor and lit up. Facing the toilet, he blew the smoke directly into the bowl and flushed. He repeated the process ten times until his cigarette was two-thirds gone.

I'm an addict. This is worse than vomiting into the toilet because smoking is voluntary. But Jeff's need for nicotine was so ingrained, smoking was probably no longer a voluntary act. He grabbed a can of air freshener. *Rose Garden,* the label said. He uncapped the can and pressed the nozzle for a full minute. After the fragrance had settled, he inhaled deeply. There was no smell of smoke, just the choking essence of a pseudogarden with way too many roses. *Perfect. Now my colleagues will just think I had to take a wicked shit.*

CHAPTER 44

HEATHER

AFTER A SLEEPLESS NIGHT, Heather struggled from bed at six o'clock. Too anxious to eat, she quickly made a cup of coffee using the hotel-issued coffeepot in her room. Opting for the paper mug rather than the ceramic one, she filled it to the brim. She left the coffee black—there was no creamer or Sweet'N Low. Besides, this cup of coffee didn't have to taste good—it just had to wake her up.

She raced downstairs and through the lobby toward the computer kiosks. Clicking past a series of colorful ads with Chinese characters, she found her way to her e-mail account. She balanced her coffee cup on the kiosk's ledge and logged on. Among the dozens of e-mails were replies from Miguel and Carol Chung. She clicked first on the e-mail from Miss Chung, expecting it would be the one most likely to explain what was happening. She held her breath and prayed silently as Carol's e-mail opened.

Dear Miss Morrison, she read. *I am sorry that you have met with delays at the Civil Affairs Bureau in Beijing. I will be honest with you. Your rush to go to China on your own to adopt Hung Wang Lin early raised the suspicions of some senior managers at the Hope for Children Adoption Agency. These suspicions have led them to want to do a more thorough investigation of your background before you will be permitted to have Lin's birth certificate certified. Knowing you and what I perceive as your suitability as an adoptive parent, I expect this additional investigation will go smoothly and quickly. At most, I expect you will be able to finalize the adoption within two or three days unless, of course, something unsavory is uncovered. I do not expect this at all in your case. E-mail me again if you have further questions. Sincerely, Carol Chung.*

Shit! Heather chastised herself. *Maybe if I'd left well enough alone and gone to China with the group, the agency never would have done a more thorough investigation. They probably never would have found out about my lawsuit against Jeff. Now they'll uncover it! What if they decide I'm an unfit parent?* She took another gulp of coffee, remembering again the lemony scent of Lin's hair and the baby skin that felt like rose petals.

There were two e-mails from Miguel. She clicked open the first one that he had written from his home account first thing the morning after she wrote him. *Hi, Sweetie,* he'd written. *Oh, poor you, alone in a big scary place, and now things aren't going smoothly! I wish I was there to help you! You know, if you'd given me any notice at all, I'd have gone with you. Try not to worry! I'm sure it's all bureaucratic bullshit. It'll probably all be resolved by the time you read this. Lin will be your baby girl forever in just a little while longer. Love, Miguel.*

She scrolled up, and noticed a second e-mail from Miguel. *Get the baby and get out!* the subject line screamed. This e-mail had been written two hours later from his office account. Praying that her friend was just being his melodramatic self, she opened his message.

Heather, I don't know what is holding things up in Beijing, but I'm afraid it could be related to an article that appeared in this morning's Post. *I don't know how this reporter could have gotten this information and how she tracked down her sources. I am praying that the adoption agency doesn't find out about this article.*

I'm going to put a link to the story here. Please try to maintain your cool. Remember, it's the Post—*it looks worse than it is.* He'd placed the link as promised. *Love you, Miguel.*

Sweat poured from Heather's entire body as she clicked on the link Miguel had provided. It seemed to take forever before the Internet settled on an image of page one of *The New York Post.* Heather hyperventilated as she read the headline: *Lung Doc Charged with Playing Doctor with Patient.*

As unobtrusively as possible, she pressed one nostril closed with a single finger, a trick she'd learned for coping with hyperventilation, and read on. *A thirty-eight-year-old asthma patient has filed charges of sexual misconduct against Jeffrey Davis, M.D., forty, a partner in the prestigious medical firm, Upper East Side Pulmonologists. The charges, made by Heather Morrison, until recently a corporate travel agent at the law firm of Peters & Andrews, also include failure to refer, improper prescribing practices, and poor record-keeping.*

Holy shit! How did the reporter get hold of this information? Heather placed her now empty coffee mug over her mouth, breathing in and out within the hollow space, hoping it would work the same way that breathing into a paper bag did to control hyperventilation. She read on. *Morrison is represented by William M. DelFlorio, a well known and hard-hitting personal injury attorney with a roster of celebrity clients and a history of winning cases. DelFlorio made only one statement to the press, saying that the* Post's *questions were premature. "If such a case has been filed—and I'm not saying whether or not it has—the case would be in its infancy," he said. "According to the filing time line the reporter provided, a defendant, if there is one, would not even have been served at this juncture."*

And then she remembered DelFlorio's words— *you would need a sharp reporter who is hell-bent on cracking a story like this to bring it into the public eye.* Could this reporter—this Dina Cavali—be what he was talking about?

*   *   *

Heather knew she had no choice but to head back to the Civil Affairs Bureau, pretending she had never seen the article in the *Post* and hoping against hope that they hadn't either. She crossed the lobby of the hotel on shaking legs, taking her place in the taxi queue. She had her purse, but there was no time to return to her room for her coat. Even seconds could make a difference now.

A bellman tipped his hat as a cab pulled up to the curbside. "Where are you going, Miss?" he asked.

"Civil Affairs Bureau," she said.

The bellman said something to the driver in Chinese. "You come back here after?" he asked. Heather nodded. The bellman pulled one of the hotel's business cards, printed in English, from the pocket of his coat. On the back of the card, he wrote some Chinese characters. "You give this to taxi driver," he said. "And do not take black car— only taxi!"

"Thank you," she said, placing twenty Chinese yuan in his hand.

*   *   *

Heather raced through the lobby of the Civil Affairs Bureau, heading directly for the grated window with the *Adoption* sign. She asked for Miss Wu as she had the day before, and again the receptionist, Lillian Chow Din, let Heather into the office by clicking open a series of locks.

"I am early," Heather said apologetically.

"Is OK," Lillian said.

Heather followed her through the labyrinth that led to Miss Wu's office. After an exchange of words in Chinese, Lillian motioned for Heather to come into Miss Wu's office. To Heather's surprise, the room was filled with four people in addition to Miss Wu.

"I am early," Heather apologized to Miss Wu. "I will come back when you finish with these people."

"No, come in," Miss Wu said, gesturing from behind her desk. "These people—they are here for you."

"For me?"

"To examine your case," Miss Wu continued.

Oh, shit. Eight o'clock in the morning and I have a team of five personnel looking into my case! I'll never be able to bring Lin home. Not ever!

"With more people, maybe we can fix your problem quickly," Miss Wu explained. "Then you and Hung Wang Lin can go to U.S. soon, as you planned."

"Oh," Heather said, sinking gratefully into the chair opposite Miss Wu. *They're here to help me?* "Thank you very much."

"Let me explain," Miss Wu continued. "When we received word from Miss Chung at our New York office that you want to come early for Lin, we become...suspicious. We do not understand why you do not wait to come to China with the group. So we feel we must investigate your background a little bit more. We must look out for our children."

It was exactly what Carol Chung's e-mail had said.

Miss Wu said, "We are all finished here except for one thing. Everything is OK. We find nothing wrong in your background. Something's a little bit fishy, but everybody has some fishy stuff if you look hard enough."

Is this fishy stuff the lawsuit? Could they possibly have found out about it and overlooked it? Or maybe they still didn't know about it.

Just then, Heather heard Carol Chung's voice on the speaker phone, but she couldn't understand her because she was speaking in Chinese. As Carol spoke, the others responded. Some of them stepped aside and spoke excitedly to each other in Chinese.

What the hell are they saying?

Finally, Miss Wu put Carol on hold. "There is some even newer information," Miss Wu said. "Miss Chung wants to send it to us by e-mail but her Internet connection is down."

It's got to be the article from the Post. *God, if I can only get out of here with Lin before Carol's Internet starts working! It's after seven at night in New York. Maybe she'll give up and go home. Maybe I can get Lin today!*

One of the men spoke to the group in Chinese. A woman ran into a room beside Miss Wu's office. A series of beeps emitted from the room before the woman raced out, making some sort of announcement in Chinese.

Miss Wu took Carol Chung off hold and lifted the telephone receiver to her ear. "Our fax is working, Miss Chung," she said in English, perhaps for Heather's benefit. "Can you send the information to us by fax?"

It took an eternity for the fax to go through. After a series of false alarms when the fax emitted its piercing sound and then broke off, the sound came again. This time the fax chugged along, transmitting whatever it was that Carol Chung was sending to Beijing in mere minutes from oceans away.

When the first page came in, the assistant rushed to Miss Wu with it. She mumbled something in Chinese and handed the shiny fax paper to Miss Wu at an angle that allowed no one else to see it. The assistant hurried back to the side room as Heather heard a second page being sliced from the fax machine. She returned, page in hand. By then, Miss Wu had read the first page and passed it on to one of her colleagues for review. Miss Wu glanced at the second page and passed it to another colleague. A series of *oohs* and *aahs* filled the room, their meaning clear in any language.

After Miss Wu read the third and final page, she shook her head as if in disbelief. "Miss Chung. She wants to speak to you," she managed to say, clutching her throat. She released the hold button and handed the receiver to Heather.

"Hello, Miss Chung," Heather said.

"Heather, I have sent an article to the team by fax. The article appeared in the Wednesday edition of the *Post*. Our intensified investigation did not uncover the filing of this lawsuit. The article just happened to appear as we were about to finalize the adoption. I'm sure you understand that, under the circumstances, we cannot allow you to adopt Lin. In fact, had we known anything about this earlier…"

"Yes, I understand," Heather said, returning the phone to its cradle on Miss Wu's desk.

"She no want to speak more to us?" Miss Wu asked.

"No, the conversation was over." Heather stood, turned, and headed to the door. *I've heard it from Carol. I can't stand to hear it again from them.* "Good-bye."

*   *   *

She fought her way back through the labyrinth of corridors like a blind woman in a corn maze until she saw the large door marked *Exit*. She raced outside, blinking tears from her eyes. A Volkswagen Jetta with a red *For Hire* sign was approaching. She stepped off the curb and waved furiously, praying that she was entering a legitimate taxi, not one of the illegal black cars that the bellhop had warned her trolled the streets of Beijing.

Inside the cab, Heather handed the driver the business card from the Hua Fu International Hotel that showed the hotel's address in Chinese and English. She reached deeper into her purse, clutching the rosary inside, and prayed that something would change, that the events of the morning had been a bad dream. But in her heart, she knew better. Her fingers grazed the pack of Parliaments inside her purse. Raising the cigarette pack so the driver could see it in his rearview mirror, she asked, "Can I smoke?"

"OK," he said. "Is OK."

Heather lit up a cigarette and brought it to her lips with a shaking hand. Exhaling a rush of smoke, she wondered, *Can you actually feel your heart breaking?*

Chapter 45

Jeff

JEFF NEEDED ANOTHER CIGARETTE. Was there no public place left in the fucking city where he could smoke a cigarette indoors? He wasn't going to repeat his earlier performance of exhaling smoke into the staff toilet. What could he do? Sit on a park bench alone and smoke like a vagrant with nowhere to go?

He didn't know which of his options was worse: trying to get through his schedule, or going home to face the music with Priscilla. There was no way he could fake his way through another session with a patient. His behavior with Clara Dixon had been about as unprofessional as he cared to get. He pressed the intercom and told Barbara, "Cancel all my appointments. I'm feeling very sick."

"Did you want to sign that letter to…" Barbara began.

"It can wait," Jeff said and hung up the phone.

\ e next call he made was to Mike Dommer. He got voice mail.

 a place to crash for the afternoon—to figure out what I'm

 Can I hang out at your place for a few hours? Call me

 me know how I can get a key from you."

 's phone on vibrate, he slipped it into the front pocket

 printed a copy of the website version of the article

 ng it in his briefcase. He put on his coat, cracked

 or, and walked softly and quickly down the vacant

 ut the back exit, he closed the automatically locking

 d took the service elevator to the main floor.

He was lighting a cigarette before he made it through the revolving door from the lobby.

*   *   *

Jeff walked down Avenue A toward St. Mark's Place. People were exercising their pets in a dog run in Tompkins Square Park. The last time he'd been in the East Village, the park had been a haven for heroin addicts and homeless people.

His hands shoved into the pockets of his overcoat, Jeff turned right on St. Mark's Place. With his left hand, he fingered Dommer's key like a worry stone as he scanned the street for Mike's building. His friend had been sympathetic as he'd slipped Jeff his spare key in the lobby at Bellevue, telling him he was welcome to stay as long as he liked. Jeff had assured him he needed only a few hours in an indoor space where he could think and smoke.

Dommer's building was a four-story brownstone with a façade that had been restored to its original glory. Jeff entered the code Mike had given him and walked up the single flight of stairs to the second floor apartment. He entered a classic bachelor pad, nicely furnished in neutral male tones with leather furnishings and an empty refrigerator—no sign of a woman in sight. *I may have to get used to this. I'll be living like this if I lose my job and my wife.*

*   *   *

Jeff spent the afternoon researching cases of medical sexual misconduct on the Internet and chain-smoking. Calls to his cell came in continuously—nearly all of them displayed his office number on caller ID. He neither answered the calls nor returned them. He didn't even listen to the voice mails.

After doing all the online research on Dommer's computer he could do for the moment to prepare for the upcoming medical board hearing and the lawsuit, Jeff channel surfed through daytime TV. An Al Pacino movie caught his interest for a while. When the film ended, he flipped through the pages of Dommer's stack of *Penthouses*. Finally, at seven o'clock, he flipped to New York One for a look at the local news.

The *Post* story had caught on like wildfire. During the second feature of the evening news, a female reporter appeared, standing outside the glass doorway of Jeff's office suite. "This is Alicia Petty reporting. I'm standing outside the office of Dr. Jeffrey Davis, one of New York's most highly regarded pulmonologists. Davis, who is on staff at Lenox Hill Hospital, has been charged by a former patient, thirty-eight-year-old Heather Morrison, with sexual misconduct." The camera panned to some stock tape of scenes around the hospital that Jeff recognized from a video the public relations department had done last year.

The reporter continued, "Morrison's civil complaint claims that Dr. Davis coerced her into a sexual relationship that started last June. According to the complaint, Dr. Davis used his influence as Morrison's physician to lead her into an affair that caused her severe emotional trauma. Morrison has also filed a complaint with the Office of Professional Medical Conduct, the agency that investigates complaints about physicians on behalf of the New York State Department of Health. She is currently out of the country and unavailable to speak with us."

The camera panned back to the sexy young reporter. Jeff felt a tug in his groin. "In an interesting twist, Davis's father-in-law, Dr. Preston Wellington, is chief of staff at Lenox Hill. Unfortunately, *New York One* has been unable to reach Dr. Davis at his home, at Lenox Hill, or here at his East 79th Street office. According to colleagues here, Dr. Davis left his office early this afternoon, claiming he was ill. He has not been seen or heard from since and hasn't responded to efforts made by his office to reach him. There is growing concern on the part of his colleagues about the doctor's well-being. Reporting from Upper East Side Pulmonologists, I'm Alicia Petty, *New York One News*."

Holy shit. This story is spreading like a cancer. Maybe my colleagues should *be concerned about my well-being.* Jeff turned off the TV and forced himself to get up from Dommer's plush leather sofa. The cereal bowl he'd been using as an ashtray was filled to overflowing. He flushed the contents down the toilet, rinsed the cereal bowl, and put it in Dommer's dishwasher along with a single plate, a glass, and a few pieces of silverware that were already inside.

Having run out of stalling tactics, Jeff opened his cell phone and said "Call home." Priscilla answered on the second ring. To his amazement, she sounded the same as she did each night when he called to say he was on his way home.

He left Dommer's spare key on the kitchen table, checked that the door was locked behind him, and headed for home feeling like a man en route to his execution.

* * *

Jeff found Priscilla in the library settled on the chaise, a tumbler of vodka on ice on the table beside her. Passing the television, he touched it lightly. It was warm.

Bending toward her, Jeff gave Priscilla the perfunctory kiss on the cheek he gave her every evening. She returned it in her usual way, lifting her elegant chin upwards and forming her lips in the shape of a kiss that touched only the air.

"Have you watched any television today?" he asked, settling on the sofa.

"That's an odd question," she replied, raising her cocktail to her mouth.

"It may seem odd, but I'm going somewhere with this." Jeff squirmed visibly. "Have you?"

After taking another gulp of vodka, Priscilla returned the tumbler to the table. "No. Of course not. You know I seldom watch television. *Especially* during the day."

Jeff took a handkerchief from his pocket and blotted his visibly sweating forehead. "Have you read the paper?"

Priscilla smoothed her hands over the tailored herringbone slacks that draped her thighs. "I read the *Times*. Just like I do every morning."

He struggled to light a cigarette with shaking hands. He cleared his throat. "There's something I need to talk with you about."

"Is there?"

"You remember accusing me of having someone else in my life when you got the bill from Tiffany's with the charge for two pearl necklaces?"

"Of course."

"What I told you then—about buying two necklaces for you for Christmas because I didn't know if you'd prefer the white pearl or the black—was true," Jeff said, searching for his story as he spoke. "And I still haven't gotten around to returning the second necklace. But I should have used that conversation as an opportunity to tell you that one of my patients—a real nut job—was making a play for me." He struggled for breath like the sickest of his patients.

"How unusual," she said sarcastically. A patient developing a crush on her doctor!"

God, she was making this impossible! Jeff was almost certain she knew everything—that she'd seen the story in the *Post* and on *New York One* and God knows where else. It would be just like Priscilla to know all but toy with him, putting him through the torment of confessing.

Jeff leaned toward his wife, but she made no gesture to move closer to him. "This woman who was interested in me—unfortunately, she's turned out to be rather…unstable."

Jeff recalled Priscilla's father's dalliances with patients. They were legendary. Although his affairs had brought on Preston's divorce from Priscilla's mother, they had never interfered with his career. Preston's heyday had been during the seventies and eighties. It hadn't been until 1989 that the American Medical Association had officially condemned sexual involvement between physicians and their patients.

Priscilla asked, "This patient—what did she do?"

"I never encouraged her, but she kept coming on to me. I hope you know that I would never do anything to put our marriage at risk, that…"

"Why are we talking about this?" Priscilla asked.

Jeff closed his eyes and spat out the words. "Because she went to the press. And the OPMC. *And* she filed a lawsuit. Clearly, she's spiting me for refusing to get involved with her. The story started in this morning's edition of the *Post*. By now, it's all over the media."

Priscilla reached toward the end table beside her and opened its single narrow drawer. Removing a folded newspaper, she opened it and asked, "Are you talking about this?"

Damn her! Damn her for putting me through the torture of confessing. I could tell she already knew the minute I told her we needed to talk.

"Since when did you start reading the *Post*?" Jeff demanded.

Priscilla didn't take the bait. She didn't want to fight. She *never* wanted to fight. "Since my father called this morning and told me my husband and his mistress were the subject of their page-one story."

Jeff leaned back against the sofa and nodded his head. His wife was really something. No doubt, she must have wanted to kill him. And yet, she sat stoically, reaching for her vodka with a steady hand.

"It's all a lie." Jeff rose to his feet and asked sharply, "Why did you tell me you hadn't read the paper today? Or watched any television?"

"Jeffrey," she said, "surely you're not comparing what you've done with my lying to you about having read all about it in the newspaper."

"I haven't *done* anything," he insisted. He returned to the couch, struggling to come up with his next move. "Priscilla," he begged, "please say you'll believe me. If not now, someday."

She swirled the nearly empty glass in her hand. "The fact is, Jeffrey, I've been expecting this for years."

"*Expecting this?*"

Priscilla sighed. "I was a psych major, remember? Do you really think I don't know enough about you to realize I married a younger version of my father?"

"What are you going to do?"

"We'll deal with it," she said matter-of-factly, as if they were talking about a child getting a failing grade in school. She stood up and headed toward the French doors. She turned back toward Jeff and said, "I've had dinner already. And Delia has made up the guestroom for you."

There was no point in arguing. Besides, the thought of sleeping without Priscilla was appealing. He wouldn't sleep a wink if she was lying beside him.

Chapter 46

Heather

THE FLIGHT BACK FROM BEIJING had been dismal. The cost to change her itinerary had been so high that tossing in another five hundred dollars for a direct flight seemed like pocket change. Heather just wanted to get home.

Despite steady doses of Valium and Ambien, Heather felt that she hadn't slept for a moment of the twenty-three-hour flight. She dragged her suitcase from the customs area, praying she could find a taxi quickly at this ungodly hour—a few minutes before midnight on a Sunday. The flight attendant had said the temperature in New York was sixteen degrees with a wind chill factor of five below zero.

As Heather headed for the exit sign, she heard a male voice call her name. Then a female called. And another man.

No, it can't be, she thought, turning her head in the direction from which the voices had come. But it had been. Trista, Miguel, and Jackson were huddled together behind the roped-off passengers-only area. Heather hurried around the ropes and landed solidly in Miguel's embrace. She felt Trista hug her from the side as Jackson placed a consoling hand on her shoulder. Together the four of them cried like the world had come to an end.

* * *

She made the appointment on Monday, the day after she got home from China.

"What is it you'd like to donate to the Salvation Army?" the male telephone representative had asked.

"A nursery set," Heather had said, fighting back tears. "A crib, dresser, changing table, and rocking chair. In white enamel. Oh, and a high chair. A walnut high chair."

"What is the condition of the nursery set?" he asked.

"It's brand-new," she said.

"Brand-new?" the man said, sounding surprised. "Never been used?"

"I *said* it was brand-new." She'd felt herself losing control and heard her voice screaming into the receiver. "Brand-new means it's never been used. It was for a baby who never made it home."

"I'm very sorry, ma'am," the flustered phone representative said. "We'll send our driver over to pick it up at your convenience. Do you need weekend pickup, ma'am?"

"No. I don't have a baby, and I don't have a job." There was silence at the other end of the line. The poor guy probably had no idea what to say. "I'd like it picked up as soon as possible."

"How's tomorrow afternoon?" he said. "Tuesday?"

Heather wanted to get the set out of the condo immediately. The empty crib was a constant reminder of the devastating loss of Lin. "Tomorrow afternoon is fine," she said.

*   *   *

A combination of jet lag, medication, and sheer misery made getting out of bed on Tuesday close to impossible. And it was freezing. At noon, Heather finally roused herself. She wrapped herself in a warm fleece bathrobe and looked outside. It had snowed—maybe half a foot. Snow still covered the small patches of grass in front of the brownstones on West 79th Street. The combination of the traffic and the noon sun had left the streets slushy but otherwise clear.

*   *   *

Now, as she waited, Heather walked down the hall to take one last look at the furnished nursery. The walls were still half painted in the bright shade of yellow that had put her in Mount Sinai. The glossy white furnishings, although tiny, filled most of the room. Soon the room would be empty. Maybe she'd turn it into a den where she could do computer work—a room where she could search for a job and figure out what she was going to do with the rest of her life.

Her severance package had been generous. Peters & Andrews had given her three weeks' pay for each of her twelve years with the firm. They'd agreed to continue to pay her medical insurance premiums for the next six months—for herself *and* her child, even though she'd only had single coverage before. Of course, she wouldn't need that now.

I've lived here for less than a year, and already this place has too many memories. She thought about moving, but it was such an expense. Maybe she could rent the place and move to Paris for a year or so. It was a dream she'd had for a long time, before it was replaced by the dream of becoming a mother. But what she had to do right now was prepare herself to watch a Salvation Army team remove Lin's things from a room that would never be hers in a world she would never share with Heather, the woman who would have been her mother.

*   *   *

When it was over, Heather called China Gold and ordered shrimp with snow peas and an eggroll. When the delivery man dropped off her food, she carried the carton to the living room and pressed the mute button on the television. Grabbing a spoon from the kitchen, she called Trista as she shoveled the food directly from the carton into her mouth.

"I need to find a way to get my prescriptions now that Jeff's knocked me off his patient list," she said.

"Right," Trista said. "Obviously, you can't get drugs from him if you're suing him."

"Do you know anybody?"

"Yes!" Trista said. "A friend told me about a doctor—Dr. Peter McGuire, I think. She says he gives her free samples and prescriptions for anything she asks for."

"But he's not a pulmonologist, is he?" Heather asked.

"No, he's a general practitioner. But I'm sure he can treat you for your asthma," Trista said. "As long as you don't go painting yourself into a corner again, all you need is some medication."

"What's this doctor's address?" Heather asked.

"He's on Bleecker Street."

"Do you know his phone number?"

"I will in a minute," Trista said.

Heather could hear the beeps from her friend's cell phone. A moment later, Trista said, "212-555-2342. The address is 114 Bleecker."

"Thanks," Heather said. "Thanks for everything. I'll call him tomorrow."

*   *   *

As Heather juggled her cigarette and her phone to access her mother's number, a hot ash dropped on her fleece robe, leaving a classic smoker's burn. "Shit!" she said, brushing the ash away. Continuing to scroll, she pressed *Mom*. Margaret answered.

"Hey, Mom. Sorry I haven't called you since I got back from China."

Margaret's response wasn't what Heather expected.

"I can't talk with you until I recover from this," her mother said in a hoarse, angry voice. "I saw that ugly article in the *Post*! Everyone I know has read that my daughter had an affair with her married doctor," she said. "An affair so ugly that she can't adopt a child. Not even a child from *China*!"

CHAPTER 47

HEATHER

IT WAS AFTER ELEVEN the next morning when Heather dragged herself from bed. She poured a bowl of cereal, brought it to the coffee table, and clicked on "The View." She noticed a scrap of newspaper on the table. *Dr. Peter McGuire, 1:30 p.m.* was scribbled in her handwriting. *Who is that? Oh! The doctor Trista told me about!* Heather could barely remember having made the appointment.

* * *

A few hours later, Heather entered Dr. McGuire's Bleecker Street office. The receptionist blew a pink bubble as she handed Heather a plastic clipboard missing its clip and a pen marked with teeth marks and the words *Learn more about once-monthly Boniva.* Heather settled into a molded plastic chair to fill out the medical history form.

Only one other patient, a paraplegic in a wheelchair, and a woman who appeared to be his caretaker occupied the waiting room. Heather was called into the exam room first. Like the reception area, the exam room was old and dilapidated with furnishings and equipment that looked like they had been there for decades. The doctor was also old and disheveled, probably at least sixty, with smudged bifocal glasses. He smelled of mothballs.

Dr. McGuire performed a perfunctory exam, told Heather she was the "picture of health," then leaned on a chipped Formica counter and pulled out his prescription pad. Heather rattled off the six medications she needed, including the dosages. Dr. McGuire asked no questions, writing the prescriptions just as she recited them.

* * *

She rode the subway back uptown, wondering where all the people riding the underground rails in the middle of the afternoon were coming from and going to. Were they out of work like her? How many, also like her, were making desperate trips to doctors—or other drug providers—in a race against time? She clutched her purse tightly when the car she was in emptied of passengers at 42nd Street, leaving behind only a derelict who had been spouting euphemisms about Jesus since she'd gotten on the train.

Exiting at West 79th Street, she went directly to her pharmacy and deposited the six prescriptions on the counter. Painkillers, sleeping pills, antidepressants, tranquilizers, and two asthma medications.

Back in her empty condo, she remembered she'd turned off her cell phone in preparation for her visit with the doctor. She felt a jolt of anticipation as she turned it back on. Nothing. She went into the kitchen and found a bottle of water. Then lining up her prescriptions on the coffee table, she took them one by one. She lay back on the couch, adjusted the pillows behind her head, and clicked on the television.

When she opened her eyes, the room was dark and the news was on. *Probably the six o'clock news.* Then as the reality of the dark night and the light from outside spilling through her windows registered, she jolted to a seated position. *Holy shit, this is the eleven o'clock news!*

She reached for a table lamp and grabbed her phone. No messages. She scrolled down to Jeff's number. Despite all that had happened, she hadn't been able to bring herself to delete it. Just for an added dose of self-torture, she pressed send. For the hundredth time, she listened to the recording. *You have reached a nonworking number at Verizon Wireless...* She clicked it off, brushed the tears from her eyes, and switched the channel to Letterman, the only man she could find to spend her lonely night with.

CHAPTER 48

JEFF

THE E-MAIL LANDED IN JEFF'S INBOX at four thirty Wednesday afternoon. *Mandatory Meeting for All Members of the Practice,* the subject line read. It was from Harvey Middleton, the senior member of Upper East Side Pulmonologists.

Jeff was amazed it had taken Harvey this long—a full week—to issue the mandate. No one had said a word to him about his disappearance from work last week, about *New York One* showing up at the office, or even about the article in the *Post.* In fact, no one had said much of anything to him for the past week.

He clicked open the e-mail and read: *All members of the practice are requested to attend a meeting at 6:00 p.m. tonight in the conference room. The purpose of this meeting is to address the management of recent negative publicity that could seriously impact the outstanding reputation of our practice. Chet Bingham, our attorney from East Coast Medical Insurers, will be joining us at the meeting.*

Each of the five additional doctors on staff was copied on Harvey's e-mail.

Jeff leaned back in his executive chair and rubbed his eyes. *Jesus Christ, why didn't Harvey sit down with me one-on-one about this? Why is he dragging the entire practice into the process?*

* * *

When Jeff arrived at the conference room at three minutes after six, all of his colleagues were already huddled around the conference table. A hush fell as he appeared in the doorway. *Perfect. They're all talking about me already.* Also present was Chet Bingham and Dr. Middleton's assistant, Mary. The only remaining seat was at the end of the table next to Chet Bingham with Harvey Middleton at the head. Jeff was sure that was no accident.

Dr. Middleton started speaking as soon as Jeff sat down. "Dr. Davis, we're here because we are all a part of this practice. What affects the professional reputation of one of us has the potential to affect all of us. Given that, we cannot ignore the allegations that your patient, Heather Morrison, has made against you. More significantly, we can't ignore the publicity that has resulted from those allegations. Last week our office was flooded with reporters. We can't conduct a medical practice under such circumstances."

"Doctors," Jeff said, looking from one to the other in the group. "Heather Morrison is a mentally unstable woman. I won't deny that I was aware that she was attracted to me. She made it obvious. But as a married man and Heather's medical doctor, I did nothing to encourage her interest. In fact, I made it clear that I wasn't open to a relationship with her. And that's exactly why she served me with papers and why we're sitting here tonight instead of heading home for dinner with our families."

The group around the table nodded in agreement. Some checked their watches.

"We've all heard the expression *Hell hath no fury like a woman scorned*," Jeff continued. Heads bobbed again in agreement—even those of the two female doctors in the practice. "And when the scorned woman is as emotionally unstable as Heather Morrison, anything can happen." As his partners murmured amongst themselves, perhaps recalling some of their own mentally unstable patients, Jeff added a little fuel to the fire. "Frankly, I'm concerned for my family's well-being."

Chet Bingham chimed in. "Denial of the charges is the most common response to charges of professional sexual misconduct. Dr. Davis, are you prepared to swear under oath that you had no relationship other than your doctor-patient relationship with Ms. Morrison?"

"Absolutely," Jeff said.

* * *

Even though he'd denied everything to Priscilla, he wasn't convinced that she believed him. Jeff needed to keep her on his side. He wasn't going to let Heather force him into confessing to Priscilla. Her suspicions alone were eroding their marriage. And there was no way Jeff would sit in this room filled with his colleagues and admit to screwing a patient.

He thought of other powerful New York women who could have ditched their cheating husbands and done fine on their own. Hillary Clinton, wife of Slick Willie. Silda Wall Spitzer, the ex-governor's wife. Jeff expected Priscilla would stand by him as well—at least in public. But he needed to ensure she never found out that Heather hadn't been the only one.

"When will the informal settlement conference be held?" Dr. Middleton asked.

"The informal settlement conference is scheduled for Wednesday, March 24, 2011" Chet said. "As for the civil trial, I have no idea when, or if, that will commence."

"Have papers been served?" Dr. Middleton asked.

"They have," Jeff replied. "As long as we're all here, you may as well see this." Jeff produced the summons and complaint from a manila folder he'd placed on the conference table. Coincidentally, they had been delivered that morning. He handed it to Dr. Middleton.

Harvey Middleton leaned toward his assistant. "Mary, please make copies right away."

"Yes, Doctor," Mary said.

* * *

After another half hour in the conference room, everyone left except Harvey Middleton, Chet Bingham, and Jeff. The three talked about their strategy for upholding the reputation of the practice while Jeff was going through the medical board hearing and a possible civil trial. Chet offered to bring in a public relations consultant to coach the doctors in responding to any media inquiries. "Chet will represent you in front of the medical board," Harvey explained. "But you'll need to have a litigator from Stewart, Greenberg, Sully and Connelly represent you in the civil case." He indicated his copy of the summons and complaint.

*　*　*

It was close to eight o'clock when Chet Bingham left. Alone in the conference room, Jeff turned to Dr. Middleton and asked, "Harvey, why did you call that meeting? It was humiliating to have everyone in the practice here."

"I expect that it was," Harvey conceded. "But the other doctors all seemed to know about it anyway. Besides, let's face it, what you've done will affect the career of every member of this practice."

"What I've been *accused* of doing. Innocent until proven guilty, boss. If it's good enough for our legal system, it should be good enough for the practice," Jeff said.

"Duly noted," Harvey nodded. "But one reason I included everyone in this meeting is that you failed to advise me when you were served with papers from the OPMC. I shouldn't have been forced to learn from the media about a serious threat to the reputation of the practice I built from nothing."

Jeff curled the legal papers in his hand into a cylindrical shape. "I understand that, Harvey. I understand because I shouldn't have learned I was being *sued* by reading about it in the paper." He tapped the summons and complaint against the palm of his hand. He breathed a sigh of relief that Barbara had signed for the complaint. All Jeff would have needed was a process server in the waiting area demanding to see him.

"Then how did the article get into the newspaper?" Harvey asked.

"If I knew that," Jeff said, "I might not be in this mess in the first place."

CHAPTER 49

HEATHER

DESPITE THE DISMAL GREY February weather, Heather walked to her Saturday morning appointment at Dr. Rosner's office. The walk turned out to be just what she needed—with one exception. She had the nagging feeling that she was being followed. At the corner of 88th and Broadway, she noticed a tall red-haired woman wearing a black trench coat walking half a block behind her. The woman stopped when Heather turned, then stepped over to a storefront window as if looking inside.

When Heather reached Dr. Rosner's brownstone, she glanced back down the street. The red-haired woman was standing on the corner of Broadway and 93rd, looking in her direction. Heather's skin grew clammy. But moments later, as Dr. Rosner greeted her with a warm hug, she felt safe and comfortable again.

"I guess you know what happened," Heather said as she settled herself on Dr. Rosner's yellow couch. "You must have seen the story in the *Post*."

"Yes," Dr. Rosner said. "I'm so sorry."

Heather touched the locket that still hung around her neck. She closed her eyes. As she recounted the story from beginning to end, the doctor listened intently.

In what seemed like minutes, Heather heard the doctor's timer let out a double chime. The session was over so fast! During the hour, they had focused on where Heather would go from here in her quest to have a family. "I doubt I can apply to adopt again with this lawsuit in my history," she concluded. "As for getting pregnant—I'm not sure I'll be able to trust a man enough to have sex ever again."

"Time will soften those feelings," the doctor promised. "Time is your friend."

Heather wondered if she should mention her suspicion that she was being followed. No, it would probably just make her look paranoid in the eyes of a psychiatrist. *If I see that woman again, I'll tell Dr. Rosner about it.*

"Here is something I want you to read," Dr. Rosner said, handing Heather a document printed on white letter-sized paper. *Sex with Your Health Care Provider is a Violation of Trust,* it was headed. "This was written by a colleague of mine. Dr. Ginsberg was concerned about unethical doctors who lure their innocent patients into sexual activity. His greatest concern was that the patients rarely, if ever, know that such conduct is unethical and even illegal. He wanted patients to know that there is no such thing as consensual sex between doctors and their patients."

"OK. Thanks." Heather folded the document in half, pressing a sharp seam into it with her fingers, and put it in her purse.

* * *

Heather frowned at the thought of going home to her empty condo. Walking down upper Broadway, she spotted a luncheonette and stepped inside. Sliding onto a counter stool, she ordered coffee and buttered whole wheat toast. She took the document Dr. Rosner had given her from her purse.

Both doctors and patients have justified sexual relations with each other by stating the acts were consensual, the article began. It went on to acknowledge that many doctors are married to former patients, and that other "thriving" relationships could develop from the doctor-patient association. The issue, it said, had to do with whether the patient's involvement in the relationship was truly *informed.*

Heather read on. *Sexual activity with your health care professional often results in the patient becoming isolated. The provider may not be in a monogamous relationship with the patient. And the provider is likely to suddenly terminate the relationship.*

This is me! Heather thought. *This is what happened to me!* She continued to read. *Often patients who become involved with their health care providers do so at the expense of abandoning moral values which they previously held with conviction. Such a shift in values may be based on an exemplary attraction called transference. Transference can cause a patient to see the provider as a powerful and trustworthy parental figure...*

The waitress placed Heather's coffee on the counter with a clatter. Next came the plate. "Whole wheat toast wit budda," she announced in Brooklynese, as if Heather had forgotten what she'd ordered.

"Thanks," Heather said, reaching for the Sweet'N Low. She hurriedly prepared her coffee and took a bite of the toast, anxious to return to her reading.

A sexual relationship with one's health care provider may ultimately result in such damaging consequences as feelings of betrayal, loneliness, confusion, helplessness, anger, confusion, guilt, and depression...

Oh, my God, she thought. *I could have written this!* She returned her coffee cup to the saucer with a clatter. "Oh, sorry," she said to no one in particular. She sat stunned, slumped against the counter. *Virtually everything I'm reading mimics what happened to me. If only I'd known.*

That was Dr. Ginsberg's point. Only if patients knew what they were getting into when a doctor came on to them—only if they were truly able to give informed consent—could they make an informed decision.

She wiped the butter from her fingers and returned to the document, reviewing the parts that most applied to her. The waitress returned and placed the check on the counter. Her thumbprint was clearly outlined in strawberry jam. "Five dollas and tirty cents," she said.

Heather slipped her coat on and dug through her purse. She left a five, a single, and a quarter.

As she stepped outside, someone was entering a bank across the street. She couldn't be sure, but she would have bet money that it was the woman she'd thought was following her earlier.

CHAPTER 50

HEATHER

DELFLORIO CALLED HEATHER FROM HIS CELL PHONE as his limo was approaching her building. "We're just pulling up," he said when Heather answered the phone.

"I'll be right down," she replied, staggering into her most conservative pair of black leather pumps. It was barely seven o'clock, and even with three Ambien, she'd been up half the night. There had been no way she could sleep knowing she'd be face-to-face with Jeff today in an OPMC hearing room.

It would take about three hours to get to Troy, a small city outside Albany where the New York State Health Department's Office of Professional Medical Conduct had its offices. The informal settlement conference was scheduled to begin at ten thirty. Heather's statement was the first item on the agenda. DelFlorio was accompanying her, not as her attorney, but as an advocate for victims of professional abuse. After Heather gave her statement, she would leave, and a disciplinary review board that had been assigned to the case would continue their investigation with Jeff and his legal team. That would be Jeff's opportunity to tell his side of the story.

* * *

As the car traveled across the George Washington Bridge and up the New York State Thruway, DelFlorio worked his Blackberry, making calls and sending e-mails as easily as if he were in his office. Heather stared out the window, feeling the pools of sweat collecting in her armpits. She tried not to bite her nails, but her fingers kept finding their way to her mouth. She wondered for the thousandth time if Jeff had been surprised when she'd reported him to the medical board's Office of Professional Medical Conduct. And how had he reacted when he'd received the summons for the civil suit? No doubt, he hated her. Yet despite all she'd learned about how he'd wronged her through sexual misconduct, her heart still ached when she thought of his rejection of her.

She counted the cars in the right hand lane as the limo sped past them—anything to distract herself from her craving for a cigarette.

*   *   *

"Heather, we're here."

She felt an unfamiliar hand touching her upper arm. She realized she'd fallen asleep. But where? She opened her eyes. The hand touching her arm was DelFlorio's, and from the look of things, they'd arrived in Troy. The limo was at the curb in front of a government building that was a few shades darker grey than the sky above it. Upstate New York was notorious for its gloomy winter weather and springtimes that didn't start until early May.

"Oh, my God," Heather stammered. "I'm so sorry." *Great timing for the sleeping pills to finally kick in! Did I snore? Did I drool? Did I say Jeff's name?*

"No problem at all," DelFlorio said. He gathered his belongings as the driver opened the door for Heather.

She looked around as she left the car, anxious to see if Jeff had arrived. There was no sign of his black Mercedes or of another chauffeured car. Heather felt her limbs tremble at the thought of seeing him within the walls of this ominous-looking building.

*   *   *

The elevator doors opened on the third floor. Heather walked unsteadily, taking DelFlorio's arm for support. The building was old and institutional, its décor stuck in the 1960s. Her heels clicked against a grey-and-green-squared linoleum floor. At the end of a long hallway, they reached a thick oak door with a sign that read *Hearing Room One*. DelFlorio opened the door for Heather to enter. As she stepped into the room, her last ounce of confidence disappeared. Jeff and his team were already positioned at one of the three tables inside.

Heather placed the flat of her hand against the doorframe to steady herself. Behind her, DelFlorio held the palm of his hand against her back for support. He helped her remove her coat and hung it, along with his own, on a mahogany coat tree. Heather recognized Jeff's black cashmere top coat hanging on the coat tree. DelFlorio had hung her coat directly on top of Jeff's.

Jeff was flanked by a grey-haired man in his forties and a blond woman of about the same age. Heather looked at him directly, taking in every detail of his clothing and features. The suit was one she hadn't seen—a single-breasted solid charcoal design that hinted at innocence. His shirt was starched and white, his tie a solid grey. His face looked slightly drawn, and there were dark circles under his eyes and touches of grey at his temples. He kept his head down and stared at the face of his watch.

DelFlorio guided Heather to the large rectangular table that faced the one where Jeff was seated. There was at least ten feet between the tables, leaving plenty of room for a third table that was set perpendicular to the others. Each table had three chairs, arranged so that the people in the room could converse with each other.

DelFlorio had explained to Heather how the medical board review process worked. After Heather had filed her complaint, the medical board's Office of Professional Medical Conduct had notified Jeff. He'd been given thirty days to respond. After receiving Jeff's response, the board had determined whether or not to pursue a formal investigation. Once the board had decided to take this step, an investigator had been assigned to the case. The investigator had obtained Heather's medical records from Jeff's office and compiled all the evidence needed to bring the case to the informal settlement conference. The investigator's evidence was then sent to a board expert who was in the same medical field as Jeff.

The procedure included a thorough study of the medical records by the investigator to determine if there were any violations in addition to sexual misconduct. Proving sexual misconduct was difficult, DelFlorio had said, and he'd advised Heather not to mention the sex tape. He planned to use that as his ace in the hole in the civil case. Making Jeff aware that the tape existed would ruin his strategy for the civil case.

Heather sat in the middle seat with DelFlorio at her right. She began to place her purse on the empty chair but overshot the seat. The purse hit the floor with a thud. Items rolled out—a lipstick, a pen, a tampon case. Perfect. She ducked under the table to retrieve them. Returning to an upright position, she caught Jeff watching her. Was the look on his face a smirk or a grimace?

She glanced at the floor-to-ceiling shelves lined with law books, at the tall industrial windows badly in need of a washing. She looked at anything but Jeff. As she examined the room, the door opened. Two men and a woman came in and took their places at the third table. *This must be the review board. I'll have to make my statement any minute.* She twisted her hands in her lap. Her palms were damp.

A bald man with furry eyebrows addressed the room. "Good morning, ladies and gentlemen."

"Good morning," DelFlorio and the twosome flanking Jeff replied. Heather and Jeff remained mute.

"My name is Dr. Henry Waterhouse," the man said. "I am both an attorney and a medical doctor and the head of this disciplinary review board. I will be acting as the board attorney to review this case and determine what, if any, disciplinary action should result from the complaints that have been identified. My colleague, Dr. Nancy Sellers, a medical doctor, is on my left. On my right is Dr. John Peabody, a board-certified pulmonologist and our panel's expert consultant."

Heads bobbed in acknowledgement at the other two tables.

Dr. Waterhouse continued. "At the table on my left are Dr. Jeffrey Davis, the physician whose conduct is under review; Mr. Chet Bingham, an attorney for East Coast Medical Insurers; and Ms. Sally Scott, a paralegal at the same firm." He turned toward Heather. "On my right is Ms. Heather Morrison, who has filed a complaint against Dr. Davis. With her is Mr. William DelFlorio, an attorney, who has joined Ms. Morrison in the capacity of an advocate."

Dr. Waterhouse continued. "Ms. Morrison has filed a complaint against Dr. Davis for sexual misconduct, improper prescribing practices, faulty record-keeping, and failure to refer." He looked at Heather with steely grey eyes. "Would you please give us your statement regarding what happened, Ms. Morrison?"

Heather cleared her throat and tried to begin. The words wouldn't come. Except for the clock ticking on the wall, the room was as silent as a tomb.

She swallowed and tried again. "I met Dr. Davis in the emergency room at Lenox Hill Hospital in May 2010." Her voice reverberated in her ears at least an octave higher than normal, almost childlike. "I was having an asthma attack. My first." She glanced at the typewritten sheet she'd prepared. She ripped tiny tears across the top edge of the paper as she continued. "He got my asthma attack under control. Three weeks later, I saw him at his office for a follow-up visit. During that appointment, he gave me his cell phone number and told me to feel free to call him at any time."

Heather looked up from the paper, now dampened from the sweat on her hands. Jeff was shaking his head, his eyebrows raised. As she continued her statement, her voice became more powerful.

"After that first appointment, Dr. Davis invited me to have coffee with him. Our relationship quickly became physical. At the time I started seeing Dr. Davis, I knew he was married. But I had no idea that his behavior was a violation of medical ethics."

Heather heard Jeff cough, but she didn't look up. "Since that time, I have learned that for a doctor to have a physical relationship with a patient constitutes sexual misconduct. I've learned such behavior is a violation of the ethics of the medical profession. I've learned about transference and the emotional harm it can cause if the person in authority violates the trust that has been placed in him by the nature of his profession. Unfortunately, I've also experienced this emotional harm firsthand."

DelFlorio touched Heather's arm for support as she continued. "Throughout our relationship, Dr. Davis provided me with prescriptions for painkillers, sleeping pills, tranquilizers, and antidepressants. He counseled me on some emotional issues. At the time, I thought these things were done out of kindness. As a result of all I've learned, I now realize he was violating the medical code of ethics in a number of ways."

Heather switched to a second sheet of paper. "Because of the emotional turmoil I experienced following my relationship with Dr. Davis, I lost my job. I've become dependent on the medications he prescribed for me. And most important, because of the publicity that resulted from our relationship, I lost the opportunity to adopt a child. Finally, despite prescribing tranquilizers and antidepressants, Dr. Davis never referred me to a therapist. In fact, he discussed my psychological issues with me, even suggesting that sexual activity with him could be therapeutic. Getting involved with Dr. Davis was one of the worst mistakes of my life, and I request that this review board do everything possible to discipline him for these violations." As she completed her statement, she felt her body turn to rubber.

"Thank you, Ms. Morrison," Dr. Waterhouse said. "I'm sure it wasn't easy for you to make your statement."

Heather nodded. She felt DelFlorio's supportive hand on her back.

"Unfortunately, for purposes of clarification, I'm going to have to ask you a few more questions," Dr. Waterhouse said.

Heather nodded again. She looked at the door, feeling the urge to race toward it.

"Are you still seeing Dr. Davis?" Dr. Waterhouse asked.

"Of course not," Heather said. "I wouldn't be sitting here if I was still seeing him."

"So the two of you broke up?" Dr. Waterhouse tapped his fingers lightly on the table.

"Yes," Heather replied.

"Who initiated the breakup?" Dr. Waterhouse asked.

"He did."

Dr. Waterhouse's next question struck hard. "Isn't it possible that you are reacting like any scorned lover might? That you reported him to the Office of Professional Medical Conduct as a means of getting even with him for ending your relationship?"

"Absolutely not," she said.

Dr. Waterhouse looked at her again, his eyes kinder this time. "Ms. Morrison, I apologize for the nature of my questions. It's simply for clarification so that we have all the facts to enable us to render the proper decision regarding disciplining Dr. Davis."

"I understand," she said.

"Can you describe any of Dr. Davis's personal bodily features that might indicate that you've seen him undressed?" Dr. Waterhouse asked.

"I can."

"Did you ever have sexual activity in his—Dr. Davis's—office?" Dr. Waterhouse asked.

"Yes."

"One last question," Dr. Waterhouse said. "Where are you getting your medications now?"

"From another doctor."

Heather saw Jeff whisper something to his attorney.

"Is there anything else you'd like to add?"

God, no, just let me out of here! "No," Heather said. "That's all."

* * *

Heather pressed the elevator call button and didn't release her finger until the elevator arrived.

"You were great in there," DelFlorio said. "I couldn't have done a better job myself."

She fixed her eyes on the panel of numbers above the elevator door. The number three lit up, then two. "It was awful," she said. "Absolutely awful."

"You're a brave woman," DelFlorio said. "The process of bringing an abuser to justice can be horribly revictimizing. That's one reason nearly all victims of sexual misconduct fail to report it. Fewer than two percent even consult an attorney."

"It would have been bad enough to just give the statement," Heather said. "But when that doctor started asking all those awful questions, I thought I'd die."

"I thought he was as delicate as he could have been, given the subject matter," DelFlorio said as the elevator doors opened.

Heather pushed her way ahead of DelFlorio through the crowd that was waiting for the elevator. As she raced toward the exit, she stopped briefly in her tracks. Someone was waving at her and walking toward her through the lobby. It was the woman with the red hair — the same woman she'd seen following her in New York. Instead of stopping, Heather walked more quickly with DelFlorio at her heels. She burst through the revolving doors, pulling her cigarettes and lighter from her purse.

CHAPTER 51

JEFF

JEFF HAD WATCHED AS HEATHER WALKED toward the door. He could see that her legs were quivering, but her ass still showed its perfect curve, even in that conservative navy blue suit. As she headed for the coat rack, she'd looked hot. He hated her for what she was doing to his career, his life—still, he'd nail her in a second. *Unbelievable that this team of assholes is going to tell me who I can and can't sleep with!* he thought.

When the door had closed behind Heather and DelFlorio, Dr. Waterhouse asked, "Dr. Davis? Mr. Bingham? Are you prepared to proceed?"

"We're ready to proceed," Chet said.

"Very well," Dr. Waterhouse continued. "Dr. Davis, although you have not taken a formal oath here, you are bound under the same sacred oath, the Hippocratic oath, that you, like every doctor, took when you received your medical degree. In taking that oath, you promised to do no harm to your patients. I trust that oath will suffice in ensuring that you tell the truth during these proceedings."

Jeff cleared his throat. "Of course," he said.

"Heather Morrison made some very serious claims against you in her statement," Dr. Waterhouse said. "Let's begin with her allegation of sexual misconduct." He looked at Jeff directly. "Dr. Davis, did you have a sexual relationship with Ms. Morrison?"

Jeff fingered the buttons of his suit jacket and repeated the prepared statement he'd spoken before. "Heather Morrison is a mentally unstable woman. I won't deny that I was aware that she was attracted to me. She made it obvious. But as a married man and Heather's medical doctor, I did nothing to encourage her interest. In fact, I made it clear that I wasn't open to a relationship with her."

"Answer the question, Dr. Davis," Dr. Waterhouse said. "Did you have a sexual relationship with Ms. Morrison?"

Jeff looked directly into each face of the trio that made up the disciplinary review board. "No," he said, settling his gaze on Dr. Waterhouse. "I did not."

"Unfortunately, the allegation of sexual misconduct—which is, by the way, the one that concerns the disciplinary review board the most—is the one that's the most difficult to prove." Dr. Waterhouse looked at his colleagues for verification. They nodded in turn. "Although Ms. Morrison gave a very strong statement, at this point it appears there is simply no evidence to prove or disprove the sexual misconduct claim."

Jeff nodded, feeling the relief flush his body.

"However," Dr. Waterhouse continued. "You noticed I asked her if she could identify your distinctive personal bodily features. After we adjourn, I will request a written statement from Ms. Morrison outlining any unique body features you may have. Additionally, I will order you to be examined by a physician who will determine if her portrayal of your physical characteristics is accurate."

"Dr. Waterhouse, I object," Chet Bingham interjected. "Subjecting Dr. Davis, a board-certified physician with fifteen years of experience and an exemplary and unblemished record to such an examination would be thoroughly humiliating."

Dr. Waterhouse shook his head. "No more humiliating than what Ms. Morrison claims she was subjected to as a result of Dr. Davis's actions," he said.

Jeff's rage tied his vocal chords in knots. The thought of having every inch of his body probed by some dermatologist or general practitioner was choking him alive.

"Would it be easier for you to simply admit to having had sexual relations with Ms. Morrison, Doctor?" Dr. Waterhouse asked.

Jeff leaned toward Chet and whispered, "Isn't this coercion? Isn't he trying to force me to admit to something I didn't do rather than be subject to the humiliation of a medical exam?"

Chet shook his head and addressed the board. "Dr. Davis will comply if so ordered."

"Thank you," Dr. Waterhouse replied. "As a result of Ms. Morrison's statement, we are also requesting materials in addition to what we have already obtained. She claimed that numerous phone calls were made between you and her on your cell phone."

"That's not true!" Jeff exclaimed. "I never gave her my cell phone number."

"In order to determine the validity of Ms. Morrison's claim, we are requesting copies of your cell phone records for telephone number 917-555-4155 for the months of June 2010 through the present."

Chet Bingham told the board Jeff would comply with the request.

Dr. Waterhouse reached for a folder containing a stack of papers. "As you know, we have already obtained Ms. Morrison's medical records and your record of prescriptions written on her behalf. Our expert has studied those records as well as the records provided by Ms. Morrison's pharmacy. These will help us to make determinations regarding your prescribing practices, record-keeping practices, and referrals for this patient. In order for us to make a determination on the claim of sexual misconduct, we will need the results of your medical examination by Monday, April 5. Are you able to comply with this request?"

Jeff nodded and glanced at his watch.

"Very well, then," Dr. Waterhouse concluded. "I believe we're finished here for now. Dr. Davis, you're free to go."

* * *

Jeff assumed a confident posture as he left the conference room. But beneath his bravado, he was a desperate man. Although his phone records couldn't prove sexual activity, they would reveal hundreds of calls to and from Heather. Would that be enough to convince the disciplinary review board that the two were having an affair? Add to that their making him—a specialist and a surgeon— strip naked in front of some general practitioner or dermatologist for a full body examination. The very idea was humiliating.

CHAPTER 52

JEFF

AS HE DROVE SOUTH on the New York State Thruway, Jeff pressed 411 on his cell. He got the name of a dermatologist whose office was just across the state line in Stamford, Connecticut, a short detour from his route home. Confirming that Dr. Fred Guinness had a Fraxel laser, the state-of-the-art equipment for removing body markings, Jeff gave his name as Dennis Jones. He told the receptionist he had no insurance but would pay cash if the doctor would see him at five o'clock that evening.

Identifying features of Jeff's private body map—a birthmark and a mole—would be history well before he was ordered to have any humiliating body scan.

* * *

By six thirty, Jeff was back on the road. His butt cheek and thigh burned like hell from the triple Fraxel treatment he had convinced Dr. Guinness to deliver. And he'd been advised to return for two more follow-up treatments. Instead, he'd made an appointment for a double treatment the following week, despite Dr. Guinness's advice that there should be three- to four-week gaps between appointments.

As Jeff handed his keys to the building garage's parking attendant, he wondered: could Priscilla look away like her mother had for so long? Preston had flaunted his affairs in Priscilla's mother's face for years.

Priscilla's need to believe that Jeff had been faithful throughout their marriage—or at least, to live as if he had—had kept his nights sleeping in the guest room to a minimum. The article in the *Post* had kept him out of the master bedroom for less than a week.

Priscilla stood and smiled as Jeff stepped through the French doors to the parlor. The light from the table lamp beside her fell softly on her face, emphasizing her patrician beauty. Silently, Jeff pledged to do everything he could to keep his marriage together. The fact was that he *liked* being married. And the level of financial comfort in this marriage couldn't be tossed away easily.

He'd told Priscilla the truth about where he was going today, sticking to the story he'd given when the article had appeared in the *Post.* He'd assured his wife he'd have no problem squelching the claim his crazy patient had made to the OPMC—that the most he might be held responsible for was some record-keeping that wasn't up to his usual meticulous standard.

"How did it go today?" Priscilla asked.

"Piece of cake," Jeff said, heading for the wet bar.

"Was she there?" Priscilla asked, clearly referring to Heather or *the crazy patient* as she was known as in the Davis household.

"Yes," he said. "She gave the opening statement, and then she was gone."

Perhaps Priscilla could endure this one infidelity. God, he hoped so. He looked at her, and he hoped so with all that was left of his heart.

Unexpectedly, Priscilla hugged him, pressing her body against his. He felt himself respond. He'd sworn to himself he'd be faithful. But instead of unbuttoning his shirt like a clandestine lover, Priscilla started to tell him about the kids' day at school. Jeff's erection vanished. It was no surprise. There was no way he could live without the excitement of new and different women in his life.

CHAPTER 53

HEATHER

"OK IF I SMOKE IN HERE?" Trista asked, looking around Heather's living room for an ashtray.

"Only if you give me one," Heather said, reaching for a cigarette.

Trista took her lighter and lit first Heather's cigarette, then her own. "God! I remember how you used to make me smoke on the fire escape when we lived together."

Heather let out a satisfied exhale. "That was a long time ago."

"Honey, it was less than a year ago," Trista said.

"A hell of a lot has happened since then," Heather replied. She wiped away a tear.

Trista shifted her weight and dug through her purse for a pack of Kleenex. "I know, sweetie," she said. "You've been through so much."

Heather took a tissue and blew her nose long and hard.

"God, I wish you'd never met Jeff," Trista continued.

"He ruined every aspect of my life," Heather said. "And I always thought doctors were supposed to be the good guys." She attempted to blow a smoke ring. "I was a fool to let him prey on me."

"That's exactly what he did!" Trista agreed. "It's crazy that people don't realize these things. Maybe your case will spare someone else this kind of agony by getting the word out there about doctor-patient affairs."

Heather stood, fighting the urge to stamp her feet on the floor in a childlike tantrum.

"Right now, all I care about is myself. And Lin. My baby girl is gone forever."

"I know, honey," Trista said. "Would it help if you tried to focus on something else?"

Heather nodded, and Trista clicked the television on. "Oprah will be on in a few minutes. It's almost four o'clock. Sound OK?"

"It's fine," Heather said. "I'm becoming quite a fan of daytime TV." The two women smoked their cigarettes in silence.

Trista sighed. "Honey, I'll be so glad when this whole thing is over. First it had you acting like a crazy woman. Now all this legal stuff! But at least you're over the bunny boiler stage."

"Oh, thanks a lot," Heather said, jabbing at nothing with the point of her cigarette.

Trista's fingers grazed the top of Heather's flailing hand. "You know, I'm not trying to insult you. I'm just hoping that once you get this legal stuff out of the way, you'll be able to be happy again. I want my friend back."

"I don't know if I'll ever be happy again," Heather said. "Not about the things that made me happy before, anyway. Unlike Jeff, who is probably going through this whole process completely unfazed."

"How can he be unfazed?" Trista asked. "He's the one who stands to lose everything—his practice, his marriage…"

"Excuse me? I lost my *daughter*!"

"You're right. You've been through the worst. I hope Jeff is running scared."

"I doubt he's all that worried," Heather said. "From what I've learned about him from the other women he was with and everything I've found out about doctors who have affairs with their patients, I expect he thinks he's above the law. It's only since it's been over between us that I've realized how narcissistic he is. I don't think he even believes he's done something wrong."

Trista reached for another cigarette. "Is he really like that? You didn't seem to think so when you were seeing him."

"I didn't *realize* when I was seeing him. I was so completely blinded by the fact that this rich, important doctor had singled me out—or so I thought—as the woman he wanted to be with. Being with him became the most important thing in my life—more important than his being married, than my job, maybe for a while even more important than adopting Lin." Heather wiped a tear from her eye.

"Aw, honey," Trista sympathized.

"He has the doctor-as-God complex down solid," Heather said.

*   *   *

After Trista left, Heather went to the kitchen to find something for dinner. She shook her head at the stacks of dirty dishes that were crammed in the sink. Spotting one of her Royal Doulton soup bowls among the debris, she noticed an edge had chipped off. *When did that happen?* She lifted the bowl and ran her finger along its jagged edge.

She opened the refrigerator and waded through its contents. From far in the back, she retrieved a carton of beef with broccoli. When she turned to where the microwave stood on the counter, she discovered it was buried under piles of pots, dishes, and towels—not worth the effort of uncovering. She took a fork from the sink, gave it a rinse, and took a taste of broccoli from the soggy carton. It was edible—barely.

Slumped against the kitchen counter, Heather washed down her dinner with a glass of wine and a handful of pills. Looking around her at the mess, she realized she was as close to rock bottom as she ever wanted to get. It was time to at least think about a solution.

She went to her computer and googled Hazelden, the world-renowned addiction treatment facility in Minnesota. Its programs were reputed to be second to none. Heather read through the clinic's website for hours. At one in the morning, she entered the facility's phone number into her cell phone. *This way I'll have the number whenever I'm ready...I'll call them when I'm ready,* she told herself.

A few years earlier, one of the attorneys from Peters & Andrews had gone to Hazelden and turned her life around. *What was her name?* Heather searched her mind for the answer, remembering that when the attorney had returned to the firm, she'd been unceremoniously fired for what P&A had termed insubordination. The fact was that Maureen McNulty—*yes, that was her name!*—had been too vocal for P&A's taste about her experience at Hazelden, encouraging her colleagues to face their demons. When she left the firm, Maureen had started a not-for-profit for professionals with addiction problems.

Heather googled Maureen McNulty. Her organization, Professionals for Sobriety, had an impressive website with testimonials from CEOs to rock stars. She entered the phone number for the group into her cell phone under Maureen's name.

Chapter 54

Jeff

JEFF CHECKED WITH BARBARA as he headed out of the office on Tuesday afternoon. "You rescheduled all my patients from between one and three this afternoon?"

"Yes, doctor. Your next appointment is at three thirty. Mr. Finkelman."

"I'll be here for Finkelman," Jeff said. "Until then, I'll be in conference. Leave a message on my cell if there are any emergencies."

* * *

An hour later, Jeff was seated across from Francis Xavier Connelly in a small but elegant conference room at the downtown headquarters of Stewart, Greenberg, Sully and Connelly.

"I've reviewed the plaintiff's complaint," Frank said. "Of course, I know you've seen it, but I've given you a copy to refer to during our meeting." He ran his finger along one of the pages. "We'll use this meeting to begin to prepare our answer to the complaint."

Jeff nodded.

"As you know, Heather Morrison is making some pretty serious allegations." Frank continued.

As Jeff reviewed the document in his hands, he noticed the papers were fluttering. His hands were shaking. He glanced at the by-now-familiar pages. What all those pages boiled down to were the charges of sexual misconduct, failure to refer, improper prescribing practices, and poor record-keeping.

*   *   *

The hot dog Jeff had grabbed from a street vendor on his way to the subway downtown lurched from his stomach to his throat. He swallowed hard against it. He stood up and walked to the window, one hand in his pocket, the other holding the legal papers. He studied the downtown skyline, fixing his gaze on the gaping emptiness where the World Trade Center had stood. Everything about Heather making these allegations against him was becoming too real. He turned to Frank and asked, "What the hell does all this mean?"

Frank smoothed the pages of his copy of the document on the conference table. "It means we have a lot of work to do," he said.

"So it seems. How do we get started?"

"We need to provide an answer to the complaint to Ms. Morrison's attorney by April 12," Frank said, furrowing his brow. He removed a silver fountain pen from his breast pocket. "How did it go in front of the medical board?" he asked.

"Fairly standard, according to the guy who handled it—Chet Bingham from East Coast Medical Insurers—a real nerd," Jeff replied.

"Most administrative attorneys could be described that way," Frank said, printing Chet Bingham's name in large letters on a legal pad. "They usually work for insurance companies—can't take the heat of a real law practice."

Jeff smiled briefly.

Frank continued. "OK with you if I give Chet Bingham a call?"

"No problem at all. I'd appreciate it," Jeff said.

Frank lifted his copy of the complaint from the conference table. "I noticed immediately Heather Morrison's attorney is William DelFlorio," Frank said.

"Yes," Jeff said. "I've checked him out. He's a real advocates' rights supporter. From what I've heard, the guy will represent anybody who ever had a gripe against a professional. Crazy women who had affairs with their shrinks. Grown up ex-Catholics who want to get money from the church by saying they were molested by priests when they were kids."

"I know him," Frank said. "DelFlorio is obsessed with victims' rights. And he's a damn good lawyer. We have our work cut out for us."

Jeff nodded as the taste of his hot dog returned once again.

"DelFlorio is sleek," Frank continued. "He has a reputation for surprising the courtroom." He poised his pen over the legal pad. "Let's go over the facts. Tell me what happened. *Everything*."

Jeff reviewed the story as he'd practiced it in his mind countless times. "I met Heather in the ER at Lenox Hill," he began. "She came in having an acute asthma attack. I was the pulmonologist on call. I took care of her, got her back on her feet, and sent her home."

"That's that?" Frank asked. "Nothing inappropriate happened during that first meeting?"

Jeff remembered how helpless Heather had been that first night, how grateful she was to him for getting her breathing under control. And he remembered how hot she had been with her sexy legs dangling from the exam table and her silky black chemise hanging from a hook on the wall. He cleared his throat. "As far as I was concerned, it was all routine."

"What happened after that first night in the ER?" Frank asked.

"Somehow she got hold of my cell number," Jeff said. "She started calling me."

Frank raised his eyebrows. "How did you handle that?" he asked.

"I spoke with her briefly when she called," Jeff said, pulling a handkerchief from his breast pocket and wiping his forehead. "Gave her a little free medical advice. Nothing more than that."

"Did you ever have sex with her?" Frank asked.

Whoa! Where did that come from? "What did I just tell you?" Jeff asked.

"I know what you *told* me. Now I'll ask you again. Did you ever have sex with Heather Morrison?" Frank asked, pressing the point of his pen against the legal pad for emphasis.

All Jeff's research had shown that attorney-client privilege encouraged clients to disclose the truth to their attorneys. The key reason for honesty was to prevent the truth from coming out for the first time at trial. More important, telling the truth from the beginning would allow the attorney to build the best case possible for his client. But could a client tell his lawyer he was guilty and expect the lawyer to work with him to build a case for innocence?

Jeff hadn't told the truth to Chet Bingham. He had no intention of changing his claim of innocence in the civil case. Or admitting to his partners that he'd violated the doctors' ultimate taboo by having sex with a patient. But maybe the truth and his plea didn't have to be the same.

"Level with me," Jeff said. "If I understand this right, I can tell you the truth—no matter what the truth is—and you'll keep it between us."

Frank nodded. "Jeff, listen to me. I'm only going to say this once." He pulled off an onyx cuff link and rubbed it between his fingers. "Even if I know you did it, I can still prepare a case that proves you didn't."

"How would you do that?"

Frank twirled his cuff link on the conference board table. "It's called skill," he said.

It was such a simple statement: *It's called skill.* But with those three words, Jeff decided to trust Francis Xavier Connelly.

"So do you want to start your story over?" Frank asked.

Jeff breathed deeply and noticed his pulse vibrating in his ears. He could feel his blood pressure rising. "Yeah," he said. "Yeah, I do want to start over."

"Good," the attorney said. "Whenever you're ready."

"OK, let's see," Jeff began. "The story starts out the same. Heather came into the ER in acute respiratory distress. She was scared—terrified, really. It was her first asthma attack, and she had no idea what was happening to her."

"Would you say you gave this patient any special treatment?" Frank asked.

Jeff cleared his throat. "I try to treat all my patients equally and professionally."

A grandfather clock framed by bookshelves stacked with law books ticked off the seconds. Frank leaned toward Jeff over the conference table. "I seem to remember you saying a few minutes ago that you'd level with me."

"OK. You've got me." Jeff shrugged and admitted, "I may show a little more concern for a beautiful young woman than for some old geezer on his last legs."

"Did you do that with Ms. Morrison—show more concern? Either on that first night in the ER or during any subsequent medical appointment?" Frank asked, still leaning forward.

"The night in the ER was standard," Jeff replied. "But, yes, there's no question that I was attracted to her."

"And was she attracted to you?"

"I thought she was," Jeff admitted. "But I chalked it up to the standard doctor-patient crush. Women develop crushes on their doctors all the time because, unlike most husbands, the doctor listens to her and makes her feel better." Jeff looked again toward the window at the hole in the skyline. "It never seems to occur to these women that doctors get paid to listen, and if they were married to them, they'd be just as much of a prick as their husbands are."

Frank smiled at the observation. "What happened next?"

"Let's see," Jeff said, tapping his fingers on the conference table. "She came to her first appointment in my office a few weeks later. The chemistry was definitely there—on both sides."

"Tell me about that chemistry," Frank said. "What were the signs?"

"Just a mild flirtatious undertone at that point," Jeff said.

Frank made a note on his legal pad. "Did you prescribe any medications during that first appointment?"

"I think so," said Jeff. "I remember her saying she was having trouble sleeping. Most likely I gave her Ambien—either a prescription or some samples."

"This complaint includes a request for all of Ms. Morrison's medical records. Have you taken care of that?" Frank asked.

"My assistant is copying them and having them delivered to you and DelFlorio tomorrow." He tugged on his tie.

"Good." Frank pushed a stray lock of hair away from his eyes. "That's where they'll try to get you—for things like improper prescribing practices and failure to refer. These are the sorts of claims that can be proven."

Jeff nibbled on a hangnail. *Failure to refer.* He knew his notes didn't show that he'd referred Heather to a therapist. That was a role he'd taken on willingly, one he hadn't wanted anyone but himself to fulfill. Chances were good, too, that he hadn't recorded every prescription he'd written for Heather and every sample of medication he'd given her. He was so busy taking care of his patients' medical needs that sometimes his paperwork suffered.

He realized Frank was still talking. "Patients who are claiming sexual malpractice invariably file additional complaints like these. They know they can't prove they had sex with their doctor, so they'll grab at anything they can claim—and prove—to put the screws to him." Frank scanned his notes. "Heather was your patient for over six months. That gave you any number of occasions to refer her to a therapist. Did you do that?"

"No." Jeff answered. "She didn't seem any more challenged by her anxieties than most of the people I see." He searched his mind for memories. "Not at that point anyway."

"Just the same, it's implicit that when antianxiety medications are prescribed, the prescribing doctor refers a patient to a therapist." Jeff knew what Frank was saying was the truth. "When did you give her your cell number?" he asked.

"I gave it to her at that first appointment," Jeff said. "But really, it was just intended to give her a feeling of security, knowing she could reach me directly if she had an asthma attack or some other sort of problem."

"How often do you give your cell number to your patients?" Frank asked, raising his eyebrows in question.

That answer was easy. Jeff knew he'd only given his cell number to the patients he'd slept with. *Frank doesn't need to know about them.* "I don't give my cell number to patients. Not ever."

Frank lowered his eyes and asked, "What happened after that first appointment?"

"She called me a few days later," Jeff said. "At three in the morning. She was having some sort of panic attack. She left a voice mail message, but I didn't hear it until much later that morning."

"What did you do about it?"

"I called her back," Jeff said. "We had lunch at Starbucks or someplace like that. It was all very tame, very aboveboard."

"Except that you were having lunch with a patient, a female patient you hardly knew. There are those who might consider that a bit unprofessional." Frank returned the cuff link to the French cuff of his stiffly starched shirt.

Jeff went on to tell Frank about how his friendship with Heather had quickly evolved from coffee to dinner to torrid sex in his office, at Heather's condo, and at the Mercer Hotel, finally ending with a crash when Priscilla became suspicious. He left out the part about reenacting Heather's childhood sexual abuse by a priest. That episode was irrelevant and embarrassing. As he replayed the scene in his mind, he realized that Frank was still speaking. "...and if your wife hadn't found out, do you think you'd still be seeing Ms. Morrison?"

"It's hard to say. It's possible the relationship would have run its course quickly. But I'm not sure."

Frank looked at him skeptically.

"You know my story has already been reported in *The New York Post*, right?" he asked.

"Yes, of course I know about that," Frank said. He opened Jeff's file and flipped through the contents. He pulled a copy of the *Post* article from the back of the file as if to prove he'd known about it from the start. "But this article is all the more reason for us to make every effort to avoid further publicity. The reporter—this Dina Cavali— clearly has a strong interest in the case. She's bound to follow it every step of the way."

Jeff returned to the conference table. He fanned the pages of his copy of the complaint. "I'm not going to be intimidated by some reporter—let alone one from the *Post*. If I have to go to trial to contest these ridiculous claims, I'll go to trial."

"But you've told me the allegations are not without basis," Frank said.

"And you've told me you could build a case for innocence," Jeff replied.

"I can," Frank said. "But settling out of court is the way to go. Only one of every twenty civil suits ever goes to trial. Why are you so hell-bent on being one of them?"

"Because I'm denying the claims," Jeff said. "And because the longer I maintain my innocence, the more likely my wife will believe I didn't have an affair. If I stick to my guns, maybe Heather will realize she has absolutely no proof this ever happened and drop the whole ridiculous thing."

Frank tugged again at his cufflink. "How do you know she has no proof?"

Jeff shrugged his shoulders and asked, "What proof could she possibly have?"

"In a civil case like this, it's not so much a matter of the plaintiff having proof as having a preponderance of evidence," Frank said.

"Like I said—she has no proof, no evidence, let alone a preponderance of evidence. I'll deny everything."

Frank spoke softly, as if sharing a secret. "As your attorney, I have to caution you that denial may well be moot at this point. With the medical board involved, it's likely they'll discipline you in one way or the other, maybe not for sexual misconduct but for the other allegations. Whether they discipline you by requiring you to work under supervision, suspending your license, or revoking your license, they've got you by the throat. The first thing Ms. Morrison's attorney will ask you is whether you've ever been disciplined by the state medical board. If you have been at that point—or expect to be—the prudent thing to do with the civil allegations is to begin mitigation."

"No way," Jeff insisted. "I came from nothing to become a doctor—a *medical* doctor. I'm not going to let some *travel agent* tear my family apart and toss my career in the shitter."

"These sexual misconduct cases are tough to fight," Frank insisted. "But luckily for you, they're also tough to prove. If the medical board disciplines you for any of the claims made in the complaint Heather filed, your civil case will be challenged."

"Why don't we cross that bridge when and if we come to it?"

"I'll do everything I can to build a case of innocence for you," Frank said. "But I need to tell you what to expect."

Jeff closed his eyes and held his head in the palms of his hands. Then as if shaking himself awake, he opened his eyes and said, "I don't get it, Frank. Your firm has defended the practice against people with claims of undiagnosed lung cancer resulting in death, surgical errors resulting in disability—really huge stuff. And you've won virtually every case for us. By comparison, this seems like a no-brainer."

"Sexual misconduct is a whole different world," Frank said. "And because there's no question that, legally, you acted in the capacity of a therapist with Heather Morrison, if only by prescribing certain medications, you've opened up a whole different area of the law—mental health care law. You gave her mind-altering medications and never referred her to a psychologist. And *those* facts are easily proven. Even if she can't prove you were involved with her sexually, she'll get you for failure to refer, faulty record-keeping, and improper prescribing."

"The sexual misconduct claim is the only one I really care about," Jeff said. "I mean, a slap on the wrist if I'm found responsible for the other charges wouldn't do my career any good. But my wife's not gonna throw me out of the penthouse because I didn't keep perfect medical records!"

"Sexual misconduct *is* the most serious allegation," Frank acknowledged.

"Damn it! I hate this!" Jeff said, pacing more quickly. "I can't believe that a patient can screw up a doctor's career like this! I mean the *doctor* is the one who's supposed to be in charge!"

"You crossed a line, Jeff," Frank said. "Can you honestly tell me that you didn't know having sex with a patient is unethical?"

"Of course I knew. I just never imagined anyone—I mean Heather—would report me." Jeff sank back into the chair, hoping his slip of the tongue hadn't told his attorney that Heather wasn't the only patient he'd slept with. "What about damages?" he asked.

Frank flipped through the pages of the verified complaint. "A lot will depend on the specifics of what Ms. Morrison claims in the way of damages. In a case like this, it's almost impossible to imagine what specific damages she'll claim."

Frank continued. "Legally, sexual misconduct is considered an intentional act. In other words, it's no accident, like the slip of a knife during surgery might be. For that reason, your insurance policy puts a cap of twenty-five thousand dollars in damages on sexual misconduct complaints. That's typical."

"So that's all she'll get if we settle?" Jeff asked. "It doesn't seem like much for all her trouble."

"No," Frank said. "That's all she'll get *from your insurance policy*. The rest will come from your own assets."

"From my *own assets*?" Jeff tugged on his tie, as if trying to pump some air back into his lungs. "Ninety percent of my assets are my *wife's* assets." He shook his head. "I never thought of Heather as a gold digger."

"If she was a gold digger, she'd be suing the practice, too."

"What could she sue the practice for?"

Frank counted on his fingers. "Negligent hiring. Inappropriate supervision. You're really lucky she didn't add that to your list of miseries. And there's not much precedent to go on. Civil cases claiming sexual misconduct against a medical professional who isn't a mental health care provider are few and far between."

"Why?" Jeff asked.

"First of all, it's seldom reported. The average person has no idea that a doctor who is providing mental health care to a patient while having an affair with her is illegal in nineteen states, to say nothing of unethical," Frank explained. "It's also extremely difficult to prove. But given that Heather has retained an attorney of Bill DelFlorio's caliber, I have to believe she's got something he believes will hold up as proof."

"I think she's bluffing," Jeff said. "Let her have her day in court. I'll come off scot-free, and she'll come off like the money-hungry whore she turned out to be."

"You won't come off scot-free, Jeff," Frank said. "Even if she can't get you for sexual misconduct, she may nail you on all the other allegations."

Jeff shook his head. "Like I said—the sex thing is the only part I really care about. So I get my hand slapped for not keeping meticulous records. Maybe I'll fire my secretary for doing poor transcriptions of my taped records and make a media event out of it."

"Is that true?" Frank asked. "Is that something we could use in your defense?"

"Not at all," Jeff said. "Barbara has been with me since I started at the practice. She's the most loyal and accurate employee I could ask for."

"And yet you'd be willing to expose her as incompetent and make a public spectacle of it to boot? How could you do that?"

"I could—and will—do anything to save my ass," Jeff said.

CHAPTER 55

HEATHER

HEATHER CHECKED HER WATCH, then headed for her kitchen and boiled water for a second cup of instant coffee. She had a few hours before her one o'clock lunch with DelFlorio to discuss her upcoming deposition with Jeff's attorney. She looked forward to the meeting, not only because it would force her to get out of the condo, but because DelFlorio had selected Restaurant 57, a four-star restaurant at the Four Seasons Hotel.

She flipped through "The Price is Right," "Martha" and "The View." After guessing the price of a dining room set exactly, she concluded that she was definitely watching too much daytime TV. She turned off the television and downed a Vicodin for pain she didn't really have.

After showering, she slipped into a yellow georgette blouse and a skirt and pulled on panty hose for the first time in weeks. It felt good to wear something other than sweats. She applied her makeup and was pleased with the result just the slightest amount of effort could bring. She shuddered as she realized there had been stretches of up to three days over the past few weeks that she'd skipped showering altogether.

She headed down the elevator and out into the sunlight. The rain had stopped, and the air smelled of early spring. As she walked along West 79th Street, she noticed tiny buds appearing on some of the trees. She checked her watch: 12:30. If she picked up her pace, she could make it to the restaurant on East 57th Street by one o'clock.

Feeling alive for the first time in weeks, Heather turned on West 75th Street. As she approached the middle of the block, she heard the happy screeches of children playing. She stopped walking. *Oh, God, why did I walk down this street?* She was passing Manhattan Borough School, the school where she had reserved a place for Lin to begin preschool when she was four. Dozens of children in tiny plaid uniforms played on swings and slides. Others raced across the concrete school yard, playing tag and catch. A few groups of mothers clustered around the grounds, having come by for a peek at their children enjoying one of the first warm days of the season.

Heather tried to walk faster, but her legs had turned to lead. She used the back of her hand to rub away the tears that were flowing down her cheeks. She turned in the direction the traffic was coming from. Mercifully, there was a taxi with its available light on. She stepped off the curb and waved frantically.

The taxi plowed through a puddle left from a predawn shower as the driver pulled to the side of the road. Mud splattered Heather's legs. She opened the door and sank into the back seat. "The Four Seasons, please," she said, wiping the muddy water from her calves, "57th and 5th."

* * *

DelFlorio stood to greet Heather as she approached his table at Restaurant 57.

"Am I late?" she asked, looking at her watch.

"Not at all," DelFlorio assured her, shaking her hand and sitting down. "I love to people watch here." He sipped a near-empty glass of what looked to Heather like bourbon.

Heather slipped off a white linen jacket, revealing the yellow georgette blouse over a flounced checkered skirt.

"Think about wearing that to the deposition," DelFlorio said. "You look almost virginal."

Heather wasn't sure that she liked being called virginal, but she got DelFlorio's implication of innocence. "Maybe I will," she said.

Over lunch, DelFlorio reviewed his strategy for the upcoming deposition and the evidence he planned to outline at the pretrial conference. "The disciplinary review board still hasn't made a decision on behalf of the OPMC," he said. "If they discipline Dr. Davis prior to a trial date, it will make an out-of-court settlement of the civil case virtually inevitable."

"It would be a huge relief not to have to see him in a courtroom," Heather said.

"Remember," he advised her as he attacked his sirloin with a fork and steak knife, "You were lucky no outsiders could show up at the informal settlement conference. If the case goes to court, the press and the public are likely to show up in the courtroom."

"I know," Heather said, pushing her scallops around on her plate.

"And your level of participation will be much more than simply making an opening statement, as you did at the ISC. As long as they can establish relevance, the defense may be grilling you on topics ranging from your childhood to your sexual history to your job."

"I know."

DelFlorio placed his large hand on top of Heather's with fatherly concern. "You may not be able to avoid being nervous," he said, "but we're going to make sure you are prepared for every eventuality. You'll have a prepared answer for any question they could possibly ask you. Will you be available next Thursday at four?"

"Unfortunately, I'm available just about all the time," Heather replied, sipping a glass of chardonnay.

DelFlorio signaled their waiter and ordered another round of drinks. "I love publicity," he said. "But judges don't like sexual misconduct cases in their courts. They're considered nasty and high profile. And since your case has had publicity already, any judge I've ever known would want to keep it off his docket. I expect Dr. Davis would want to limit additional publicity as well."

"You would think," Heather said.

"And what about you?" DelFlorio asked, mopping up the juices from his steak with a roll from the bread basket. "Do you really want any more dirty laundry hanging on your clothesline?"

Heather shrugged. "It doesn't matter to me. The harm is done. All that really mattered to me was Lin and my job."

"I never imagined you were adopting," DelFlorio said, a flicker of sadness crossing his face.

Heather raised a single hand in dismissal. "Why would you ask a single woman if she was in the process of adopting a child?"

"Well, I do feel at least partly responsible," DelFlorio said.

Heather waved his comment away. "As for my reputation, if I ever want to work in this city again, it would be good not to have prospective employers knowing I've been involved in this case the minute they hear my name."

"Your reputation will be fine," DelFlorio insisted. "The way I'll present the case, your reputation should remain spotless to anyone who remotely understands medical ethics. The onus, the blame, everything, will all be on Jeff Davis."

Heather reached into the pocket of her jacket that hung on the back of her chair. As unobtrusively as possible, she reached for a Valium. Feigning a cough, she covered her mouth, placed the pill on her tongue, and reached for her wine. After a long swallow, she asked, "What kind of reputation will I have if that sex tape is shown as evidence?"

"Remember," he said. "Our strategy is to push Davis as far as possible toward a large settlement before the tape is entered into evidence. That way, when the tape is introduced, he'll raise an already high settlement figure to ensure that it isn't shown."

"A smaller settlement would be okay. I just want to get this over with!"

"Every plaintiff wants to get it over with. That's why so many of them settle for monetary amounts that are far less than they deserve."

"How long is this going to last? I feel like it's going to take forever."

"I know how hard this is on you," DelFlorio said. "Try to remember that you're not just doing this for yourself but to protect other women—and men—from predators like Davis."

Heather cut a scallop and nibbled on a small bite. "I'm just so uncomfortable about when—and if—that tape is going to be introduced as evidence. I hate the way not knowing is hanging over me."

"I understand," DelFlorio said. "But it's our best strategy. I'm going to hold off on introducing that tape for as long as possible."

She frowned.

"Once the subject of that tape comes up, Jeff will be crying for a settlement," DelFlorio said. "Believe me, Heather—that tape is our ace in the hole."

Chapter 56

Heather

THE WOMAN SEATED IN THE RECEPTION AREA of Stewart, Greenberg, Sully and Connelly was dressed in head-to-toe Chanel. Her sleek black dress was cinched at the waist by a wide patent leather belt. She groped around in a huge Hermes handbag and retrieved a Blackberry, clutching it in her left hand. Her ring finger was surrounded by at least six carats.

Heather knew immediately that the woman was Jeff's wife, Priscilla. She remembered her from the photo on Jeff's desk.

As she and DelFlorio stood at the reception desk, Heather whispered to him frantically, "I thought no one was allowed at the deposition but the opposing sides and their attorneys."

DelFlorio glanced at the woman in the waiting area, then returned his gaze to Heather. "Anyone from either side can wait in reception," he said. Apparently, he, too, had easily determined that the woman was Jeff's wife.

As DelFlorio told the receptionist that he and Heather were here for the deposition in the case of Morrison v. Davis, Heather stole another glance at Jeff's wife. Priscilla sat erect, staring at her Blackberry as if willing it to ring. She was large boned, her dark hair gathered in a chic chignon at the nape of her neck. And there was something else— a single white pearl rested against her collarbone, suspended from an almost invisible gold chain.

Bastard! That's the same style necklace he gave me!

"Let me see if Mr. Connelly is ready for you yet," the receptionist was saying. *Oh, God, please let him be ready. Don't make us have to wait in reception—with her!*

Heather barely breathed as the receptionist spoke into a wireless headset. "May I bring them in?" The receptionist ended the call and stood, indicating a door to their right. Heather and DelFlorio followed the young woman toward a closed door marked *Boardroom*. The receptionist tapped lightly and opened the door.

DelFlorio had explained that both sides had the legal right to be present at the other's deposition. Heather had opted not to attend DelFlorio's deposition of Jeff—she only wanted to be in a legal setting with him when she had to be. DelFlorio had told her that Jeff would be present today while she gave her deposition to Frank Connelly. Priscilla's presence in the reception area had confirmed that he was already inside.

Heather froze as she attempted to follow DelFlorio into the boardroom. She thought she'd overcome the hurdle of seeing Jeff at the informal settlement conference. But laying eyes on Priscilla for the first time was something she hadn't anticipated. It had thrown her off.

She grabbed the flowing sleeve of the receptionist's peasant blouse. "Where is the ladies' room?" she asked. The receptionist pointed. Heather stumbled across the hall and into the ladies' room, chiding herself for being so visibly shaken. Once alone, she used her inhaler until it was empty. Then cupping her hands to catch water from the faucet, she swallowed two Valium. She dabbed on some lipstick and ran a comb through her hair before returning to the boardroom.

This time she was able to make it across the floor and drop into a chair at the conference table. The two attorneys were seated at either side of the long table. She sat next to DelFlorio, directly across from Frank Connelly. Jeff sat behind his lawyer in one of a row of chairs placed against the wall. At the head of the table was a court officer who was introduced as Richard Belcourt.

Frank Connelly stood and reached across the table, shaking Heather's hand as he introduced himself. Jeff remained in his chair, pressing his head against the gleaming mahogany wall behind him.

"Although we will conduct a brief deposition on the allegations of faulty record-keeping, improper prescribing practices, and failure to refer, our focus today will be on the allegation of sexual misconduct," Frank began. "All evidence related to the allegations has been identified. We have Ms. Morrison's medical records, prescription records, and cell phone records. During this deposition, I'll be referring to Ms. Morrison's cell phone records from telephone number 646-555-7279."

Frank turned to Richard Belcourt, the court reporter. "Mr. Belcourt will administer the oath to you, Ms. Morrison, and also record the proceedings. Are you ready?"

Heather nodded and stood, her knees knocking against the table, while Belcourt stood and instructed her to put her left hand on a bible he presented and raise her right hand. Next he asked, "Do you swear to tell the truth, the whole truth, and nothing but the truth so help you God?"

"I do," Heather said. After stating her name, she sank back into the chair.

For the next hour, Frank Connelly grilled Heather on the details of her professional relationship with Jeff. He started with the terrifying night at Lenox Hill and worked his way through to her last appointment and the letter terminating her as a patient.

DelFlorio had prepared her well. There was not a single question she couldn't answer quickly and factually. Even though Jeff was in the room, a constant presence over the shoulder of his attorney, Heather remained focused.

Frank Connelly quickly moved into the subject of the affair. "Ms. Morrison, you allege that you had a six-month sexual relationship with Dr. Davis. When did that relationship begin?"

"June 2010," Heather replied. Her voice was tiny and high. She repositioned herself in the hard wooden chair. *Why don't they have leather chairs around this conference table?*

It was two more hours before Frank finally said the words Heather longed to hear. "That will be all." Belcourt switched off his tape recorder. Shaken and exhausted, she longed to race from the room.

At least there had been no humiliating questions about the sex tape. She wondered again if and when DelFlorio was going to introduce it as evidence. She felt her armpits dampen. In some ways, her lawyer's behavior was making no sense.

Heather left the boardroom alone, DelFlorio having opted to stay behind. Jeff's wife remained in the reception area, exactly where she'd been seated over three hours earlier. Her posture was erect as she thumbed through a huge magazine, probably *Vogue*, Heather surmised. Priscilla didn't lift her eyes as Heather walked quickly past her and headed out the door.

Chapter 57

DelFlorio

AS BOTH SIDES AWAITED TRIAL, DelFlorio realized that Jeff had been lulled by his own certainty that there was no evidence that could prove he'd been sexually involved with Heather. Jeff had continued to play the crazy card, insisting that Heather had stalked him for months and made so many calls to his cell number that he'd been forced to change it. DelFlorio, meanwhile, adapted his strategy as Jeff held fast to his refusal to settle out of court.

When the disciplinary review board had finally come down with its decision in mid-November, it had fueled Jeff's belief that the civil case was certain to result in a finding of his innocence. As expected, the disciplinary review board had given him a slap on the wrist for faulty record-keeping, improper prescribing practices, and failure to refer. But the board had concluded that the sexual misconduct charge lacked the evidence to prove there had been an affair between Jeff and Heather. That was exactly what DelFlorio had hoped for—for now. Recordings of telephone messages had led the board to conclude that Jeff's friendship with Heather had escalated beyond what is proper for a medical professional and a patient. But sexual misconduct? No, they'd said. Just the slap on the wrist.

* * *

DelFlorio mulled all this over while he waited for the long-anticipated civil court proceeding to begin on the morning of Wednesday, December 1. The courtroom was just as he had anticipated. The room was packed with press, the tension thick in the air and on the faces of everyone present. *No wonder,* DelFlorio thought as he navigated the noisy courtroom. *No one here knows what's about to happen—no one but me.*

A bailiff who appeared to be barely out of his teens entered the courtroom. "All rise," he shouted above the din. "The court is now in session, the Honorable Matthew Forester presiding."

It took longer than usual for the judge to bring the court to order and give instructions to the jury. DelFlorio juggled in his seat as he waited. Finally, Judge Forester called DelFlorio up to make his opening statement.

DelFlorio smoothed his jacket as he walked to the front of the room. He could feel dozens of pairs of eyes fixed on him, almost searing heat into the back of his custom-made suit jacket. He pressed the bulky item in his inside jacket pocket as he stepped forward. Still bulky. He tugged at the edge of the starched white handkerchief peeking from his outer pocket and gave it a fluff. Better now.

Turning to face the courtroom, DelFlorio began. "Your Honor, ladies and gentlemen of the jury, and all here present, we are here today in this courtroom to prove that the defendant, Dr. Jeffrey Davis, a pulmonologist, endangered the well-being of my client and his patient, Ms. Heather Morrison. When Ms. Morrison began treatment for environmentally-induced asthma in May 2010, she was an otherwise healthy young woman with a bright future. She held an excellent job as director of corporate travel at Peters & Andrews, one of the largest and most prestigious law firms in the world. She had a secure income and an exemplary work record. She was in the process of adopting a baby girl from an orphanage in China. It appeared that everything was going her way. However, the happy ending she was working toward was not to be.

"I am here to establish that, as a direct result of the negligence and misconduct of Dr. Davis, my client sits before you now as a woman who has lost everything. She's lost her job and perhaps the likelihood of finding another. She's lost her chance to be the mother to a child she waited years to find, flew halfway around the world to bring home, met, bonded with, and then was told she would never see again. She lost her will to live—attempting suicide in an effort to see Dr. Davis one last time after he had turned her away emotionally. As a result, she required psychiatric care.

"My mission here is to prove Dr. Davis's neglect in the areas of prescribing, referring, and record-keeping, as well as an even more serious allegation—that he violated both medical ethics and the law by seducing Ms. Morrison, having a six-month affair with her, and treating her for emotional issues in the guise of lovemaking.

"Over the course of this case, it is my intention to prove that Dr. Davis knowingly neglected his primary obligations to the plaintiff— to put the medical needs of Heather Morrison above any needs and desires of his own and to do her no harm. Contrarily, Dr. Davis initiated a lascivious, almost predatory sexual affair with Heather Morrison—an affair that he carried on and ultimately terminated with callous disregard for Ms. Morrison, the laws of the State of New York and the AMA's Code of Medical Ethics.

"I will prove that Dr. Davis not only violated medical ethics and state law by having an affair with a patient, but he opened for this case a whole additional host of medical law, that of mental health care law, by treating Ms. Morrison's psychological issues with mood-altering medications and outrageous psychotherapeutic techniques, even incorporating this so-called therapy into his sexual activities with Ms. Morrison. I will prove that Dr. Davis acted in the role of psychiatrist in a perverted effort to help her to deal with issues related to childhood sexual abuse—an effort that was, in truth, motivated solely by Dr. Davis's own callous and unrelenting quest for sexual release."

As DelFlorio returned to his seat, he checked the pallor of Jeff's skin. Ashen. Good. His opening statement had gotten to him. In the row behind him, Jeff's wife sat solemnly, a balled-up tissue clutched in her hand.

A few rows back on the plaintiff's side of the courtroom, DelFlorio noticed a well-dressed Hispanic man seated beside a woman dressed in bohemian style, her dark blond hair curling down her back. They had to be the dear friends Heather had mentioned often—Miguel and Trista. In the row behind them was a forty-something woman with distinctive red hair. DelFlorio was sure he'd seen her before but couldn't place where.

DelFlorio's chair scraped against the linoleum of the courtroom floor as he pulled it from the table and settled in beside Heather. She glanced at him with a weak smile. Her black tailored suit over a crisp white blouse was perfect for the courtroom. The blouse was buttoned high. A single black pearl hung over the neckline. He could see beneath her collar that there was a second fine chain around her neck, but whatever was hanging from it wasn't revealed.

A plastic pitcher filled with water sat beside a stack of plastic cups in the middle of the table. As Heather reached for a cup, DelFlorio lifted the pitcher, took the cup from her hand, and filled it. She smiled in gratitude as she took the cup from him with a shaking hand. A moment later, he noticed that both her hands had disappeared into the purse on her lap. As he saw her fumbling, he heard a rattling sound, as if she was trying to shake some Tic Tacs from their plastic case. She coughed, lifted a hand to her mouth, and took a sip of water. *Drugs. God only knows what she's taking to get through this.*

Despite the crisply tailored suit, DelFlorio had never seen Heather looking so bad. Months of searching for a job in a dead economy had resulted in her giving up the search for a while. Her eyes were glazed with the look of someone who had detached from life. DelFlorio wondered how often she was taking the drugs Jeff Davis had gotten her hooked on and where she was getting them. The only good thing about Heather's worn appearance was that she looked like what she had become—the woman he'd described in his opening statement.

DelFlorio turned from Heather to the front of the courtroom where Frank Connelly was preparing to begin his opening statement. Connelly cleared his throat and began to speak.

"Ladies and gentlemen of the jury, attendees, Your Honor," Frank said. "My client, Dr. Jeffrey Davis, is a medical doctor and a board-certified pulmonologist. He is a partner in the medical practice Upper East Side Pulmonologists, one of the premier pulmonologist practices in New York or, for that matter, the entire country. He is on staff at Lenox Hill Hospital, one of the most prestigious hospitals in the nation. Dr. Davis has dedicated his life to healing people affected by such traumatic illnesses as lung cancer, chronic obstructive pulmonary disease, and, of course, asthma.

"Prior to this occasion, Dr. Davis's record as a physician and as a member of the community had been unblemished. It is my intention that, when this trial ends, the doctor's record will remain unblemished. It is also my intention to prove that, contrary to the allegation, it was the plaintiff, Heather Morrison, who unsuccessfully attempted to seduce Dr. Davis in an effort to realize financial gain. I intend to prove that Heather Morrison was fully aware that a physician having a sexual relationship with a patient could result in a malpractice lawsuit, sanctions by the medical board, and even loss of the doctor's license to practice medicine. I will show that despite—in fact *because of*—that knowledge, Heather Morrison attempted to seduce Jeffrey Davis, who was not only her physician but a married man, with the intention of threatening him with lawsuits, the settlement of which could result in payment to her of millions of dollars in damages.

"During the trial, I intend to demonstrate that the plaintiff, Heather Morrison, was already emotionally scarred when she initially presented to Dr. Davis in the emergency room at Lenox Hill Hospital in the throes of an acute asthma attack that was initiated by a combination of paint fumes and her already fragile mental health."

DelFlorio struggled to keep himself from jumping from his seat to object, knowing that his objection during an opening statement would mark him early as a troublemaker with both the judge and the jury. He forced himself to sit tight. Jeff Davis's moment in the sun was about to fade. Not only would DelFlorio's case destroy his credibility as a doctor, it would reveal him to be a lecherous philanderer who liked to play shrink.

"Furthermore," Frank was saying, "I will show the court that Ms. Morrison's suicide attempt and resulting need for psychiatric care were the result of her already shaky mental health. I will show you that Dr. Davis did all that can be expected of a medical doctor to help the patient to manage her asthma. I will prove that there is no evidence whatsoever that sexual activity ever occurred between Heather Morrison and Jeffrey Davis, despite the fact that Heather Morrison pursued him, stalked him and fabricated charges with the intention of obtaining a large payoff."

Frank turned on his heal and returned to his seat, where Jeff greeted him with a handshake and a broad smile. *To think that idiot doctor thinks he has a prayer of winning this case when I'm representing the other side,* DelFlorio thought.

"Your first witness, Mr. DelFlorio?" Judge Forester asked.

DelFlorio stood. "I call the defendant, Dr. Jeffrey Davis, to the stand."

Jeff stood and approached the witness stand. DelFlorio had to hand it to him. Jeff exemplified grace under pressure, striding toward the stand as if it was a chaise in his study. But he was about to knock the wind out of the doctor's sails.

After Jeff was sworn in, DelFlorio began his interrogation. "Dr. Davis, during what period was the plaintiff, Heather Morrison, under your medical care?" he began.

"I first saw Ms. Morrison in the emergency room at Lenox Hill Hospital on May 27, 2010," Jeff replied in a strong voice. "On January 26, 2011, I sent her a letter advising that I was terminating my care for her and giving her a standard four-week window during which to find another pulmonologist. She was given the opportunity to return to Upper East Side Pulmonologists for the purpose of a final appointment with one of my colleagues."

Frank Connelly had prepped Jeff well. Exact information the first time. No scrambling for dates or details. But none of it mattered. In fact, the better the doctor came off on the stand, the further he'd fall. DelFlorio would bring him down in a blaze of glory!

DelFlorio continued. "As you know, Dr. Davis, this has been a highly publicized case. The accusations have been written up in newspapers and touted on news broadcasts. There appears to be a question surrounding whether you treated Ms. Morrison as a pulmonologist or as a therapist—or some combination thereof. Has anyone other than myself, your counsel, or Ms. Morrison herself ever mentioned to you that Heather Morrison was molested as a child?"

"Objection!" Frank Connelly shouted, springing to his feet. "Permission to approach the bench."

Judge Forester nodded and signaled for Frank Connelly and DelFlorio to come forward.

"Your Honor," Frank said, "my client has been cleared of any unethical sexual activity by a disciplinary review committee appointed by the Office of Professional Medical Conduct. Why are we putting him on trial again here for accusations for which he has already been exonerated?"

Judge Forester replied, "Mr. Connelly, certainly you, as an attorney, realize that discipline by a disciplinary review board and a proceeding in a civil case such as this are two entirely different things." Raising his voice, he added, "I'll allow Mr. DelFlorio's question."

DelFlorio repositioned himself in front of Jeff and said, "Again, Dr. Davis, has anyone other than myself, Ms. Morrison, or Mr. Connelly ever mentioned to you that Heather Morrison was sexually abused as a child?"

Jeff paused. It looked as if Frank Connelly hadn't given him the answer for this question. This time, he was on his own.

"The only mention of something like that came from some random phone call I received," Jeff replied.

"When did you receive that phone call, Dr. Davis?" DelFlorio asked.

"Sometime earlier this year. In March, I believe. I don't know the exact date." Jeff shifted in his seat.

"Objection," Frank Connelly said, clearly aware that his client was out of his comfort zone. "Relevance?"

"I'm going somewhere with this," DelFlorio said.

Judge Forester leaned forward in his chair. "Mr. DelFlorio, you have permission to proceed. But I'm warning you, sir, you'll need to reach your point quickly."

"I will." DelFlorio turned back to the defendant. "Dr. Davis, please tell us about this phone call."

"The call was from a woman," Jeff began. "Caller ID was blocked. Usually I don't answer calls unless I know who is calling, but this time I just didn't notice."

"What did the caller say, Dr. Davis?"

"The caller was a woman," he said. "She claimed that Heather had a DVD of us having sex together. And that the sexual activity included a reenactment of a sexually abusive experience Heather had had as a child."

"And is it true that you and Ms. Morrison recorded your sexual activities on tape, Dr. Davis?"

"Mr. DelFlorio, there was nothing to record." Jeff's voice was angry. "There was never a sexual relationship between Heather Morrison and me in reality or on DVD. Recorded or not recorded."

DelFlorio reached into his breast pocket and pulled out the bulky object. "I request to enter into evidence a DVD that will refute Dr. Davis's statement that there was no sexual relationship nor any recording of such a sexual relationship," he said. He heard a buzz from the swarm of reporters gathered at the back of the room. He felt his heart pound in his chest, the adrenaline rushing through him like a baseball player about to pitch with the bases loaded.

Frank Connelly sprang to his feet. "My client never had sexual relations with Heather Morrison, let alone captured them on tape. This whole ordeal is becoming a media circus!"

"Please remain seated—and quiet—Mr. Connelly, until Mr. DelFlorio has completed his examination of your client," Judge Forester said.

DelFlorio had tried cases that Forester had presided over before. He was sure Forester remembered his approach—that ingenious way he had of introducing rebuttal evidence and watching the defense hang themselves with it.

"May I have the evidence, please?" Judge Forester asked.

DelFlorio approached the bailiff and handed him three copies of the DVD—one for the judge, one for the jury, and one for the defense. The bailiff distributed the tapes to Judge Forester, the forewoman of the jury, and Frank Connelly.

Turning to the jury, Judge Forester said, "Ordinarily, all evidence and all witnesses are identified prior to the commencement of a trial. But in his own testimony, Dr. Davis himself mentioned something that was not identified during the discovery period."

The judge turned toward Jeff. "Dr. Davis, you've raised the issue of a telephone call, a call during which an unidentified woman told you that a tape existed that shows you and Ms. Morrison having sex together. Nowhere in the preparation of this case during the months of discovery was this phone call referenced. Therefore, the plaintiff's side is at liberty to introduce rebuttal evidence."

Judge Forester turned back to the jury. "For those of you who may not be familiar with the term *rebuttal evidence*, when a witness brings direct testimony that was not anticipated, the other side may be granted a specific opportunity to rebut it. In rebuttal, the rebutting party may generally bring witnesses and evidence that were never declared before, so long as they serve to rebut the prior evidence. Dr.

Davis mentioned a phone call that we were not aware had taken place. Therefore, we are permitted to introduce new evidence—rebuttal evidence. As required by law, rebuttal evidence must be confined solely to the subject matter of the evidence rebutted. New evidence on other subjects may not be introduced during rebuttal."

DelFlorio recalled the phone call Jeff Davis had brought up in his testimony. When DelFlorio had told his assistant, Catherine Mason, to place the anonymous call to Dr. Davis, she'd done so immediately. Catherine had been his loyal legal assistant for fifteen years. Herself a victim of a professional boundary violation two decades earlier, she was as passionate as he was about punishing professionals who took advantage of those who had placed themselves in their care.

DelFlorio had instructed Catherine to go to a phone booth at the corner of 42nd Street and Seventh Avenue and call Jeff's home number. It was a Wednesday evening, a time when busy doctors are more likely than usual to be at home. As always, Catherine had followed his instructions to the letter. Within minutes, she'd left the office, bringing along a pair of leather gloves.

When Catherine had recounted the story to DelFlorio, she'd said that Jeff had answered the phone on the first ring, probably before noticing caller ID had been blocked.

Who is this? he'd demanded.

I'm a friend of Heather's, Catherine had said, as DelFlorio had instructed her. *You better settle this case quickly. She has a tape of the two of you having sex together.*

Who is this? Jeff had demanded a second time. He'd paused, as if trying to remember Heather's friend's name. *Is it Trista?*

It doesn't matter who it is, Catherine had said. *What matters is that Heather has it all on tape. Not just the sex, Dr. Davis, but the reenactment. You remember. Where you acted out the part of the priest who had abused her as a child?*

That's impossible! Jeff had insisted. *Who is this?*

That was when Catherine had hung up. Then she removed the leather gloves that had kept her fingerprints off the phone.

Of course DelFlorio knew this setup was hardly by the book. But he had bent the rules before in his efforts to hang professionals who abused their powers. As he'd told Heather at their first meeting, it was nothing that kept him awake at night.

* * *

"The court will recess in order to give the jurors the opportunity to evaluate this additional piece of evidence," Judge Forester said, holding the tape in his long, elegant fingers. "Court will reconvene tomorrow morning at ten o'clock." He pounded his gavel and stood, his robe swirling around his lanky body.

DelFlorio stole a look at Heather. She was reaching into her purse again. Next he sneaked a peek at the doctor's wife. All color had drained from her face. He took Heather's arm, and they made their way through the crowd. He tried to mask his satisfaction with himself as he ushered her from the courtroom. As they stepped into the hallway, they were assaulted by a barrage of flashing cameras. Microphones and tape recorders were shoved toward them from every direction.

DelFlorio held Heather's arm and ushered her into an elevator, pleading with the reporters to remain behind. As he turned in the elevator to press the button for the lobby, he glimpsed Jeff and his lawyer, who were now under siege by reporters and photographers. Jeff's wife appeared frozen at his side.

When the elevator doors finally closed, DelFlorio's face broke into a broad grin. The way he had set up this case was nothing short of genius.

Chapter 58

JEFF

"STOP TALKING TO THAT REPORTER!" Frank Connelly whispered harshly into Jeff's ear as the two men left the courtroom. Priscilla clung to her husband's side like a strip of Velcro.

"I was just telling him that Heather is bluffing about the tape," Jeff said, his voice low but sharp.

"I have my copy right here," Frank said, patting the side pocket of his jacket. "Let's step into an empty courtroom and take a look."

Jeff jabbed his attorney with an elbow and rolled his eyes toward his wife.

Frank got the message. "Or if you prefer, I'll take a look at it when I get back to my office."

"That's fine with me," Jeff said. "I don't see any reason for Priscilla to have to spend an extra minute in this courthouse." He smiled at his wife. "Besides, I assure you, there's nothing on that tape that has anything whatsoever to do with me."

"OK," Frank replied. "But we do need to talk about our strategy." He looked into a courtroom whose door was ajar. The room was empty. "Come in here. It won't take long."

Frank pulled out a chair at the side of the table for Priscilla. She smiled awkwardly and sat down as Jeff settled into the chair beside her. Frank took the seat at the head of the table. He pulled the DVD out of his pocket and tossed it on the table. The words *Morrison v. Davis* had been hand printed on it with black magic marker. "Why in the name of God didn't you tell me about this thing?" Frank asked Jeff.

Priscilla sniffled and reached into her handbag for a tissue.

"She's bluffing," Jeff insisted. "There can't be a tape containing the stuff DelFlorio described. That sexual encounter never happened. *No* sexual encounter ever happened."

"OK. Say this is a recording of *American Idol*." Frank tapped a single finger on the tape. "I still want to know why you mentioned that phone call on the witness stand—a phone call you never told me about."

"I didn't even think about mentioning the phone call," Jeff said. "DelFlorio led me right into it."

"I warned you about him." Frank said. "I told you he was sly. Jesus, Jeff, how many times did we discuss sticking only to those topics we'd discussed in discovery? What happened to you up there on that stand?"

"I don't know." Jeff lowered his head. "Maybe I wasn't thinking clearly."

"Do you think clearly when you're performing surgery?"

"Of course."

Frank pressed his back firmly against the chair. "Going forward in this trial, keep in mind that when you're on the witness stand, you need to think just as clearly—and be just as careful—as when you're in the operating room. Have you got that?"

"I've got that," Jeff said.

Priscilla shrank back, her figure framed by the back of the wooden chair.

"OK," Frank said. "For the record, did the phone call happen?"

Jeff looked at Frank directly, avoiding Priscilla's gaze. "Yes, the phone call happened."

"Why didn't you ever mention it to me?"

Jeff let out a loud breath. "It never crossed my mind to mention it to you. At the time of the call, I figured it was one of Heather's friends trying to scare me. But of course she didn't scare me at all because I knew such a tape could not possibly exist." He took his wife's hand in his and squeezed it tightly.

"You do realize that if you'd told me you had gotten a phone call and the caller had claimed that a sex tape existed, we could have requested the tape as evidence before we got into the courtroom?" Frank asked. "Before the publicity grew out of control by the case going to court?"

"Yes, I realize that," Jeff said. "I realize that now. This whole hideous event has been an education for me in how the law works. But once again, Frank, there is no tape of sexual activity between Heather Morrison and me." Jeff felt his wife's hand dampen inside his grip. "There was never anything of that nature to record. And if there was, why would I want it to be entered into evidence? Evidence like that—if there were any—would only stand to strengthen her side."

"Exactly," Frank said. "And if you had told me someone had claimed there was a sex tape, I'd have done everything possible to ensure that Bill DelFlorio had produced it during the initial discovery period— not when we were sitting in a courtroom filled with reporters from every New York media outlet and gossip rag in the country."

Jeff let go of Priscilla's hand and twisted his fingers. "I know that all evidence is supposed to be marked before the commencement of the trial. I really think DelFlorio saved this intentionally and led me right into bringing it up when he examined me."

"You're damned right that's what he did!" Frank said. "It was the last weapon in his arsenal, and he didn't bring it out until the world was watching!"

Jeff grimaced. The case had already brought him to his knees. He recalled the humiliating body exam performed by a lowly general practitioner when his only gratification had been that the doctor had found no trace of the birthmark or the mole that Heather had remembered. The idiot hadn't even noticed the patches of dry skin that were left by the Fraxel laser treatment.

"How about I swing by your office late this afternoon?" Jeff asked. "We can map out our strategy then. My wife has had more than enough of this thing."

Priscilla smiled at Jeff gratefully and blew her nose.

Frank looked at his Rolex. "Can you come in at five?"

"I'll be there," Jeff promised before whisking Priscilla away through the crowd of reporters and photographers waiting outside the door for them.

* * *

By the time Jeff had gotten Priscilla home and left his place again, the lunch crowd had deserted the streets and sidewalks and returned to their offices. He raced along the nearly empty streets, desperate to get to his office.

When he'd gotten the phone call, he had believed that Heather had put her friend Trista up to making the call. But he had wondered why the subject of the tape he'd filmed had been brought up by Trista—or anyone. He'd been so careful—he'd been sure that Heather had had no idea. Her only moment of suspicion had been explained away with his story of filming medical procedures for students.

He had meant to check the file cabinet to make sure the tape was still there. But instead, he'd convinced himself that the call had been a hoax or a coincidence, denying even to himself that there was any chance his perversion would be revealed. Now he wondered if his denial had cost him everything.

He entered his office and raced past his staff without saying hello. Knocking on exam room B, he heard Dr. Cooperman's voice. "Just a moment. This room is in use."

For the next ten minutes he paced the hall. Finally, Dr. Cooperman appeared. A few minutes later, her patient exited the room. Jeff went into the exam room and locked the door behind him.

Hiding his pornography in Dr. Cooperman's exam room had seemed the perfect spot. From the day she'd arrived at the practice, she'd complained that she didn't have a key to the file cabinet in the room. That was because Jeff had a key—the only key.

Jeff slipped his key easily into the lock—too easily. As he slipped the file drawer open, he realized that the lock had seemed loose for a while. When he'd first noticed, he figured a janitor on the night crew might have picked the lock and discovered his porn collection. He'd shrugged the idea off, never checking to see which, if any, of his DVDs had disappeared.

But now that the sex tape of himself and Heather reenacting her childhood abuse had been ordered into evidence, he had to know if somehow Heather had managed to get her hands on it. DelFlorio would never introduce evidence he hadn't confirmed to be real. If there was a DVD, the judge and jury would see it. Maybe they'd show a portion of it at the trial. Priscilla would see it! The world would see it! There might even be snippets of it on the evening news and the Internet.

His hands shook uncontrollably as his fingers scanned the alphabetized files. When he got to H, to where the DVD of Heather had been stored, he dropped to the floor. It wasn't there. And if it wasn't there, there was only one place it could be.

What am I going to do? He reasoned that he might be able to hold onto his marriage if Priscilla believed that Heather had been the only one. What about his job? Most of his colleagues were married men. They might not condone an affair with a patient, but wouldn't they understand a little infidelity after ten years of marriage? But kinky sexual activity with a patient in the guise of therapy? If that came out, he'd be lucky to get a job cleaning bedpans at the VA hospital.

* * *

I've got to keep that DVD from being shown! He left his office and raced outside, breaking into a run as he passed the Whitney Museum. He glanced at his watch. The jury had probably reviewed the new evidence by now. The only way to keep the images from leaking beyond the courthouse was to settle immediately.

But how could he explain his sudden willingness to settle without looking guilty? He stopped running and leaned against a lamppost, trying to catch his breath. *I know! I'll say I'm more frightened than ever for the safely of my family—that Heather's claim that a tape exists of us having sex together with me pretending to be a Catholic priest proves that she's even crazier than I thought.*

Yes, that was it. The public story would be that his fears for his family's safety had escalated, driving him to settle.

He pressed Frank Connelly's number on his cell phone. "Have you viewed the evidence yet, Counselor?" he asked.

"I thought I'd wait until you got here at five," Frank said.

"Why don't we skip it?" Jeff suggested.

Jeff heard the exaggerated sigh in Frank's voice. "Why would we do that?"

Jeff stopped walking and leaned against a bus stop shelter. "I want to settle."

"Are you kidding?" Frank asked. "After all we've gone through? Jury selection. Going to court. The media circus. If you're going to settle now, why didn't you do it before they dragged you into a courtroom?"

"Because I didn't know about the DVD," Jeff said.

Jeff could hear Frank moving around at the other end of the connection. "Let me put this thing in my DVD drive right now and…"

"Don't do it," Jeff said.

"Jesus, Jeff, why not?" Frank demanded. "I have to review the evidence!"

"I know. Sorry." Jeff's grip tightened around the phone. "But there's something I have to tell you that I couldn't say in front of my wife."

"And what is that?" Frank asked.

Jeff's voice cracked as he said, "That DVD could be real."

"No shit, Sherlock," Frank replied. "There's got to be something tangible here. DelFlorio's a brilliant attorney. He's not going to introduce fabricated evidence."

"But what they say is depicted on the tape, well, it did actually happen," Jeff stammered.

"It *happened*? I'm sorry to say this, Davis, but sometimes I think it's you—not the plaintiff—who's crazy," Frank said.

Jeff pushed the hair from his eyes as he turned into the wind on Fifth Avenue. Holding the phone close to his lips, he said, "I have no choice. I have to settle."

"The judge and jury have probably seen the DVD already," Frank said. "The damage is done."

"If I don't settle, they'll show portions of that DVD in the courtroom," Jeff said. "My wife will see it."

"Your wife will hear about it anyway."

"I'll handle it, Frank. It's not your problem anymore."

"As you wish," the attorney said.

Jeff glanced at his watch and picked up his pace. "Priscilla believes what she wants to believe—what she can handle believing."

"For some people, denial is the only way to go," Frank said before clicking off.

Chapter 59

Heather

HEATHER AND DELFLORIO TOOK THEIR SEATS in the already crowded courtroom. It was just before ten in the morning. The jurors' seats stood empty, and there was no sign of Jeff and his lawyer. What was going on?

Heather nibbled on her fingernails as she waited for what seemed like hours. She glanced at the clock on the wall. Two minutes after ten. Still nothing. She looked at DelFlorio and raised her eyebrows. He shrugged his shoulders in response.

Above the chatter of the room full of spectators, Heather heard the clipped sound of footsteps approaching the front of the room. Frank Connelly arrived, leaned over, and whispered something in DelFlorio's ear. DelFlorio smiled like a child on Christmas morning.

Frank signaled for Heather and DelFlorio to follow him out of the courtroom. DelFlorio took her arm, all but lifting her out of the chair as he stood. *What the hell is going on? Where is the judge? Where is the jury? Where are we going?*

As she rose, Heather heard the bailiff's announcement. The jurors funneled into their seats. "All rise," he said. "Court is in session. The Honorable Matthew Forester presiding."

As the judge came into the room, Frank continued down the aisle toward the exit. Heather and DelFlorio turned and returned to their seats. A moment later, Frank hurried back up the aisle with Jeff at his side. The two took their seats across the aisle from Heather and DelFlorio.

"The jurors have examined the evidence, a tape marked rebuttal exhibit 1-A," Judge Forester said. "We will continue at the point in the testimony being taken by Mr. DelFlorio from Dr. Davis when the court recessed yesterday."

DelFlorio stood. "May counsel approach the bench, your honor?" he asked.

Judge Forester nodded. Together, DelFlorio and Frank Connelly approached the judge. "Your Honor," DelFlorio said softly, "Mr. Connelly has just informed me that the defense wants to settle."

Judge Forester raised his eyebrows and turned toward Frank. "Is that true, Mr. Connelly?"

"Yes, Your Honor," Frank said. "We have decided to settle. After the recent bizarre claims about a sex tape made by the plaintiff, Dr. Davis fears for his family's safety more than ever."

The judge nodded. "Gentlemen, you may return to your seats."

"What happened?" Heather asked as DelFlorio took his seat beside her.

"The good doctor still claims you're crazy—so crazy that he fears for his family." He shook his head and broke into a broad smile. "So crazy that he's agreed to settle."

Despite her relief, Heather seethed. She didn't like being portrayed as a crazy woman. If the tape was shown, she would be mortified. But she wouldn't be ruined. Jeff would be.

Judge Forester spoke. "Court is adjourned until eleven fifteen," he said. "That means, gentlemen, that you have one hour during which to work out the terms of this agreement with your clients. Your agreement is to include the damages to be awarded. The terms are to be agreed to by both parties. If not, we will return to this courtroom and have the jury decide for you."

*   *   *

DelFlorio led Heather through the crowd to an adjoining courtroom. Somehow Jeff and his lawyer had managed to arrive in the room before them. Just as well. Judge Forester hadn't given them much time.

They sat at a rectangular table as they had the day before. This time Priscilla wasn't at Jeff's side. Heather had seen her in the courtroom.

She knew Jeff's wife couldn't be far away. Jeff stared at the wall beyond Heather's head, barely moving his eyes.

DelFlorio took the lead. "Mr. Connelly, please repeat for my client the sum you just mentioned to me in the courtroom in settlement of this case."

"Two point eight million dollars," Frank said.

Heather's body jerked visibly when she heard the number.

"Let me discuss this with my client," DelFlorio said. He stood up and motioned for Heather to join him. Together they walked to the back of the room out of earshot of the others. They stood so close Heather could hear him breathing.

"Should we accept it?" she asked.

"Accept it?" DelFlorio said. "We should grab it!"

"What about proving he's at fault for sexual misconduct? And what about my reputation? I can't stand that he's suggesting he fears for the safety of his family. That's absolutely ridiculous. I wouldn't kill a bug!"

"Please don't tell me you're going to stand on principle when you're looking at a settlement of this size." DelFlorio shook his head.

Heather felt the urge to fight any further drain from her body. "It does sound like a huge amount of money," she agreed.

"Let me put it into perspective for you," DelFlorio said. "What you've just been offered is the highest malpractice settlement in the history of the State of New York for a plaintiff who can still walk, talk, or breathe on her own."

"Amazing," Heather agreed. "But the principle…"

"The first thing I'm going to do when we leave here is call Dr. Henry Waterhouse, the head of the disciplinary medical review board," DelFlorio said. "I'll overnight a copy of the tape to him. Hell, I'll drive it up to Troy myself! Once Waterhouse sits down again with the disciplinary review board for an addendum meeting, it won't take months for them to revoke Jeff's license—more like minutes!"

"But won't Jeff think the settlement takes care of the civil case? And that the disciplinary medical review is over?"

"He'll think that for a while," DelFlorio said. "A very short while. Until they notify him of the change in their findings."

"The change?" Heather asked.

"Yes," DelFlorio said. "The change by which they'll find him liable for sexual misconduct with a patient in the guise of psychotherapy. It will cost him his license."

* * *

When Heather and DelFlorio returned to the table, Frank already had the legal papers spread out before him. It was as if he knew Heather would sign. Frank handed her a fountain pen. Jeff's signature was still damp on the page.

Heather sat down. She did her best to read the agreement with Jeff sitting across from her. DelFlorio stood behind her with his copy. When she finished reading, she turned to him. He nodded. She removed the cap from Frank Connelly's pen and signed the page.

The group filed back into the courtroom so that the judge could formally dismiss the case. As they stood before the judge, Heather's knees knocked together so hard she was certain the others could hear them.

* * *

When it was finally over, DelFlorio offered Heather a ride home, but she declined. She could feel the tears welling up in her eyes as she elbowed her way past the wall of reporters outside the courtroom and hurried down a back stairwell. Bursting from the building, she pulled her sunglasses from her purse and put them on. She needed to be alone. She'd even left Miguel and Trista behind in her race from the courthouse.

The rain splashed on her bare head as she descended the courthouse steps. It was a classic December rain in New York—a rain that would have amounted to half a foot of snow if the temperature were just a few degrees lower. Raindrops blurred the lenses of her sunglasses. She peered over the glasses to find her way down the slippery courthouse steps. When she reached the sidewalk, she sighed, relieved that she had neither slipped nor been accosted by the media.

As she walked on, Heather wondered why, although she had just been awarded a fortune, she felt as if she had lost everything. The settlement would make her a wealthy woman. The publicity surrounding the case would be enough to set a precedent that would scare other doctors from even thinking about having sex with a patient. It was a case likely to be cited in ethics classes at medical schools across the country. And it would send a message to women everywhere that if their doctor came on to them, he was violating a code of ethics that had been around for as long as the medical profession. The case had accomplished all this. Yet Heather felt empty.

Her life had been changed forever. She'd lost her job. Far worse, she'd lost Lin and the chance of ever adopting a child. And she'd lost the ability to get through the day without self-medicating.

She reached under her collar behind her neck and unclasped her locket with a single gesture. Cupping the locket in her hand, she let it fall into a puddle on the sidewalk.

As she headed down Centre Street, a woman appeared before her, locks of red hair peeking from beneath a black rain hat that matched her trench coat. She shoved a microphone in Heather's face.

"I'm Dina Cavali from the *New York Post*," the reporter was saying. "You won! How does it feel to be awarded a multimillion dollar settlement?"

Heather recognized the name immediately—it was the reporter whose story had cost her Lin's adoption. Just as quickly, she recognized her as the woman who had been following her.

Heather pushed Dina's microphone away and trudged on through the puddles, not caring that cameras from all the major news outlets were focused on her. As she glanced over her shoulder, Heather saw a homeless-looking woman in a grimy grey sweat suit stoop down in the spot where she'd dropped her locket a moment before. As Heather watched, the woman fastened the locket around her neck, Lin's picture still inside.

Heather darted into the street in the direction of a sleek chauffeured limo. Too late, she noticed that there was a caravan of news trucks from various media camped at the curb and that one was just pulling away. Brakes screeched loudly as she crossed the double yellow line in the middle of the street. She didn't even look at the news truck that had screeched to a halt within inches of her.

Stepping up the curb, she turned toward White Street. Only then did she see Jeff and Priscilla walking toward the limo, waves of reporters being held at bay by a trio of large men who looked like bodyguards. A third man walked behind Jeff and Priscilla, holding a beach-sized umbrella over them. Unless Heather stopped dead in her tracks, they'd walk directly past each other.

Drenched and frozen, Heather put her gloveless hands into her coat pockets. Her hand touched her cell phone. Its hard metal surface felt like a gun against her bare skin. *If I had a gun, I wonder if I'd use it,* she thought.

Jeff and Priscilla were within a few steps of Heather. She stole a glimpse of them from behind her sunglasses. Jeff tightened his grip on his wife's arm.

Heather walked past them, determined not to turn and look back. She turned the corner at White Street on legs of jelly—legs that wouldn't carry her another step. Stumbling toward the stone walls surrounding the Manhattan House of Detention, nicknamed the Tombs, she sank to the ground. A murky puddle surrounded her. *I'm sitting outside one of the most notorious prisons in the city,* she thought. *Why do I feel like I'm a prisoner?*

*   *   *

The rain had begun to freeze, the sky spitting sleet onto Heather's already drenched body. She reached again into her pocket, this time for a vial of Valium. She knew she'd brought enough to do herself real harm. As she groped through the deep pocket of her trench coat, her hand once again grazed her phone. *Maybe now I'm ready. Maybe I'll call her,* she thought. Removing the phone, she scrolled to the number of Maureen McNulty. She pressed *Call.* Within seconds, Maureen was on the phone.

"It's Heather—Heather Morrison from Peters & Andrews," she managed to say. "I need your help getting off pills."

"I remember you," Maureen said. "Where are you?"

Heather leaned against the stone wall at her back. "I'm on the corner of Centre and White. In front of the Tombs. I'm the one sitting on the sidewalk, leaning against a prison wall and crying my eyes out."

"My office is on lower Broadway—I'll be there in ten minutes," Maureen said.

"Hurry," Heather pleaded, one hand on the phone, the other on the full vial of Valium. She flipped the vial open with her thumb. "Please hurry."

As she closed her phone, two familiar sets of feet stepped into the puddle—Trista's black stiletto boots and Miguel's unmistakable Cole Haan wing tips. Miguel extended his hand, gently pulling Heather from the pavement as his hand closed around the vial of pills, removing it from her hand. She collapsed against his chest sobbing as Trista rubbed her back.

"It's over, sweetie," Miguel whispered. "Now you can get on with your life. Nothing bad can touch you ever again."

Heather shook her head against his chest. "No," she sobbed. "No, it'll never be over. I'll never have a baby—I'll always be alone!"

"We won't let you be alone," Trista promised. "Not even if you want to be."

Miguel slipped the vial of pills into his coat pocket. He took Heather's face in his hands, his leather gloves framing her cheekbones. "Shhhh," he said. "It's all going to be OK."

"How?" Heather asked. "How can it be OK?"

Miguel glanced at Trista and winked before returning his warm brown eyes to Heather. "I know someone who would make a great dad," he said.

"A dad?" Heather asked. Miguel's broad smile conveyed his message. "*You?* My own baby? You'd help me have my own baby?" she stammered.

Miguel's smile warmed giving Heather all the confirmation she needed as Trista literally jumped for joy.

"Oh, my God," Heather breathed, embracing one friend with each arm. "Oh, my God, what an incredible idea!"

"It's not just an idea—it's a deal." Miguel said.

From the corner of her eye, Heather saw Maureen approaching. "I'll need just a little time," she said. "There's something I need to take care of first." She clung to her friends as Maureen headed toward them.

Miguel opened his umbrella to cover Heather's head. "Now nothing bad can touch you, sweetie. Not even the rain."

MORE GREAT READS FROM BOOKTROPE

Scars from a Memoir by **Marni Mann** (Contemporary Fiction) Sometimes our choices leave scars. For heroin addict Nicole, staying sober will be the fight of her life. But having lost so much, can she afford to lose anything else?

Deception Creek by **Terry Persun** (Coming-of-age novel) Secrets from the past overtake a man who never knew his father. Will old wrongs destroy him, or will he rebuild his life?

I Kidnap Girls: Stealing from Traffickers, Restoring their Victims by **Pamela Ravan-Pyne and Iana Matei** (Fictionalized Biography) How a phone call to one woman resulted in the rescue of over 400 victims of forced prostitution.

Dismantle the Sun by **Jim Snowden** (General Fiction) A novel of love and loss, betrayal and second chances. Diagnosed with cancer, Jodie struggles to help her husband Hal learn to live without her. As Hal prepares to say goodbye to his wife, he discovers the possibility of happiness—in the arms of one of his students.

Friends or Lovers by **Rory Ridley-Duff** (General Fiction) A young HR professional gets a harassment case all wrong and finds romance in unexpected places.

Dizzy in Karachi by **Maliha Masood** (Memoir) An intimate account of the experience of living, working and traveling within a country teeming with contradictions.

Suitcase Filled with Nails: Lessons Learned from Teaching Art in Kuwait by **Yvonne Wakefield** (Personal Memoir) Leaving behind a secure life in the Pacific Northwest, Yvonne Wakefield finds both joy and struggle in teaching art to young women in Kuwait. A colorful, true, and riveting tale of living and coping in the Middle East.

Discover more books and learn about our
new approach to publishing at **booktrope.com**.

31772526R00195

Made in the USA
Lexington, KY
24 April 2014